SHARKBAIT

When Pat Tallon had friends, a fishing yacht and a future, he'd been hired to go after the shark they called the mako. This time Tallon is a stranger in a strange city, the killers he is hunting have two legs and are more deadly than any mako...and he is the sharkbait.

Moving from Melbourne to the East Indies, Sharkbait is a fast-paced thriller with all the tension of the shark hunt itself.

SHARKBAIT

SHARKBAIT

by

Richard Butler

Dales Large Print Books
Long Preston, North Yorkshire,
England.

British Library Cataloguing in Publication Data.

Butler, Richard
 Sharkbait.

A catalogue record for this book is
available from the British Library

ISBN 1-85389-570-9 pbk

First published in Great Britain by John Long Ltd., 1970

Published in Large Print May 1995 by arrangement with
Richard Butler.

Dales Large Print is an imprint of
Library Magna Books Ltd.
Printed and bound in Great Britain by
T.J. Press (Padstow) Ltd., Cornwall, PL28 8RW.

To Miles and Charles

The author wishes to express his gratitude to Captain I MacRobert for the technical assistance he gave when this book was being written, and to thank the Bureau of Meteorology, Melbourne; the Department of Shipping and Transport; the Victoria Police Force and the Commonwealth Police Force for the information their officials so generously provided.

CHAPTER ONE

The Trans-Australia Airline service from Tasmania to Melbourne spans the Bass Strait like a bridge three hundred miles long and three miles high, across which the blue-and-white propjets with the red kangaroo insignia shuttle serenely to and fro, busily compiling the statistics that prove their passengers to be safer in their high-backed seats than in their armchairs at home. They're certainly more comfortable. For how many homes are equipped not only with free service for baby, lie-back comfort and air-conditioning, but also with two slim, golden-tanned hostesses to fix your drink, fetch your magazine, or just add to the décor in those uniforms that are as white and smooth and well-filled as the paper on a cigarette? Sitting in my well-upholstered, statistically-safe seat on the afternoon flight from Hobart, I should have felt pampered, relaxed, literally on top of the world.

I felt like jumping out.

Through the oval window of the TAA Super-Viscount I could see white-hot sunlight dancing on the starboard airscrews of the Dart 525 turboprops that displayed the black Rolls-Royce monogram so re-assuringly on their burnished inboard sides. Ten thousand feet below, a white comet trailed across midnight-blue water...the wake of a power-boat cruising off Wilson's Promontory, the southernmost tip of mainland Australia. The vast land-mass of the island continent, hung with heat-haze and the smoke of distant bushfires, stretched away to the north like a gigantic green-and-brown relief map. It was a sun-drenched, spectacular view.

But all it meant to me was that it would be as hot as the hobs of hell in Melbourne. The fountains would be playing in the public gardens and the trees would be green and cool in Collins Street, but it was going to be murder tramping the blocks looking for work—any sort of work. Because you can't pick and choose, once you've done your time in the Scrubs and come out cashiered, divorced and branded as a killer. They'd called it manslaughter because it had been a weak heart that had killed the man I'd found with my wife, and it had all been a long time ago on the other side of the world, but not many prospective employers had given me time to explain all that. I dug a hand into the side pocket of my shabby jacket, then pulled it out again, empty. From now on, I had to remember I was a non-smoking non-drinker who was liable to become a non-eater if things didn't go right.

It had been to avoid that very thing that Two-tooth Harry Lamb—ex RAN P/O, ex-deserter, ex-safebreaker, ex-con, in that order—had let me talk him into a half-share in *Lorelei*, the sixty-foot motor-yacht that was to have taken us from rags to riches in the big-game fishing business. It had sounded fine, that afternoon in the pub when I'd met up with the big, bearded Sydneysider after God knows how long and sold him the idea. Instead of grovelling for jobs, we'd hire out our piscatorial paradise to those millionaire tourists we happened to like the look of, live rent-free, and learn all about Income Tax avoidance. We'd buy the yacht on the easiest of easy of terms, the repayments coming out of the profits we'd make.

But there hadn't been any profits—only losses. I'd lost the ship with every cent

13

I'd put into her and, more important, Two-tooth's savings as well. Not only that, but the finance company had promised to sue for the cost of the yacht's salvage and repairs after a wild episode off the south-west coast of Tasmania when we'd got involved in the cold war. So now I was on my way to a career in dish-washing or ditch-digging—if I was lucky. Two-tooth had been trying for a berth in the engine-room of one of the Port Line fruit-boats out of Hobart when last I'd seen him. I sat and stared unseeingly out of the window while the Super-Viscount, flaps down, drifted across the flat landscape of northern Melbourne. The suburbs floated up to meet us, there was the usual interminable moment just before touch-down when you begin to think that the law of gravity has been repealed, then the aircraft, her jets shrilling, was taxiing to her parking area.

The blast of heat that hit me as I went down the steps felt like a fire-box door opening. Melbourne's notorious northerly wind, coming straight from the super-heated deserts of the interior, made my eyelids shrivel and the glare of the sun on the white concrete was like a physical blow. I trudged along a glassed-in covered way, where the hot wind eddied and blew dust in my eyes, towards the shelter of the air-conditioned terminal building. I'd got my jacket off before I was halfway there and already I could feel the sweat trickling between my shoulder-blades. There was the usual knot of grinning, yoo-hooing plane-meeters waiting behind the barrier but I hardly gave them a glance since nobody would be likely to be grinning and yoo-hooing for me. So I didn't see the stout, middle-aged woman with the tray and collecting box until I walked into her. She took the collision better than I and said, 'Buy a button, sir?' She clashed her tin box under my nose.

I looked down at her cerise flower-pot hat, with the matching face beneath it. She was perspiring lavishly in her respectable summer coat and a strand of hennaed hair was stuck to her left eyebrow. She bared her false teeth at me and said heartily, 'Aid the Distressed Mariners?' I got another marimba solo from the box which bore a highly-coloured picture of a heavily-whiskered, and presumably myopic, sea-dog peering through a telescope at a large rock a yard from his face.

I grinned in spite of myself. Distressed

Mariners seemed a pretty worthy cause just then, and the sea-dog reminded me irresistibly of Two-tooth. I fumbled in my trousers pocket and came up with a ten-cent piece. 'Ta very much,' she said absently, already casting about for fresh prey. She pinned a large round metal badge firmly on to the lapel of the coat I was carrying over my arm, and moved aside.

As she did so, the man who'd been standing behind her said, 'Mr Tallon?'

He was about twenty-five, medium height, medium build, in an inexpensive dark-grey suit with a subdued tie and a grey snap-brim hat. The only noticeable thing about him was that he was the only man in sight with his jacket on. No, I was wrong. There were two other men standing unobtrusively by the glass doors that led into the building—big, impassive men, and they had their inexpensive dark-grey jackets on, too. That's the trouble with shoulder-holsters: they tend to lose their secrecy if you're in shirt-sleeves. I said, 'Yes, I'm Tallon. You'll be from the pest-control people, I suppose?'

He frowned. Flashing a small plastic folder so that I was the only one who could see it, he said briefly, 'Sergeant Sprott, Commonwealth Police. We'd like you to come to Headquarters to...'

'...assist you in your inquiries,' I said unpleasantly. This meant they were going to rake over the Tasmanian business again. The Australian police system is similar to that of the USA in that each State has its own police force and has no authority outside its own territory except under extradition agreements. The Commonwealth Police, roughly equivalent in function to the FBI, is an overall body concerned with crime at a Federal and international level. And the Tasmanian business had been very international indeed. 'Look,' I said. 'They told me in Hobart I was in the clear. What's it about this time?' I grabbed the sergeant's wrist to make sure it wasn't a credit card he was holding. At the sudden movement, the two heavily-built men came to life and started to move in on me.

'I'm not at liberty to say.' Sprott put a hand under my elbow. 'Just get into the car. We'd like to go over one or two details again, if you're agreeable.'

'And suppose I'm disagreeable?' I shook his hand off. The heat was making the newly-healed .45 bullet scar on my scalp itch and, having had only myself to blame recently, it was a change to have somebody else to pick on.

'Then we do it the hard way, if that's how you want it,' he said indifferently. He took my arm again. 'But you've got to get into the city somehow. So why not save the bus fare?'

He had a point there and, anyway, there was nothing to be gained by being frogmarched around on a day like this. I followed him through the coolness of the passenger lounge and out into the heat again through the self-opening doors on the far side. I picked up my battered suitcase and climbed into the powder-blue Ford Falcon whose two-way radio was hissing with static. The interior of the car was like an oven and, sandwiched between Gog and Magog on the back seat that had been heated unbearably by solar energy, I felt like the filling in a hot-dog. Sprott got into the front passenger seat and the plain-clothes driver swung the flat nose of the Ford towards the exit where slick, highly-polished cars whispered along the dual carriageway, their windscreens flashing in the sun. When we were out in the south-bound traffic stream Sprott said over his shoulder, 'Find anything?'

Magog shook his bullet head. 'No, sarge. Nothing in his bag,' they said. He grinned at me. 'Except dirty washing.'

The sergeant grunted, unhooked the radio microphone and, without using any call-sign, said, 'Bringing him in. No fuss, no weapons, no contraband.' He listened, staring ahead at the Calder Highway intersection where the Bendigo traffic was boring in with the single-minded determination that keeps so many Melbourne panel-beaters in business. Beyond it, the highway was divided by tramtracks that ran between grass strips set with rows of neatly-spaced Phoenix palms. With the single-decker trams, the palm trees and the deep Mediterranean blue of the sky, we could have been driving into Naples or Barcelona. Sprott said, 'Yes. About a quarter of an hour.' He hung up and said to the driver, 'Come on, Dave. You'll get booked for a parking infringement if you go much slower.'

The driver said thoughtfully, 'Just checking, sarge. I reckon we're being tailed.'

'Tailed?' Sprott whipped the glove-box open. 'Nobody looks back, OK?' He fixed a small mirror with a suction cup to the dash. As he adjusted it I caught a glimpse of the roadway behind us, cluttered with cars. Sprott said, 'How can you tell? And which one is it?'

'Black Mini-Cooper, sarge. Parked just across from us at the airport. Bloke sat watching us, left when we did, and now he's tucked behind the semi-trailer two cars back. Not like a Mini-Coop to stay behind a truck that's doing less than thirty.' He accelerated to overtake a bread-van, checking his wing-mirror as he pulled out. 'Yeah. He's coming out from behind the truck now, but he's staying two cars back all the time.'

Sprott grunted. 'Just stay with the traffic. I want to find out who he is.' He gave me the hard eye. 'Pal of yours, maybe, Tallon?'

I shook my head. Nobody spoke for a mile and a half, and all the way the little black car stayed two or three places in line behind us. Melbourne lost its Mediterranean air as the road narrowed and became an ugly, tramtracked street lined with dingy, peeling shopfronts and small factories. Sprott said suddenly, 'Right, Dave. Pull in here.'

We stopped outside a milk bar. 'Funny,' said Dave, his eyes on his mirror. 'See that, sarge? He stopped before we did. Hundred yards back, with a side-road handy for an escape route.' Sprott nodded, crossed the pavement where empty ice-cream cartons and chip-bags blew about in the hot wind, and disappeared through the fly-screened door of the shop. I studied the newspaper placards. 'BANK HOLDUP: MAN SOUGHT,' they said loudly. 'US PRESIDENTIAL VISIT: OFFICIAL MOTORCADE ROUTE,' and 'POP-STAR TO WED IN SEWER.' Two teenage girls, wearing more makeup than clothes, dawdled past and their transistor radios yeah-yeahed monotonously until they were swamped by the roar of a tram that passed us, the air-blast making the Falcon rock slightly. Sprott re-appeared, tearing the wrapper off a pack of Viscount cigarettes. He got into the car without looking at the Mini and lit up. I almost managed to convince myself that I wouldn't have taken one of his fags anyway.

'Been on the phone,' he said, exhaling pleasurably, 'just in case smartie back there can monitor our radio. The State Police are going to have a car waiting for him at Flemington Bridge and a motor-cycle patrol down a side-street a quarter of a mile this side of it. There are no side-turnings in between, so once he's past the motor-bikes he's in the bag.' He looked at his watch. 'Get rolling, Dave. And, everybody, eyes front. He might just get suspicious if he sees a row of grinning faces in the back window.'

We pulled out, the Mini tagging behind, and cruised gently along until Sprott said grimly, 'Any minute now.' He leaned forward to stub out his cigarette. Ahead lay an open stretch that ran past waste land backed by grey, twenty-storey blocks of flats. I had a fleeting glimpse of two Victoria State Police patrolmen astride their 120 mph Kawasakis, the big white Japanese machines parked unobtrusively down the last of the side-streets. Then we were past and leading our little black sheep to the slaughter.

Suddenly, the sergeant stiffened, stared disbelievingly at his mirror, then twisted round to peer, tight-lipped, out of the rear window. So did I, tight-lipped too, because I didn't want to be one of those grinning faces he'd mentioned. To judge from his expression, he'd book me if I as much as blinked.

Behind us, there were plenty of cars to choose from. But not one of them happened to be a Mini-Cooper, black or otherwise.

Cursing bitterly, Sprott picked up his mike. 'Turned off before he got to the motor-cycles... No, he couldn't possibly have seen them... No, they won't have Buckley's chance of catching him. And you know how much use a registration number'll be.' He turned to glower at me. 'Right. We'll bring him straight in.'

We slunk shamefacedly past the State Police Chrysler's blue flashing light and drove on dourly into the city and the start of the evening rush-hour. Under the perpendicular cliff of a building in Elizabeth Street, Sprott climbed out, snapped, 'Dave, see to his bag. Come on, you in the back. We haven't got all night,' and slammed the door of the Falcon in a way that did nothing for its resale value. The coolness of the building was like a cold shower, and I put on my jacket as we went up in the lift. Leaving Gog and Magog at the reception desk, Sprott led me down a corridor and into

23

a big, comfortable office that was done up in satin-polished blackwood panelling and midnight-blue wall-to-wall Axminster. Some police station, I thought. A glass wall faced south to the white office-blocks and long-shadowed spires of the city, framing the man who sat at a big desk with his back to the view. He glanced up from the file he was studying and a pair of expressionless blue eyes, not unlike those of a Siamese cat I used to own, photographed me from head to foot.

'Sit down, Mr Tallon,' he said politely. 'Be with you in a moment. Take a chair, sergeant.' The eyes switched off, went down to the file again, and I sat down obediently on the tubular-steel chair that was set squarely in front of the desk.

The man facing me was fiftyish, with a strand or two of sandy-grey hair brushed back from a freckled forehead, and so tall that his long spindly legs stuck out on my side of the desk. He was wearing a snowy-white shirt with the sleeves rolled up halfway to the elbows, a Melbourne Cricket Club tie and the bottom half of a fawn lightweight suit. His voice was quiet and slightly nasal and his accent was Australian without being markedly so.

He looked up from his file at last and said amicably, 'Now, Mr Tallon. Perhaps you won't mind telling us what it is that brings you to Melbourne?' He took a pipe and a goat-skin tobacco-pouch out of a desk drawer.

'I'm here to get a job,' I said briefly.

'To get a job.' He watched me as he stuffed tobacco into the bowl of his aluminium-stemmed Falcon pipe. 'And what sort of job had you in mind, Mr Tallon?'

'Anything at all.' Seeing where that could lead, I added, 'Anything legal, that is.'

'Sure,' he said smoothly. 'Plenty of legal jobs here in Melbourne. And you'll have contacts here, of course. Somebody who's going to fix you up with this job?'

'No. I don't know anybody here at all.'

'That so?' He lifted a sandy eyebrow. 'Where are you planning to stay, then?'

I shrugged. 'The YM, I suppose. I hadn't made any...'

'There's a place just round the corner from here. The Galatea Guest House,' he said helpfully. 'Cheap and very clean. You could try there.'

'Thanks,' I said guardedly. 'I might do that.'

'That's fine, because I've already had your bag sent round there. Only thing is,' he concentrated on packing his tobacco evenly, 'if you stay there, nobody'll know where to get hold of you, will they?'

'I don't think that'll matter,' I said evenly. 'I don't know anybody here, remember?'

'That's right. You did say that.' He struck a match and regarded me over the flame. 'But somebody seems to know you, wouldn't you say? Followed you all the way from the airport.' He sucked the flame down on to the tobacco and puffed little blue jets out of the corner of his mouth. 'Who was he?' he asked gently. 'What sort of job was he going to offer you?'

'He followed Sprott all the way from the airport, too. Why not ask him? He knows as much as I do.'

'Oh, well,' he said off-handedly, 'it'll keep for the time being.' He blew the match out, giving me the benefit of a cloud of rich, aromatic tobacco-smoke that made my nicotine-starved blood run cold. 'And how long,' he asked without altering his tone in the least, 'were you working for the Communists in Tasmania, Tallon?'

The unexpectedness of the attack made me jump. I stared at him, but he was busy tamping down the glowing ash on the top of the bowl. 'Look,' I said wearily. 'They told me in Hobart I was finished with all this. Now you drag me off a plane to start all over again. Why? And who are you, anyway?'

His head came up slowly. 'I'll ask the questions,' he said bleakly. 'You just answer them. OK?' He stuck his pipe between his teeth without taking his eyes off me. 'You were working for the other side in Hobart, weren't you?'

'No. All I did was...'

'No?' He pretended to consult his file. 'Maybe I've got it all wrong. I thought it said here that you'd smuggled a Russian ashore. A Russian naval officer.'

'He was drowning, twenty miles out, so I picked him up. What was I supposed to do—drop a wreath?' I throttled back on my temper. 'Anyway, I've explained all that. In centuplicate.'

'Not to me, you haven't. So you picked up this Russian. But you didn't report the incident on your radio.'

'No. He said he was defecting and that

27

his own people were hunting him down. If I'd used my radio...'

'OK. So you didn't use your radio. Then he got ashore undetected. How long did it take you to inform the police?'

'I didn't. If you'll let me get a word in...'

'You didn't go to the police?' He sat back, staring at me. To Sprott he said, 'He brings a Russian ashore—a member of the Soviet armed forces, no less—and turns him loose. But he wasn't working for the other side. I hope you can find some sort of logic in that, sergeant.' He leaned forward. 'And why didn't you go to the police, Tallon?' When I didn't answer instantly he snapped, 'There's no need to cook up a story. It was because you were bringing in contraband, wasn't it?'

'It's all there in the file,' I said angrily. 'I'm not trying to cover up. We were carrying...'

'Forged currency,' he said, nodding. He tapped the file. 'At least, that's what you said at the time. But you were working for a dope peddler, weren't you? Bringing in consignments for...'

'That's a damned lie!' I came to my feet, scared out of my self-control. They'd never accused me of that before. 'I had nothing to do with the filthy stuff. I knew nothing about it, not until after...' I stopped when I saw the satisfied look on his face and I gripped the edge of his desk, cursing myself for letting him needle me. 'Look,' I said, forcing myself to speak quietly. 'I know what's in that file better than you do. There's nothing there about narcotics.' I stood back. 'So let's stop playing games, shall we? If you're going to charge me, get on with it. If not...'

'I only wish I could,' he said coldly. 'It would save a hell of a lot of trouble. But, for some half-baked political reason that I don't pretend to understand, I can't touch you. Not yet, anyway.' Behind him, the blue-and-gold evening sky was dappled with high cirrus. One or two early neons were already gleaming palely on the roofs below, and the big swivelling cranes on the partially-constructed buildings were motionless, outlined against the sky like long-necked birds of prey. 'All I can do is give you the gypsy's warning, Tallon. If you as much as commit a parking offence, I'll have you. And one more incident like today's—one more attempt to contact these subversives you've been mixed up with...'

'Then I haven't a thing to worry about.' I turned to the door. 'Since I've no car to park and nobody, subversive or otherwise, to contact.'

'Don't give me that,' he said contemptuously. 'There was somebody waiting for you today, all right. Somebody with a proposition who...' He stopped dead.

I turned back to face him. As I did so, his china-blue eyes settled on the round metal badge in the lapel of my coat. Slowly, he came to his feet. As I'd expected, he topped my six feet one by a good three inches. 'Of course,' he said, his voice dangerously quiet. 'And there was only one person waiting for him apart from you, wasn't there, sergeant?' Before Sprott could reply, the tall man's arm had snaked out and whipped the badge from my coat.

'The button-seller?' I said incredulously. 'You can't be serious. She was...'

'AID THE DISTRESSED MARINERS,' he read slowly, walking back to his chair. He looked at me, his face hard, as he put the badge down on his immaculate blotter and picked up a paper-knife. 'By God,

Tallon,' he said savagely. 'If this is what I think it is, you're going to have some explaining to do.'

I stared at him, mystified. 'How,' I asked, 'do I explain buying a button?' He was prising at it with the paper-knife.

There was a tiny metallic clatter as the gaily-painted front came off and rolled across the desk. Silently, he laid the rest of it down on the blotter. I looked at it, dumbfounded, recognising it for what it was even as he reversed the paper-knife and smashed the handle down on the compactly-stowed mass of miniature components and circuitry as viciously as if he was crushing a spider.

'Just,' he said softly to no one in particular, 'as I thought. A complete radio-transmitter—and not one of your bleep gadgets, either. Mike in the front section, pin doubling as an antenna. A lovely bit of work.' He pushed the shattered bits around on the blotter with the point of the knife. 'Range of about four hundred yards. Far enough, if the receiver's in a car. And everything you've said since you landed, every word we've uttered in this room, has been picked up and broadcast by this.' Oddly enough, he didn't seem to care. He grinned at Sprott. 'No wonder the Mini was able to dodge you so easily.'

'I'm very sorry, sir.' Sprott gave me a vindictive look. 'But I could get you the woman who sold him the button, I reckon. And the bloke in the car can't be all that far away.'

'He'll have skipped as soon as the radio went dead. And the button-seller'll have taken the first flight out after you left. Don't let it worry you, sergeant.' The tall man re-lit his pipe and surveyed the sergeant benignly. 'My report's going to be favourable—very favourable indeed.' He searched in a drawer for a manilla envelope and scooped the bits of radio into it. Then he looked at his watch, stood up, put on his fawn light-weight jacket and slipped the envelope into an inside pocket. 'And now, sergeant,' he said, 'I'll leave you to lock up.' He collected a green snap-brim hat and a copy of *The Australian* from the top of a filing cabinet and made for the door. 'I'm going to have a swim before dinner.'

I stared, astounded, at his retreating back. What about the explanation he'd said I'd have to give? And wasn't the possession of a listening device enough for him to charge me with? 'What,' I said cautiously, 'do I do?'

He turned, his hand on the door-knob. 'Have one too, if you like,' he said genially. 'There's a public baths not far from the guest house.' He strode down the corridor and I heard him whistling cheerfully as he waited for the lift.

CHAPTER TWO

After dining off a meat pie I went out into the hot, brilliantly-lit streets to look for the Galatea Guest House. It was a couple of blocks away from the café where I'd eaten, in an area where all the shop-signs were in Greek. Its entrance was sandwiched between a glass-and-chromium-fronted electrical retailer's, still open for business in below-cost refrigerators, and one of those gents' outfitters that always seem to be having a closing-down sale. Dark-haired, olive-skinned characters stood gesticulating energetically outside the shop doorways, and a snatch of bouzouki music floated plangently from an upstairs window on the warm evening air.

The boarding-house had its name lettered in Greek and English on the fanlight above an open, electric-blue door. I went inside and along a narrow, brightly-lit passageway that ended in another electric-blue door marked PRIVATE. In the wall on my left was a closed hatchway, painted electric-blue, with a bell-push and a neatly-printed card that said: RECEPTION. PLEASE RING. SERVICE IS OUR WATCHWORD. A flight of carpeted stairs led up on the right, the woodwork recently painted in a tasteful shade of electric-blue. I pressed the bell-push.

Instantly, the hatch flew up with a crash that made me leap a foot in the air. It revealed a sloping shelf with a receipt-book on it, a calendar on the opposite wall with a picture of a blonde baring her teeth and most of her chest, a small switchboard, and another door. Whoever stocked the electric-blue paint around here was making a fortune. I waited for five minutes, but nothing happened except that when I closed my eyes everything went bright yellow. I shouted, 'Hey! Anybody there?' and beat impatiently on the shelf with my fist.

The door at the far side of the hatch opened and a fat, bald man in shirt-sleeves came through, wiping his mouth with a tartan handkerchief. He grinned broadly at me, still swallowing, and waved his handkerchief at the hatchway. 'Is neat, eh?' he said, closing the door behind him. 'You press the button, the hatch go up, and there am I, Dimitrios Karonides, waiting to attend to your needs. The instant service. My own idea.' The grin faded as I looked expressionlessly back at him and he came and put his fat elbows on the shelf, peering up into my face. 'There is no bell, you understand?' he said anxiously. I gathered that fried onions had played a dominant role in the meal I'd interrupted. 'Is the hatch that goes up when you press...'

'...the button,' I said, nodding. 'My name's Tallon. Have you got a room?'

'But of course!' He beamed again. 'Your friend, he booked it for you. Your bag is already 'ere. A moment.' He pulled down the hatch and re-appeared through the door that said PRIVATE. 'For a week only, yes? Number eight. He has already paid—for the room only, since he said you would eat out. This way, if you would be so kind as to follow.' He began the ascent of the staircase, hanging on to the banister that flexed dangerously as he heaved at it. 'There is a telephone in the room,' he said, breathing hard. 'You come and go as you wish.' We reached the summit and he paused to wipe his sweating head and neck with his handkerchief. 'But, please,

36

no visitors of the fair sex in the room, eh? An' no grog. This is a quiet house, and you are not offended if...?'

'I like it quiet,' I said, thinking of the seven dollars in my wallet. 'Which room is it?'

When he'd gone I took off my shoes, tie and jacket and lay down on the bed in the hot, clinically-neat little room whose high-voltage colour scheme I was quite getting used to already. To celebrate my release from custody I'd bought a pack of Churchman's and smoked one after my pie. Now, feeling abandoned, I lit another and blew smoke rings at a solitary fly that was patrolling slow jerky triangles round the yellow plastic lampshade. I had a lot to think about, and it all added up to the fact that somebody was taking a lively interest in me, quite apart from the police, and I didn't like any of it. I'd got across quite a lot of people recently; I had no friends in this sprawling cosmopolitan city; and if I vanished overnight who would know—or care? Maybe Melbourne wasn't the place for me. Maybe I ought to go down to the docks tomorrow and see who wanted their decks swabbed. But in the meantime, I thought, yawning, it was very warm, and the bed wasn't at all uncomfortable. I closed my eyes.

Straight away, I found myself running down an endless corridor, pursued by a black, driverless Mini-Cooper. The car filled the corridor exactly, like the piston in a cylinder, and I knew I couldn't outrun it so I stopped at an electric-blue hatchway and pressed the bell-push desperately. I could hear the bell ringing insistently as the Mini came nearer and nearer, but Karonides wouldn't open up. 'There is no bell, you understand,' he kept saying every time it rang. The black car, as big as a locomotive, loomed over me, about to squash me like a bug as I awoke, sweating, and fumbled for the phone that was shrilling in my ear. Groggily, I rolled over on to my elbow, picked up the handset and gave my name.

A cheerful Aussie voice said, 'Police HQ Russell Street, Mr Tallon. We've picked up a black Mini-Cooper whose driver claims he knows you. We'd like you to confirm that, if you can.'

Russell Street is the headquarters of the Victoria Police and Interpol Australia. 'He can't know me,' I said. The burnt-out ash of my cigarette on the rim of the ashtray looked like some obscure fungus. 'What's his name?'

'Can't give it over the phone, sir? We'll be sending a car to pick you up. Sorry it's so late, but you know how these things are. Five minutes be OK?'

I looked at my watch. Five to eleven. 'I'll be ready,' I said. I hung up, sloshed cold water on to my face in the clean but primordial bathroom, put on my jacket and shoes, and snapped off the light.

When the Greek, who was talking with both hands at a thin, alert man in a dark suit and felt hat, heard me on the stairs he swung round ponderously, sweating like a ton of wet cement. 'Mr Tallon, I do not like the queer goings-on in my house,' he said crossly. 'I do not fear rivals, you understand, but there are those who will say, "Ha! Behold the police at the house of Karonides! It must be a den of iniquity, and..."'

'They'll be right, Mr K,' said the thin man, grinning. 'You can tell yer mates you've got a guest who's helping us crack one of the biggest cases since the Shark Arm Murder.' He winked at me. 'Might even get yer picture in *The Herald*. People would fight to stay here then.'

39

'Truly?' Karonides waddled with us to the street door. 'In that case, of course... The newspapers, did you say? I had no wish to unco-operate, you understand, but this is a quiet, respectable house and...'

'Goodnight, sir.' Leaving the Greek burbling happily on his doorstep, the thin man led the way across the pavement. 'I'm Senior Constable Egger,' he said crisply. 'This is Constable Macreedy.' The tubby man in the driving seat of the blue Falcon GT half-turned and lifted a hand off the wheel in greeting.

I put a foot inside the car. Then I paused. If I hadn't been half asleep I'd have realised before now that this was all just a little too smooth. 'Maybe,' I said, 'it might be an idea if I checked your identification?'

'Too right,' Egger said agreeably. His right hand went under the left lapel of his jacket and came out wrapped round the butt of an automatic pistol that gleamed dully in the street lighting. Holding it so that Karonides couldn't see it, he said in the same amicable tone, 'How about checking this? Bearing in mind that, if you start anything, I'll have to blast fatguts over there as well.' He flicked the gun-muzzle at the car.

The shops had all closed long ago and the street was empty. I climbed into the back of the Ford and Egger shouted goodnight cheerily to the Greek while shielding the driver, who turned round to frisk me expertly. Egger got in beside me, he and his gun never taking their eyes off me for a second, and the tubby driver started his engine. We crossed Collins Street in thin, late-night traffic, Egger sitting well away on the wide seat where I couldn't reach the .38 Bernardelli that poked its tapering snout at me from down by his right leg. The driver said politely, 'Anything else you'd like to check, Mr Tallon, sir? Tyres, oil, water?' As he sniggered I recognised the man who'd said he'd been speaking to me from Police Headquarters.

I was cold with fury at the ease with which I'd been taken. I was also cold with apprehension, remembering what I'd been thinking about before I'd dropped off to sleep. The siren of a diesel locomotive wailed mournfully from among the twinkling red, green and yellow lights of a railway yard away to the right. I said between my teeth, 'Very smart. And what else did they teach you in the nick besides ventriloquism?'

'Bit more'n they seem to have taught you, you stupid pom,' said the stout driver, chuckling. 'Jeez, yer musta come down with the last shower, falling for an old dodge like that.' He accelerated as we came on to a wide, well-surfaced stretch that cut through open parkland, darkly mysterious under the stars, and I recognised the rotunda-like bulk of the Melbourne Cricket Ground as it looked up out of the darkness and fell behind. There was very little traffic about. Gradually, my panicky rage gave way to a feeling that was almost relief when I reflected that, for the time being, I could forget about jobs, money, the police—everything except the immediate present. My life had suddenly simplified itself into a straight-out duel between me and the man on the other end of the gun.

Wire-fenced factory premises and small shops with blind windows began to crowd us as we ran through one of the older, more industrialised suburbs. Black alleyways yawned like open graves. If these two got me into one of those...I said, 'OK. So what's it all about? Where are you taking me?' It was time to start working out just how I was going to jump Egger.

The trouble was, Egger looked as spring-loaded and watchful as a taipan, and the odds against jumping him and getting away with it were about the same as for jumping an anti-personnel mine. He was a pro—calm, confident and competent. His voice was almost bored as he said, 'We're taking you to see somebody, that's all. Somebody who can put you on to a goldmine. Now relax, will you, and enjoy the ride.'

'So that's the way it is,' I said slowly. 'A proposition.' For a moment I was almost tempted to go along with it, if only to find out who it was who was so desperate to make my acquaintance, but then wiser counsels prevailed. If my lanky friend in the Commonwealth Police found out about this joyride he'd throw the book at me.

'You could say that,' Egger agreed. 'A proposition.' To the driver he said, 'You turn off here, remember.' The car slowed and I saw the driver flick his indicator for a turn to the right. I reached into my pocket, but not too fast.

Egger reacted instantaneously. 'Keep your hands still!' The gun caught the light from a street lamp as it shifted a fraction. 'What the hell are you trying to do?'

'I only wanted a fag. You said relax, didn't you?'

He nodded, knowing I wasn't carrying a weapon. 'But slowly, right? I got orders to deliver you in one piece and I'd like to carry them out.'

I took my right hand out of my pocket with my nearly-full packet of Churchman's in it. Then I groped with my left. 'Match,' I explained. Egger nodded again, irritably. I selected a cigarette and put it between my lips as the driver started to swing his wheel for the turn. Egger was watching every move I made. I pushed the matchbox open with my thumb, feeling with my fingertips for the rounded heads of the tightly-packed matches. 'You smoke?' I asked.

'No,' he said curtly. 'I don't use them.'

I struck a match. 'Very wise,' I said. Then, while the match was still flaring, I rammed it back into the box and threw the lot in his face. As the whole boxful exploded in a hissing mass of phosphorus I hurled myself forward, helped by the heeling car, and grabbed for the gun.

He yelled and struck out to protect his eyes from the ball of yellow-orange flame that flew at him in a cloud of acrid smoke and I got his wrists as he batted the blazing matchbox down to the floor. Blinded and thrown off balance in the car's turn, he fell back and the .38 went off twice under my nose, the reports sounding like the crack of doom in the confined space. With a second, minor crash, the windscreen turned into an opaque, milky wall with a small, whistling hole in it level with the driver's face. The fat man shouted and stood on his brakes. I tore the automatic out of Egger's jerking hand, reversed it, and clubbed him over the head. The driver flung his door open, baled out while the wheels were still rolling, and the Ford climbed the pavement, made a half-hearted attempt to get through a three-foot-wide gateway, and stalled.

It was very quiet. No windows flew up; nobody seemed anxious to be informed about what the hell was going on down there. This was obviously the kind of neighbourhood where people liked to keep themselves to themselves. Across the street a wrecker's yard crouched misshapenly behind a high wire fence and, on this side, a fluorescent street lamp picked out the abandoned chapel whose gateway we'd partially demolished. Beside the gate, a board carried a faded poster pointing out that strong drink was a mocker. Somebody who didn't go along with that had added a spherical footnote in spindly white paint. The smell of burnt hair and carpeting inside the car was horrible, but I took my time about getting out in case the driver was planning a come-back.

But I needn't have worried. He was a full-bodied man, such as sleep o' nights, and his job was to drive cars, not to leap out of them in a hail of bullets. The NO STANDING AT ANY TIME signpost he'd run into hadn't done much for him, either. I found him at the foot of it, obeying its instructions by crouching on his hands and knees in the gutter and looking like a fat St Bernard getting acquainted with a lamp-post. He was far too busy spitting out pieces of broken denture to give me any trouble. I checked that he had no gun, towed him back to the car and stacked him against the rear bumper. I was leaning against the offside door at the rear, panting and wishing I'd saved a match to light the cigarette that was still dangling from my mouth when the engine of the Ford came to life with a hissing roar.

Somebody screamed, and went on screaming. The car's door-handle slammed agonisingly into my left hip and catapulted me into the gutter. I got a split-second impression of a fire-blackened face protruding from the driver's window as the man who'd called himself Egger reversed the Ford, fast.

And his mate had been behind it.

There was a hideously soft crunching noise, like breaking eggs, and the rabbit-like screams from under the car were cut off abruptly as one and a half tons of automobile surged forward and went over the fat man again. I rolled clear as a radial-ply tyre brushed my face. The car leapt off the footpath, skidded, then straightened up as its 225 h.p motor slung it down the street like a runaway rocket. Propped on my stomach, I lifted the Bernardelli. Then I lowered it again. To be found with one corpse—I'd already seen what had happened to the fat man's head—was bad; to have another on my hands, with a bullet in it, would be suicidal. They still employ a hangman in Victoria.

It could have been the smashed windscreen. Or perhaps Egger was still blinded, or maybe he just couldn't control the power under his bonnet. Whatever the reason, the Ford was doing something like eighty miles an hour when it raced across the T-junction at the end of the street and smashed into the brick wall on the other side with an impact I felt through the length of my body as I lay watching. The car rebounded in a shower of displaced brickwork and there was a second grinding smash as it fell back on to its roof. I scrambled to my feet. But, even as I ran, the petrol tank ignited in a whoomf of hot air that blasted me in the face from two hundred yards away, and the wreck bloomed into roaring red-and-yellow fire.

I got as close as I could. Then I turned away and limped slowly down the street. From the city, the sirens were already wailing like lamenting bagpipes in the distance.

CHAPTER THREE

It took me well over an hour to get back to the guest house. The only two taxis I'd seen had slowed, taken a look at my crumpled suit with its bulging side-pocket, and driven off smartly so that, by the time I'd slogged across the city in the hot, sticky summer night that smelled of over-cooked pavement, I was dog-tired, sweaty and shaken by the sudden death I'd witnessed. If, I thought as I fumbled for the keys Karonides had given me, I'd been a good little citizen I'd have stayed to tell the police about that. And they, naturally, would have taken my word for it that I'd never set eyes on Egger or his fat friend before. Like hell they would. I opened the front door, looking forward to a cold shower followed by as much sleep as I could get before they threw me out to make the beds.

Shutting the door behind me was like being sealed up in a tomb. I couldn't find the light switches but, as my eyes adjusted to the dark, I was able to make out a blue glow coming from a bulb at the top of the stairs. An electric-blue bulb, I thought, sniggering light-headedly. I went up, my feet silent on the stair carpet, and along the top corridor. It was, as the Greek had claimed, a quiet house...so quiet that, with the crepuscular lighting and the soft carpeting, I had the feeling that I was spending the night in a waxworks for a bet. Somewhere a church clock chimed and then struck once, sounding as if it was tolling from the bottom of the sea, and then there was only the deep velvety hush again, with none of the muted radios, unmuted snores and other sound effects of a cheap hotel late at night. It occurred to me that I might be Karonides' only guest, and I was annoyed to find myself holding my breath and listening for evidence that there was somebody else alive behind one of those gaily-painted enigmatic doors. A floorboard creaked sharply and I jumped, cursing under my breath. Then I relaxed sheepishly when I saw the line of light between a badly-fitting door and its jamb. Somebody else was awake after all in this shadowy, silent house. Somebody in number eight who couldn't sleep and

50

who...I froze, my keys in my hand and my heart in my mouth.

Number eight was my room.

And it was no good trying to kid myself I'd left the light on when I'd gone out earlier, or that I'd imagined that creaking floorboard. I knew I hadn't...just as I knew it was hardly likely to be Karonides in there, waiting up for me with a nice hot cup of ouzo. No, far from being alone in the house, it now looked as if I had all the company I could handle. I leaned against the wall, wondering if this was all some conspiracy on the part of the citizenry of Melbourne to kill me off through lack of sleep. Then I hauled out the Bernardelli with one hand, inserted my key into the lock with the other, turned it, kicked the door open with a crash that nearly unhinged it, and leapt to one side, all in what they call one swift, flowing movement. I then waited for things to start happening.

Nothing happened at all. No shots, no knives of intricate Oriental design thudding into the woodwork, no shouts of baffled fury even. I stood for what seemed like half an hour while I confirmed that the rapid, sinister ticking I could hear was coming from the watch on my wrist. Finally, coming to grips with the impracticability of spending the night jammed up against the wall like a terrified hatstand, I poked my head cautiously round the door-jamb.

After the corpse-light of the corridor, the forty-watt bulb hanging from the ceiling was almost blinding. My bedspread had been draped across the window which, judging from the motionless strata of blue tobacco-smoke that hung at head-height, was firmly shut so that the atmosphere had all the heat and aroma of a well-established bushfire. My bedside table had been dragged to a position facing the door. And, sitting beside it on a wooden kitchen chair, was the tall, balding quizmaster from the Commonwealth Police.

His long legs were crossed comfortably and he was wearing a cream linen jacket with a dark-green sports shirt, charcoal-grey slacks, and an interested expression. 'With an entrance like that,' he said, removing his aluminium-stemmed pipe from his mouth as I peered coyly round the door at him, 'you could make a fortune in the horror-movie business, Tallon.' He eyed my rag-bag suit and the gun in my hand as I limped into the room feeling every bit of six inches tall. 'Dressed for the part, too, right down to the murder weapon. You feeling OK? You're limping a bit, I see.'

'I never felt better,' I snarled. I was hot, harassed and humiliated and his nasal voice had the same effect on me as a roomful of mosquitoes. 'I walk this way because I'm a little saddle-sore from being shoved in and out of cars all day, that's all.' I stood over him and pushed my face into his. 'Of course I'm not OK,' I said between my teeth. 'D'you know what happened to me tonight?'

He gazed up at me, unmoved. 'Sure. You were picked up by two men who'd just stolen a car and who were posing as police officers. Their car crashed, probably because of a fight started by you, and they were both killed. And now you're in possession of a pistol for which you can't possibly produce a licence.' He exhaled a cloud of tobacco-smoke into my face. 'Right?'

I backed off, coughing. 'Right,' I said bitterly. I put the gun on the table beside him. 'But it wouldn't be any use trying to tell you my side of it, would it? You said you'd get me sooner or later, and this is your big moment. So let's get it over. I'm...'

'I'm only trying to show you how Sprott would look at it.' He stood up, brushed past me, and closed the door. 'He's under the impression that you're mixed up with a narcotics ring, so it's only natural that he should want to take you in. That's his job.' He sat down again and tilted his chair on to its rear legs. 'After all,' he said reasonably, 'if I were a policeman, I'd probably feel the same way.'

'If you were...?' I was beginning to get the baffled feeling between the ears again. 'You mean, they've retired you since last we met?' I tore off the jacket and tie that were slowly strangling me, and tossed them on to the bed.

'I mean,' he said placidly, 'that I've had a lot of help from the Commonwealth Police, one way and another. The loan of one of their offices this afternoon, for instance, plus,' he grinned at me round the pipe-stem, an annoyingly likeable grin, 'the co-operation of your old cobber Sergeant Sprott. But I'm not a policeman, Tallon. I thought you'd have been on to that by now, with all the experience you've had.' He took out a small blue perspex-covered card from the inside pocket of his linen jacket. 'ASIO,' he said briefly as he hung it under my nose.

'ASIO?' I took the card and sat down on the edge of the bed, watching him as carefully as if he'd turned the Bernardelli on to me. The Australian Security and Intelligence Organisation is not—unlike the CIA and what used to be called MI5—a much-publicised secret service. It is small, a comparative newcomer to the international cloak-and-dagger scene and, unlike its big brothers in Western Intelligence, it manages to avoid making the mistakes that make the headlines. ASIO is, however, very well known in certain quarters. To the Russians, for example, whose *Ministerstvo Vnutrennik Del* was hopelessly out-manoeuvred by ASIO in the Petrov affair of 1954, and again in 1959 when the Soviet agent Ivan Fedorovich Skripov was unmasked and trapped by a blonde agent of Australian counter-espionage.

'Fenner,' I read aloud from the card. 'Alexander George. Captain, RAN.' I looked up, comparing him with his photograph. 'Which of those do I use when we're going over my shady Communist past?' I flipped the card back at him and lay down on the bed. This looked like being one of those long, hot, sleepless nights they'd told me I'd get in Melbourne.

'Fenner will do.' A floorboard creaked as he came and stood at the foot of the bed with his hands in his pockets, looking down at me in a way that, with the cream linen jacket, made me feel I ought to have a temperature chart hanging up for him to check. 'And it's your shady Communist future that interests me, Tallon, not your past.'

'Now, look,' I said tiredly. 'Don't let's start that all over again. I told you this afternoon, I may have done some pretty off-beat things in my time, but I've always steered clear of the big stuff like drugs and politics. A career in subversion wouldn't interest me at all.'

'Pity,' he said, still with that oddly-clinical look on his face. 'With qualifications like yours, you could go straight to the top.' He went back to his chair, spun it round, and sat astride it with his arms along the back, checking off points on his fingers with the mouth-piece of his pipe. 'Five years' Regular Army experience with weapons and explosives, including a detailed knowledge of all the tricks the terrorists got up to in Malaya during the Emergency; prison record for violence; expensive tastes, but no income; good with cars and boats; reasonably intelligent, physically fit—hell, I could go on all night. You've even done one job already for the other side—I know, I know.' He waved me down as I came up on one elbow. 'You were tricked into it. But isn't it conceivable that a man who's helped out the USSR might be persuaded to do the same thing for somebody else as long as the price is right?'

'Not in this case,' I snapped. I swung my feet on to the floor. 'Now, it's very late, so...'

'So those two in the car tonight didn't come up with a proposition?'

'They told me they were taking me to somebody who could put me on to a goldmine, yes. But, if you were expecting me to go along with them, you'll have to try some other kind of trap, Fenner, because that one's bust a spring. I wouldn't get mixed up with a bunch like that for all the tea in Red China.' I took my squashed pack of Churchman's out of the jacket on the bed, groped frustratedly for the matches I hadn't got, and he came across to light my cigarette for me.

'No?' He grinned at me as he blew the match out. 'They'll be very disappointed. Because they've been watching you for months—checking up on your background, tailing you, finding out how you stand with the law. We knew they'd make you an offer sooner or later.' He went back to his chair and propped himself against its back, his arms folded. 'We knew they'd be waiting to pick you up when you entered the State, so we arranged to have the police meet you. Routine narcotics investigation. And, when I heard how you were being tailed, it seemed pretty obvious that the opposition had made the mistake of planting a voice mike either on you or in the car—and I settled for you, since a police wagon isn't the easiest thing in the world to fool around with at a crowded airport. Now, a bug's like a boomerang, Tallon. It can turn round and kick you in the teeth once it gets out of your control. And I was able to use this one to feed our friends some really good information on how you stood with the law. All I had to do was borrow an office, put on a tough cop act, and give them the kind of programme they wanted to hear.'

'Wait a minute.' I was tired, but not that tired. 'How d'you know you're not doing exactly the same thing now? If these characters can bug a police office, this place should be a push-over. For all you know, that Greek freak downstairs has got this place so festooned with microphones that we could be doing the late late show for Radio Pekin.'

He cocked an eyebrow at me. 'I hope,' he said good-humouredly, 'that you're not going to turn out to be one of those Englishmen who think we poor colonials spend all our time riding around in big hats and singing *Waltzing Matilda*, Tallon. We can do other things beside play cricket and raise the best sheep in the world, you know. And our people have come up with an anti-monitoring device that'll take care of anybody who's listening. Dimitrios'll see to that.' He grinned at the expression on my face. 'That's right. Fat, foolish old Karonides, the garrulous Greek. Only he isn't Greek and he's a hell of a long way from being foolish. He's naturalised Australian, he's one of the best brains in the game, and he's worked for us ever since the terrorists wiped out his family in Cyprus. You don't think I put you in here by accident, do you?'

Half an inch of ash fell on to my trousers and I brushed it off mechanically while I tried to adjust to the fact that a good deal of what I'd said and done recently seemed to have been of interest to at least two different sets of observers. It made me feel like a rat in a laboratory cage. I said, 'But who are these characters I seem to fascinate so much? Somebody other than the Russians, you said. The Red Chinese?'

He stared at me. 'You were in the fishing game,' he said. 'What does the name "mako" mean to you?'

'It's a shark,' I said, surprised at this sudden change of topic. 'The one they sometimes call the Blue Pointer. Open-ocean species, blue in colour. Runs to about thirteen feet as a rule. And,' I added, 'it's one of the most bloodthirsty brutes in existence. A streamlined, fearless killer that attacks on sight and can rip a man open in seconds. They'll even attack small boats, those bastards, and...' I stopped. 'Why? Who's talking about shark?'

'We are,' he said sombrely. 'Because the

lot we're up against call themselves the Mako, too. And you've just given a pretty accurate description of them. Dangerous, cold-blooded killers, lurking beneath the surface of our society and waiting to tear the guts out of anybody who stands in the way of a Communist-dominated South-east Asia.' He straightened up and came to the foot of the bed again. 'Have you stopped to think,' he said quietly, 'how accident-prone our politicians and key men generally seem to be, compared with those of the other side? A liberal cabinet minister, famous for his anti-Red views, jumps out of a skyscraper in Tokyo; a South Vietnamese general dies in a car smash in Saigon on the eve of an all-out offensive; in America...' He shrugged. 'We've had a hell of a lot of that kind of thing lately. Fatal accidents, motiveless suicides—and most of them were arranged by the Mako. Because that's their speciality—political assassination, carried out by small task forces of highly-trained professional killers. A kind of Marxist Murder Incorporated, except that they're on hire to Governments instead of private individuals. Where they're getting their money from at present is anybody's guess, but they seem to have plenty of it. They only go for the really big stuff, the VIPs who are usually considered impossible to hit, and they never miss. If you can imagine an organisation with the international network of the Mafia, the political dedication of the Viet Cong, and the technological aids to murder of Himmler's Gestapo, then you're beginning to get some idea of what the Mako is like.'

'And those two tonight.' My flesh crept as I realised how close I'd been to getting mixed up in all this. 'They were trying to recruit me?'

'If they had been,' he said grimly, 'you'd either be working for them now or occupying a drawer in the city mortuary. No, the whole thing was set up to test our reactions—to see if you were being tailed, if you'd go quietly, maybe even to test whether I was trying to palm you off on them. According to Dimitrios, they were just local boys, hired for the occasion. If you'd gone along with them you'd have ended up at an empty house. They'd have hung about for a while, waiting for their employer to turn up and, when he didn't they'd have pinched your wallet and left you stranded. They probably didn't even know who was paying them.' He eyed me thoughtfully. 'But it was you I was really interested in, Tallon. Not them.'

'Me?' I stared up at him suspiciously. 'What for?'

'Well, for one thing, we know where you stand now, don't we?' He smiled down at me disarmingly. 'You're what I'd call a good risk.'

I felt as if a weight like an anchor had been lifted off my mind. I put my feet up on the bed again and tapped a little ash off my cigarette. 'I'm glad to hear it,' I said, more convinced than ever that jumping out of that car had been the best night's work I'd done for a long time. 'Not that there was ever any...'

'Of course there wasn't.' He chuckled amusedly. I could grow to like this character, I thought, given time. 'And there's no question either of the Mako thinking we were trying to pass you off as an infiltration job.'

'I should say not.' I chuckled too. With a bottle of the right stuff, we could pass a jolly evening like this. 'Knocking hell out of the two who were supposed to be taking me to their leader would be a highly original way of infiltrating their organisation, wouldn't it?'

'Too right it would,' he said, yuk-yukking a bit more. 'It's a method that appeals to me very strongly, Tallon.'

'It does?' I grinned. 'You tortuous-minded old devil. I only hope it works out all right for...' A bedspring twanged as I sat up abruptly. 'Now wait a minute,' I said. In spite of the furnace-like heat of the room, the shirt that had glued itself to my back felt like an ice-pack and the phrase 'a drawer in the city mortuary' began to flit through my mind with the phrenetic insistence of a soap-powder commercial. 'You couldn't get away with it, even if I was stupid enough to let you try. As soon as this Mako bunch find out that I refused their invitation tonight they'll drop me like a botulinus cocktail. They...'

'Then you haven't a thing to worry about, have you?'

'But...' I stared at him, stymied. 'Suppose they do try again...'

'In that case, I want you to help us bust that organisation wide open from the inside. One operation, Tallon. That's all I'm asking.'

'But how do you know it's the Mako

that's after me? And what is it they want me to do?'

'While they've been watching you, we've been watching them. We know who it is we're dealing with. We could even pull in a few of them now. But, if we did—even if we got their whole Australian group, they'd have another lot here within twenty-four hours and we'd have to start all over again. We've got to wait until they're committed—until it's too late for them to make a change of plan. Then we'll take them—the big fish as well. As for what they want you to do,' he looked at me oddly, 'you'll find that out for yourself.'

'Who are they planning to assassinate, apart from me? Or do I have to find that out as well?'

'Have you,' he asked quietly, 'read your newspapers lately, Tallon?'

'No. I haven't been...' I stopped. I recalled one of the newspaper placards I'd seen outside the milk bar on my way into the city. 'The United States President,' I said slowly. 'He's coming here, isn't he?'

'In a fortnight, as part of his South-east Asia goodwill tour. The biggest, most heavily-guarded target in the Western world. The one that only the Mako could go for. And it's my job to help guard him.'

'But it's not mine.' I was appalled by the chasm that was opening up under my feet. 'Hell, I wouldn't know an assassin from an aspidistra. Why pick on me? What about that army of CIA men he'll have with him in Melbourne? Why can't one of them...?'

'The Mako won't try anything in Melbourne. Or in Sydney, for that matter. We and the Americans can sew the cities up so tight that not even the Mako could get at him. I can't tell you about it, but I give you my word he's completely safe while he's on Australian soil.'

'So?' I frowned. 'Then what are you worried about?'

'I'm worried about the one place in Australia where he's out of our control. In transit. In the air.'

'You mean they might try to shoot down his plane? But that's fantastic. How could...?'

'Sure, it's fantastic. It was fantastic when the United States Air Force shot down Admiral Isoroku Yamamoto, Commander-in-Chief of the Japanese Navy, back in 1943. He had a fighter escort, he was only ten minutes from his destination at Bougainville, and he was supposed to be out of range of any American plane. But they got him all the same.'

'But they could re-route the President's Boeing, surround it with fighter aircraft...'

'How the hell,' he snapped, his nerves showing for the first time, 'can we re-route him when we don't know where they're going to strike? We might fly him through the very area they want.' He walked back to his chair and sat down, getting his self-control back. 'I want you to find out where that area is. We'll do the rest.'

I dragged on my cigarette. 'You talk as if you know that the Mako are definitely planning this. How many other stooges have you used and lost before me?'

'None. All I can tell you is that we've had a couple of people in our sights for some time now. A man called Bellamy and his wife who live down the coast. Her brother was sent up the river by the Indonesians in '66 for complicity in the murder of an anti-Communist general in Djakarta. Typical Mako stuff. Before that, he was an engineer. In rocketry,' he said quietly, 'and he was trying to get the Indonesians to finance a missile he'd designed. Now, not only has he escaped from prison with outside help, but he's been in touch with this Mrs Bellamy. We picked up a courier who'd delivered a letter to her but he couldn't—or wouldn't—tell us what was in it. Bellamy himself is a layabout, living off his wife's money, and he's said to have a strong feeling for the Red Chinese.'

'But, I've told you, all this isn't in my line. Besides,' I said cunningly, 'how do you know you can trust me, with the record I've got? That fight in the car could have been faked just to...'

'What,' he asked pityingly, 'is it you think I'm running, Tallon? A Boy Scout troop? I don't trust you. Trust isn't a word I use in my business, any more than a finance company manager uses it in his. Like him, I merely assess risks against,' he grinned thinly, 'adequate security. And in your case, the security consists of a series of pending prosecutions by the Treasury, the Taxation Department, the Department of Immigration, and a hire-purchase firm up in Sydney. At the moment, we're blocking all that. But,' he added nastily, 'if we as much as nod, they'll all be down on you like a pack of famished dingoes. Think about that, Tallon, before you start playing hard to get. And bear this in mind as well: if you co-operate, we can not only get all that straightened out. We can guarantee that you'll get your yacht back—and a clean slate to go with it.' He unscrewed the bowl of his pipe to rake out the clinkers. 'I'm not going to give you the God-bless-Australia bit,' he said quietly, 'but, quite apart from the life or death of one man, this means a lot to us. The whole future of the SEATO Alliance could depend on it.' He blew down his pipe-stem, watching me. 'It isn't as if,' he said persuasively, 'we were asking you to do anything beyond your ability. You won't have to do any acting. You've a background that can be checked from here to Wormwood Scrubs and back and found completely authentic—which is why I can't use one of my own men. All you've got to do is what you did when you were in the big-game fishing business—take whatever client comes along, with the difference that, this time, you'll be...'

'On the wrong end of the hook,' I said gloomily. 'This time, I'll be the sharkbait.' I crushed out the cigarette that had suddenly taken on a nasty taste of gunsmoke. 'Hell, you're not risking much, are you? If I don't play ball I get put away until I'm eligible for a pension. If I do co-operate, it won't cost you a cent anyway, because the only corpse I know of who needs a ship is the Flying Dutchman.' I stared at him defeatedly. 'OK,' I said. 'What do I have to do?'

CHAPTER FOUR

I drifted up from the depths of a dreamless sleep to the realisation that my phone was ringing again. White-hot sunlight blasted me between the eyes like a laser beam as I stretched out an arm, knocked the phone to the floor with a crash, and groped for it among the bed-fluff. A faint voice said politely from under the bed, 'Good morning. Is that Captain Tallon, please?' I found the receiver and grunted into it while I hauled the rest of the apparatus on to the pillow. 'My name,' said the voice confidentially into my left ear, 'is Smith. Mrs Smith. I heard you are looking for a job, Captain?'

'Not Captain,' I said thickly. 'Just Tallon.' It was a warm, beautifully-modulated voice, with the careful clarity of someone to whom English is still a foreign language, no matter how well-learnt. A husky, sexy voice—the kind of voice, I thought, that ought to go with long, honey-blonde hair, an eye-popping figure, and a taste for indoor sports. I came awake on the instant—but not on account of my caller's physical possibilities. For all I cared, this Smith could be a balding ninety-nine with a silhouette like a decaying bollard. What had got my adrenalin moving was her use of the in-word 'job', the one that all the switched-on set were using these days. 'What,' I asked, breaking out in premonitions all over, 'makes you think I need a job, Mrs Smith?' Be suspicious, Fenner had said. Don't make it easy for them. I only wished I could think of a way of making it impossible. 'And how did you know where to find me?'

'I think you are still in bed,' she said, somehow contriving to make it sound highly indecent. 'Your voice sounds rough and unshaven, and you have certainly not read your newspaper this morning. You are front page news, Mr Just Tallon. I thought perhaps we might meet and discuss...'

'I'm sorry,' I said curtly. 'You'd be wasting your time. There's nothing I want to discuss.' I swung my legs out of bed, wondering just how many people were tapping my line at that very moment.

'From what I hear,' she said, letting her voice purr a bit, 'you are a man of some initiative. I think some way of occupying my time would occur to you.' She paused to let me think up a few ways and I yawned silently, waiting for her to go on. 'There is a restaurant in Collins Street called the Palermo, where they have little tables with gay umbrellas set out on the pavement. On a beautiful morning like this...'

'It sounds fascinating,' I said brutally, 'but, on this particularly beautiful morning, I happen to have other things to do. Like building a raft.'

'Building a...?'

'Raft. I'm leaving the country, Mrs Smith, as soon as I can arrange a passage.'

'From what I read,' she said calmly, 'I cannot say I am surprised. But please do not make any arrangements until I have had a chance to talk to you. I think I can help you, and I know you can help me. Shall we say in ten minutes, for lunch?'

I counted up to five slowly. 'OK,' I said at last. 'I can't see what you can do for me, but I don't mind having lunch with you, as long as you pick up the bill. We'll say in half an hour.' I hung up on her. Having been uncouth enough to discourage any genuine prospective employer, I sat for a moment scratching the mosquito bites on my wrist. The sharks, too, were biting early this morning, it appeared. Then, somewhat cheered by the reflection that, whatever kind of entertainment she had in mind, her style was going to be a little cramped in an open-air restaurant in the middle of the city, I got my Shavemaster out of my bag and plugged it into the skirting-board.

It was, as she'd said, a beautiful morning—what was left of it. I'd opened my window to let out Fenner's atmospheric pollution before going to bed, and now the yellow plastic curtains swung gently in the warm northerly breeze, revealing a pock-marked fly-screen backed by a strip of brassy blue sky and the dusty sun-baked roofs of the buildings across the street. A mixture of Australian and Hellenic accents came up to me above the distant susurration of midday traffic, together with the latest hit from Athens played in the radio shop next door. I shaved and showered and I was breaking out my only clean shirt when there was a sudden loud thump on the door. I spun round nervily as Karonides ballooned in, his button nose twitching desperately to dislodge the fly that he couldn't brush off because he was carrying an enormous tray that held a dinner-plate overflowing with ham, eggs and fried potatoes, a toast-rack packed with thick golden slices, half a grapefruit, about a pound of butter, a cream jug, a sugar basin, and an earthenware coffee pot. He dumped the lot on my bed. 'A light breakfas' only,' he announced, scratching his nose ecstatically, 'since it is so late. The grapefruit 'as been soak all night in port wine. You like it, yes?'

'I like it, no,' I snapped ungratefully. His offering put me in mind of the hearty breakfasts they used to hand out just before they asked you what size you took in nooses. 'I never eat breakfast. Take it all away, apart from the coffee, and feed it to the mice.'

'Your voice sounds rough and unshaven,' he quoted, leering horribly at me. 'For a woman like this Smith, it is evident that a man needs all the strength he can get. 'Owever, if you do not wish the 'amaneggs, I have a very good friend who sells little tablets that...'

'Get out, you fat faker.' I couldn't help grinning. 'Before you get fatty degeneration of the ear. And bring me a paper.'

'Already I have one.' With an effort, he

hauled out the rolled-up copy that was stuffed into his hip pocket. I grabbed it from him, poured out a cup of black coffee with one hand and shook out the paper with the other. The caption halfway down the front page caught my eye at once:

LUXURY YACHTSMAN ATTACKED FOLLOWING POLICE PROBE FIGHT IN STOLEN CAR

The former captain-owner of a luxury yacht was lured from a Melbourne guest house late last night in a Chicago-style abduction bid that ended in a desperate fight for life in a speeding car.

The man, Patrick Tallon, an Englishman, at present unemployed, had been questioned by Commonwealth Police officers earlier in the day in connection with alleged activities on behalf of a political group in Tasmania.

According to the proprietor of the Galatea Guest House, jovial local identity Dimitrios Karonides (pictured), Tallon left the hotel in the company of two men who had posed as police officers. It appears that a struggle developed inside the car in which the assailants sped off with their intended victim, and the vehicle, a late-model sedan said to have been stolen from an adjacent car-park, crashed into a wall and burst into flames. Tallon was thrown clear, but the driver and his companion, as yet unidentified, were trapped in the blazing wreckage.

Shaken by his ordeal, Tallon stated in an interview with our reporter that the abduction was an attempt at murder to prevent him from assisting the police further with their inquiries. 'They were killers,' he said. 'They had a gun and they said they would use it. I know too much for my own good.'

A police spokesman at Russell Street was unable to comment on Tallon's statement but...

I dropped the paper on to the bed, the smirking picture of mine host lying uppermost. 'Very authentic, you jovial local identity, you,' I said, sipping my coffee. 'So now Mrs Smith is able to contact me openly without having to go to all the trouble of kidnapping me again. Very considerate. But what happens if, having lured me from my city hotel, she too speeds off with her intended victim? How am I supposed to report back?'

'Report? You report to no one. Not unless you are looking for a quick way of committing suicide.' Suddenly the fat buffoon seemed to dissolve in front of me, and a very different man looked out from the chocolate-brown eyes—a tough, hard-faced character with a build like an Olympic wrestler and a mind like a diamond drill. 'Listen to me, my friend,' he said crisply. 'I have had much experience of these matters. And one of the things I have learnt is that, while any fool in the right place at the right time can get information, it takes a trained agent to relay it without being caught. So you are not to attempt to contact us, no matter what happens, understand? We will be watching you discreetly, and we will find the means of approaching you at the proper time.' He grinned at me and clapped me on the back with a hand that felt like a sledge-hammer. 'An' now,' he said, reverting to his simple inn-keeper role, 'get out there an' see what this Mrs Smith 'as to offer. But not to let Mr Smith catch you taking it from her, eh?'

The temperature was already into the high nineties and climbing when I left the guest house and, by the time I reached the top end of Collins Street, my jacket was off and I'd have agreed to lunch with Chairman Mao himself if he'd thrown in a couple of beers. Under the trees, in the dancing, dappled patterns of shade thrown on the pavement, it was a little cooler and the striped umbrellas outside the Palermo looked cooler still. I checked the clientèle as I sat down gratefully at a vacant table facing the street. I got three shirt-sleeved clerks, three elderly biddies, a brace of young matrons complete with ice-cream-coated offspring, one very old Italian reading *Il Globo*, and two naval ratings with a high-octane blonde apiece. Will the real Mrs Smith please stand up? I thought. I ordered an iced coffee and sipped it while tanned Melbournians, clad in everything from beach gear to lightweight business suits sauntered or hurried past. I checked out every female in sight, getting some unexpected reactions, and it was while I was avoiding the speculative eye of a ringleted brunette in a pink pleated shirt and lime-green slacks who had turned out to have a pipe sticking out of his hip pocket that a warm, slightly-husky voice said from just behind my right shoulder, 'Mr Tallon?

My car is just round the corner, if you are ready.'

For a moment, until I realised she'd been waiting inside the restaurant, I thought she'd come up through the pavement. Then, following the eyes of the three clerks, the two naval ratings and the ancient Italian, who was making no attempt to retrieve the newspaper he'd dropped, I turned without getting up, eyed her from head to foot in a way that would have earned me a smack across the chops from most of the girls I'd known, and said, 'Ready for what? I'm not going anywhere, sweetheart. But, if you want to take the weight, feel free.' I took a swig of my iced coffee.

After looking her up and down I needed the stuff as a coolant. It wasn't that she was panting in my face or waggling her hips at me—nothing like that. It was merely that she conveyed, overwhelmingly, a kind of modestly-suppressed sensuality that was far more disturbing than any overt parade of sex. The summer-weight woollen dress she had on was plain and virginally white against her café-au-lait tan, and no shorter or tighter than the average, but it was cut so cleverly that it showed off the high pointed breasts and the long smooth curve of the thighs as effectively as a bikini. She was a little under medium height, and her shoulder-length auburn hair, brushed until it shone like burnished copper, framed a heart-shaped face that, even partially concealed behind big square Zeiss sunglasses, was a strikingly beautiful blend of the innocent and the earthy—a face that would have looked as tranquil as a carved madonna's, with its broad, intelligent brow and smoothly-tanned schoolgirl skin, had it not been for the slightly-flared nostrils and the wide, invitingly full-lipped mouth that was about as tranquil as a bongo rhythm. She looked like the kind of girl you'd be glad to take home to mother—as long as you were careful not to leave her alone with father.

She touched me caressingly on the shoulder with the tip of a slim, golden finger. 'Across the street,' she said softly, so that her entranced six-man audience couldn't hear, 'there are two men in a car who have been watching you ever since you sat down. But if you prefer to talk here...'

I jumped to my feet, cursing Fenner under my breath. If this, I thought as

81

I followed her round the corner into Exhibition Street, was his idea of discreet observation, we weren't going to get very far. I climbed into the passenger seat of her pillar-box-red Chrysler Valiant while she slid behind the wheel, keeping her knees correctly together so that, when her mini-skirt rode up, the view was aesthetic rather than anatomical, but her modest tug at the hem merely served to underline the fact that she had long and completely perfect legs. In the car, I was also exposed to the kind of perfume that ought to be marketed in lead-lined containers, but it was all rather wasted on me, since I was far more concerned with my own skin just then than with hers. As she slid the key into the ignition, I put my hand on her wrist. 'Just a minute,' I said. 'How far are we going? As I said on the phone, I've got things to do when I get back.'

She smiled at me, a slow secret smile, as she removed my hand. 'You'd be surprised,' she said, 'how far I can go.' She switched on the motor, moved the selector to Drive and, without looking to right or left, hit the accelerator pedal. The car surged out into the traffic amid a bedlam of screaming tyres, oaths, and blaring horns. Unconcernedly, she said, 'And you won't be coming back, Mr Tallon. This is a one-way trip.'

'A one-way...?' I braced myself as she stood on the brake-pedal to avoid ramming the Yellow Cab in front. 'Listen, I've got a bag at the guest house with all my...'

'You won't need it. We'll provide everything you want.' She turned left into Flinders Street, the aerial array of a local radio station towering above us on the roof of the *Herald-Sun* building. 'You will be quite safe with us. You need help, Mr Tallon.'

'I can look after myself,' I said toughly. 'Those two opposite the café didn't worry me. They...'

'No?' She looked sideways at me from behind her big sunglasses. 'There were no men opposite the café. But you got into the car fast enough, didn't you?'

'And I can get out again, too,' I snapped. I was genuinely annoyed to think that she'd managed to put one over on me in the opening moves. 'Stringing me along with a false name and showing me how clever you are isn't exactly the best way to get me to work for you. If there's one thing I hate, it's a bird who's got to keep proving that her

IQ's bigger than her bust measurement.'

She shrugged. 'If names are important to you, mine is Bellamy. Christina Bellamy. I had my own reasons for not giving it over the phone. And you won't get out of the car. You're curious, aren't you? You want to know why I'm doing this, and what's in it for you.' She turned north into Spring Street, into the hot sun that beat on to my knees through the windscreen. 'What is it you know that made those people want to kill you last night?'

'Now you're the one who's being curious,' I said sourly. We passed the tall rectangular ICI building. 'And are we going anywhere in particular, or do we just cruise around until we run out of petrol?'

'Oh, we are certainly going somewhere. But first, we have to do a small disappearing trick. Everything has been arranged, and all you have to do is exactly what I tell you. We know precisely what we are doing.'

The disappearing bit sounded slightly ominous, but I was reassured by the fact that Fenner seemed to know what he was doing as well. And if she was hoping to shake off a tail in a car this shade of red, she'd have to be pretty smart. We drove on a little way until, without warning, she turned left down a ramp and pulled up in the cool gloom of a basement filling-station underneath a multi-storey parking block. On the far side of the pumps an attendant was checking the tyres of a dove-grey Dodge Phoenix that had a big aluminium caravan, glittering under the fluorescent lights, in tow. The Dodge was on our offside, facing the way we'd come and, as we stopped, its driver got out, spoke to the attendant, and the two of them walked across to the office.

The girl said quietly, watching them, 'Don't ask questions. Just get into the caravan when I tell you.' She switched off her motor. At the same time, a door in the side of the caravan opened and a man and a girl jumped out. 'Now!' Mrs Bellamy said. 'Quickly!' A flash of tanned leg, and she was out on her side of the car.

I climbed out more slowly. 'Hurry!' she hissed. I went round the front of the Valiant, nearly colliding with the tall man in shirt-sleeves who pushed past me without a word and got into the seat I'd vacated. Mrs Bellamy shoved me into the caravan, climbed up, and shut the door quickly behind her—but not before I'd seen the other girl, in a white dress and with big square sunglasses and auburn, shoulder-length hair, who was now sitting behind the wheel of the Valiant. Footsteps echoed hollowly on the concrete outside, a car-door slammed, and the floor lurched beneath my feet as the Dodge pulled the caravan up the ramp and out into the sunlit street. Mrs Bellamy casually put a hand to her head, pulled off her auburn wig, and shook out her cap of short, raven-black hair.

'Very ingenious,' I said hollowly. I'd had a sudden, unpleasant cut-off feeling as I pictured Fenner assiduously tracing the movements of two complete strangers in the pillar-box-red Valiant that would shortly emerge into the street. I sat down on the leather settle as we turned right. The caravan was well-equipped and well-insulated, cool and twilit behind its closed venetian blinds.

'Ingenious, yes.' The girl took off her sunglasses and smiled down at me, wrinkling her rather flat nose. 'It is also illegal to travel in a caravan. But you won't mind that, I'm sure.'

I was so taken aback that I forgot all

86

about Fenner. 'Well, what do you know?' I said, staring at her. 'You're...'

'Chinese,' she said, still smiling. 'My name was Christina Chan before I married. But don't let it worry you. I have no colour prejudices—in fact, some of the Englishmen I have met have been almost civilised. And now, will you please take off your clothes?'

'My what?' I wondered whether it was her English or my mind that was slipping. The latter, I thought, since she was already unzipping her dress and kicking off her shoes.

'Your clothes,' she said impatiently, pulling the dress over her head in a flurry of lace underwear that was startlingly white against her golden skin. 'Your shirt and trousers. Then...' She shook her head free and caught my eye. 'If this,' she said coolly, 'is the first time you have seen a girl undressing, you must have led a very sheltered life, my friend.' She padded lithely past me, holding on to a built-in wardrobe as the caravan swayed round a corner. 'And, if you have ideas, forget them.' She tossed me a bundle of clothing. 'The middle of the street at midday is neither the time nor the place.'

She proceeded to encase herself in a pair of stone-coloured skin-tight pants and an ensign-red shirt.

Not to be outdone in permissive behaviour, I whipped off my shirt and slacks and got into the navy-blue sports shirt and off-white Koratron trousers that fitted as if they'd been made to measure while she combed out her gleaming blue-black hair and checked her makeup in the tiny bathroom. 'Good,' she said, eyeing me critically as I transferred my belongings from my suit. 'A pair of sunglasses, and you are ready.'

She separated the slats of the venetian blinds as we stopped. I had a brief glimpse over her shoulder of a phalanx of pedestrians crossing Swanston Street, and of a white-helmeted shirt-sleeved traffic cop sweating it out in the hot sun with the unlovely Kremlin-like mass of Flinders Street railway station behind him. We crossed the Yarra River on Princes Bridge, and a few minutes later we stopped again. This time, the driver of the Dodge touched his horn-button gently, and I put on the Polaroids the girl had given me as we got out into the grilling afternoon sun. The car and caravan moved off smartly and we crossed the broad tree-lined road to where a white Mercedes Benz 280SE was parked opposite the sloping lawns of the Botanical Gardens. 'Where,' I asked as I strapped myself into cool, air-conditioned luxury, 'are we going?'

'I own a boatyard down the coast.' She took a slim gold cigarette-case from her bag, lit two Dunhill's King Size with the lighter on the dash, and passed me one. 'It is very lonely there—a place where the Red Star will never find you.'

'The Red Star?' It sounded like a shipping line.

'The Communists, then,' she said impatiently. 'You know what I mean. They are the ones who are after you, aren't they?' She strapped herself in, started the motor and did a U-turn. Luckily, the road happened to be clear of traffic just then. 'You see, I have heard something of your activities, as the newspaper called them, in Tasmania. They are trying to get rid of you, as they usually do with people who have outlived their usefulness. You were working for them there, yes?'

I shrugged, staring out of the side window as we passed the Shrine of

Remembrance, Melbourne's imposing granite memorial to the war dead of Australia. 'I just make a living where and how I can,' I said guardedly. 'I can't afford to be choosy about the people I work for. All that interests me is how much I get paid and what I have to do to get it.'

'Good. And so what you are going to do for me will interest you greatly, I think. You see, Mr Tallon, in addition to my boatyard, I also own a boat. I want you to sail it for me.'

'What sort of boat?' I began to show a little of the interest she'd predicted. 'And how's she registered?' When she glanced at me uncomprehendingly I said, 'Is she a freighter, or a sailing dinghy or what? If she isn't registered privately I can't touch her without a master's ticket.'

'Oh, *Victoria* is a motor yacht, registered privately. I have only just bought it, and I can tell you little of the technical details, but I know it has two diesel engines, and radar. And a crew,' she added helpfully.

'Oh, sure.' I thought we'd get round to the strong-arm brigade sooner or late. 'How many?' About fifty, I guessed, and Red Guards to a man.

'Two. One is a Frenchman, Max, who

runs the boatyard for me. The other worked for the yacht's last owner, so he knows it well. He says there will be little to do before we sail.'

'Fine,' I said. 'and where are we sailing to?'

'To Hong Kong,' she said, as off-handedly as if she was proposing a trip round the Bay.

CHAPTER FIVE

'Hong Kong?' I said sharply. This I hadn't bargained for. I wondered if Fenner had and, if so, what possible use I could be to him while I was bobbing about in the South China Sea. 'What for?'

'For two thousand Australian dollars,' she said smoothly, 'plus a free passage out of the country. Afterwards, you could change your name, go where you please, start a new life. That is an offer that would interest you, I think?'

'It depends,' I said slowly, 'on what your own interests happen to be. Why do you want to go to Hong Kong?'

'Does it matter? You said yourself that all you care about is the money.'

'And what I have to do for it. Don't misunderstand me, Mrs Bellamy, but I've had some pretty kooky clients in my time, and your interests could include getting me to peddle little packets of castor sugar round the Wan Chai nightspots for all I know.'

'It is nothing like that,' she said distantly. 'This is a pleasure cruise, nothing more. I was born in Taiwan, but my parents now live in Hong Kong and I am going to visit them.'

'I see. And who else goes on this slow boat to China? Your husband?'

'Yes,' she said, without sounding wildly enthusiastic about it. 'He runs a small manufacturing chemist's business. He hopes to get export orders in Hong Kong.' She flicked me a quick, slant-eyed glance. 'His work leaves him very little time for me.'

The ante was rising. First, a ship to sail under the blazing tropic stars, then two thousand for doing it, and now a beautiful neglected wife as a fringe benefit. It sounded fine—if you happened to be making a B picture—but it wasn't getting me anywhere. I had to have something to tell Fenner, and soon, because it was highly unlikely that I'd be allowed unrestricted use of the yacht's radio once we were at sea. 'And that,' I said, 'is why you've gone to all this trouble with the cars and the decoy and the slow trip in the caravan—because you and your husband would rather travel to Hong Kong in a smallish craft in the middle of the tropical

93

cyclone season than go P & O or Qantas?'
I grinned at her as I drew on my cigarette.
'Don't let's kid ourselves, Mrs B. There
are plenty of skippers in Melbourne with
better qualifications than mine, and most
of them would jump at a job like this.
You didn't have to pick one who's on
the run—not unless you wanted him for
something that no other skipper'd touch
with a grappling-hook. So let's hear what
that something is. And you don't have to be
all Oriental and devious about it. I've been
in crooked deals before, and I don't shock
easily. It's just that I always like to know
what the maximum sentence is, that's all.
And they have a quaint local custom here,'
I added, watching the crowded intersection
that was racing at us, 'of stopping when the
lights go red. How about...?' I grabbed for
the padded dashboard as the power-assisted
brakes came on with a shriek.

'You are trying my patience, Mr Tallon.'
She set the hand-brake with a rasp like
an angry rattlesnake. 'You are also being
very stupid. Two thousand dollars is a
great deal of money to a man like you.
Enough, I think, to prevent you inquiring
into my private affairs. However, if you
think otherwise...'

'...I can leave my name at the desk. OK. But you'd have had to tell me sooner or later what it is you're up to.' I reached for the door-handle. 'I can find my own way back.'

'Wait!' She gave me a look that put me in mind of the Death of a Thousand Cuts. 'There is no need to be so hasty. I will tell you what you want to know. But then,' her face hardened, 'there must be no more talk of backing down. You will be fully committed, you understand?'

I understood all right. She was telling me that this was the point of no return. Once I knew what the score was, my life wouldn't be worth a cardboard cent if I turned her offer down. 'I'm not backing down—not from two thousand dollars.' I took my hand off the door-handle. 'But I'm not working in the dark, either.'

'Very well.' She rolled the Mercedes forward. 'We are going to Hong Kong, as I told you. We are even going to visit my relatives there. But, on the way, we are taking on another passenger. My brother, Peter Chan. We are going to smuggle him into the Crown Colony.'

This, I thought as I remember what Fenner had told me about her brother, was more like it. I sat back and smoked my cigarette as she said, 'He went to Djakarta six years ago to work on an engineering project there. He is older than I, and he means a great deal to me. We wrote often. He even came to visit me once, here in Melbourne. But then after September 1965, his letters stopped.' She looked sideways at me. 'You remember the abortive Communist coup of that time?'

I remembered. It had been on the night of 30th September, 1965, that Indonesia had come within a whisker of ending up as a Red Chinese province—a fate that had been averted only by the prompt action and personal bravery of a handful of her leaders. I felt slightly sick as I recalled some of the things I'd read about that hibiscus-scented night of horror in Djakarta—how six anti-Communist generals had been murdered in a planned, cold-blooded massacre. Four of them, together with a junior officer, had been thrown to a pack of screaming women fanatics who had tortured them obscenely and then flung their mutilated bodies down a well. I said casually, 'Was your brother mixed up in that business?'

'Of course not,' she said warmly. 'But he was foolish enough to become involved with a woman who was an active member of the terrorist group that planned the coup. She persuaded him to become a member, too. Then, when she was tried for her part in the murders, she implicated my brother because he had refused to have anything to do with them. He was arrested, tried, and imprisoned.'

And lucky not to have been hanged, I thought. Because the only part of her story I believed was the bit about her brother being a member of a terrorist group—and that group was almost certainly the Mako, who had now got him out of gaol because they wanted to use him again. I said, 'So? You're not suggesting we try to spring him from a prison in the middle of Djakarta, I hope?'

She shook her head. 'Recently, an Indonesian student at one of the universities here brought me a letter from Peter. It said that he and another man had been able to escape from a ship that was transferring them to a prison in Surabaja, in Eastern Java. The letter was written from Selaru, in the Tanim-bar Group, where Peter intended to steal a fishing boat and hide out on the Pulau Mati.'

'Pulau Mati? Where's that?'

'In the Kepulauan Aru—the Aru Archipelago, the eastern-most tip of the Indonesian island chain. It is a strange, remote place, more like Northern Australia in many ways than anywhere else.'

I nodded. I'd heard of the naturalist's phenomenon called Wallace's Line, the division down the Lombok Strait that splits the flora and fauna of Indonesia in two. West of it, in Bali, Java and Sumatra, are the tigers and jungles of tropical Asia; to the east, in the Lesser Sundas, Timor and the Moluccas, are to be found the marsupials and rare plants of Australia. I said, 'There are supposed to be kangaroos in the Aru Group.'

'But not on Pulau Mati,' she said quietly. 'It's name means Dead Island. There, the only animals are the rats.'

'Rats?'

'It is a place where the people of the neighbouring islands used to bury their dead. So the rats did well there, until the burial ground fell into disuse. Nowadays, having killed off everything else, they keep alive on the sea-birds—and on each other. The natives believe they are devils sent to guard the souls of the dead. And so no one chooses to live on Pulau Mati, or even go near it.'

I crushed out my cigarette. 'And that,' I said, as casually as if I ferried hot convicts up and down the South China Sea every day of the week, 'is all there is to it? We sneak in there one dark night, take off your brother and ferry him to Hong Kong. Nothing else?'

'Nothing,' she said, with an open, earnest sincerity that convinced me of one thing—that I was dealing with the most accomplished actress since Anna May Wong. 'My family has influence there and, once he is ashore, he will be safe.' She paused. 'I bought the yacht as soon as I received Peter's letter, but it was difficult to find the right man to sail it. Then, this morning, I saw your name in the newspaper. The crewman I spoke of, the one who came with the yacht, says you have done this kind of thing before and that, in a difficult situation, you are the best in the business.'

'That,' I said, 'was nice of him.' I didn't bother to ask how her sailor had formed this flattering opinion. I just settled back in my seat like one who has been bribed, flattered, and fed the best story since the

Three Bears. 'And you need look no further, Mrs Bellamy. You've got yourself a skipper.' I yawned. 'And now, suppose you give me a call when we reach the end of the line? You got me out of bed early, remember?' I closed my eyes.

Not, I thought grimly as I listened to the hot dry wind whispering against the heat-insulated glass beside me, that I was likely to get much sleep. What I wanted was time to think—time to try to fit into Fenner's jigsaw the various jagged little bits I'd been presented with, and see what kind of picture emerged. One scene I knew I wouldn't get, and that was one of a manufacturing chemist and his charming wife snatching an erring brother from misdirected justice. Even without Fenner's briefing I'd have had to be pretty hard up for two Gs to believe that one. That we were bound for Pulau Mati, yes. That we were picking somebody up there, yes again. But I was prepared to bet that that somebody was a man who had played a substantial part in the events of the night of 30th September, 1965, in Djakarta—a Mako assassin, and a rocket expert, to boot.

And we weren't taking him to Hong

Kong. If this Peter Chan was a convicted Red terrorist, known to Australian security, then the Hong Kong authorities would know about him, too. It would be impossible to smuggle him ashore, no matter how much pull his sister might have. On the other hand—and the interior of the air-conditioned car seemed uncomfortably chilly all of a sudden—it would be the easiest thing in the world to land him anywhere on the thousands of miles of lonely, unguarded coast between Cape York and Wilson's Promontory.

And the time of his arrival in Australia would be spang in the middle of the Presidential visit.

We ran through Frankston, a pleasant Bayside beach resort alive, at this time of the year, with brown little boys clutching inflatable rubber ducks and with bigger, browner boys clutching equally pneumatic birds of their own. I sat up and said liverishly, 'How much farther, for God's sake?'

'Not far.' She spoke absently, as if she had thoughts of her own that certainly didn't include slobs like me. Obviously, there was no more need for the hard sell now that she'd got what she wanted. 'I said it was a lonely spot.'

We went on, south on the Nepean Highway, driving fast down the Mornington Peninsula that encloses Port Phillip Bay on its eastern side like the claw of a crab. The open sea was very close now. When I wound my window down I got the old familiar tingle as I sniffed the lovely clean saltiness of it and saw, in my mind's eye, the surf creaming on the ocean beaches with the Bass Strait rolling restlessly out to the purple-hazed horizon. The neat suburban houses had given way to the gaily-painted weekend retreats they call shacks in Australia. Soon, even these began to thin out until, when we turned off the main highway towards the Bay, we were driving through thick bush—a belt of tall eucalypts and tea-tree, charred and blackened in places where the bushfires had gone through earlier in the summer. Behind us, the choking red dust rose up like a wall, making me roll my window down as we lurched along a narrow rutted track that got worse as the trees closed in overhead. I said, as I bounced jerkily on my seat, 'This is a hell of a place to pick for a boatyard.'

'I bought it for my husband. He was

working on a carbon monoxide absorption unit for marine engines, and he used this place to test it out.' She added with a touch of contempt, 'It didn't work, of course.'

We jolted round a bend into a cleared space where the track came to a dead end and a two-storeyed weatherboard building, sagging and neglected and with a tall paling fence running off to left and right, blocked off my view of the water. A peeling sign painted on the side of the building said BEL-AMI CHEMICALS PTY LTD, and another, newer notice fixed to a double gateway advised us to KEEP OUT. DOGS GUARD THIS PROPERTY. To prove they weren't fooling the baying of what sounded like a pack of famished mastiffs came from beyond the fence. The gates swung open as we approached, and we drove straight through without stopping into the shade of the building where a smallish, dark-skinned character in a singlet and khaki pants nodded briefly in reply to the girl's wave. Straight ahead, a concrete ramp led to a covered slipway and what looked like a tin-roofed workshop beyond which the dogs clamoured hungrily. We turned the corner of the main building into the sunlight and came to a halt under a bougainvillea-fringed verandah that looked out on to the Bay across a turning-circle of red gravel. The girl switched off the motor and turned to me. 'Well?' she said. 'What do you think of our boat, Mr Tallon?'

Directly opposite the house, on our left, was a solidly-constructed wooden jetty where big yellow-beaked Pacific gulls perched and preened their jet-black tail-coats. And, lying quietly alongside the jetty, was a sixty-foot motor yacht that had been freshly tricked-out in ice-blue and white. She was moored stern-on to me and her name and port of registration, VICTORIA—MELBOURNE, stood out clearly in black.

I stared at her. And, for an instant, the whole scene—the trim, pale-blue yacht with the deeper blues of sea and sky behind her—seemed to blur into a blue-grey mist and then swung back into focus with a lurch. The gulls screamed sardonically from the jetty as I said stupidly, 'It's *Lorelei*. The yacht I used to...'

'...own,' she said softly, watching me. 'I know. And it's nice to know you recognise it, Mr Tallon. It would be awkward if we'd got hold of the wrong man, wouldn't it?'

I recognised the yacht all right. I recognised her the way you'd know your own home, even when it had had a new paint job and its name changed. From where I was sitting, I could see straight into the flying-bridge that, mounted hansom-cab fashion above and aft of the saloon, gave her the slightly ungainly appearance I knew so well—an appearance that was entirely at variance with the way she handled. More things, pleasant and unpleasant, had happened to me aboard that yacht than I cared to think about, and I hardly heard the girl when she said, 'You are to go straight aboard. We will follow shortly, but in the meantime you are not to leave the yacht, you understand?' There was the clunk of the car-door closing, and the crunch-crunch of her high heels on the gravel as she went into the house.

After she'd gone, I sat and looked at the yacht and thought about Fenner. I'd underestimated the lanky, casual Australian —badly. In the first place, I'd dismissed his promise to get my yacht back for me as so much bull-dust. How, I'd reasoned, could he have known that *Lorelei* would be on the market when this job was over? I saw now how he'd known. Her ownership after she'd passed out of my hands would have been checked by ASIO as a matter of routine. That was why he'd been so sure the Mako would contact me. I was the logical one to pick as skipper for a job like this. And the Mako's elaborate precautions to avoid being tailed had been a monumental waste of time. Fenner had known, without even leaving his desk, where I'd be taken. And not only that. The entrance to Port Phillip Bay is so narrow that you can't float as much as a beer-can through the Heads without its being noticed. Fenner would know, to the minute, when we put to sea. Slightly cheered by this, I went aboard the yacht and down the companion to the saloon.

I ought to have known it would all be different. But I'd got used to picturing *Lorelei* as she'd been when I'd left her, forgetting that, while whatever is stored in the memory remains forever fixed and unchanged, only a fool expects reality to do the same. To Two-tooth and me, *Lorelei* had always been a working vessel, as reliable as her chronometer and as comfortable as we could make her. We'd had neither the time nor the inclination to do much about the décor. But now there were navy-blue curtains with gay aboriginal motifs on the big laminated-glass windows, and the carpet had been replaced by a thick-piled job in white Acrilan. There was a television set mounted on the after bulkhead where my bookcase had been, cushions with go-go patterns were scattered on the settle whose mahogany had been changed to a glossy teak veneer and, over the cocktail cabinet, there hung a highly-coloured abstract that looked like an unsuccessful appendectomy. You had to pay out a barrel of money these days, I reflected vindictively, to get anything as hideous as that. I went down the short ladder to the galley.

There had been changes in here, too, I thought grimly, staring at the steel watertight door that led for'ard to the crew's quarters in the fo'c'sle. Because, the last time I'd seen that door, it hadn't been clipped back, as it was now. It had been shut tight—all that had stood between this bright, well-equipped galley and the sea. The tiled deck had tilted dangerously then and, in the darkness of the flooded fo'c'sle, there had floated a dead man who had bumped gently against the bulkhead as the yacht rolled, as if knocking to be

let out. I could almost hear him now if...
My scalp prickled.

Quite clearly, from beyond the open watertight door, I could hear once again the splash of water, together with a soft, fleshy bumping noise.

Angrily, I pulled myself together. Somebody was running the shower in the crew's bathroom, that was all, and jumping around underneath it. One of Mrs Bellamy's homicidal hirelings, no doubt. Well, I thought coldly, the captain has his little privileges on most vessels and, in my case, not sharing the cramped, noisy fo'c'sle with a professional cut-throat was going to be one of them. I opened the door of the spare cabin that opened off the galley on the port side.

To my annoyance, the cabin was already tenanted. A vast dark-blue T-shirt with VICTORIA across the chest was draped over the neatly-made-up lower berth, together with an outsize pair of jeans. On the dressing-table were a Timex wrist-watch, a pocket transistor radio, a paperback with an improbably-stacked female panting on the cover, and a wicked-looking sheath-knife.

I was in no mood just then to discuss

problems of accommodation. I scooped up all the personal belongings, bundled them up in the shirt, and was on my way out with them when the doorway seemed to darken all of a sudden. I had a fleeting glimpse of what looked like a monster baboon clad in a bath-towel, then a hand like a hydraulic ram closed over my face and shoved me back into the cabin.

CHAPTER SIX

I staggered backwards. A deep Australian voice said coldly, 'Jeez, wouldn't yer know it? Peace and quiet all these weeks, but the minute you come aboard we have to have the practical bloody jokes. Gimme me togs, yer silly bludger, before I catch me death.'

I collapsed on to the bunk, wondering if I was going out of my mind. 'Two-tooth!' I said, gaping at him. 'What the hell are you doing here?'

'Trying to find me clean underpants,' he said testily, rummaging in a locker. 'Unless, of course, you've got there first.'

I must be really slipping, I thought. Why hadn't it occurred to me, as soon as I saw *Lorelei*, that Two-tooth Harry Lamb was the crew member the girl had told me about—the one who'd come with the yacht? Suddenly, with an overpowering sense of relief, I realised that nothing aboard had changed, really. *Lorelei* could change her name, be re-painted, even have her saloon papered with psychedelic paintings, but as long as Two-tooth was around she was still the same as ever. 'What,' I said, grinning like an idiot, 'went wrong with the Port Line job? They decided they'd rather have somebody in their engine-room who knew what he was doing, is that it?'

'Gotta better offer, mate.' Grunting, he forced his hairy torso into the T-shirt. As his bearded face popped out he said, 'La Bellamy asked me to stay on after she bought the old bucket. I even put in a word for you although,' he avoided my eye as he strapped on his watch, 'I never thought you'd come back as a chauffeur. Not after...'

'I didn't have much choice. Like those sentences they handed out in the old days, it was either the navy or the nick.'

'Yeah?' His steel-grey eyes held mine for a moment but, characteristically, he asked no questions. 'Well, you'll be all right here. We're off to Honkers, soon as Mrs B gives the word, did you know that? Holiday cruise. Happy Valley Racecourse, Nathan Road at night with the shops all lit up. Just the job, eh? And, in the meantime, it's the life of Reilly. All I got to do is keep the diesels on the top line, flop around in the sun and catch up with me reading. Quiet, peaceful set-up they got here.' He held out his paperback. 'Lend it to yer, if yer like,' he offered. 'Been banned in two States.'

I wondered how long the set-up was going to stay quiet and peaceful. 'Is that so?' I said grimly. 'And it hasn't struck you that there might be something queer about it?'

'Queer?' He stared at me. 'Hell, no, I don't go in for those boy-meets-boy books, you should know that. No, this is just ordinary, straightforward porn about a sex-mad bishop on the loose in a convent. Yer want to try page forty-seven. Cor! There's this gorgeous young nun in the shower, see, and while she's got her eyes all bunged up with soap he...'

'Let's go on deck.' Rather belatedly, I recalled my recent experiences with hidden microphones. I pushed past him. 'Maybe we could kill a couple of beers.'

'Suit yourself.' He tossed his book on to a bunk. 'We can't all be avid readers, I reckon.' He scooped two cans of Victoria Bitter out of the fridge in the galley and followed me up through the saloon and out on to the narrow shaded strip of deck on the port side.

'OK,' I said. 'This'll do. But I couldn't take any chances in your cabin. It might be bugged.'

He paused in the act of unzipping a beer-can. 'Bugged?'

'Bugged,' I said impatiently. 'Monitored. Little fella bokkis, you speakum, he hear. And, for crying out loud, stop looking at me like a retarded wombat. I know what I'm talking about, believe me.' Briefly, I filled him in with the details of my forcible enlistment in to ASIO.

When I'd finished he poured half a can of beer down his throat, quickly. 'You're not trying to tell me,' he said incredulously when he'd surfaced, 'that you're working for the fuzz, Tallon? Jeez, you can't be serious?' He took on some more beer, staring at me over the rim of the can as if he'd never seen me before. 'And what did you expect to find down here—the headquarters of this Mako mob, and Bellamy running it with a black eye-patch and a swimming-pool full of sharks? In your gum-boots, mate.' He started a derisive snort, burped instead, and excused himself absently. 'Bellamy couldn't run a bloody kindergarten. A no-hoper, that's all he is, living off his wife's money. And she's as nice a kid as you'd find anywhere. When I saw your name in the paper this morning and told her you'd do a good job but you were in a bit of trouble, like, she and Max were off like a dose of salts, organising her pals to get those Commos off your back. You should be bloody grateful.' He drained the can and tossed it over the side. 'She told me herself, she's going to Hong Kong to visit her old Mum and Dad. They've got a place on Des Voeux Road—in Victoria there. That's the Victoria she's named the boat after. Thinks the world of them she does.'

'She does?' I repressed the urge to grab him by the beard and shake him till his dentures rattled. 'Well, I wouldn't get all choked up about that, if I were you. And I wouldn't look forward to this holiday cruise you were telling me about, either. Because one of our ports of call is going to be a God-forsaken island that used to be a burial ground, it's supposed to be haunted, and we're putting in there to pick up an escaped Red convict who's been doing time in Indonesia for political murder.'

'Yeah?' He took his short black pipe out of his pocket and stuck it into his beard, eyeing me sceptically. 'And who told you all this? Your bird-brain security mates?'

'That nice kid of yours told me so herself. Not in as many words—according to her version, we're picking up her brother who was framed because he wouldn't play ball at the time of the September Plot of 1965. She wants to smuggle him into the Crown Colony.' I drank some of my own beer, getting a certain satisfaction out of the rapidly-changing expressions that were flitting across what could be seen of his face. 'But if, as I strongly suspect, this brother of hers is a big wheel in the Mako, it won't be Hong Kong he'll be heading for. He'll be coming here. And, with the US President around, it won't be to throw confetti, either.'

He struck a match to light his pipe and stared at me in silence until it drew. 'OK,' he said at last. 'But I know these people better than you do, Tallon, and I just can't see them as subversives. Bellamy hasn't got what it takes, and as for the girl...' He paused. 'She might believe this stuff she's been telling you, have you thought of that?'

'What difference does it make? We can't tangle with the Indonesian Government. Whichever way you look at it, she's got to be stopped.'

'Then you will have to be quick about it.' He jerked his pipe at the house. 'Here's the new radio we've been waiting on. Once that goes in, we're away.'

A white VW Kombi van with the name of a radio firm on its side had stopped on the gravel in front of the house and I saw Christina Bellamy's ensign-red shirt flash like a Chinese good-luck banner as she came out of the cavernous gloom of the verandah. With her was a tall, dark and handsome number in a gleaming white shirt, white shorts and white knee-high socks. A slim, deeply-tanned man in a white singlet and khaki slacks—the man who'd been on the gate—was standing talking into the driver's window. 'The one in the whiter-than-white outfit's Bellamy,' said Two-tooth gloomily. 'Fancies himself as a naval type. He'll be sporting a yachting cap as soon as we sail, you mark my words. The other bloke's Max. French, but he can't help that. He's all right.' He snorted. 'Will you look at that. Bloody typical.' The photogenic type in the shorts had climbed

116

up beside the driver, leaving the other two to follow on foot as the van reversed slowly on to the jetty. 'Lazy bludger. Won't walk across the room if he can help it.'

The VW pulled up alongside and Bellamy lowered himself out, staring up at me. In close-up, he wasn't quite as good-looking as he'd first appeared. He was tall and tanned, with the kind of features that used to be described as clean-cut in the boys' magazine I read at one time. His hair was thick and black and beautifully waved and his moustache was neatly clipped along his upper lip. But, although he was only in his late twenties, he already had a perceptible pot belly and his eyes, even behind his wrap-around glasses, looked cold and mean and set just a fraction too closely together. I got the feeling of being appraised by a shark through murky water as he stood with his hands on his hips, surveying me aggressively. 'You'll be my new skipper,' he said, in a voice that had had an imitation Guards accent sprayed on top of its native Australian. His eyes went pointedly to the beer-can in my hand. 'Hasn't taken you long to make yourself at home, has it?'

'No, it hasn't,' I said agreeably. 'And

who might you be? From the whites, I'd say you're the ship's cook, right?'

'Cook?' His bronzed cheeks flushed a muddy pink. 'I happen to be the owner. What the hell...?'

'I see,' I said quickly. I was trying not to show the shock I'd had when the white-overalled driver had climbed out of the VW and gone to open the doors at the back. He was a big, powerfully-built man with a sweaty bald dome and he carried with him, I was prepared to swear, a faint odour of fried onions. For a man of his weight, Dimitrios Karonides covered a lot of ground fast. To the indignant, red-faced Bellamy I said, 'I'm very sorry. But I couldn't be expected to know who you are, could I?'

He pursed his rather thick lips, considering this. 'Right,' he said, when he'd kept me in suspense long enough. 'Just as long as we know who's boss around here. And you'll address me as "sir" from now on. Now, I don't want to catch you with a beer in your hand on deck again, understand? I'm not having my ship run aground because the skipper's half stoned. No smoking on the bridge, either, and the owner's accommodation is out of bounds to the crew at all times. Is that clear?'

'Perfectly, I should think.' Christina Bellamy had come up to stand beside her husband, followed by the man called Max. She said coolly, 'But do we have to have the Captain Queeg impersonation, Robert? Mr Tallon is just...'

'Tallon is just finding out where he stands.' Bellamy turned his cold stare on to her. 'Unless, of course, you object? Perhaps,' he sneered, 'it might suit you better to have him prowling round the cabins at night?'

She shrugged. 'It's all the same to me. I always keep my door locked. As you know,' she added silkily, 'very well, Robert dear.'

Bellamy flushed again, but before he could sound off Karonides came round from the back of the van carrying the 80-lb weight of an SP Sailor radio transmitter as if it was a box of chocolates. 'Here,' he said to Two-tooth with an accent that was no more Greek than my own, 'grab hold of this, mate, while I fetch the receiver.'

Max vaulted the rail and held out a hand. 'M'sieu Tallon? I am Max Perrin. I do all the work around 'ere.' He grinned, showing a row of white, even teeth in a face like that of a friendly monkey. Behind him, Karonides climbed aboard, the receiver tucked under his arm, followed more slowly by Bellamy.

'All the work?' I gripped Max's hand. 'That's nice to know. We'll try to keep it that way.' The girl put up a hand, I took it, and she swung neatly on to the narrow deck so that she, her husband and Max were all between me and Karonides.

In the wheelhouse, too, they continued, unobtrusively but effectively, to shield him from any contact with Two-tooth or me. Mrs Bellamy stood on his right, Max on his left, and Bellamy peered over his shoulder while he worked. Short of violence, it looked as if my chances of getting a message to him were nil.

When he'd finished he straightened up, wiping his sleeve across his forehead. 'My word,' he said to no one in particular, 'she's a warm one today, all right. Real beer-drinking weather, this is.'

'You finished?' snapped Bellamy unsympathetically.

Karonides nodded. 'Set up on the channels you wanted, and I've wired up the lead you asked for to the extension speaker in your cabin. If you'll just sign for it, Mr Bellamy.' He passed a clipboard and a ball-point to my employer, who frowned judicially as he read the small print on the work docket. He was just about to sign when Karonides said casually, 'Nice boat you've got. You'll be skippering her yourself, I reckon? You don't employ a captain?'

Bellamy looked up irritably. 'Why? What the hell's it got to do with you? Don't I look as if I can afford one?'

'Aw, it's not that, sir. It's only that, if the owner employs a captain, it's the skipper's signature they've got to have in the office.' I pricked up my ears. 'As an acknowledgement,' said Karonides smoothly, 'that the set's satisfactory. Department of Shipping and Transport regulation, sir. Legally, it's the captain who's responsible for the vessel's communications, you see.'

'I've never heard such bloody rubbish,' said Bellamy testily. As a matter of fact, neither had I, but it sounded plausible enough to get past anybody who didn't know much about maritime law but who wanted to get all his paperwork in order. Bellamy shoved the clipboard back at me petulantly. 'Here,' he said. 'Sign it, then,

Tallon, since I don't seem to be important enough.'

I glanced cursorily at the slip of paper. Then I wrote 'Pulau Mati' with a flourish on the dotted line. I passed it back to Karonides. 'Fine,' he said, without looking at it. He tucked the clipboard under his arm. 'Now I can go and get myself a nice cold beer.' He looked hopefully at Bellamy and made no attempt to leave.

'You do that,' said Bellamy grimly. 'Max can see you to the gate.' The Frenchman made a wry face at me behind his boss's back and followed Karonides ashore. Bellamy said to Christina, 'I'm going back to the house. I'll see you at dinner if,' he gave me a nasty look, 'you can tear yourself away.' At the door he turned and glowered at Two-tooth and me. 'And nobody uses that radio without my permission, regulations or not I've got an extension speaker in my stateroom, so I'll be checking up on you.'

When he'd gone, the girl said, 'I must apologise for my husband. He and I...'

'It's none of our business,' I said briefly. The last thing I wanted was to get mixed up in any domestic trigonometry. 'When do we leave?'

'Tonight. The weather forecast is good.' She looked at Two-tooth. 'Tallon has told you,' she said, a trifle hesitantly, 'what we are going to do?'

'Yeah.' He took his pipe out of his mouth. 'And I think you could have told me yourself before now. I can't say I'm all that keen on chancing a stretch in an Indonesian gaol just to pick up a bloke who's worked for the Commos. If it wasn't for Tallon...'

'But it isn't like that at all,' she said earnestly. 'I know my own brother. He would never have taken part in the things of which they accused him.' She looked at me, then at Two-tooth again. 'If everybody,' she said quietly, 'who has worked for the Communists is to be condemned, then where would you two be? My brother is no different from you. And there will be no risk in this. The island is remote, with no patrol vessel within several hundred miles.'

But that, I said to myself, would be remedied before long. Yet, somehow, I felt a stupid sense of betrayal as I looked at her intent, serious face. What if she was telling the truth? What if her brother was just another sucker like me, who'd been manoeuvred on to the wrong side of the law?

But that, I told myself, was none of my business. I followed Two-tooth down to the galley to fix a meal—and to explain to him just why it was so essential that an electrical firm had to have my autograph on its work docket.

CHAPTER SEVEN

We slipped quietly out of Port Phillip Bay soon after midnight, under the last half of the moon and with the five stars of the Southern Cross flying like a kite to the south-east. By six o'clock the following morning we were off the south-east Cape. I came on to the bridge after four hours' sleep to a cool morning and a slight south-easterly swell that swung the yacht's stubby mast in gentle arcs across an overcast sky. Ahead and to port the Cape dropped sharply into the jade-green sea from two thousand feet and, on our port quarter, the rocks of the Glennie Group reared their strangely-castellated boulders out of the water like the ruins of some medieval fortress. By this time, Bellamy had got us all into uniform—white drill trousers, white deck shoes, and navy-blue T-shirts with VICTORIA in white letters across the chest. It made me feel like a deck-hand out of *HMS Pinafore*. Max, perhaps as a Gallic send-up, had added a French matelot's hat with a red pom-pom to his outfit. He sat, relaxed, in the big padded control seat, the Martinet auto-pilot switched in and the wheel moving eerily in front of him as he smoked a small Dutch cigar. I checked the echo-sounder, got a reading of thirty fathoms and said, 'You can go and eat. I'll start the run to Cape Howe.'

He said, 'Like you, I don' eat breakfast. but if your *copain* Two-tooth knows 'ow to avoid ruining good coffee, then I will 'ave a cup.' He made no attempt to go and get it, however. He looked up at me, his olive-brown face expressionless. 'Tallon,' he said slowly. 'Are you quite 'appy about this trip?'

'It's a living,' I said cautiously. 'Why? What's on your mind?'

He lifted his hands, then let them fall on his knees. 'I don't know. This brother of Madame's, now...'

'Yes,' I said thoughtfuly. 'This brother of hers. What do you know about him?'

'But nothing. That is the trouble. All I know is that Madame had a letter from him that had been brought by a student who...'

'You read it?'

'I? Read the correspondence of Madame?

126

I am a man of principle, *mon ami,* in spite of appearances.' He grinned at me suddenly. 'Besides, it was in Chinese.'

'And Bellamy. Why is he in on this? He doesn't exactly strike me as being the adventurous type.'

He twisted his mouth down like a bit of rubber. 'That crétin! Madame has friends, important business men, in Hong Kong. His affairs have gone badly and he hopes to get the export orders for his malodorous chemicals if he does as Madame wants.' He cocked his head on one side. 'But why the questions? Is it that, beneath the British upper lip, you too have the suspicions?'

'That,' I said, 'isn't where I'd keep them if I had any. What about yours?'

He turned to rest his forearms on the back of the seat, pointing his cigarillo at me. 'Understand, I have known Madame for some time, from before her marriage to this film-star type. She is above suspicion, that I know. But this brother, who draws his sister into possible danger of prison, he is another pair of sleeves altogether. At best, he is an idiot to get into this mess. At worst...' He shrugged. 'Has it occurred to you,' he said softly, 'that he may be, in truth, an agent of a terrorist organisation?

And that, if he is, he and his friends can take over the yacht and run her, not into Hong Kong, but into Swatow or Amoy or any other Red Chinese port where this Peter Chan would be safe?' He sat back, watching me. 'An' what would happen to us then, Tallon? I tell you, I don' like the idea one bit. Do you?'

'But she says she knows her brother and...'

'Pouf!' He snapped his fingers. 'Since when does she see him? five, six years? A man can change much in that time—and the communists have ways of making him change, too. No, I think we have to protect Madame against that possibility, my friend. Ourselves also.'

I looked at him with interest. This wasn't quite the way I'd expected Mrs Bellamy's right-hand man to turn out. On the other hand, I thought grimly, had anything turned out the way I'd expected since I'd landed in Melbourne? 'So?' I said. 'What do we do about it?'

'Nothing—at present. But we prepare a plan.' He looked round conspiratorially with all the Frenchman's love of intrigue. 'You have a gun?'

I shook my head. How could I, after

his precious Madame had made me strip almost to the buff in the caravan? 'No?' He said. 'I would have thought that, in your line of business—but no matter. I have one. A P-38. So, we pick up this Peter Chan as arranged, and if all goes well we take him to Hong Kong. But if he tries the funny business, I blow his head off an' we radio for assistance. OK?'

I said sceptically, 'If this boy's a trained terrorist it'll take more than one automatic to hold him off. Let's just play it by ear, eh?'

'But, of course. You are in charge, and I take my orders from you.' He stood up. 'Only, I want you to know that I too am on the side of the law and the order, an' you can rely on me.' He gave me a wink and a mock salute. 'An' now, she is all yours, *mon capitaine.*' He went below.

I chewed over this interesting conversation as I swung the yacht's gently-rolling bow round on to an east-nor'-easterly heading. Why had Max thought that, in my line of business I ought to be carrying a gun? Why did he want me to know that he was on the side of law and order? Was there a double meaning in what he'd said, or was I imagining it?

129

The wooded, undulating coastline receded and disappeared over the horizon during the morning as we crossed the shallow bight where, off Ninety-Mile Beach, the rigs of the booming Marlin, Barracouta and Kingfish oil-fields stood up to their steel thighs in forty fathoms to bring up real-life buried treasure from the sea-bed, and I was still no nearer to knowing what the amiable Max was trying to prove. All I could be sure of was that I wouldn't trust him any further than I could throw the Eiffel Tower—particularly now that I knew he packed a gun.

In the evening, the land came up out of the sea to meet us again—Cape Everard with its tall sandy peak, Ram Head and Gabo Island and, finally, in the diffused glow of a saffron sunset, Cape Howe on the border of Victoria and New South Wales, its haystack-shaped hill silhouetted against the yellow sky. Two-tooth, who had insisted on taking the wheel for the run into the waters of his home State, sat stirring sugar into the mug of milkless tea I'd brought him as I switched our lights on and the night, warm and humid and starless, closed in on us. 'Well,' he said, clinking the spoon against the mug to get rid of the drips, 'that's one quiet day to go down in the log, anyway. Calm sea, engines running like clocks and, as a bonus, bloody Captain Bligh down in his cabin all day. Haven't seen him, have you?'

I shook my head. The girl, too, now I came to think of it, had kept out of our way, appearing briefly for lunch and then sitting silent and preoccupied in the saloon afterwards, pretending to read a book.

'Not,' said Two-tooth, swigging his tea, 'that I'm complaining. If I never saw that gigolo again it'd be too soon.' He watched my reflection in the windscreen. 'Whatcha doing?'

'Weather forecast.' I flicked the receiver switch and spun the station selector. 'If we run into a Southerly Buster I want to know about it in advance.' Before we'd acquired the yacht she'd weathered a full typhoon in the South China Sea. I had no worries about her. But a Southerly Buster—the sudden blast of cold air liable to accompany a cold front in summer off the New South Wales coast—can give a sixty-foot yacht a shaking, and I didn't want to miss any strong wind warnings that might be going, not with the ominously-named Disaster Bay looming up to the north-east. I hunted for 2BA and, as I found the station, there was a sudden loud crash from below, followed by a muffled shouting. 'What the hell,' said Two-tooth in alarm, 'was that?'

Before I could say I didn't know, the bridge intercom started buzzing continuously like an angry chain-saw. I switched it on. 'You bastard!' shouted Bellamy thickly. 'I told you to leave that radio alone. Think I don't know what's going on, you...?' He threw in a string of obscenities that made Two-tooth raise his eyebrows respectfully, then there was another crash, followed by the shattering of broken glass.

'Jeez,' said Two-tooth, awe-struck. 'And he's the one who did his block when we had a can of beer. He's as full as a bloody boot. You'd better get down there before he starts digging holes in the hull.'

I dropped down the bridge ladder, down the short companion that led to the passenger accommodation aft, and along the miniature carpeted corridor to the owner's cabin that took up the whole width of the yacht for'ard of the cockpit. Mrs Bellamy, wearing a short, sky-blue towelling bathrobe, was standing in the doorway of the guest cabin on the starboard side, staring at the sliding door of what her husband called his state-room. I said, 'OK. I'll look after him.'

She turned to me, looking scared. 'He's been drinking all day. I was hoping he'd knock himself out—he usually does. But...'

From inside his cabin, Bellamy shouted, 'I tell you he was using the radio. I'll teach that layabout to disobey me. He and that Chinese tart are...'

Another voice interrupted him, a soothing mutter. Then Bellamy said, his voice slurred and truculent, 'To hell with that—and to hell with you, too, you bloody frog. Get away from that door. I'm going up there to...' There was a sound like a butcher's cleaver going through a leg of lamb, then silence.

A moment later the bird's-eye-maple door slid open and Max appeared, rubbing his knuckles. He grimaced ruefully when he saw us. 'I'm sorry,' he said to Christina. 'But he was becoming difficult.' He shrugged. 'It is a pity you permitted him to bring the whisky aboard, Madame.'

She pushed back a lock of blue-black hair from her forehead. 'How could I stop him? He puts it in with his chemical samples. You know what he's like.'

He nodded curtly. 'Like a pig with the brain of a monkey. *Eh bien,* there is no 'arm done, apart from the broken glass. But we make sure 'e gets no more in Sydney, eh?' He made for the companion.

I watched him go. Then I said, 'How often does your husband go on these jags?'

'Quite often,' she said steadily. 'Especially when things get complicated. He's lost a lot of money lately and if he doesn't sell some of his stuff in Hong Kong his company's finished. And what we are going to do frightens him, I think.' She'd come straight from the shower, I guessed, and she smelt wonderful. The short blue bathrobe made her look absurdly young and appealing, and against it her skin was like sun-drenched apricots. Suddenly, like a knife turning in my heart, she reminded me of somebody else—of another girl who'd sailed with us and stood in this very spot talking to me. A girl who'd called herself Lucky Silvera when she'd been working for Naval Intelligence in Hobart, and whom I thought I'd managed to shut out of my mind for ever. Lucky had been just as dark, with skin tanned to the same honey-gold, and...I turned away abruptly and Christina put a hand on my arm. 'Are you all right?' she asked concernedly. 'You look...'

'Of course I'm all right.' I pulled away from her. 'I'm going to see what the damage is in your husband's cabin. Any objections?' As good an excuse as any, I thought, for a little quiet snooping.

'Why should I object?' she asked quietly. 'I want to see if he's got any more whisky hidden away. But I don't want to go in there by myself.'

She padded in after me, barefoot, carefully avoiding the smashed whisky bottle under the washbasin. She looked away hurriedly after a quick glance at her husband who was lying on his back on the double bed, his white shirt stained and open to the waist and his face a mottled khaki. He was snoring stertorously, and the cabin smelt like a shebeen. Together, the girl and I went through his expensive American luggage and through ever locker, drawer and cupboard in the cabin. We found nothing more intoxicating than a stack of well-thumbed girlie magazines at the back of the built-in wardrobe. I looked at the two wooden packing cases that stood against the after bulkhead. 'Suppose,' I suggested, 'we take a look at the chemical samples?'

She tried the lid of the first box and it came off easily—much too easily. It revealed a wooden tray of tins, bottles and plastic containers, all labelled Bel-Ami Chemicals and all, as far as I could tell, labelled correctly. Underneath the tray, however, there were two dozen bottles of Johnny Walker Black Label, less the three that Bellamy had been using for his experiments that day. Clearly, only the best was good enough for my employer.

The lid of the second crate needed a claw-hammer. I fetched one, taking the whisky to my cabin at the same time. The three-inch nails that held the lid down were hard going and, when the last one came out with a screech, I thought I'd been wasting my time after all. The cases held nothing but Laboratory apparatus packed in shredded paper—boxed microscopes, Pyrex test-tubes, Bunsen burners, two large portable gas cylinders, and all the paraphernalia that took me right back to the dear old stinks lab at school. The only difference was that, at my school, a microscope box could usually be counted on to hold a microscope.

These didn't. They contained money, lots of it, all used and all neatly packed in brown-paper wrappers—Indonesian rupiahs, Japanese and Filipino bank-notes, several packets of British and French currency, and Australian and American bills of varying denominations.

'But Robert was supposed to be penniless.' Christina stared, fascinated, over my shoulder at the money as I packed it away again. 'He's sunk all his money into that firm of his, and a good deal of mine as well. And yet there must be over a hundred thousand dollars there.'

'And genuine, at that.' I shovelled every scrap of paper back into the crate and nailed it up. Bellamy didn't even stir. Then I went out through the after door to the cockpit where the fishing chairs had been in the old days. I wanted to clear my head of the smell of R Bellamy.

Christina followed me out into the warm night wind that *Victoria* was creating as she sliced through the dark sea with the phosphorescence creaming under her stern and her exhausts rumbling like distant thunder. 'Where does all that money come

137

from?' The girl's voice was slightly off-key. 'And what is he going to do with it?'

'How should I know? Maybe he's saving up to buy you an F-111 for Easter.' I lit a cigarette and spun the match into the sea. What I'd been looking for was explosives or guns or some connection between Bellamy and the Mako. His nest-egg was no concern of mine. 'I'm not paid to be curious,' I said. 'I only work here, remember?'

'Will you stop that?' she said tightly. Her hair gleamed as the moon rode out from behind a cloudbank and I saw her face—puzzled and worried and scared. 'You know as well as I do that there's something odd going on. Even Max has been evasive lately. I just don't know whom to trust any more.'

'Perhaps,' I said carefully, 'you ought to start asking yourself whether you can trust your brother. He could have been got at since you last saw him. He...'

'Do you think I haven't thought of that? And do you think I'd lift a finger to help him if I thought he was working for the terrorists?' She shook her head. 'But, even discounting what I know about him, it just wouldn't make sense. If they wanted to use

138

him, why would they have had him sent to prison?'

'Maybe they didn't know they'd need him, at the time.'

'All right,' she said quickly. 'Then answer this. Why are we involved? If he's needed so badly by the other side, surely they could have got him out of Indonesia weeks ago without bringing us into it at all?'

She had a point there. Why bring a girl nearly three thousand miles to do a job that could be done much more easily and quickly by a submarine or fishing boat? It was becoming increasingly obvious, I thought uneasily, that Fenner had been wrong; Christina Bellamy was no more involved with the Mako than I was. None the less, she was going to get hurt when we sprang the trap on her brother—and I was the one who'd set it. I put my hands on her shoulders. 'Listen,' I said. 'Why don't you get off at Sydney and take a plane to Hong Kong? We could go on and pick up your brother. Then...' The yacht rolled, she fell forward, and the next minute I found myself holding her warm, sweet-smelling body in my arms. The very last thing I'd intended. She felt both soft and firm at the same time, and it was pretty apparent that the bathrobe was all she had on. I swallowed. 'Then, if anything goes wrong...'

'Tallon!' Max's shout from the bridge was sharply urgent. I released the girl, jumped for the ladder, crossed the diminutive sun-deck in two strides, and I was in the wheelhouse almost before the shout had died away. Two-tooth was still at the wheel, and Max was leaning over the radio, listening to the news broadcast.

It said, '...and other alleged irregularities. It is believed that Mr Robert Bellamy, the managing director of Bel-Ami Chemicals, is at present cruising off the New South Wales coast in his private yacht. Two Fraud Squad detectives left Melbourne by air this afternoon, and it is expected that Mr Bellamy will be asked to assist them with their inquiries on his arrival in Sydney... In the Sheffield Shield Match in Brisbane today...' Max snapped the set off.

Two-tooth said expressionlessly, 'He's run off with the bloody till. Jeez, Tallon, we do pick 'em, don't we?'

'The fool!' Christina had come on to the bridge behind me. 'The stupid, greedy, selfish fool. He's ruined everything—

140

everything.' She stared at me and, for an awful moment, I thought she was going to cry. 'The yacht's in his name,' she said helplessly. 'He insisted on that when I bought it. And so they'll hold it in Sydney until...'

'*Alors!*' Max's monkey face was a mask of anger. 'That is why he did not want the receiver used. When the money was missed he did not want us to know—in case we wanted a share of it, maybe.' He ripped off a short burst of French, the kind they don't put on those gramophone records. 'And now, when we dock in Sydney, we will find *les flics* waiting for us.'

'I knew something like this would happen.' The girl's face looked as if it had been carved out of stone. 'I said to Tallon...'

'Wait a minute.' I thought fast, trying to get my priorities into some sort of order. Much as I'd have liked to run into Sydney and put an end to the whole wretched business, I still had a job to do. If I was the bait it was up to me to land the big shark, not just a pilot-fish like Bellamy. He could be thrown back and netted later. I said slowly, 'We don't have to put in at Sydney.'

141

'Sydney, Newcastle, what's the difference? We gotta have fuel, mate,' said Two-tooth reasonably, his beloved engines first in his mind as always. 'This isn't a bloody sailing yacht, you know. They know we gotta put in somewhere for oil, and every cop and harbour-master on the east coast'll have been notified about us. They...'

'OK,' I said. 'So our first move is to clear the coast. We'll take a swing to the north-east—out into the Pacific, well clear of the coastal traffic, fishing radar and so on. Then...'

'*C'est ça!*' Max snapped his fingers, grinning excitedly. 'We refuel at sea, yes? Of course! And I have a frien', a tug-master, in Noumea—a French port in New Caledonia, you understand. A place where these things can be arranged without stupid questions.' He shrugged. 'It will be an undertaking of some expense, *bien entendu*, but...'

'That,' said Christina, her black eyes crinkling as she smiled, 'will be no problem. My husband can afford it.' She looked at me, the smile vanishing. 'But won't they start looking for us if we don't turn up in Sydney?'

'Sure. But not right away.' I drew on the cigarette I was still holding. 'As Two-tooth says, they know we have to take on diesel fuel. I think they'll sit back and wait for us to show up, at first. But, even if they decided to lay on a full-scale air-sea search for us, a sixty-foot yacht isn't as easy to find in the South Pacific as you might think.'

'An' the time we spend on our detour,' said Max confidently, 'will be no more than the time we would have spent in Sydney. We will still keep our rendezvous.'

'Yeah?' said Two-tooth gloomily. 'But I won't be able to keep mine with that blonde in King's Cross that I was counting on. Tray bloody bong, that is.'

'Don't worry,' said Christina. 'In Hong Kong we will have the biggest party you have ever seen.' Impulsively, she came forward and kissed him on the port side of his beard. 'Thank you, all of you,' she said gratefully. 'You don't know what it means to me to know that Peter is going to be all right after all.' She smiled at the three of us and went below.

I avoided the reflection of Two-tooth's eye in the windscreen as he put a hand to his face. I knew exactly what he was thinking—that there wouldn't be any party in Hong Kong. And Christina wouldn't be handing out any kisses either—not when she found out who'd pulled the plug on her brother's bid for freedom.

CHAPTER EIGHT

Now there was no land to the west by day, no shore-lights or coastal beacons to be seen by night. There was only the flat, unruffled immensity of the Pacific all around us, a perfect circle of deepest blue neatly bisected astern by the white snail-track of *Victoria's* wake as she crawled steadily up the parallels towards the Tropic of Capricorn. By day, the ocean shaded to a misty purple where the heat-glaze met the white, milky sky from which the sun glared down like a magnesium flare in a steam-bath. The only wind was an occasional fiery breath from the north-west that hardly disturbed the dancing shimmer of hot air on the coach-roof. At night, the humidity made the cabins unbearable. Tempers splintered with sleeplessness and, on the afternoon of the third day out, when we were pushing into the Australia Current 200 miles from the land with the fuel levels dropping, I was in no mood for a tête-à-tête with Bellamy.

He came up on the bridge looking a mess. I hadn't set eyes on him since the night of his drinking bout, and I hardly recognised him. The bronzed, matinée-idol features were yellow and puffy and unshaven, and his eyes were baggy and blood-shot. With his thin moustache and long black hair hanging round his face, he looked like a Restoration hell-rake who'd come down with a touch of fowl-pest. 'Hi, skipper,' he said, with a sort of nervous bonhomie as he sat down at the chart-table, a glass of beer in his fist. 'Mind if I have a word?'

'Not,' I said briefly, 'as long as the word is good-bye.'

'Aw, now, look,' he said placatingly. 'No need to rub a feller's nose in it, you know. Had a spot too much, that's all. It can happen to anybody. As a matter of fact, I wouldn't touch the stuff if it wasn't for the pains I get in my stomach. You see, I've got an ulcer, and I get the most awful...'

'I'm just the hired hand around here. Not the ship's doctor.'

'I know, I know,' he said humbly. 'You've got a lot of responsibility, and I can't expect you to be interested in my troubles. All I want to know is where we are.'

146

'The chart's right in front of you,' I said shortly. 'We're somewhere under your right elbow.'

'We're a hell of a long way out.' He studied our track. 'About seven hundred miles south-west of New Caledonia. And only three hundred miles from French territorial waters, right?' He looked up at me, his eyes craftily calculating.

'More or less.' I had the figures in my head already, since the ocean-going tug *Natalie*, now a day and half out from Noumea, was due to rendezvous with us the following morning. 'So?'

'So we could call in there.' He drank some beer, trying to appear offhand and casual, but his hands were trembling on the glass and he looked about as offhand and casual as an Al Fatah guerrilla-fighter caught in a synagogue with a bomb up his *galabia*. 'How about it?'

'And you think the Fraud Squad won't be able to catch up with you there?' I grunted. 'You want to get with it, pal. Haven't you ever heard of Interpol?'

'Interpol?' He frowned. 'What the hell's Interpol and the Fraud Squad got to do with it?'

'Everything. They want you for that

147

money you've run off with. The money in that packing-case in your cabin.'

'Packing-case?' His eyes narrowed. 'But there's no money in there. There's only...'

'Oh, grow up, Bellamy,' I said disgustedly. 'I've seen it. I heard the news broadcast. The police are waiting for you in Sydney. They want you for embezzlement. Why d'you think we're keeping so far from the coast?'

'You're crazy,' he said angrily. 'I haven't got any money. My firm was a one-man band and it went bust, so how could I run off with any?' He stared up at me. 'What the hell's the angle here, Tallon? If you're trying to put the bite on me, you're wasting your time. I haven't a cent.'

'No?' After the fortune I'd found in his cabin, I ought to have found that hard to believe. And yet I couldn't help the crazy feeling that he was telling the truth. Bellamy was the kind who would lie automatically, but never convincingly. The look of angry bafflement on his face was genuine, I was sure of it. 'Then why,' I said slowly, 'do you want to go to Noumea?'

'That's my business,' he snapped.

'And what,' I asked, shooting in the dark, 'are certain people going to say when they find out you've run out on them?'

As a shot in the dark, it was a lulu. His jaw sagged, beer slopped from his glass as he set it down, and the aggression in his eyes changed to pure fright. 'How the hell do you know about them?' he asked thickly.

It was as easy as that, I thought incredulously. All you had to do was ask. Why hadn't I tried it before? 'I'll ask the questions,' I said, remembering Fenner's technique. 'Why do you want to go to Noumea?'

He stared at me for a second. Then he picked up his glass and drained it. 'OK, Tallon. No harm in telling you, since I'm not going through with it. Fact is, my business went downhill a while back through no fault of my own. Christina wouldn't help, and I was in a hell of a spot. Well, one afternoon, a couple of Chinese turned up at my office. They were very complimentary—said their people had been following my work for some time, and it looked pretty good to them.' A touch of boastfulness crept into his manner. 'They said first-class, experienced chemists were few and far between in the People's

149

Republic, and that I'd be really well looked after if I went there to work. Then they came up with an offer. Executive post in a big chemical plant they're building outside Pekin. Fat salary, apartment on the Chang An Avenue. Car of my own, even. All I had to do was take...' He paused fractionally. '...Take some samples for them to copy, and they'd see me across the border at Lo Wu when we reached Hong Kong. But then...'

'What samples did they want?'

He grinned slyly. 'You've seen them, haven't you? Just some stuff I've developed. But they're not going to get it.' The fear came back into his eyes again. 'I've been thinking things over. What's to stop them pinching my stuff when I get there, and then getting rid of me? I've heard stories about what they do to defectors they don't want any more. So I've got to get off this boat, Tallon. They'll be waiting for me in Hong Kong, but if I can get to Noumea...'

'You'll be arrested the minute you set foot ashore.'

'Don't start that again,' he snapped. 'What is it you want—a deal? OK.' He leaned forward. 'Listen. I may not be worth much at present, Tallon, but I know how to lay my hands on quite a lot of money. So here's the deal. You take me to New Caledonia, and there'll be five grand waiting for you at any bank in Hong Kong you care to name. US dollars. What d'you say?'

'I say you must be out of your mind.'

'OK,' he said quickly. 'I know what you're thinking—that I'll welsh on the deal. But I'll sign over the yacht as security. I'll even...'

'We've got a deadline to keep. I couldn't divert, even if I wanted to.'

'But you'll have to refuel,' he said angrily. 'So, instead of putting in at an Australian port, why not get your oil in New Caledonia and do yourself a bit of good at the same time?'

'We're refuelling at sea,' I said curtly. 'Now shove off and get rid of your hangover. There's a tug meeting us at first light tomorrow and I'll want you on deck to throw a few oil-drums around.'

'You bloody fool!' He stood up, the sweat shining on his putty-coloured face and his voice shrill with fury. 'You mean you're turning your back on five Gs just because you're hoping for a roll with that Chinese...?'

'Watch your mouth, Bellamy.' I came to my feet, fast. 'Before I spread it all over your face. You signed on for this cruise and, by God, you're going through with it. And if your Commie pals are waiting to put a bullet through you at the end of it, that'll be all right by me. Now get to hell out of here.'

'All right,' he hissed, his mouth twisted with rage. 'But you're making the mistake of your life, turning me down like this.' He went down the ladder and, at the foot of it, he looked up at me, his eyes as mean and venomous as those of a stone-fish. 'I know how to fix you, Tallon. You're the one who won't live to see the end of this trip, you bloody gaol-bird, and that's a promise.'

Then I was alone again with the monotonous, tribal-drum note of the diesels and the sticky, enervating heat. Bellamy was, beyond doubt, one of the slimiest infestations I'd ever sailed with. He was stupid, selfish, and as unpredictably vicious as a tiger-snake. But the thing that annoyed me most of all about him was that these charming traits were the very reasons for his not being part of the Mako

152

set-up. For no organisation as formidable as the one Fenner had described would have any use at all for an alcoholic who defected, changed his mind and, in the process, called down a man-hunt on his own head, and all the publicity that went with it.

And he hadn't stolen that money, either. If he had, he'd have been waving it under my nose as a bribe. So how had it got into his packing-case? And, if he and Christina weren't working for the Mako, who was left? Max? I got my imagination to work, trying to see him forging a letter in Chinese so that Christina would buy a hundred-thousand-dollar yacht, put her boozy husband on it to be framed on an embezzlement rap, and then sail it three thousand miles to pick up a man who was going to knock off the US President.

Not for the first time, I asked myself whether Fenner was fishing in the wrong pond.

Then I heard the shot.

Once you've heard an automatic fired in a confined space, you don't mistake it for anything else. So, when I heard the flat, cracking report from somewhere for'ard, I didn't have to sit around wondering if it was a door slamming, or if Two-tooth was opening a bottle of vino for dinner. I shoved the auto-pilot in after a quick 360-degree look round, and then dived for the ladder. I raced across the saloon and, as my feet hit the rubber-tiled galley deck, I heard Bellamy say, 'And you'll get it as well if you don't do exactly as I say.'

He had Two-tooth bailed up in the corner between the fo'c'sle and the spare cabin. The big Sydneysider had his hands locked behind his neck, and Bellamy was digging a long-barrelled, blued-steel pistol into his stomach. Through the fo'c'sle hatchway I could see Max hauling himself up on to his bunk, his face grey with pain and a trickle of bright-red blood running between his fingers as he gripped his shoulder.

'Stay right where you are, Tallon.' Bellamy looked sideways at me. His face was bloodless beneath the two-day growth of black stubble and his left eye was twitching uncontrollably. With a small, eerie shock, I realised that drink, fear and nervous tension had pushed him over the edge. Temporarily, at least, he was paranoic—a killer. His eyes were blank and empty, and the hand holding Max's P-38 was shaking like a loose propeller blade at high revs.

He saw the look of shock on my face and he grinned at me in a way that made my blood run cold. 'Aha!' he said, with a horrible high-pitched giggle. 'The situation has changed somewhat, eh, Tallon? Not so free with our bloody orders now, are we?' He chuckled softly and leaned on the gun. Two-tooth, who had been glowering at him, his face red with rage, looked down as the pistol bored into his stomach. Bellamy said, 'I'm the one who's giving the orders now. And you're going to take me to Noumea, or else I'll blast your pal's guts right through his backbone.'

He'd do it, too—by accident, if no other way. From where I stood, I could see his finger alternately flexing and slackening inside the trigger guard as his hand shook. 'OK,' I said quickly. 'OK, Bellamy. You win. Put the gun down, and we'll take you anywhere you want to ...'

'Like hell we will!' Two-tooth's eyes came up from the P-38. 'The only place we'll be taking you is to a padded cell. Get out of my way, yer nong, while I see to Max.' He lowered his hands, gave Bellamy a shove that sent him staggering, and headed for the fo'c'sle.

I'd always known that Two-tooth wasn't deficient in physical courage. He'd been in Bomb Disposal when he was in the RAN, and you don't lack moral fibre if you're in that game. But, with Bellamy like this, it wasn't physical courage that Two-tooth was exhibiting. It was a tendency towards suicide. 'All right!' Bellamy's voice rose to a shriek. 'You've asked for this!' He aimed the pistol at Two-tooth's back, holding the butt with both hands to steady it.

I jumped him. I got my left arm round his neck and my right hand on to his wrist, forcing it down. I squeezed, and he sagged like a deflated tyre as the gun thumped to the deck.

'Don't hurt him.' Two-tooth turned and surveyed him unconcernedly. 'Poor bastard's not responsible for his actions. Lock him in his cabin and tell the girl to come and give me a hand with Max.'

'My God!' My throat was dry and I could feel the sweat running down my back as the reaction hit me. 'You played that pretty cool. What's the matter with you—tired of life?'

'Naw.' Two-tooth grinned at me. 'Like I said, he's crazy. Doesn't know what he's doing. Who but a nut-case would stick somebody up with an empty gun?'

'Empty?' I released Bellamy and he collapsed, crying softly to himself, against the cooker. I picked up the pistol and examined it, putting on the safety catch.

'Sure. Saw it as soon as I got over the surprise of being held up by a little ratbag like him. Yer see,' he said condescendingly, 'I happen to know a bit about guns, mate. The P-38's got a loading indicator, see? A little rod just above the hammer that sticks out when the chamber's empty.' He pointed it out to me, smiling smugly. 'There it is, sticking out like a sore thumb. Thought you'd known about that, Tallon.'

I looked at the gun, then at him. 'You idiot,' I said softly. 'You've got it the wrong way round.'

The confident smile disappeared among his whiskers and was replaced by an expression of dawning apprehension. 'The wrong way round? How d'yer mean?'

'I mean,' I said, slowly and clearly, 'that the loading indicator retracts on a P-38 when it's empty. If it's out, there's at least one round up the spout. Take it on deck and try it if you don't believe me.'

'Gawd!' He backed up against the watertight door, his face an interesting shade of beige and every whisker standing on end. 'And I shoved him in the chest. He could have...' Words failed him and he gaped at me in horror.

'Keep an eye on Bellamy,' I said. 'But don't hurt him, will you? Remember, he doesn't know what he's doing, either.' I went into the fo'c'sle to see to Max.

CHAPTER NINE

'He said you were sending 'im to 'is death.'
Max's Gallic pride had been hurt far more
than his shoulder. Fully rested after a
night's sleep and with a hypodermicful
of antibiotics inside him, he sat at the
chart-table, his bandaged left arm resting
carefully on it and an after-breakfast
cigarillo between his lips. Through the
starboard bridge window, the dawn was
coming up out of the South Pacific like
a rising souffle—a streak of pale yellow
along the horizon that swelled and grew
minute by minute, spilling its ochreous
reflection towards us across a sea that
was more like a stagnant pond than the
open ocean. 'He'd already foun' the gun
when I go to the fo'c'sle. I ask him what
the hell, an' he tells me that everyone is
against him and he 'as to 'ave protection.
He was *comme un fou*—like a madman,
you know? So, I try to take the gun from
him and—pouf!' He started a shrug and
winced. 'What more could a man do?'

'You could have made damn sure,' I said curtly, with one eye on the radar and the other on the barometer, 'that you hadn't left a loaded P-38 lying around.' I was, I knew, being unreasonable in implying that the whole thing had been Max's fault, but I didn't feel reasonable. *Victoria*, with only a teaspoonful of oil in her tanks, felt and sounded dead, the way a ship always feels and sounds when her engines are cut after days of continuous running, and I was getting more worried by the minute. We'd heard nothing from the tug *Natalie*, there wasn't anything resembling an echo on our radar and, worst of all, the previous evening's weather report had included a Tropical Advisory. A low, they had said, that showed signs of deepening indicated the possibility of a tropical cyclone developing in the central Coral Sea about seven hundred miles from Cairns. I felt strung up and jittery after a night without sleep, I didn't like the look of the sky, I didn't like the way the barometer was beginning to wilt, and I wished Max would go to hell and leave me to gnaw my fingernails in peace.

'What was that about a loaded P-38?' Two-tooth eyed me suspiciously as he heaved himself up the ladder, balancing three mugs of coffee on a tray.

'Nothing to get excited about.' I looked into the saffron eye of the sunrise as if expecting the tug to surface out of the oily grey-and-yellow water like a submarine. 'Try VIB Brisbane and see what they've got to offer.'

He nodded, setting the tray down. As he twiddled the knobs, Max said, 'You are thinking of the Tropical Advisory? But surely we are too far south to be in danger. Even if...'

'Don't kid yourself,' said Two-tooth, always the ray of sunshine. 'A cyclone travels south-west and then re-curves south-east, as a rule. In '54, one hit the coast a long way south of where we are now, and then went on down into New South—worst they've ever had. Dozens of lives lost, and ships fifty times the size of this going down like paper boats. Besides, we'll be heading north-west, right into the track they usually follow, and a cyclone can cover a front of a thousand miles, don't forget. And the wind velocity...'

'Talking of wind,' I said, gritting my teeth, 'why don't you just shut up and go and sandpaper the propeller blades or

161

something? I know how much fuel we've got, and I know how long we'd stay afloat without power in the middle of a cyclone. But we don't even know it's developed yet, do we? So...'

'All right, all bloody right,' he said huffily, turning up the radio volume. 'I was only telling Max here...'

'...following gale warning was issued to shipping at 1900 hours GMT by the Bureau of Meteorology in Brisbane,' said the loud-speaker offhandedly. 'Tropic cyclone Helen, 998 millibars, centred at 1700 GMT near 17 degrees South, 158 degrees East, is moving south-west at 5 knots. Gales within 100 miles of centre in southern quadrants, with gusts to 50 knots near centre. Central pressure is expected to fall to 995 knots near centre. Central pressure is expected to fall to 995 millibars by 0500 GMT, with gales within 200 miles of centre.'

Nobody said anything as Two-tooth switched off. He turned our lights off as a blood-red sun came up out of the sea. A ripple ran across the ocean as if, far away beyond the sunrise, a giant had tossed a rock into it, and *Victoria* rolled gently to a breath of wind from the east.

'D'you think,' I said to Max, 'that this pal of yours is going to turn up? Now that he knows what the weather'll be like?'

'He will be here.' Max reached for his mug of coffee, his face crimson in the red glow of the sunrise. 'For such a sum as he was promised, Captain Giraud would sail to hell and back. Perhaps he has to search a little, because of the radio silence, but he will be here.' He remained leaning forward and his white teeth showed suddenly in a triumphant grin. *Et voila!* He pointed with his mug of coffee. 'You see?'

On the extreme edge of the radar screen, a small green blip had materialised, blurring as the trace revolved through three hundred and sixty degrees and springing into sharp definition again as the echo came back to us. The echo of a smallish vessel, almost due north and twenty-five miles away, and coming straight for us with every revolution of the scanner. Thank God, I thought, sinking back into my padded chair, suddenly aware of how tired I was. If we had to fight a cyclone, at least we'd do it with our engines running.

'And he's in a hurry.' Two-tooth watched the trace spin round once or twice. 'Twenty-five, maybe thirty knots he's doing. Be here in less than an hour.' He looked at me. 'I'm going below to get organised.'

'I'll give you a hand.' I stood up. to prepare for our rendezvous with Tropical Cyclone Helen, there were the shutters to be fitted to the big windows in the saloon, doors and hatches to be checked, and the china and glassware to be secured, just for a start. With Max unable to help with the refuelling, we were in for a busy morning.

'You bloody won't,' said Two-tooth positively. 'Max and the girl can do the light jobs. We've had some sleep; now you push off and grab what you can.'

I didn't argue. 'Call me when the tug shows up,' I said. On my way to my bunk, which got more luxurious with every step I took, I looked in on Bellamy. He was fast asleep, still under the influence of the tranquilliser his wife had given him, so I locked his door again and went groggily for'ard.

No sooner had I put my head on the pillow than I felt somebody shaking my shoulder. Or so it seemed. 'Sorry, Tallon,' said Max sympathetically. 'But *Natalie* is ready to come alongside.'

The engines were running again and *Victoria* was rolling, but very slightly. Something to be grateful for; in a rough sea it would have been no fun rigging lines and risking a collision with every gallon of oil we took on. Christina, in a white short-sleeved linen shirt and a pair of attenuated navy-blue shorts, was getting a driving lesson from Two-tooth in holding the yacht steady. A good idea, I thought, now that we were short-handed, and it wouldn't be beyond her capability on a day as calm as this. The morning sun had disappeared behind the haze of a grey, overcast sky and, although it was still hot and sticky, a light easterly wind was holding the temperature and humidity down to a workable level. The tug, fenders rigged, stood off our port beam at a cable's distance, a wisp of smoke floating away from us and the tricolour of France floating gently from her ensign staff.

She was a long-distance salvage vessel of the latest type, a big powerful job three times our size, with a high, sharply-raked bow and a funnel so squat as to be almost lost behind the streamlined bridge that rose a good thirty feet above her waterline. And, clearly, she spent more time at sea than in port. Brown rust-stains had already begun to mar her once-smart black-and-white paintwork, a line of singlets and underpants fluttered like a distress signal from her foretopmast stay, and her sleek, futuristic lines were broken by the netted stack of oil-drums that cluttered the flat deck-space aft of the towing bitts. *'Bonjour, messieurs,'* rasped a genial, mechanical voice from the loudspeaker mounted on the wing of her bridge. 'Giraud speaking. 'Ave you, by chance, a lecherous son of a diseased goat named Perrin aboard?'

'Tell him to shut up,' I said patiently to Max, 'and get on with the job.' what I wanted was oil in our tanks, not a lot of French chit-chat. I took the wheel from Christina and she went on deck to watch the tug.

Max seized the battery-operated loud-hailer, grinning. *'Pas de grossièretés,'* Giraud!' he bawled tinnily. 'Watch your language. There is a lady aboard. And now, stand by. We come alongside.'

There was an annoying pause while binoculars were focused on Christina's legs, and heads sprouted from hatchways aboard the tug. A long-drawn whistle of appreciation floated across the water.

'My apologies,' boomed Giraud gallantly, 'for keeping such a beauty waiting. And it is we who shall close you, on your leeside, to keep our smoke out of the lady's lovely eyes. 'Ave no fear, *mes amis*. We shall touch with the delicacy of an angel's kiss.'

The angel belched a jet of sooty exhaust smoke out of her dumpy funnel and began to close the gap between us as her Kort nozzle units propelled her crabwise. At a hundred yards, I could make out a fat figure on the bridge hastily combing its hair while another man ran for'ard to take in the washing. The plume of smoke died and the tug drifted smoothly towards us, her power shut off. At fifty yards, the hand with the washing had disappeared below and Giraud was no longer visible through the bridge windows. The gap narrowed. Thirty yards. Twenty. Ten. But nobody appeared on deck to throw us a line, no captain leaned over the bridge wing that was now towering high above us. 'Giraud!' shouted Max, out on our foredeck. 'The line, idiot!'

There was no answer. The tug, her steel plates looming over us like the side of a battleship, wallowed on and the sea slopped loudly between her hull and our own. *Victoria* rolled uneasily. Then *Natalie* touched with a gentle thump, the yacht heeled slightly to starboard, and the gap between the two vessels began to increase again. And still no line was passed from the tug. 'Bloody frogs!' muttered Two-tooth censoriously. 'Bet they're all below, queueing up for a go at the scent-spray.'

Christina, out on deck, looked at the tug, then at me. 'What's the matter?' she asked, puzzled. 'Why are they all keeping out of sight?'

There was certainly something very odd going on. There should have been a face or two at the portholes that were level with our bridge, a shouted order, a bustle of activity. Instead, the tug, with no way on her, was rolling helplessly, her masts drawing great arcs against the steel-grey sky. I handed over to Two-tooth and went out on deck. 'Giraud!' I bawled. 'Is anything wrong?' My voice was thrown back by the dirty black hull of the *Natalie*, now a good twenty yards away.

Her bridge windows were at such an angle that I couldn't see into them. Nobody shouted back. Nobody moved on the deck of the tug. All I could hear about the gentle mutter of our own diesels was a girl's voice singing hauntingly in French from a radio on the other vessel. It sounded eerie and inexpressibly lonely, out there on the open sea, like music from an empty house that you know has been empty and dead for years.

And, suddenly, my scalp crawled with an intuitive sense of danger—the feeling the Ancient Greeks called *panikos*, after the god Pan who was able to inspire sudden, groundless fear in lonely places. What Giraud was up to, I had no idea but I badly wanted to get away from that uncannily silent, inexplicably deserted vessel before I found out. So did Max. From his position up on the foredeck he said nervily, 'Tallon. I don't like this. Let's get the hell out of 'ere.'

The sight of his face had the effect of steadying my nerves. He'd gone a milk chocolate colour, and the hand by which he was holding on to the coach-roof was shaking like that of a man in a fever. I said, 'I don't like it, either, but we need that fuel. I'm going aboard her.'

Christina said, 'Max. I think it might be a good idea to break out that gun of yours. Don't you, Tallon?' She looked at me, her dark eyes wide.

'But...' Max shook his head. 'Giraud would not...'

'Get it,' I said curtly. 'It can't do any harm unless it's fired, can it?' He went below as Two-tooth touched the throttles and brought the yacht up to the low, flat stern of the *Natalie* with the casual dexterity of a long-service nanny parking a pram. I jumped aboard the tug, secured a line for'ard to one of the big steel hoops that were there to keep a towline clear of the deck gear and then I went aft to take the line that the girl passed me from the yacht's cockpit. 'You three stay here,' I said. 'Christina, go below. You stay at the controls, Two-tooth. Max, I want you here on the after-deck where you can cover me. If anything goes wrong you'll cut the lines and get the yacht clear. OK?' He nodded and I ran for'ard past the stacked oil-drums, the patter of my rubber-soled shoes sounding very loud in the silence. I went straight up the ladder to the weather-deck. Then I stopped abruptly.

There was a man lying there, sprawled out on his back flat and relaxed near the lifeboat davits, staring up reflectively at the sky. He didn't turn his head when I dropped to one knee beside him, and he didn't even blink. He hadn't been dead for very long, because his wrist was flexible and still warm to the touch.

He was an elderly man in a blue fisherman's jersey and faded denim trousers and he had a red-and-white knitted cap on his bristly grey head. His face was peaceful and there wasn't a mark on him that I could see, but his lips were an odd, cold, bluish-purple colour. Without knowing a great deal about heart attacks, I was prepared to bet that that was what had killed him. He'd just dropped in his tracks and died, without any sort of struggle or violence. OK, I thought, listening to the slap-slap of a loose halyard and the voice of the girl singing huskily about l'amour from somewhere for'ard. So an elderly man has a heart attack. It happens, even to sailors. But, in that case, what the hell were all the other sailors doing? Looking for canvas and scrap iron and mugging up the burial service? I went up the enclosed bridge ladder to ask Captain Giraud.

He looked as puzzled as I did. He stared at me, frowning, when I went into the wheelhouse, as if I'd interrupted him in the middle of a tricky problem. And so

I had, I thought with the crazy lucidity that comes with shock, since he was busy solving the last and greatest puzzle a man is ever confronted with.

He was as dead as a Bombay duck.

He was sitting comfortably on the deck, where he'd slid down the bulkhead, and his cap was swinging gently from a hook over his head. In falling, he'd pulled down the canvas-covered log-book from its shelf, and he still had a rather hairy comb in his hand. His lips were a cold bluish-purple. By the slowly-revolving wheel, the helmsman lay curled up on the deck where he'd collapsed, his face hideously serene in death and his lips the same colour as his captain's.

I ran out of the wheelhouse, feeling as if I was acting out some madman's nightmare and that I knew exactly what I was going to find when I went round the ship. And I was right—incredibly but irrefutably right. In the galley, a bald, ferociously-bearded man in a white soiled apron sat propped sideways against a table, peacefully dead, with a half-peeled apple and a knife in his hands, a dead cat at his feet, and his lips the colour of violets. So were those of the engineer who'd been struck down in the act of lighting a cigarette. There was another blue-lipped corpse on the foredeck, still smiling happily and lying just where he'd sagged from the rail after ogling Christina. And all the time the music played softly and the girl sang of love and life and living men in her husky contralto voice.

I tracked her down to the fo'c'sle, a taped voice on a cassette that was running through a Japanese tape-recorder. There were two men there—one caught with his head in the shirt he'd been pulling on, the other slumped across his bunk with his arms full of freshly-laundered singlets and under-pants. And, when the girl's voice died, the ship seemed to die, too. There wasn't a living soul left on board except me.

Apart from checking that they were all dead, and switching off the tape-recorder, I'd touched nothing. I began to walk aft, deliberately at first, then more quickly until I broke into a run, sprinting as if the devil was after me through that silent, accursed ship with its crew of corpses I burst out on to the after-deck, and Max levelled his pistol indecisively at nothing after taking one look at my face. Then I vaulted the rail to fall into a chair aboard my own familiar, blessedly-alive little world.

'What the hell!' Two-tooth twisted in his seat and stared at me in alarm. 'What goes on, Tallon? My oath, you look as if you've seen a...'

'Don't say it.' I got out a cigarette and lit it after only one or two tries. 'For God's sake, don't say it, Two-tooth. Just get me a drink, will you? And never mind a glass. You won't find one big enough.' I called to Max who was still standing irresolutely on the deck of the tug. 'You can come aboard. They can't hurt us, Giraud and the others. They're all dead. Every single one of them.'

Max shook his head, looking back at the tug's bridge. He climbed over the rail. 'Maybe I don' understand so good. Who is dead?'

'The whole bloody lot of them right down to the cat.' I took the bottle of whisky from Christina, who had come up quietly from the saloon. 'Eight, I counted.' I tilted it back and let the smooth golden liquid glug down my throat.

'Jeez, mate,' said Two-tooth, watching me. 'Never seen yer do that before.'

'You've never seen anything like that

ship before, either. It's like a cross between the *Mary Celeste* and a morgue, back there.' I re-corked the bottle. 'They all seem to have died natural deaths,' I said, more rationally. 'Right in the middle of what they were doing, all over the ship. And their lips are a sort of purplish colour, all of them.'

'I'm going to take a look.' Two-tooth stood up, his face grim. 'Maybe there's something we can...'

'No!' Max grabbed his arm. 'If Tallon says they are dead, then there is nothing we can do for them. But we must get away from here, fast.' He stared at me, his eyes wide with fear. 'You say they died naturally? And their lips—a purple colour?'

I nodded. 'In every case. Why? Do you know...?'

'Then it can be only one thing.' He drew a deep, shuddering breath. *'C'est la peste!'* he whispered. 'That is what has killed them. It is the plague—bubonic plaque!'

CHAPTER TEN

'Bubonic plague,' he repeated. He released Two-tooth's arm while the three of us stared at him in fascinated horror. 'I saw it once in Macao—faces that turned blue, just as you describe, then black and swollen. If they had that on board...'

'You're wrong, Max,' I said steadily, fighting down the cold fear I could feel rising within me. 'I don't know much about bubonic, but one thing I'm sure of—that you don't die quickly or peacefully when you get it. And eight men couldn't die of it at the same instant.' I paused, seeing those dead faces again. 'One of them had died in the middle of a smile, and it was still there on his face. They were all like that—alive one minute, dead the next. It was if they'd all been painlessly electrocuted.'

'Electrocuted?' Two-tooth sat down again at the wheel. 'You think that might have...?'

I shook my head. 'They were all over the

ship. The whole of the hull would have had to be live for that to happen. No, it wasn't electricity and it wasn't sickness—not even radiation sickness, if you're looking for something really way out.'

'Me, I do not look for anything.' Max looked apprehensively at the tug's deserted decks. 'You say they die naturally, not of violence. But they do not die of sickness, either. *C'est surnaturel*—supernatural, yes? All I want, therefore, is to get out of here as soon as...'

'As soon as we've refuelled.' I stood up. 'We've got to have that oil. We can square the payment with Giraud's next-of-kin later on.'

'And then what?' Two-tooth rubbed thoughtfully at an imaginary scuff-mark on the polished wheel. 'We just sail off and leave 'em?'

'No.' Christina spoke for the first time, leaning back with her hands gripping the chart-table behind her. 'We can't do that,' she said slowly. 'Those men came to help us, even though there was a cyclone warning out. Some of them will have families who will want to know what happened to them. We'll have to report it.'

There was a small silence. 'You realise what you're saying?' I said finally. 'If we report this, there'll be a plane over here in half an hour. Touch that radio, and your trip's a wipe-out.'

'But of course we don't report it, Madame,' said Max excitedly. 'Giraud was a frien' of mine, and I don't want to leave him like a dead dog by the roadside. But it is of the living we mus' think not of the dead. Your brother, he mus' come first. *Natalie* will be found by some other ship and...'

'And, in the meantime,' said Two-tooth, 'she's drifting and a danger to shipping. Besides, she's a French vessel, and you know how touchy they are. What I mean is,' he said hurriedly as Max bristled, 'there could be a bloody international incident over this. What d'you say, Tallon?'

'I agree with Max,' I said slowly. 'We go on.' All the same, I couldn't help wondering why he was so concerned about Peter Chan, after what he'd said about the girl's brother earlier. I saw Two-tooth open his mouth, then shut it again as he watched me. 'By midnight, we'll be two hundred miles away. And then we'll send off a signal on the distress frequency, giving the tug's position but leaving *Victoria* out of it. They won't find her until daylight tomorrow, and by that time we'll be four hundred miles to the north-west.'

'*Impossible!*' snapped Max. 'On an SOS they will take a D/F bearing, and then...'

'That,' I said evenly, 'is a chance we'll just have to take, isn't it? And now, the sooner our tanks are full, the better.'

It took all morning to get them full and part of the afternoon as well, with the sweat pouring off Two-tooth and me as we worked. When the levels were as high as they could go, there were spare drums to be swayed into the yacht's cockpit and chocked and stacked and secured. Then we left Christina to fix a meal while we went wearily aboard *Natalie* for the last time, the quiet, dead eyes of her crew seeming to follow us reproachfully as we moved among them.

Max went below with Two-tooth to close down the engine-room while I hoisted the flags NC—international code for 'I am in distress and in need of assistance'—and switched on the tug's navigation lights to minimise the risk of somebody running into her in the dark. I checked the ship's log which was lying open on its sloping shelf near the radio. As I'd expected, *Victoria* didn't figure at all. I paused in my reading to stare at Giraud, whose sightless, puzzled eyes were already taking on the yellow film of approaching decomposition. There was something odd about his log, but for the life of me I couldn't work out what it was.

Then it came to me. The last time I'd been here, Giraud's log-book had been lying on the deck beside his dead body. Now, it was back on its shelf again, and open. So, since Two-tooth had been with me all the time and Bellamy had been locked in his cabin, it had to be either Max or Christina who had been up here. OK, nothing wrong with that. Whoever it was could have been checking, like me, that the yacht wasn't mentioned in the record.

But there were other things out of place, I realised, now that I was looking for them. A block of wood with a spike, on which were impaled a number of signals flimsies, had materialised mysteriously on top of the radio. A locker was half-open. And, lying on Giraud's trouser-leg, was a small fragment of burnt paper. I didn't need a crystal ball to work out that it was the remains of a radio message from the stack on the spike.

I switched on the wireless-operator's lamp and, holding my breath, I slid the end of a foot-rule under the charred piece of paper and lifted it to the light. All I could make out were five-letter groups. A coded signal. I put the paper down, feeling cheated. As I did so, my eye caught the light from the lamp as it reflected off the open pages of the log and I smiled smugly to myself. Somebody had saved me a lot of speculation—somebody who had been in a hurry, and careless. For what's the good of burning a signal that you've just decoded with a ball-point on top of an open log? I held the book at an angle and read the transcription that had been impressed into the paper in hurried but perfectly legible block letters. It was the text of a message only, with no time of origin or sender's name, and it was in French. I translated it.

And the grin disappeared abruptly from my face. It said: INFORM AGENT DESTROYER *BANDUNG* PREPARING DEPART AMBOINA PATROL DUTIES ARU GROUP.

Now, I thought as I replaced the log-book and switched off the lamp, I really had something to think about. Who was the agent mentioned in the message? Christina, Max or me? Not me, surely, unless Fenner had gone crazy, and I didn't think it was Christina. On the other hand, it had been Max who had suggested employing Giraud in the first place. But, in that case, if he'd decoded the signal and he knew we were to be intercepted by the Indonesian Navy, surely his reaction should have been to show us the message, with some appropriate yarn, and get the trip called off?

I gave up. I was tired and dirty and hungry, and Max could be any sort of agent—insurance, estate or even news—for all I cared as long as I could get outside a cold beer and a plate of sandwiches. I turned to the door with that in mind.

He was standing there, his P-38 trained straight on my heart. 'You are finished?' he asked.

For a moment, I thought I was. 'Yes.' I swallowed. 'But why the gun?'

'Gun?' He looked down at it. 'Forgive me.' He thrust it into his belt. 'But this ship, she gives me the creeps to go about alone.' He stepped aside politely to let me go first down the ladder. 'Below, all is completed.'

'Fine,' I said heartily. 'so now we've got enough fuel to take us all the way to Pulau Mati.' I watched him closely.

'*Naturellement.*' He nodded agreeably. 'Now, nothing can stop us, eh? Not even Hèléne.'

'Who?' For a moment I wondered who this new subversive element might be. 'Oh, the cyclone?' I'd forgotten about that.

I was reminded of Helen as we cast off from the tug and I felt the yacht, stern-heavy with the weight of the extra fuel, roll in the long swell that had developed from the north. The distress flags that flew from *Natalie's* foremast stood out stiffly in the breeze that had backed nor'-east and her lights glowed pallidly against the grey sky, although it was still only two in the afternoon.

And, by nightfall, Helen wasn't at all easy to forget. All afternoon the weather had thickened until, by five, we had the lights on in the bridge and the wind, backing constantly to the north, had risen to half a gale. It keened shrilly in the aerials, it hammered gustily on the windows, it whipped the sea into a desolate grey waste of white-caps—a cold, clammy wind, like the touch of a dead man's hand. And this was only the beginning, a mere waft of air from Helen's skirts, as, clothed in black thunderclouds and jewelled with lightning, she gyrated in her dance of destruction across our path—a clockwise-spinning giant, packed with appalling energy and forty thousand feet tall.

On land, they were ready for her, tracking her with radar as if she was an incoming thermonuclear missile, measuring her strength, reporting her progress as she bore down on the Queensland coast. 'Cyclone warning,' said the radio, on every channel. 'Tropical Cyclone Helen, 28.40 inches, centred at 3 pm Eastern Standard Time 200 miles east of Mackay, is moving south-west at 15 mph. Wind gusts to 80 mph near centre. Gales extend along the coast between Mackay and Double Island Point. Centre is expected to be near Sandy Cape at 1 am tomorrow with gales along the coast between the border and Mackay with gusts to 60 mph. Flood rains are likely in south coast districts, with storm surges along the coast south of Sandy Cape.'

And, in the language of the sea, Radio

VIR Rockhampton said much the same thing in its broadcasts to shipping so that, by midnight, our speed was down to eight knots, with the wind screaming like a fiend from the pit above the thunder of torrential rain and the yacht behaving like a cork in a washing machine. As she soared upwards, the gale tore the tops off the twenty-foot seas and slammed them at her like concrete blocks. When she dropped into the troughs with spray exploding from her bows, the rain hit her so that all I could see through the spinning clear-view disc was water—sloping Everests of water that gleamed greenish-white one minute, then swung dizzily upwards and vanished behind a solid curtain of rain the next.

Christina said rather breathlessly after a particularly stomach-wrenching descent, 'The yacht—I suppose it can stand up to all this?' She was sitting wedged against the chart-table, wearing a yellow sweater and navy-blue jeans. She didn't look scared or even sea-sick—just a little excited, like a teenager at her first all-night party.

'She's stood up to worse.' But not, I reflected as I hung on to the wildly-kicking wheel, with a deck cargo dragging her stern down. 'We're two hundred and fifty miles from the centre, so, we'll be all right. And while we're heading north-west, the cyclone's going south-west in a great curve because of the earth's spin. We're cutting across the inside of that curve like a matador stepping inside the rush of a charging bull. As long as we keep heading into the wind and sea, we can ride this one out.' If we couldn't, we'd have to jettison the oil, and that would mean we'd never reach Pulau Mati, but I didn't tell her that.

'Nothing to it,' Two-tooth bawled above the roar of the storm, the reek of his noxious pipe preceding him up from the saloon. He peered disparagingly out through the wind-screen as the yacht soared up to the crest of a wave, stood on her rudder, and then dropped like a bobsleigh down the next slope. 'Hell, I've wrung worse seas than this out of me socks. I remember once, off Luzon...'

The bridge intercom buzzed at my elbow.

It was Bellamy, and he sounded bad. 'Tallon,' he said, gasping, 'you've got to get down here. I can't stand much more of this...'

'Take it easy,' I said reassuringly. 'It's a

bit rough, I know, but by morning...'

'By morning, I'll be dead!' he shouted hysterically. 'He's going to kill me. He keeps whispering all the time...'

'Who does?' The naked fear in his voice was setting my teeth on edge. 'And what's the...?'

'Max?' he said, in a despairing wail. 'He's in here with me now. He's trying to...'

'Take her, Two-tooth!' I waited until his big, capable hands had closed over the wheel, then slid out of the seat and dropped straight down the ladder with the pitch of the yacht. I landed in a crouch in the darkened, shuttered saloon as Max, a big thermos in his hand, came out of the galley for'ard and stared up at me. 'Steady, *mon ami*,' he said warningly. 'To break a leg now would not be...'

But I was already going aft, fending myself off the bulkheads and thinking that, if Max had been in Bellamy's cabin a moment ago, he'd gone for'ard a damn sight faster than I could have done. And Bellamy's door was still locked. I used my key and slid the door open—carefully, in case Bellamy was waiting for me.

But he was half-sitting, half-lying on his

double bed with his knees drawn up to his chest and his hands braced sideways on the pillows. He looked terrible. His clothes were filthy, his bristly black beard was wet with saliva, and his eyes were halfway out of his head with terror. 'For God's sake, Tallon, help me,' he croaked when he saw me. 'Don't let him get in here again.'

'Max? Look, Bellamy.' I hung on to the doorpost. 'He's in the galley.'

'Maybe he is—now.' He nodded jerkily, his hands plucking at the bedclothes. 'But, if you go, he'll be back. He's very clever, you know. He can get through the walls, through the floor, anything.' He listened for a moment to the howl of the gale, his head on one side. Then he said, his voice suddenly and weirdly normal, 'And he knows what I did to those men on the tug.'

'What you did?' I grabbed for the foot of the bed as the yacht rolled. 'What,' I asked reasonably, 'did you do to them?'

'Aha!' He grinned at me cunningly. 'I'm not telling you that. If I did, you'd side with Max. You're all against me.' He brushed something invisible off the bed. 'Damned spiders,' he muttered. 'You'd wonder how they get in. And all different colours, too.' Abruptly, his voice went off into a high, keening whine. 'I didn't mean to kill those men, Tallon. I swear I didn't. But Max won't believe that. He keeps getting behind me and whispering what he's going to do...'

'Listen to me, Bellamy.' I'd had about as much of this Human Jungle stuff as I could take. The mad scream of the gale was beginning to make me hear people whispering behind me, too. 'You didn't kill those men. And nobody's going to do anything to you while I'm around. I'm going to get you something to settle your nerves.' I made for the door. 'I'll lock you in, and I'll be right back. You can talk to Two-tooth on the intercom if you like.'

But he was lying huddled on the bed when I left, his head in his hands. I locked the door ostentatiously behind me and reeled up to the saloon. Max was coming from the galley four mugs dangling from the fingers of one hand and the thermos under his undamaged arm. 'What is it with Bellamy?' he asked. He timed the roll nicely and nipped across the saloon to hang on to the bridge ladder.

'He's off his head. Says you keep sneaking into his cabin to murder him.'

'*Alors*. First he says you are trying to kill him, now me. The delusions of persecution, eh? He is a very sick man.' He climbed the companion and I followed.

'Sick, is he?' asked Two-tooth alertly from behind the wheel. 'Then how about me fixing him some of me seasick remedy?' He turned to Christina. 'Bit of hot, fatty pork,' he explained, 'washed down with strong cocoa. Yer can't beat it. This time off Luzon I was telling you...'

'Break out another dose of that sedative you've been giving him,' I said to the girl. 'I'll see he gets it.'

'He had two tablets an hour ago,' she said doubtfully. 'I don't know... Is he very bad?'

'Hallucinations.' I looked at her. 'Did you tell him about the tug?'

'He asked me if anything had happened. He became violent when I wouldn't tell him. So...' She shrugged. 'Why? How has it affected him?'

I looked at Max. 'He says he killed those men.'

'Poor devil.' He wedged the mugs on the table. 'Did he say how, or was he...?'

The bridge intercom rasped sharply.

'It's OK, Bellamy,' I said soothingly.

190

'I'm coming right down. Just relax and...'

'He's here again!' he screamed. 'He's come for me, Tallon. Max is here and he's going to...'

'He's up here with me,' I snarled, the hair crinkling on the back of my neck at the sheer insanity in his voice. 'Now knock it off, will you? I've told you I'll be down...'

There was a howl like a soul in torment from the other end, followed by a splintering crash. 'Bellamy!' I shouted. 'Listen to me!'

'He 'as knocked himself out,' said Max. He clambered down the bridge ladder. 'I'll go.'

Before I could tell him I had the only key, another scream ripped across the roar of the wind. And this one came from just behind me. I spun round, my nerves jangling like a steel band gone crazy, to find Christina, her hand to her mouth, staring at the sliding door that led out to the tiny scrap of sundeck aft of the bridge. 'Look!' she gasped.

Bellamy's face, like something out of a bad dream, was pressed against the glass, looking in at us.

'The bloody fool!' The streaming-wet,

staring face disappeared as I pushed past the girl. 'He's broken out through the cockpit. He'll kill himself.' I slid the door open.

Instantly, I was sent staggering by a deluge of icy sea-water that felt like a dam bursting. Everything movable in the wheelhouse took off in a cloud of charts and papers and the wind screamed like a demon as it fought to keep me in. I forced myself through the door, bent double, and shut it behind me. And there I was, out in the wet, howling blackness with only a madman for company.

He was down in the cockpit where the oil-drums were lashed, his soiled whites glimmering palely in the light from the bridge. 'You lied to me, Tallon,' he shrieked above the clamour of the wind and sea. 'You said he was with you.'

'Max was with me. He went below.' The wind tore the air out of my mouth when I opened it, half-suffocating me. I put a foot on the ladder and he yelled, 'Get back, Tallon!...don't trust you...'

I got to the foot of the ladder just as a wave like the side of a house fell on me. I couldn't breathe, see, hear or even think. I hung on, as mindless as a limpet, while the stunning weight tried to prise my grip loose. When I surfaced I peered out into the blackness, coughing up seawater. He was still there. 'Let me take you back to your cabin,' I yelled.

'You're not getting me...that cabin. He's waiting. Keep away...jump over the side!'

'Don't be a fool!' It's not easy to be calm and reassuring when you have to shout at the top of your voice and your teeth are chattering like maracas. 'Take my cabin.' I clung on to the lashings and eased myself towards him as the yacht soared up to a crest. One false move and we'd both be over the side into the roaring black maelstrom that kept reaching out to grab us. 'I'll stay with you. I won't let Max...'

'Yes, you will!' I'd got within three feet of him. 'I see it all now...both of you in it together. The Mako's sent you to get rid of me.'

'The Mako?' Taken by surprise, I forgot to be cautious. I made a grab at him. And missed.

He had the roll of the yacht behind the wild swing that got me right in the throat. Choking, I was lifted off my feet to land on my back on the steel rim of an oil-drum. I nearly blacked out with the agony in my spine, but I had the sense to clutch the lashings with my left hand as Bellamy fell on top of me, clawing and punching and getting in a few kicks at my shins as well. 'Yes, you swine,' he shrieked into my face. 'And that's how you knew about the Pekin job, wasn't it? But now the Mako want me out of the way, and they've sent you and Max to do it.'

It was like fighting a combine harvester on a corrugated iron roof, except that I couldn't fight back. All I could do was hang on to his shirt-front with one hand and grip the ropes with the other as *Victoria* roller-coastered downhill. If I let go to hit him we'd both go overboard. He was still bashing me when we hit the trough with a crash, and he made no attempt to hang on. I felt his shirt rip, and he was half over the side when I seized his flailing left hand and hauled him back. He clouted me in the face with his right by way of acknowledgment as I steadied him, then he ran for the ladder and went up it, shouting incoherently.

Feeling very old, I dragged myself up after him, the warm taste of blood in my mouth. I'd have thought that, after all this healthy exercise in the fresh air, a sick, maladjusted industrial chemist would have been ready for his bed by now. But he was still as full of punch as a pound of chillis and, as I reached the top of the ladder, he aimed a kick at my head that would have taken it off if I hadn't ducked. Instead, I took his size nine in my left shoulder and it didn't do much for me at all. What the hell are the others doing? I thought bitterly, forgetting that Max had only one arm, and Two-tooth was at the controls. I clutched at Bellamy's leg to bring him down, but he stamped on my hand and went blundering off for'ard along the narrow deck outside the wheelhouse. Through the streaming windows, I saw Max making for the bridge door to cut him off. Bellamy must have seen him too, for he stopped. He beat on the windows. 'Christina!' he screamed. 'Help! They're going to kill me!'

I staggered along the reeling deck. 'It's all right, Bellamy,' I croaked, wishing everything was. 'Get inside, and...'

'No!' Bellamy wrapped his arms around me as soon as I came within reach. 'Leave me alone, you bastard, or I'll take you with me!' He hung on to me like an adhesive plaster, dragging me to the rail.

There was only one way out of this—a short, sharp jab to the chin that would work as well as any sedative for the time being. I wrenched my arm free to administer it.

Max slid the bridge door open. 'Hold on, Tallon,' he shouted. 'I'm coming!'

I saw Bellamy turn his head, his eyes frantic with terror in the light from the wheelhouse. 'Get back, Max,' I said sharply. 'Let me handle this.'

But it was too late. Even as my fist connected with the side of Bellamy's jaw, he gave a tremendous leap and went straight over, backwards, into the sea.

CHAPTER ELEVEN

For an instant I could only stare disbelievingly at the patch of boiling sea into which Bellamy had vanished as if he had never been. Then, as I put a foot on to the rail, Max seized my arm. 'No!' he shouted. 'We have had insanity enough, Tallon. You know you could never find him.' He pulled me into the bridge and slid the door to. 'What is done is done. Here, sit down and drink this.' He pushed a mug of scalding coffee into my hands.

It seemed very quiet in there, with the fury of the wind reduced to a muffled shriek. And nobody spoke. Two-tooth was scowling intently through the clear-vision disc and Christina was sitting motionless, her head in her hands. I sat down opposite her, wondering what I could find to say. But, before I could speak, she looked up at me, her black eyes blank with shock. 'You killed him,' she whispered. She stared at me as if she'd been hypnotised. 'I saw the whole thing. You sent him overboard.'

'Killed him?' I said slowly. Suddenly, with horrible clarity, I saw how, after Bellamy's plea for help, our struggle must have looked from inside the bridge. I saw how unsavoury I must look, too, with blood trickling down my chin and soaking into the front of my shirt. I was soaking wet, and filthy from rolling about on Giraud's grimy oil-drums. 'Now wait a minute, Christina. You've got it all wrong.'

'Of course,' said Max sharply. 'Madame, your husband was *aliéné*—insane. He was trying to pull Tallon over with 'im—I saw it. Tallon did all he could—you see the state 'e is in. But, in the end, it was either his life or that of a madman. He had to defend 'imself, and so...'

'It wasn't like that,' I said impatiently. 'It wasn't a question of self-defence. I was trying to knock him out, that's all.' I had a fleeting vision of what a Crown lawyer could make of that statement. When the girl's expression didn't change I said, 'But there isn't time for all this.' I stood up. 'Here, Two-tooth, give me that wheel.'

'Whatcha going to do?' Two-tooth stared at me in alarm as I shoved him aside. 'You can't put about in this. Jeez, you're crazy, too.' He grabbed the back of my chair as the yacht lay over on her beam ends.

And how we didn't founder after that I'll never know. I broke every law of man and nature by bringing the unstable, stern-heavy yacht about in the teeth of a Force 9 gale and trying to search in that black, shrieking bedlam for Bellamy, knowing all the time that we'd as much chance of finding him as he had of being alive. Two-tooth was right—I was crazy. I was deliberately endangering the ship and the lives of three other people, and all for nothing. But I had to do it. I tried to tell myself I was doing it for Christina, to prove to her that I hadn't killed Bellamy. But I knew that wasn't the reason. The one I had to convince was myself.

We didn't find him, of course. Instead we lost the radar scanner, the dinghy and a section of the stern rail with the ensign and its staff as the following seas pounded us like a herd of elephants going over a paper bag. The only consolation was that, afterwards, weathering the diminishing fury of the cyclone seemed easy. The wind was still strong when daylight came, but the sun came up out of a watery blue sky to show us the ragged grey banners of the storm's rearguard retreating to the south-west.

'You gotta go below, mate.' Two-tooth had stayed on the bridge all night and so had Max. Christina had gone below without another word after we'd abandoned our futile search. 'You'll catch bloody pneumonia, sitting there like that.'

I looked up at him dully. I was still wet, stiff and encrusted with dried blood from the lip Bellamy had split open. 'Listen,' I said. 'Did I send him overboard or not?'

'Of course yer didn't. Now lemme fix you a drink and...'

'You didn't see, did you?' I said levelly. 'You were too busy fighting the wheel. For all you know, I could have dismembered him and thrown the bits over the side.'

Max said soothingly, 'Do not unquiet yourself, Tallon. When the people you work for hold the inquiry, I can swear...'

'You'll swear to damn-all,' growled Two-tooth, 'except that Bellamy fell overboard during the storm.' He paused. 'What people?'

'The Australian Government, *naturelle-ment*,' Max spread out his palms in a self-explanatory gesture. 'Surely it is they who will want an account of...'

'The Government?' I looked up at him sharply. 'What,' I asked quietly, not feeling at all tired any more, 'are you trying to say, Max?'

'Only that,' he said, as if reasoning with idiots, 'since you are both agents of the Australian security service ASIO, there will have to be an inquiry into how Bellamy died, yes?'

'Agents?' I stared at him. 'What gives you that idea?'

'But it is obvious!' Max's black eyes went from one to the other of us. 'I am not a fool, *mes amis*. And I am not a big mouth, either, so there is no need to make the pretences with me. There were many things to give me the idea. That newspaper item, for example. It was too...'ow you say? Too opportune, yes? Figure for yourself, at exactly the time when Madame needs a skipper of a certain type, he appears. You were planted on Madame, very cleverly, to make her think she had chosen you for the job.'

'And those men who died in the car,' I said grimly. 'They were planted, too, I suppose. But go on. What else have you got?'

'That you wanted to shield Bellamy by

not putting in at Sydney, and that you agreed with me when I said we should not report the affair of the *Natalie*. Why should you risk such trouble for the sake of Bellamy and his wife's brother? But, most of all, there was the message that Giraud brought for you.' He took out a packet of his small Dutch cigars and lit one. 'He had been careless. When 'e decoded it, he left an imprint of the text on 'is log-book. I was looking among 'is signals for a reference to the yacht when I saw it. It was about an Indonesian destroyer that is to intercept us.'

'So naturally,' I said, 'you told Christina about that?'

'No,' he said. 'No, I 'ave not told her about that.' He drew on his cigar, letting the smoke trickle slowly out of his nostrils as he watched me thoughtfully. 'You remember I told you, once, that it is my job to protect her—from herself, if necessary. *Eh bien* I think she will be glad to see this destroyer coming over the horizon before we are finished. She will regret being involved with this organisation of her husband's.'

'Organisation?' I kept my face frozen. I thought, when Bellamy had died, that I'd

202

lost the only man who might have been able to tell me something about the Mako. Now, it looked as if everybody on board knew about it. 'And what,' I asked, 'is this organisation, Max?'

He smiled faintly. 'I tell you, I am not a fool, Tallon. But, if you want it spelt out, it is a subversive group, a kind of political Mafia, dealing in assassination. I 'ave 'eard of it on many waterfronts in many countries.' He shrugged. 'And that is why you are here, to break this Mako, this syndicate of murderers.'

'And Christina's a fully-paid-up member, is she?' asked Two-tooth sarcastically. 'A sorta Lucrezia Borgeois?'

'Borgia,' I said abstractedly.

'OK, Borgia, then,' he said impatiently, 'although I thought that was one of those Russian dogs with long hair. Anyway, I don't believe a bloody word of it.'

'Of course she is not a member,' said Max sharply. 'But her husband was.' He leaned forward. 'He used her regard for her brother to trick her into helping the Mako. It was by him that all the arrangements for this trip were made. Even the yacht is in his name. And, afterwards, he was planning to defect to Red China, did you know that? I tried to warn Madame, to tell her she was stupid to...'ow is it? To sup with the Devil, yes? But she is very strong-willed and, when it concerns her brother...' He grimaced ruefully. 'It 'as been very difficult for me, very difficult. It is a good thing that you are 'ere.'

'What is it that the Mako wants her to do?' I asked.

'I don't know,' he said frankly. 'Most of my information I got from Bellamy, when 'e was drunk. But even he did not know the object of this trip.' He blew out a cloud of smoke. 'Do you?'

'No,' I said.

He grinned. 'An' you would not tell me anyway. OK. But you have a plan? Some arrangement for contacting this destroyer, perhaps?'

I stood up stiffly. 'At the moment, my only plan is to catch up with some sleep.' I started down the ladder. 'Call me if you need me, Two-tooth.'

But I didn't sleep. I wouldn't sleep for a long time to come and, when I did, Bellamy would be there with me in my nightmares. Because I'd been through all this once before. Bellamy was the second man who'd died after I'd laid hands on him, and you don't sleep all that well with a thing like that on your mind.

And, if they got me in the dock, I'd had it this time. They'd say I'd murdered Bellamy to get the yacht, the girl, her money—all three. And, if the *Natalie* hadn't gone down in the cyclone, they'd tie me in with that, and then they'd have the trial of the decade—murder, piracy plus all the old charges thrown in for comic relief. It would be better all round, I thought grimly, if the Mako got me first. But, either way, all I wanted now was to get to Pulau Mati and put an end to the whole wretched business.

It seemed to take a lifetime to get there—altering course every time we saw a puff of smoke on the horizon, and holding our breath every time we sighted a plane. Wearing sunglasses against the blinding dazzle of the Great Barrier Reef, we skirted the eastern seaboard of Queensland, where almost every physical feature on the chart from Cape Byron in the south to Banks Island and Cape York had been plotted and named with meticulous care by that incredible man Captain James Cook. In tropical sunlight that seemed to soak through the skin and into the very bones, we passed through the shallow, discoloured waters of Torres Strait, unchallenged by the few fishing vessels we encountered. Then, with the jungles of West Irian to the north, we put our watches back half an hour as we crossed the Arafura Sea and left Australia behind.

All this time Christina kept out of my way with a success I wouldn't have thought possible on a vessel the size of *Victoria*. She arranged to have her meals while I was on the bridge and, when I was below, she stayed on deck—usually with Max, so I didn't see a great deal of him, either. Since Two-tooth and I were either sleeping or eating while the other was standing his watch, I pretty soon began to feel like Captain Bligh with a deodorant problem.

And so we came to Pulau Mati, the Island of the Dead, on a sultry moonless night with the sea like black glass and *Victoria* floating among the mirror-images of a thousand stars that flared as sharp and bright as welding-arcs. It was sunset on our ninth day out of Melbourne when we sighted the low hump of the island silhouetted against the golden glow of the western sky beyond which the three thousand islands of the Indonesian archipelago stretched like a jade necklace all the way to the Indian Ocean. The sun went down in such a blaze of pyrotechnics that you found yourself listening for the hiss as it met the sea, and night overtook us like the pall of smoke that follows the extinguishing of a fire. There was no twilight. The sea glowed red like molten lava, then turned ash-grey and faded to black as the stars were switched on and the island vanished from sight.

We were showing no lights and nobody smoked—not so much as a precaution against detection; on a night as calm as this we'd show up on a radar screen like a floodlit polar bear in a coal-cellar. But, with our own radar out, I wanted all the night vision I could get. The only light on board came from where Two-tooth sat in the hooded glow of the echo-sounder. Christina was standing aloofly at the rear of the wheelhouse with Max beside her and, when I spoke to her, it was for the first time since the night her husband had died. I said, rather formally, 'Mrs Bellamy. This is where I have to advise you on the risk we're taking. With no radar and not even a dinghy to pilot us in, we stand a good chance of piling up on a reef. I'd like to lie off until dawn and then go in.'

'Perhaps you would,' she said coldly. 'But you're being paid to take risks, aren't you? By dawn, I want to be well away from here. We'll go straight in.'

I checked the bearing I'd taken before the island had disappeared into the darkness. 'OK,' I said. 'You're paying the insurance premiums.' I touched the throttles and the purr of the diesels rose half a note as we began to feel our way in, *Victoria's* screws swirling in the dark water with barely a ripple. Ahead, I could make out a black, humped mass that blotted out a patch of stars. 'Max,' I said. 'Get up in the bows as far as you can. Two-tooth, watch that reading. What've you got now?'

'Five fathoms, and shelving slowly.' Two-tooth raised his head and sniffed as Max went for'ard. 'Phew-ee! You breathed in lately, Tallon? There's something on the bloody nose out there, all right.'

I smelt it, too. A breath of wind like the sigh of a sleeping leviathan blurred the reflection of the stars in the sea, bringing with it the dry, sickly stench of death and decay—the kind of smell that must have greeted the first people to open up the Great Pyramid. 'Four fathoms,' said Two-tooth. 'Strewth, it's like a camel-driver's bedsocks. At this rate, we're not going to miss the radar. When the air turns blue, you're there. If we...' He stopped. 'Two fathoms and shoaling fast—'

At the same time there was a shout from Max. 'Reefs, Tallon! Back your engines!'

Instantly, I switched to full astern and, as the diesels responded with a full-throated roar, I caught a glimpse of what looked like white lace in the sea dead ahead. A vessel of seventeen tons displacement takes a lot of stopping, however. As the pale line of froth disappeared under the rake of *Victoria's* bows I waited, my fists clenched, for the jolt that would tell me she'd had the stem ripped out of her. But, after what seemed like an eternity, she lost way and began to go astern. Sweating, I cut the engines when we'd stood clear and, trailing the lead of the twelve-volt handlamp, I went up into the bows and flashed its powerful beam out over the water.

The long white shaft of light settled on the line of jagged rocks we'd nearly struck, and Max grabbed my arm. '*A gauche,* Tallon...to the left. I thought I saw...' I heard him catch his breath as the beam settled fair and square and the sea ran, bubbling, off a vast brown-and-white striped dome that reared out of the gently-heaving swell in front of us. *'Mère de Dieu!'* he whispered. 'What is it?'

In the harsh glare, it had all the quality of nightmare—a bald, eyeless head, gleaming with wet slime, that gnashed grinning jaws at us before the sea engulfed it again. It was a shell—an enormous shell, three feet across, lying on a mat of frilly bright-red algae. There were dozens of them on the rocks that jutted out from the water's edge, and they opened and shut their serrated, ore-crusher jaws slowly as the tide washed over them, revealing an obscene pink wetness within. I said, 'They're clams. Tridacna gigas, the giant clam of the East Indies. They're harmless enough—unless you happen to step on one, and then God help you. Because, if the quarter-ton weight of the shell doesn't take your leg off, you stay there until you drown.' I swung the light in an arc. 'I'm going to stay here with the light. You take the echo-sounder. Tell Two-tooth to circle the island until I can find a way in. If I can't, we'll stand

210

off until daylight whether Christina likes it or not.'

I wasn't impressed by what I'd seen of Pulau Mati, and our patrol round the island did nothing to make me change my mind. The shoreline was infested with stranded, decaying jellyfish, spider crabs and thick growths of blue-green seaweed. A collection of flying bugs that would have made an entomologist's fortune rose up into the beam of the spotlight until it became a silver, writhing mass of wings and legs and feelers, and I beat myself black and blue trying to keep the mosquitoes at bay. I saw nothing in the scrub that fringed the shore except, once, a pair of red eyes that gleamed briefly in the light before something went scuttling and squealing off into the bushes, and all the time there was the hothouse humidity and the dry, acrid smell of decay. If Peter Chan, I thought, had preferred this place to a nice cosy gaol, he must have been crazy.

After something like three-quarters of a circuit of the island, I picked out a dirty grey strip of tree-fringed beach split like a hare-lip by an inlet that was wide enough to take *Victoria's* beam. Prodding with a boathook, we felt our way in to where a moss-covered mudbank formed a natural mooring, sufficient for the yacht's three-foot draught at low water. I secured her for'ard to a reliable-looking tree, left the light on deck, and jumped ashore with a line into the tough, spiky bushes to moor her aft. I got the line round a tree-trunk and straightened up, sweating and itching.

Something rustled behind me. I spun round and, silhouetted against the light I'd left on the yacht's foredeck, a claw-like hand, its fingers outstretched, reached out of the darkness for my throat.

I lashed out instinctively, hit nothing, and over-balanced. I grabbed for *Victoria's* port rail and hung on to it, arched across the gap between the yacht and the shore. I kicked myself aboard and ran for'ard to get the light, pushing past Two-tooth and Max who were both trying to get through the bridge door at the same time. 'Keep the lights off and your heads down,' I snapped. 'There's somebody out there. He tried to grab me.' I swung the brilliant white beam aft and Christina screamed—a scream that was cut off short as she jammed her knuckles into her mouth.

There was somebody out there, certainly.

But that's all he was now...just some body. The naked corpse of a man who'd once been Chinese. He rotated slowly, his head tilted quizzically to one side by the rope that was embedded deeply into his neck and that stretched as taut as a bowstring from a branch on the tree I'd used as a mooring-post. Framed in the glare that cast a slowly-moving shadow behind him, he looked unforgettably hideous with his face half-decomposed and the yellow teeth snarling in the lipless, exposed jawbone. His eyes were missing. His scrawny arms stuck out imploringly, the fingers outstretched like twigs. And his legs had been torn away by something that had jumped and jumped to gnaw them off halfway up the thighs.

I snapped the light off quickly. Max and Two-tooth stood shocked into immobility in the starlight, and I heard the girl release a long, shuddering breath. She said shakily, 'How horrible! Who could have...'

I went aft, the lamp still in my hand. I said gently, 'Was it...anybody you knew?'

'It wasn't Peter.' She shook her head. 'I could see that, in spite of...' She stopped.

Two-tooth grunted. 'I'm glad to hear it.' From the tone of his voice I could tell that

213

he was thinking along the same lines as I was—that, if Peter Chan wasn't the victim, he might very easily have helped carry out the execution. 'Did you notice,' he said to me, 'that the hands weren't tied?'

I'd seen that. And that was probably the worst thing of all, because it meant that the hanging had been as much an entertainment as a punishment. With his hands free, the poor devil would have been able to cling to the rope and take the weight of his body off his neck, so that he could breathe and maybe even scream and beg as well. But he wouldn't have been able to undo the knots. You need two hands for that. If he tried to use both hands, the rope would be too taut to unfasten. After a time, his arms would reach the stage of agonised numbness where he'd have to let go. Then, choking his life out, he'd grab for the rope again and this would go on and on until, with his lungs bursting, he'd be left scrabbling at the rope with fingers too feeble to grasp it. It must have taken him quite a while to die, with the red-eyed rats waiting for him in the dark and...

Feeling sick, I switched the light on again, carefully avoiding the tattered horror that hung in the trees. 'OK,' I said. 'So we've arrived. What do we do now, Mrs Bellamy?' I flashed the lamp along the bank.

And I nearly dropped it as it spotlit the line of brown-faced men in ragged jungle-green uniforms who had, apparently, sprouted out of the ground. Their Kalashnikov assault rifles were levelled unwaveringly at me.

I heard Max spit out a bitter oath in French and I remembered that this was exactly the kind of situation he'd predicted. Then a voice said, 'You turn your light on to yourselves, please. And stand quite still. We come aboard now.'

Slowly, I turned the lamp inboard. There was a soft thump as somebody vaulted our rail. 'Downstairs, please,' he said politely. 'All people downstairs. There we can talk, friendly.'

I hoped he was right. But, as something hard and round and definitely unfriendly jabbed me in the kidneys, I didn't think I could count on it somehow.

CHAPTER TWELVE

It was an oddly-contrasting scene in the saloon. The navy-blue curtains with the natty tan-and-white aboriginal motifs were drawn tight and all the lights were on, including the strip over the meaty abstract that not even a cyclone had been able to dislodge. With its switched-on colour schemes and expensive furniture, the salon looked gay and welcoming and all ready for a few white dinner-jackets and gowns by Balenciaga. Christina, in a white shirt and black stretch pants, stood by the companion as if ready to receive guests, with Max beside her. Two-tooth and I sat on the settle like early arrivals at a party waiting for the fruit cup to start taking effect.

But the characters we'd collected wouldn't have been considered good party types, not even in Chelsea, London or King's Cross, Sydney. They both wore torn, sweat-stained jungle-green overalls, flat peaked caps that bore enamelled red star badges, and mud-caked, calf-length rubber boots. One, who was thin and Chinese, with a drooping stage-Chinaman's moustache, sat with a leg draped over the side of a saucer-shaped black leather chair, watching us like an elderly roué sizing up a chorus line, and picking his gold teeth with the foresight of a Tokarev automatic pistol. I wondered if he knew that the Tokarev doesn't usually have a safety-catch. He had a gilt charm-bracelet on his right wrist and a gold wrist-watch on his left, together with a wrist-compass. He also wore a verdigris-stained British Sam Browne—the wrong way round—and a collection of medal ribbons on his chest that, with its two Victoria Crosses, three Purple Hearts and a Croix de Guerre, would have been most impressive had it not also included several strips cut, rather forcibly, from Japanese neckties.

His companion didn't look like anything I'd ever seen before. He was only five feet tall, but so well-developed that he was the same distance across the shoulders, with arms that hung to his knees. His head swelled out at the ears to join his body with no neck at all, and he was as bald as a lizard. Facially, too, he was more reptilian than human, with an unwinking eye set on each side of his brown, leathery head and two small slits instead of a nose. His lipless mouth was slightly open and he made an unpleasant hissing noise as he watched me.

The man in the chair said, chinking his bracelets as he ran a hand over his cropped black head, 'Pay no attention to Choong-sun, please.' He had a high-pitched voice with the pseudo-American accent favoured by many mainland English-speaking Chinese. 'He is from North Korean People's Republic—not a smart guy, and he speaks no English. He is, however, very good guy at getting information out of silent prisoners.' He showed his gold teeth at us. 'I am Colonel Kung Wang-mao, officer of Indonesian People's Army of Liberation, and supreme commander of this area. Since this is war zone, I could have you shot as spies and anti-revolutionary elements, under international law. But, instead, I treat you well if,' he thought for a moment, 'you play ball game with me, yes? You will now bring all papers. Go one by one.' He pointed his pistol at me and spoke rapidly to Choong-sun. 'You first.'

Accompanied by the lizard-like Korean,

we got our mixed bag of Australian, British and French passports, plus the ship's papers. Kung examined them all carefully, looking up suspiciously from time to time to check names with photographs. He was, I reflected, the terrorist arch-type—the flamboyant, unstable street-corner hooligan who would, under normal conditions, be safely tucked away in one of those institutions where they make you eat with a plastic spoon. With his phony ribbons and bangles, he was a classic case of the psychopath playing at soldiers to liberate his lust for killing. Hitler's SS had been full of men like Kung. 'So!' he said at last, dumping all the documents on to the cocktail cabinet at his elbow, where there was a silver box of cigarettes. He helped himself to one, lit it, and dropped the match on to the carpet. 'And what,' he asked, grinding it out with his boot, 'are you doing on Pulau Mati?' I was nearest and he aimed his cigarette at me. 'You. Answer, please.'

I shrugged. 'You're the one who got us here,' I said. 'Suppose you tell us?'

He didn't even nod to the Korean. He just gave him a look. The next instant, I was sent staggering by a swipe across

219

the face that was like being hit by a bus. 'What,' asked Kung pleasantly, 'are you doing on Pulau Mati? Answer, please.'

Christina said impatiently, 'There's no point in trying to be smart, Tallon. All you have to do is tell him what he wants to know.'

I rubbed my jaw, looking at her. 'OK,' I said angrily. 'Then why don't you do the talking? After all, you set this up with him.'

'Set it up?' She frowned. 'I don't know what you're talking about.'

'Don't give me that. I know all about this organisation you've been burning your fingers with. Your husband told Max about it.' I snorted. 'You know what they're planning to do? Bring off one of the biggest killings of the decade, that's what. And it's probably your precious brother who's behind it all.'

'How dare you!' she said quietly, her black eyes snapping. She turned to Kung. 'I don't have to listen to this. He...'

'You listen,' snapped Kung, 'if I say. I give orders here. Who is this brother? And what is this organisation he works for?'

'His name is Peter Chan, but he isn't working for anybody. He escaped from a prison ship that was taking him to Surabaja. I was told in Melbourne that...'

'Chan?' The cigarette stopped halfway to Kung's mouth. 'The man who, with a companion, swam ashore from wreck of fishing boat?' He fixed the girl with a cold, cobra-like stare. 'He is your brother?' he asked, his voice dangerously quiet. 'And you have come here for him?'

'Yes.' She clasped her hands together nervously in front of her. 'Why? Is there anything...?'

'Why?' Kung's face flushed a muddy red and his voice went up to a shout. 'You ask why? You think I am stupid, woman? You think I let prisoner go, just for you?'

'Prisoner?' she said slowly.

'Yes, prisoner,' snarled Kung. 'I treat him and his companion well when they say they are refugees from the Djakarta clique. I give them clothes—food, even, when we have so little. But,' his face darkened still further, 'this companion, he was very bad guy. In misguided attempt to defect, he sank my motor-launch. So, I court-martial him, under international law. Choong-sun carried out sentence.' He jerked his head at the shore. 'Out there. And this Chan I punish also. With prison.' He looked at

221

the Korean. 'And questionings,' he said softly.

I stared at him, then at the girl. I was beginning to get the nasty feeling that Max's theory about Christina innocently helping out the Mako for the sake of her brother had blown a fuse somewhere. If she and Kung were working hand in hand to get Chan off the island, they were going about it in a very Oriental way.

Kung said grimly, 'Now, woman. You will tell me of the organisation your brother works for.'

'He isn't working for anybody. He was an engineering apprentice in Djakarta, and he was imprisoned because he was framed by a member of the revolutionary group there. Now...'

'Do not lie to me!' Kung's voice rose again. He flung out an arm at me. 'This man has already betrayed you. He says your brother belongs to an organisation that is to bring off a killing. Which capitalist spy system is it? The CIA? That of the British?'

'No.' She looked him straight in the eye. 'He doesn't belong to any spy system.'

This was going horribly wrong. If Chan wasn't working with Kung's Mako group, then I'd got the girl into a hell of a spot, and her brother as well. Suspicion was all these people needed. I said, desperately trying to get her off the hook. 'She's right. I was just shooting my mouth off. I made a mistake.'

Kung merely looked at me contemptuously. Then, as he turned to the Korean, I added quickly, 'But not as big a mistake as you'll make if your pet ape lays a finger on that girl. If he touches her, you stupid peasant, I'll kill you, gun or no gun.'

That certainly got Kung's attention off the girl. He froze and time stood still while he stared at me as if he couldn't believe his eyes. Then, slowly, he flipped my passport open with the muzzle of the pistol. 'Of course,' he said viciously. 'It is the Englishman, Tallon. An imperialist pig who thinks he still deals with coolies, maybe.' He came to his feet with the smoothness of a snake uncoiling. 'Very well, Mr Tallon. We will see who makes the mistakes here, you or me. We will all see.' He glared round at us, his voice rising shrilly as he flogged himself into a fury. 'You are spies, all of you. Lackeys of the puppet Government in Djakarta. I treat you well, under international law, and what is my reward? Lies. Insults. Insolence.' He stamped up and down the saloon, waving his pistol, his face working. 'OK. So I tell you what I do. You have boat—I have none. You have food—I have none. So I take all—boat, food and woman also. And you men will hang, outside in the trees.' Abruptly he stopped, pointed a quivering gun-barrel at me and shouted, 'But first, Englishman, I teach you lesson in obedience and get truth out of woman.' He snarled a harsh, staccato command to the Korean.

Before I could blink, I was spun round, grabbed by an arm like a steel hawser that pinned my elbows to my sides, and swung around again to face Kung. Another arm clamped across my forehead and pulled my head back so that, with the squat Korean's face jammed into the base of my skull, I was held against his evil-smelling body as effectively as if I'd been tied to a tree. I lashed out backwards with my right foot but all I got was a grunt from Choong-sun. Then his grip tightened, my ribs creaked ominously, and I found that my air was shut off. Through the flecks of black that began to swirl in front of my eyeballs I saw Two-tooth jump forward. Kung said, breathing fast with excitement, 'Back, you! Move again, and the woman takes his place.'

He drew on the cigarette he was still holding in his left hand. It glowed brightly. Then he came towards me, held the red-hot tip about a foot from my face and began to move it, very slowly, towards my right eye. 'Speak, woman,' he said softly. 'And be quick if you wish to save his sight.'

I heard Two-tooth swear horribly. At the same time, Max said resignedly, *'Eh bien, m'sieur le colonel,* there is no need to go further. Clearly, the time has come to tell you everything.'

The heat that was scorching my right cheek eased off. I opened my eyes to see Kung staring malevolently at the Frenchman. 'Tell me?' he barked. 'Tell me what?'

'That what you have so cleverly guessed is true,' said Max, reluctantly. 'We are, as you say, agents of the Djakarta Government, here on a mission of vital importance.'

He's gone mad, I thought dazedly. Right off his trolley. What was he trying to do—give Kung an iron-clad reason for stringing us up? I tried to shout him down, but I could hardly breathe, let alone speak. I gasped and struggled in Choong-sun's iron grip like a fish on a line. 'It's no good, Tallon,' said Max regretfully. 'We must admit we 'ave come up against a superior mind.' He shrugged, a picture of chagrined defeat. 'Evidently, it is useless to try to deceive Colonel Kung.'

'You are right,' snapped Kung. 'I tell you, I always get information from silent prisoners.' He gestured to the Korean, who released me, and I stood drawing in deep lungfuls of lovely, body-odour-scented air while Kung strutted back to his chair and sat down, tugging importantly at his drooping moustache and trying hard to conceal his gratified surprise. 'People's Army has best Intelligence system in the world. I knew, of course, that you were enemy agents even before you landed. And now you will tell me the purpose of your mission here. To confirm,' he added quickly, 'what I already know.'

Max nodded humbly. 'It is obvious that you know all about Peter Chan, the man who was posing as an escaped convict so as to expose any Communist

226

groups who might be foolish enough to help him. But you, of course, were not taken in. You saw through him instantly and imprisoned him. Our mission, as you have undoubtedly guessed, was to take him secretly back to Djakarta without destroying his cover. He is, you see, a counter-espionage agent of the first class, with important information concerning the activities of the anti-Government groups in this area.'

Christina uttered an involuntary gasp. 'No,' she said. 'That's not true. They'll kill him if...'

'Silence, woman!' rapped Kung. 'It is useless to deny it.' Surprises were coming thick and fast for the Colonel, but he hid the fact well. With a face so impassive that it might have been carved out of cheese, he said thoughtfully, 'I saw through his cover immediately. But, if he is wanted in Djakarta...' Slowly, an expression of pleasurable cunning spread over his yellow face as he watched us. He sniggered unpleasantly. Then, abruptly, the crafty grin vanished and he snapped, 'But why have you come for him?'

Max said, surprised, 'But I have just told you. He has information...'

'You lie!' Kung's bracelets clashed as he banged the cocktail cabinet with his pistol. Why it didn't go off, I couldn't think. 'Why would they send you for him? When, as you all know very well,' he stared round at us, 'there is a Government destroyer, the *Bandung,* waiting offshore that could have performed the task so much better than you bunglers?'

Clearly, that was a nasty blow for Max to take. He'd done well to take the heat off me—playing for time, hoping to string Kung along, apparently, with a Scheherezade-like succession of stories until the sailors from the destroyer came to the rescue. But, if Kung already knew about the ship, he'd take good care we were all dead when they arrived. Max said, looking stunned, 'The *Bandung?* Here?'

'Sure.' To my surprise, Kung didn't seem at all put out by the presence of the naval vessel. In fact, he was having a ball in his role of master-mind. He grinned his gilt-edged grin at the shock on Max's face. 'As you say, it is difficult to deceive Colonel Kung.' The grin faded and he frowned, once again the razor brained interrogating officer. 'Answer my question. Why have you come for Chan, instead

228

of the misguided sailors of the Djakarta imperialists?'

It was a good question. I was wondering the same thing myself. But Max had only just started, it appeared. 'The fools,' he said softly. His face took on a hard, bitter look. 'So that explains everything. I thought, when we found you here, that something had gone wrong.' He stared dejectedly at Kung. 'I...'

'Say no more,' said Kung condescendingly. 'I see it all. When your capitalist bosses found I was in control of situation here, they were compelled to use force against formidable opponent. They brought in their toy boat. But they omitted to recall you.' He laughed—an unpleasant sound, like a dingo with a bone in its throat. 'Ridiculous mistake of your stupid political system. But unfortunate for you, eh?'

Max nodded miserably and Kung laughed again. 'Because now you hang as spies, under international law. Except,' he said with a leer, letting his eyes wander round the curves of Christina's stretch-pants, 'for the woman. She is going to...'

'A moment, *m'sieu le colonel, je vous en prie*—I beg of you.' Max appeared to think for a moment, and a sly expression crept over his face. He looked sideways at the rest of us. 'There is something else I 'ave to say. Something for your ears only. Perhaps, if you sent these...?'

'No.' Kung shook his cropped head. His face, I noted with surprise, wore exactly the same look as Max's—a kind of crafty anticipation. 'You want to make deal, you all make same deal.' He surveyed Max, smiling to himself as he lounged back in his chair. 'You wish to save your life, eh, is that it?'

'The lives of all of us,' said Max eagerly. 'Yours, too, because tomorrow, when the landing parties from the *Bandung* come ashore, you will die. Your men also...'

'My men do not enter into this,' said Kung dismissively. 'They will die when they are told, that is all. And I do not die. I have other plans. If this Chan is so valuable to your employers, we can do a deal, maybe. But on my terms, not yours.'

'I'm not sure they'll like this in Djakarta, Max,' I said, playing up. 'I don't think...'

Kung gave me an evil look. 'The sailors,' he said, ignoring my protest, 'will do nothing until daylight. They will not land in the dark, when they can come ashore by day. So, tomorrow at dawn, you will go out to the *Bandung* in your yacht.' He pointed at Two-tooth. 'You will take that man to help you, and one of my men who will remain out of sight with gun. You will tell the captain that I hold Chan as hostage. I let him go only if they withdraw ship and leave me alone.'

Two-tooth growled. 'Why should they do that? If they want Chan, all they gotta do is come and get him.'

'True,' smiled Kung. 'But they get him dead, once they set foot ashore. I think they agree.' The smile broadened. 'You two,' he said to Max and Two-tooth, 'are not bad guys. You have been co-operative. You will go with Chan, on *Bandung.*' He paused. 'But Tallon and the woman and your boat, they do not leave Pulau Mati.' He looked at Christina and me. 'I have uses for them,' he said softly.

Two-tooth's beard bristled. 'To hell with that,' he said. 'I'm not going without me mate. And you're not keeping the girl, either. I'll see you in hell before...'

'So?' purred Kung. 'Instead, you wish to die slowly, like that bad guy out there? The choice is yours.'

I gave Two-tooth a look. 'Do as he says.'

I used the Australian phrase he was so fond of. 'She'll be right.' How, I didn't know, but anything was better than the alternative Kung had in mind.

Kung stood up. 'OK,' he said briskly. He clapped his hands, and immediately two stocky men in jungle-green appeared in the saloon doorway, unslung their Kalashnikov rifles, and took up positions watching Max and Two-tooth. Followed by Kung and the Korean, Christina and I were hustled ashore and into the low, stunted scrub that seemed to cover most of the island. Kung said from behind me, 'Tonight, my men eat for the first time in days. So we have entertainment for them. A *tjatji*. You know what that is?'

'No.' I stumbled uphill along the starlit path through the bush, tripping over roots and stones. 'But, if it's your kind of entertainment, I bet it's something pretty kinky.'

Kung said something to Choong-sun, and the Korean let out a croak that was probably the nearest he could get to a laugh. It sounded ominous to me, and to Christina too, evidently, for she said quietly, 'Tallon. Whatever happens, I want you to know I'm sorry I said what I did about my husband. I know you didn't mean it to happen.'

'I was trying to get him under control, not push him over.' I almost forgot about Kung and Choong-sun, who were jabbering loudly behind me, in the relief of hearing somebody tell me I wasn't a two-time killer, on my way to becoming something like them. That, I realised, as I dragged it into the open, was what I'd really been afraid of—not the Mako or Kung or even Fenner. 'It's just that I seem to be accident-prone with people. Like getting you into this. If I'd kept my mouth shut...'

'I got myself into it.' She paused as we tramped along. 'But I'm relying on you to get us out of it. They said you were useful in an emergency, didn't they? So now it's up to you to prevent Kung from handing Peter over to the authorities, and to get us all away from here.'

'I can't do that.'

'Of course you can,' she hissed. She took my arm as Kung paused suspiciously in what appeared to be a string of instructions he was giving to the Korean. When he went on, she said in an undertone, 'Convince him his deal won't work. Tell him that Peter really is an escaped convict and

233

not a spy. Then offer him an alternative deal—money, or even a passage on the yacht if he'll...'

'I can't,' I said again.

'Why not?'

I sighed. It had to come sometime. 'Because,' I said into her ear, 'I'm doing a sort of sub-contracted security job for the Australian Government. That destroyer's here because of me, and it's my job to get your brother on to it.'

I felt her stiffen. 'A security agent? I don't believe it.'

'It's true. They're trying to crack an organisation called the Mako that's planning to murder the US President. Your husband was working for it. He told me so.'

'And you think my brother is, too? That he's like Kung, and that I'm helping him?' When I tried to speak she shook my arm away. 'But it doesn't matter, now, what you think. It's all over, isn't it? Peter goes back to Djakarta, and you and I...'

A high-pitched challenge rang out ahead where yellow firelight flickered among the trees, and Kung replied. I could smell woodsmoke, tangy and welcome after the all-pervading stink of the island. Shouts

234

and raucous singing came from not far away. then we came out of the trees into a brightly-lit clearing that seemed to be about the size of a tennis-court. Four huge fires blazed in its corners and the spaces between them were packed with Kung's troops, lying or sitting in the scrubby grass, among opened packing-cases and tins that I recognised as having come from the yacht. In the shadows that came and went and the smoke that swirled about them, the terrorists looked like fiends from the pit, their mouths opening and shutting as they sang and shouted and their eyes showing whitely against faces like Oriental devil-masks that glistened with sweat in the yellow-orange glare. They were all blind drunk. Cups waved and clinked and, from the bottles I saw littering the grass, I realised that they'd got at the cases of whisky I'd put away in my cabin. A shot rang out and there was a burst of laughter—a laugh that changed to an animal howl when they saw Christina. A man staggered to his feet and ran, weaving drunkenly, at her. Choong-sun came from behind me to hit the man once, a contemptuous backhander that lifted the soldier off his feet to crash in a limp heap.

'And now,' said Kung in the comparative silence that followed, 'we have *tjatji.*' He clapped his hands and one of his men stumbled away into the darkness. Kung turned to me. *Tjatji* is a game,' he said, 'played in the remote parts of eastern Indonesia. The English are fond of games, I think. This one you should enjoy as a test of your skill and courage.' The orderly returned, grinning, with an armful of colourful paraphernalia which he dumped at Kung's feet. 'These are *tjatji* helmets,' Kung said, smiling wickedly, 'from the island of Flores. I collect such things.' He picked one up. It was hand-carved from a single block of hardwood, a masterpiece of native patience and craftsmanship, with a thick projecting peak that extended out over the eyes. Gaily painted in red, blue and yellow patterns and decorated with masses of dyed horsehair plumes and clumps of feathers, it looked like a cross between a motor-cycle cop's skid-lid and a witch-doctor's mask. 'Put it on,' snapped Kung. I did so, in a roar of drunken laughter from the troops.

Kung held up a hand for silence. 'And these,' he said evilly, 'are the other things you will use. Whips.' He picked them up.

One was a wicked-looking yard of rattan half an inch in diameter, as flexible as a fishing-rod, with another three feet of rawhide at the end of it. The other was shorter by two feet and of rattan only, tapering to a point like that of a rapier. 'Both have advantages. The longer has the reach. The shorter enables blows to be struck with greater speed.' He flicked the short whip and it sliced through the air with a vicious whistle. 'And both...' his gold teeth gleamed in the firelight, '...can take out an eye or tear off the tip of a nose. It is customary to change whips frequently during the duel.' He offered them to me. 'Choose one.'

Christina said coldly, 'Don't do it, Tallon.' She turned to Kung. 'I, for one, don't intend to take part in any of your perverted games, in public or private. If you're going to get rid of us, you might as well do it now with a gun. But, tomorrow, you'll hang for it, I promise you.' She looked him straight in the eye. 'You're stupid, Kung Wang-mao. Stupid and sick. My brother isn't a Government agent. And so there won't be any bargaining tomorrow, because you've nothing to bargain with. We mean nothing to the Djakarta Government. They'll come ashore and wipe you out, that's all.'

Kung stared at her. Then he giggled—a high-pitched, crowing noise. 'You are right,' he said. 'There will be no deal. I know that. I know, too, that you are not agents of Djakarta. But the sailors will not come ashore.' He flicked the whip again enjoyably. 'For woman, you have intelligence. I have intelligence also. We do well together, I think.' He looked at me. 'Your European friends, they think they have intelligence too. But that is not so. Tomorrow, they go out to the *Bandung* to save their worthless lives—and to give me the double-cross, maybe. They tie up alongside.' He giggled again. He was having a hell of a time. 'When we took food from your boat, we set explosive charges. With radio-controlled detonators. So, when I pull switch—boom! No more friends. No more *Bandung*.' Conscious of the growing restlessness of his men, he turned to Choong-sun, still grinning his head off, and spoke to him rapidly.

Christina said, 'Can he do that? Would it work?'

I nodded, feeling the heavy mask wobble

on my head. 'It'd work all right. A radio-controlled detonator's expensive, but much less complicated than the radio-control on a toy boat. With one of his men on board on suicide duty to stop Max or Two-tooth going below, he can blow a hole in the destroyer the size of a barn-door. We've got to warn...'

In response to a brief command, the orderly grabbed the girl and hustled her away. 'To my quarters,' smiled Kung, 'where she will be put in chains. She will not escape to warn your friends, if that is what you hope.' He pushed the shorter of the two whips into my hands, together, with a small, round, buffalo-hide shield. 'And now,' he pushed me forward into the rectangular clearing and his men fell silent with expectation, 'Choon-sun is ready.'

CHAPTER THIRTEEN

Lit by the leaping flames of the four big fires and standing on the black cross formed by his own shadows, the Korean looked like a voodoo devil-dancer. He had stripped to the waist, and his squat, hairless body gleamed with muscle. On his head, the horsehair plumes and feathers of the brightly-painted *tjatji* helmet waved like the questing antennae of some nightmare insect, and his eyes glittered out of the shadow cast by the peak of his mask. He stood motionless in the centre of the arena, with his whip trailing on the ground and his shield hanging at his side. For a long half-minute there was dead silence, broken only by the crackling of the flames.

Then, suddenly, he leapt a yard in the air with a hoarse shout, to land in a crouch with his shield up and his whip back ready to strike. In answer, the soldiers responded with a roar of encouragement. A hand shoved me violently in the back and I was sent staggering forward. At the same time, Choong-sun danced towards me, I heard his whip whistle, and the buffalo-hide shield was ripped out of my hand, to go spinning through the air straight into one of the fires.

The crowd bellowed its appreciation of this feat as I stood staring foolishly at the Korean, who was jigging in a circle round me, hissing like a snake. His whip slashed again, a blur of movement in the firelight. What felt like a red-hot branding-iron touched my chest, and the front of my navy-blue T shirt fell away as if it had been cut by scissors, to reveal the long welt across my ribs that turned suddenly into a foot-long, bleeding gash. Another agonising slash, this time from behind me, and the back of my shirt was torn in half. At the prospect of seeing my clothing removed bit by bit, the terrorists were in hysterics, rolling on the ground, pointing and howling with glee.

Choong-sun stopped his jigging and stood revelling in the applause, his shield down and his body running with sweat. I tilted back the helmet that was falling over my eyes. Then I jumped forward and slashed inexpertly at his naked chest—a cut that, by its unexpectedness, drew a yell of pain from the Korean.

There was a sudden, ominous silence. That hadn't been a popular move at all. For, not only had Choong-sun been struck; he'd lost face by crying out—a disgrace that was shared by all. The drunken, grinning faces went grim and hard as they stared accusingly at their champion. A voice from the top end of the clearing shouted something, and you didn't have to be a linguist to know that it was the local version of 'chicken!'

Choong-sun looked down at the blood running from the cut on his body. Then, very slowly, he raised his shield and came at me.

No jigging this time. He advanced like a flail-tank, his eyes murderous in the yellow glare of the flames, and I staggered back, striking out ineffectually under the hail of biting, slicing blows that struck fresh agony wherever they landed. His whip made a non-stop piercing whistle as it slashed at my arms, legs and body. A cut ripped across the front of my helmet like a razor searing across the bridge of my nose. I felt the heat behind me and I realised dimly that he was driving me into one of the fires. Wild with blood-lust, the men were on their feet, screaming like animals. I struck at Choong-sun with arms that felt like lead weights. Then my whip was torn out of my hand, as my shield had been. Panting with the exertion, the Korean paused, surveying my bleeding, tattered body as he made up his mind where to strike next.

Without really thinking what I was doing, I turned, picked a blazing branch out of the fire, and threw it at his head.

He yelled again, this time a scream of terror and pain as the horsehair and feathers ignited and his head was enveloped in flames. He dropped his whip, wrenched his mask off, and it fell hissing into the grass. Then he rushed at me blindly, his arms extended, to get me into that deadly, hugging wrestler's grip of his again. I was in a corner with the roaring fire behind me and the terrorists, howling with rage at my unsporting tactics, hemming me in. Hands struck at me from behind as the Korean came in for the kill.

Almost within arm's length he stopped, an expression of devilish fury on his lizard's face. He put his hands to his stomach, clutching what seemed to be a handful of feathers from his *tjatji* helmet. He went back half a dozen tottering paces and stood stiffly on his toes, his elbows pressed to his sides and his hands still holding his middle. Then, as his knees gave way, he collapsed like a dynamited house and writhed shrieking on the ground.

There was a moment of shocked silence until, shouting and pushing, the men crowded forward like spectators invading a football pitch, elbowing me aside as they surrounded their fallen hero. A hand grabbed at me out of the mob. As I fended it off, a voice said in my ear, 'Follow me. Quickly, before they recover their drunken wits.' I threw my mask away and followed, only too gladly. I could see what was coming to me when Choong-sun got over his attack of dyspepsia.

It was pitch dark under the trees and blessedly cool after the heat and glare of the fires. Feeling as if I'd been dipped in acid, I staggered after the small, slim figure of the man who'd rescued me, falling over branches, rocks and my own feet until he wrapped one of his arms round my neck and let me use him as a crutch. When the unholy row that was going on behind us had subsided into the distance, I stopped and leaned against a tree. 'What,' I asked weakly, 'happened to Playful?'

'Choong-sun?' The small man showed his white teeth in the gloom as he looked up at me. 'Kung collects native weapons, as you discovered for yourself. And they have a very nasty one in the islands—an arrow to whose point they fix dried chicken-bones that splinter on impact, like a soft-nosed bullet. It makes a hole in a man that you can put your fist into. I took a bow and one of those arrows from Kung's quarters, and I shot Choong-sun with it. In the guts.' He grunted. 'Even so, he died more quickly than the poor devil who swam ashore with me. I had a debt to settle with Choong-sun.'

'You got me out of a spot.' I took a deep, painful breath to fight off a wave of dizziness. 'And don't tell me, let me guess. You're Peter Chan.'

'Correct,' he said briskly. 'And you are Mr Tallon—an Australian secret agent. But we must keep moving. You've got to return to the yacht before it goes out to the *Bandung* and destroys it.'

'I'm not Australian, I'm not secret, and I'm not an agent. But otherwise you seem to be pretty well informed.' I fingered his denim uniform. 'I thought,' I said suspiciously, 'you were supposed to be a prisoner, not one of Kung's little green men. How do you know about the *Bandung?*'

'They had me shut up in a tomb, but my guard was drunk tonight when he brought me food. I went to Kung's quarters with the intention of killing him. I was hiding there when they brought my sister in. You can imagine how I felt.' He was silent for a moment. 'I managed to talk to her, but I couldn't get her away. She told me all about the *Bandung*—and about you. Now, if that allays your suspicions, can we...?'

'No.' I wiped some blood off my mouth. 'I'm not going anywhere until we've got her out. Kung's...'

'You couldn't get the cork out of a bottle,' he said gently. 'You need medical treatment, Mr Tallon. And Chris will be OK for a while. Kung will be too busy chasing you to think about her.' He grabbed my arm on an open wound and I winced. 'Sorry. But I must get you away. Kung knows you'll warn the *Bandung* and that, if you do, he'll die. He'll tear the island apart to find you.' He put an arm round my neck. 'You OK now?'

I started to shuffle forward like a geriatrics case trying to get to the john ahead of Mother Nature. 'Sure,' I said. To prove it, I sank down on my knees. Then, almost with a feeling of luxury, I slipped down into the black abyss of unconsciousness that opened up beneath me.

I came round to a feeling of appalling urgency—the feeling you get in those nightmares when your feet are encased in concrete and you're being chased by monsters, Income Tax inspectors, or whatever your particular aversion happens to be. There was something I had to do—something that involved Two-tooth and Max and was of desperate importance. Suddenly, I remembered. The two of them plus part of the *Bandung's* crew, were due to be blown to fragments in a few hours' time. And all I'd done about it so far was lie down and go to sleep. I started to heave myself to my feet, only to collapse again, biting back a groan as the red tongues of pain burnt into every square inch of me. I lay still, sweating and clenching my fingers in the wet sand.

Sand? And wet? Where had that...? A voice said into my ear, 'Come on, Mr Tallon. You can make it.'

'Go to hell,' I snapped. My head was splitting. More cautiously this time, I levered myself off the ground and stood up. I was on a narrow strip of beach, with the sea shining quietly under the stars and breaking with a soft, grating hiss of pebbles a few yards away. I put a hand to my throbbing head and felt the dried blood in my hair. I said to Chan, who was hovering about solicitously, 'How did I get here?'

'I carried you.' Out of the scrub, I could see him more clearly. He wasn't an inch over five foot six, and he was as thin as a noodle. 'We Chinese,' he said modestly, 'are a lot stronger than we look. And Kung began to search the area round the camp, so...' He added, when he saw me look up at the sky. 'You are on the west side of the island, a quarter of a mile from where the yacht is moored.'

But it wasn't my bearings I was interested in—not after I'd seen the position of the stars. I felt for my watch, but somewhere along the line I'd lost it. I said urgently, 'My God, it's nearly dawn. What happened to me?'

'It's almost five o'clock. You have been out for some time. You passed out from loss of blood, I think, and in falling you struck your head on a *peo*, a stone fetish, that was lying in the grass.'

'And the sun rises at six or thereabouts. That still gives us an hour. But,' I said grimly, 'in the meantime, Kung's had time to sober up his men and get them in position. Hell's bells, you should have gone back for Christina while he was still disorganised.'

'I couldn't leave you. Pulau Mati swarms with rats, and they'd have eaten you alive. Now listen. Your job is to reach the yacht, warn your friends, and have your injuries fixed. Then you must take *Victoria* round to the northern tip of the island where there is a rocky outcrop covered with giant clams.'

'I know it.'

'Good. Chris and I will wait for you there.' He was oddly like his sister in the way he said that—as matter-of-factly as if he was ordering a taxi. But getting the girl out of Kung's clutches wasn't going to be as easy as all that.

I said doubtfully, 'Maybe we'd better go to the yacht together. Then we'll all go back for your sister. You haven't even got a gun.' On the other hand, boarding the yacht would be no picnic, either. Kung would expect that to be my first move, and he'd have slapped a guard on *Victoria* that would make the Bank of England look like open house in comparison.

'No, I've no gun. But Kung has plenty. You don't have to worry about me, Mr Tallon.' I saw the gleam of teeth in his dark face. 'We secret agents are trained to look after ourselves.'

'I told you, I'm not a secret agent,' I said impatiently.

'But I am,' he said quietly. 'Internal Security of the Republic of Indonesia. My mission was to penetrate an organisation called the Mako. You've heard of it?' When I nodded dumbly he went on, 'I was set up some years ago, when it became known that the Communists might attempt a take-over, as a discontented rocket engineer with Red inclinations. I got into the Mako. But, at the time of the September Plot, I had to turn down an assassination assignment and the woman I was living with had me sent to prison as a terrorist. Then the Mako got me out again, and I was told they had a use for me on Pulau Mati. I never found out what it was, because the man who escaped with me—a former bandit and a very good friend, as it turned out—tried to get away and Kung hanged him. That wrecked my operation completely.'

'I think,' I said slowly, 'I can guess what they wanted you for.' It was like a light coming on in a darkened room. 'Will the United States President be flying in this area while he's on his south-east Asia tour?'

'The US President?' Chan watched me, puzzled. 'I know he's visiting Djakarta before going on to Australia. There's...'

'So that's it,' I said. This was exactly what Fenner had anticipated—but in Indonesia, not Australia. 'They're going to shoot down his plane. From here. And they're going to use a missile. That's what Kung's doing—running an anti-aircraft missile unit, and the Mako got you here to...'

'Just a minute, Mr Tallon,' he said gently. 'It's an ingenious theory, and I don't doubt that the Mako would do it if it were possible. It would discredit this country very much if such a thing happened—perhaps bring down the Government. But it's out of the question. Before Kung put me away I went over this

251

island with a magnifying glass. There's no rocket-launcher here. And do Kung's men look like technicians? Any fool can fire off a missile, but it takes an expert to prepare and arm one.' He shrugged. 'The Mako don't employ men like Kung for key jobs, believe me.' He looked at me. 'And they don't employ me, either, if that thought's crossed your mind.'

I said awkwardly, 'I did think that, at one time. But...'

'Then you were wrong.' He turned to go. 'My sister said to make sure you were convinced about that. Good luck, Mr Tallon.' He vanished into the trees like the Cheshire Cat in *Alice*, his grin being the last I saw of him.

I turned north and hobbled along the beach my cuts opening and shutting like man-traps with every step. It was a calm warm night with only the stench of the island to spoil it—the end of the night, the quiet hour when the stars' batteries begin to run down and the birds stir their feathers and cheep sleepily, ready for the dewy-fresh, brightly-packaged, brand-new day they're going to get. Only, here on the Island of the Dead there weren't any birds. There was only the hiss of the Arafurua

252

Sea breaking on the beach, and the chuckle of pebbles as the waves retreated—a noise, I hoped, that was covering the crunch of my feet on the sand.

I hadn't gone a hundred yards before I knew I was being followed.

I turned, and saw nothing. The beach stretched, pale and empty, into the gloom with the trees edging it on one side and the sea on the other. I plodded on a few more steps, then I heard it again—a soft, spiky rustle behind me, like leaves blowing along an empty street. A shadow moved over the sand as I turned—a shadow thrown by nothing. A shadow, moreover, without any light-source except the soft, diffused glimmer of the stars. Then I realised what it was. Not a shadow at all, but a black mass of rats stalking me along the beach, drawn by the smell of the dried blood that was caking my body.

Without so much as a splash, I turned and waded out into the sea, gritting my teeth as the salt got into the hamburger meat of which I seemed to be very largely composed. I started a slow, cautious dog-paddle, floating along silently with my nose just out of the water as I kept an eye on the trees for Kung's sentries. Equally silent, the rats surged along the shoreline, keeping pace with me like eager boat-race fans trotting along a towpath. They knew I'd have to come ashore somewhere. They knew, too, that in my condition I couldn't have gone three rounds with a pair of white mice. All I needed now, I thought with a jab of fear as something—probably a rock—scraped my leg was for a shark to get a whiff of what the rats were missing and then I'd really have decisions to make. But, in the meantime, I had a use for those rats.

They turned out to be very useful indeed. Because, if it hadn't been for them, I'd have trodden on the men who were lying out on the open beach, buried in the sand and so well concealed that even the rodents were taken by surprise.

The pandemonium of yells, thumps and squeals shattered the silence not fifty yards away as, in a cloud of flying sand, the three men erupted out of the ground, lashing out at the black, furry wave that washed over them. The rats fled, squealing like steam-whistles, into the trees as I submerged, grinning painfully as I imagined Kung's fury when he heard the racket. As I'd thought, he wasn't going to look for me.

Knowing my objective, he would let me come to him. The area round the yacht would be thick with his men. But I had to get through—not only to warn Max and Two-tooth, but also to use the yacht's radio. Whether there were missiles on Pulau Mati or not, the US aircraft would have to be alerted.

Surfacing only when I had to, I wallowed slowly towards the mouth of the inlet where the yacht was moored. The current was setting northwards, which helped. When I came across the bough of a tree bobbing along beside me, I hooked up on to its seaward side and let myself drift with my nose up against the wet, rotting bark, grateful that there was no moon. Opposite the narrow inlet, I paddled gently with my feet to steer myself in to the yacht.

I couldn't see any lights, but I hadn't expected to. Kung was making it easy for me, luring me into the trap he'd set under the trees. At the first splash I made, there'd be all the light he could muster to catch me like a floodlit flounder—and all the firepower, too. I stopped paddling and let the log's momentum carry me in, inch by inch, towards the yacht's mooring. It was odd, I thought, peering between the branches, that I couldn't see the gleam of her ice-blue hull in the gloom.

It wasn't odd at all. I could make out the trees, and the muddy bank where Kung and his men had stood. But *Victoria* wasn't there.

CHAPTER FOURTEEN

It was, I reflected bitterly, characteristic of Kung that, when he baited a trap, he wouldn't even risk losing the cheese. Now, I had to go back to square one and find the yacht before I could board her—and I had about half an hour in which to do it. Cursing, I released my grip on the floating bough. To see it drift in and then out again would be just what Kung was waiting for. I could almost feel the dozens of pairs of slit eyes peering over the gunsights in the gloom. The water-logged chunk of timber rolled as I let go. One of its branches struck the water with a loud slap.

I dived a split second before the twin searchlights flashed on. They grabbed greedily for the log like the silver feelers of some enormous insect and held it, turning the dark sea into a blaze of underwater colour. Thankful for the thick growths of weed, I burrowed among them on the muddy bottom clutching a rock as the water was lashed to fury overhead and the rotting log disintegrated in a chaos of bubbles. I began to feel the need for air but the light stayed on, switching suspiciously to and fro and pausing to illuminate the chips of wood that bobbed and spun in the green, frothing water. My ears began to sing and a small, bright-green crab came out of the mud, stared at me with eyes as bulging as my own, and vanished into blackness as the lights went out.

Desperate for air as I was, I didn't budge, remembering an old terrorist technique. And, sure enough, the lights flashed back on again to catch any poor sucker who'd popped up to the surface. They roamed around the inlet while I tied my throat muscles in knots to keep the air in my lungs. At last, the searchlights went off again, their lenses glowing redly in the dark as they cooled. Very carefully, I rolled on to my back, floated up, and let my nose protrude out of the water. It wasn't shot off, so I used it blissfully. Then, inch by inch, I propelled myself out to sea.

I came ashore again near the spot where I'd left Chan, and by that time the sky to the east was already taking on a mother-of-pearl luminescence that paled the stars and outlined the treetops as sharply as if they'd been drawn in Indian ink. The sun was about to come up out of the sea on the other side of the island, and there was only one way of stopping Kung. Instead of running away, I had to find him and smash up his radio-control unit—and him with it, if possible. The question was, where would he set up his transmitter in order to observe the *Bandung* from whatever quarter she approached? Limping, I set off through the scrub that lashed my face, and headed uphill at a shambling run for the highest point of Pulau Mati.

It wasn't a very high point, at that. A mere hundred feet, and in the centre of the island. But, with the sky now tinged to an ominous wax-flower pink and the trees becoming more clearly defined every minute, it seemed like the ascent of Everest. Abruptly, I stopped as I reached the edge of the scrub that surrounded the crown of the island like a monk's tonsure. I'd heard an odd, whickering noise, like that of a returning boomerang, from somewhere ahead. But all I could see in the rapidly-growing light was an expanse of hummocky, knife-bladed *lalang* grass and small stunted bushes. I went out into the open, feeling the first breath of the new day on my cheek as I left the trees. The whickering drone I'd heard increased in volume.

Then I saw it—the Bell Ranger helicopter that was flying parallel with the coastline and half a mile to the north-east, its glass nose held down questingly like that of a hungry mosquito. It was painted a matt blue-grey and, on its side, it had the red-over-white colours of the Republic of Indonesia.

I ran to the middle of the open stretch of grass, tore off my ragged, blood-stiff T-shirt and waved it frantically. The Ranger held its course, heading for the southern end of the island, its blades spinning a transparent silver halo as they caught the rising sun and its torque rotor flashing like a gold coin. It was flying at two hundred feet and, as it came level with me, I could see the pilot, dark-skinned and white-shirted, staring ahead through his perspex dome. I screamed and jumped up and down like a madman, but he didn't so much as turn his head.

Then something that sounded like an

angry hornet plucked at the shirt I was waving, and the flat crash of a rifle-shot echoed across the plateau. I threw myself flat into the spiky grass as the reports blended into one another and the Kalashnikovs pumped their shells at me, hissing through the *lalang* like snakes. Kung's men burst out of the trees behind me, firing from the hip as they ran. I stuck my face into the ground, almost crying with frustration. This time, there was no way out. I'd be cut to ribbons before I even got to my feet.

In addition, I was under heavy machine-gun fire from my right. I could hear the sewing-machine racket of a .5 Browning, and the vicious zipp of big stuff whipping overhead. Unless...I raised my head, in time to see the line of green-overalled men break as they scattered for cover. One flung up his arms and fell as the chopper, at treetop height, came angling in with blue flames bannering from the twin barrels in its nose. The *lalang* was blown flat all around me as the pilot cut the power on his main rotor and a door in the Ranger's side opened. Feeling as if I'd been caught up in a tornado, I stood up and grabbed the hands that reached out for me as the helicopter dropped to the ground, bounced, and took off again with a shattering roar while my legs were still dangling in space.

There was a metallic clang, and a large jagged hole appeared in the door as it was pulled shut. Through it, I saw leaves and branches, frighteningly close as the Ranger clawed for height with its engine bellowing on full power. Then the trees gave way to a strip of grey sand, and I was looking down at the royal blue of the Arafura Sea, ruffled out of its flat calm by the morning breeze. A voice behind me said, 'Is neat, eh? You press the button, the chopper go up, and there am I, Dimitrios Karonides, waiting to attend to your needs. The instant service. My own idea.' There was a deep chuckle.

I turned, wondering if the crack on the head had given me hallucinations. But, in his spotless white shirt and neatly-pressed stone-grey slacks, the big bald pseudo-Greek looked real enough. He said, suddenly concerned, 'But your chest—your arms. You look as if you have been...'

'Never mind that,' I said urgently. I grabbed his arm. 'The yacht's down there, stuffed with high explosive. When she goes alongside the destroyer, it's going to be detonated by remote control. We've got to...'

'Explosives?' Karonides leaned forward. 'Lieutenant,' he snapped. 'Call up the *Bandung*. Tell them the yacht carries explosive charges. On no account must it approach...' He broke off, staring for'ard over the pilot's shoulder. 'I think,' he said grimly, 'we have left it rather late, Tallon.'

He pointed for'ard. And, as the Ranger came round in a curve, I saw the *Bandung*—long, sleek and pearl-grey in the morning sunshine that threw back a sequinned dazzle off the blue water. She was lying at anchor half a mile from the island with a wisp of smoke drifting lazily from her two stubby stacks. I saw something else, too—the vessel that was tied up on the destroyer's windward side. A yacht with a bent radar mast above her flying bridge and empty davits where a dinghy should have hung. I couldn't make out any sign of activity on the deck of either vessel. *Victoria* looked as if she'd been alongside for some time, and it was as peaceful a scene as you could wish. Karonides said flatly. 'Please cancel that message, lieutenant. Instead, ask your controller to have the yacht searched for possible explosives.'

I said weakly, 'I don't get it. By this time, they...'

'Relax, my friend.' Karonides patted my knee. 'You are overwrought,' he said soothingly, 'that is all. Take it easy. You have done well—very well, for one with no experience. But now your part in this is finished.'

'Listen,' I said angrily. 'I'm not crazy, if that's what you think. They were planning to blow up...'

The pilot said over his shoulder, 'Sir. I cannot raise the *Bandung*.'

Karonides shrugged. 'They will be busy this morning. Keep trying. Obtain permission to land.' He turned to me. 'Of course you are not crazy. If the Mako could knock out this destroyer, they would certainly do so. But all seems to be in order down there.' He stared down at the *Bandung's* decks as we flew at three hundred feet over her main radar array. 'She is a highly-efficient, up-to-date vessel—given to Indonesia by the Russians when they wished to impress the previous anti-Western regime. And she is here to protect the Boeing of the United States President, who is due to fly over here in an hour's time on his way to Djakarta.' He turned, watching me. 'The Mako plan to shoot down his plane, exactly as Fenner predicted.'

I stared back at him woodenly. 'With a missile, I suppose. One that's hidden on the island?'

'You discovered it? Excellent, Tallon. You can show us the exact location...'

I shook my head. 'You're wrong,' I said quietly. 'I thought that, too, at one time. But there's no missile site down there.'

He smiled at me. 'OK. So you didn't find it. But Pulau Mati lies on the exact track of the aircraft. And we have information—definite information, which we have passed on to the Indonesian Government...'

'And I,' I said grimly, 'have information, too. There's nothing there except a bunch of terrorists run by a thug called Kung who was supposed to be sabotaging the destroyer. He couldn't operate anything more complicated than a thumb-screw. Not,' I said tiredly, 'that it really matters, since they'll re-route the plane now, anyway.'

'And fly it over another island, where there may be another missile that we know nothing about? No, it is better to make this route safe than to take such a chance. Besides, it would be a major propaganda victory for the Reds if they could tell the world that Indonesian air-space is unsafe for American aircraft. To cancel the visit altogether would be an insult to a friendly nation.' He looked across at the island—a green-and-brown, apparently lifeless lump on the sparkling sea. 'But don't worry, Tallon. The situation is well under control.'

The pilot said as we circled, 'Still no contact with my controller. But I am in touch with strike force. They were warned that *Bandung's* transmitters would be out temporarily because of minor generator failure.'

'Land anyway.' Karonides peered down. 'They will flag us off if it is unsafe.' He fingered his seat-belt as the Ranger dropped smoothly to the raised helipad on the destroyer's stern. 'And I do not wish to be up here when the attack begins.'

The pilot gunned his motor, and the helicopter's rubber pontoons touched down. I said, 'When are they going ashore?

I want to go with them. There are some friends of mine...'

'Ashore?' Karonides looked at me in astonishment as he unfastened his belt. 'You are not going ashore, Tallon. And your friends are here, safe on your yacht. Nobody is going ashore.' With the engine shut off, the rotors swished idly in the silence as he looked at his watch. 'Because, in a few minutes' time, the Indonesian Air Force will launch a massive air strike on Pulau Mati. With napalm and high explosive. Nothing and nobody on the island will survive.'

I stared at him, shocked into immobility. Then I turned to the young Indonesian lieutenant. 'Take off again,' I snapped. 'I'm going back.'

'Back?' Karonides snorted, opened his door and began to scramble out. 'What you need is a doctor, Tallon. That is obvious.'

I grabbed his arm as his feet touched the deck. 'The girl's still on the island. And her brother. They'll be...' I stared at Karonides, transfixed. For a mad, hideous second, I thought he'd grown another eye. As I swung him round to face me, his brown eyes stared at me blankly together with the small blue one that had suddenly appeared in the middle of his forehead. Then, as the crack of the pistol shot came to me, he collapsed against the fuselage.

It was only then that I saw Max, down on the stern deck beneath the helipad. 'Look out, Max!' I jumped out of the Ranger. 'Somebody's shot...'

'The radio service-man.' Grinning, Max took his P-38 from behind his back. Stripped of its friendliness, his monkey face looked like the mask of a snarling, predatory ape. 'I wondered how you managed to get word out that we were coming 'ere. And now come down. You also, *mon lieutenant*. But very slowly, eh? We don't want to dirty these nice clean decks.'

It just didn't seem possible. I looked for a moment at the limp bag of clothes that had once held a man called Karonides. Then, stunned, I lowered myself down the ladder. But the Indonesian pilot was neither disbelieving nor stunned. As he dropped to the deck he went for the intercom phone that was mounted on one of the helipad supports, tore it off its hook and shouted into it in his own language, his brown face still with shock.

'There is no one to hear you,' said Max gently. 'You are wasting your time. So put down the phone and stand over there, if you please.' He wagged the gun-barrel. 'Against the rail. A little further. Good.' The kid stood where he was told, defiantly upright with his back to the sea.

Carefully, Max shot him through the heart.

For a second, the body remained on its feet. Then, tiredly, it toppled over backwards. The rail caught it in the middle of the back, the legs shot up, and it vanished from sight. There was a pause, followed by a flat splash.

CHAPTER FIFTEEN

I stared at the little round eye of the P-38, and it didn't mean a thing. 'You bastard,' I said quietly. At that particular moment I was in such a state of cold fury that I didn't care, one way or the other, what he did just so long as I could get my hands round his throat. 'You treacherous, murdering bastard. You...' I took a step forward. For once, I was going to kill with intent and, as I thought of Karonides and the boy I'd just seen die, I was going to enjoy it even though it would be the last thing I'd ever do.

Then I stopped. The red mist of murder cleared as I looked at the destroyer's silent, deserted decks and superstructure. Nobody stirred. Apart from the spinning radar scanners, and the thin trail of exhaust smoke against the duck-egg-blue sky, there was no life, no movement. It reminded me forcibly of...

'The *Natalie,*' I said slowly. 'You killed Giraud and those seven others. But how?'

'I did not kill them,' said Max contemptuously. 'Giraud was one of us. One of the Mako. It was that drunken pig of a Bellamy who killed them—as he told you.' He grunted. 'But what he meant to do was murder us—all of us on the yacht. He wanted to get out, to sail to Noumea on the *Natalie*.'

'Because he'd stolen that money? But...'

Max grinned at me over the gun. 'That money was planted by me. In 'is packing-case before we sailed.'

'But he stole it. They said on the radio...'

'A tape-recording, *mon ami*.' He was enjoying this—and enjoying even more his power to stop this conversation whenever he chose. 'I was operating the radio on that occasion, you will remember. I 'ad to make sure we did not put in at Sydney where Bellamy could betray me. He had lost 'is nerve, the fool. That is why he tried to kill us. But, like the incompetent 'e was, 'e miscalculated the wind.'

'The wind?' Suddenly, it all seemed so hideously simple. 'A gas,' I said slowly. 'He used the gas...'

'...that was disguised as industrial gas in 'is samples. *Exactement*.' Max sneered at the stupefaction on my face. 'A nerve gas that he had developed—an agent, as it is called—of truly remarkable properties. A gas not only as efficient as Sarin and the other GB agents already invented, but one that is also completely non-contaminative and immunisable. The two cylinders in Bellamy's packing-case contained the agent, in two different forms. One, a G agent, is lethal. The other, a V agent, is an incapacitator an' brings about temporary paralysis of the nervous system. Both are absorbed through the skin, and both act almost instantaneously. It was the G agent that Bellamy tried to use on us.' He shrugged. 'But, when 'e took his immunisation capsule on top of all the liquor and sedatives he'd had, who knows what 'appened? In any case, when the *Natalie* came in on our lee side, the agent blew across to her.'

'So that's why you were so scared.' I had to keep him talking. And I had to keep my eyes on him without letting them shift to the slow, silent movement behind him where a big, bearded figure was edging inch by inch from behind a winch housing. 'If the agent had seeped up from below, or if the wind had veered, you'd have died

272

along with the rest of us.'

'My dying, that was not important,' he said quickly. 'It was the danger to my mission that scared me—and made me careless with the message Giraud had brought for me. I was able to cover up for that, and you agreed not to report the *Natalie* affair. But Bellamy had to die—sooner than I had originally intended. And so I exchanged his tranquilliser pills for some containing LSD. The usual results followed—apparent insanity, with aural an' visual hallucinations in which 'e saw me pass through the walls of his cabin to get at 'im. He knew I would kill him for what he had done. So, finally, when 'e saw me coming out on deck that night, he threw himself overboard out of sheer terror.'

Two-tooth had retreated behind the winch again, and I could see why. He had problems. If he came out to rush Max, the long shadow he cast in the early morning sunlight would arrive before he did and, with the gun-muzzle a yard from my stomach, I wouldn't live to see what happened after that. He couldn't try another approach because there was no cover. If he went off to burgle the armoury, I could be dead by the time he returned.

No, it was up to me to trundle Max back ten yards so that Two-tooth could grab him and the gun simultaneously.

I eased my weight on to my right foot and moved my left forward experimentally. 'And now,' I said, 'you've released his gas into the air-conditioning system of a foreign naval vessel and murderd its entire crew. You'll hang for this, you stupid...'

'Don't call me *stupide*, Tallon,' he snapped. 'The crew are unconscious, nothing more, and so is your friend Two-tooth—for the time being. I used the V agent, the incapacitator, on them.' He jabbed at me with the P-38, moving back to keep it out of my reach. 'It is you who have been the stupid one, you and your ASIO chief Fenner. He thought we were trying to recruit you, the fool. It did not occur to him that, all along, we were arranging for you to be recruited into ASIO so that we could use you. The microphone at the airport, the fight we knew you would put up in the car that night—all was planned with that end in view. We used the Bellamy woman also. We assisted her brother to escape and headed him for Pulau Mati. He brought the girl here, and she brought you. And

274

you, *mon ami,*' he grinned triumphantly, 'as an agent of ASIO, brought the destroyer here. I knew that, once you reported that you were going to Pulau Mati, it would be sent to intercept us. It is the only one east of Java. As for Bellamy, I persuaded him that the Mako was taking him to the People's Republic where his nerve gas would give him a new life, new prestige. I was in control of everything. And it was all done with one objective—to get Bellamy's gas and this destroyer to meet here.'

'Bloody clever,' I said. 'So you're in control of a ship full of doped men. But what's the next objective, master-mind? To go through their pockets?'

Luckily, it wasn't hard to keep Max talking. He had to have somebody to brag to and, the more I needled him the more he tried to impress. He said boastfully, 'I, Maximilian Perrin, am in control of history, Tallon. In control of Governments, nations.' He laughed out loud, carried away by his own cleverness, and he took a step backwards as I nudged his gun-muzzle with my bare chest. 'It is a ship full of doped men, yes. But it is also a *Krupnyi*-class destroyer,' he grinned wolfishly, 'supplied a few years ago by the

USSR and still equipped with one of its SAM-1 surface-to-air missiles.'

I went cold all over. So Karonides had been right, and there was a guided-missile installation. Only, instead of being hidden away on the island, it was out here on the open sea in front of everybody. I said, 'But that's a heat-seeking missile. A highly-specialised weapon. You can't...'

'Do not delude yourself, Tallon. At one time, I served with a North Vietnamese missile unit, 'andling these very same weapons. I am not French—although they tell me my father was. But my mother was Tonkinese, and killed by American bombs. So it is fitting that I should be the one to execute the US President and 'is staff when they fly over this spot in three-quarter of an hour's time.' His grin widened as he watched me. 'I've already explained to the Indonesian aircraft that they can expect no radio contact with the *Bandung*. If necessary, I can signal visually, using the correct codes. The planes will attack the island an' leave, convinced that the path is clear for the American Boeing. Then it will appear—an' be wiped out. And then...'

'And then their Vice-President takes over.' I moved my right foot forward, feeling as if I was doing the Hoki-Koki. 'So what's the difference? This game of knocking off the President's been tried before, you know. But they always...'

'Idiot!' he sneered. 'This President is of no more importance to us than was the Archduke Ferdinand at Sarajevo. But his death will separate the Djakarta Government irrevocably from the West. That is our aim—for them to be completely discredited, at home and abroad, so that my employers can take over. Then, from this front-line position in Asia, plans can be made for a confrontation with Australia. And stop crowding me, Tallon,' he snapped. 'You think I don't know what you are trying to do? But, if you make one move for this gun...'

'Who d'you think you're kidding?' I'd pushed him three yards towards the winch where Two-tooth was lurking, but it looked as if that was my lot. 'I collect a bullet whether I go for your gun or not, so...'

'We are both going to die,' he said quietly, 'so what you do is really of no importance, my friend. When my mission is completed, I will end my life in the sea.' Far from being depressed by this prospect, he chuckled, his eyes fixed on me and shining with a kind of unholy devotion. 'One day, when your drug-addicted, sex-crazed society has been eliminated, I may live again in history like Gavrilo Princip, who changed the world when 'e pulled the trigger at Sarajevo. But, in the meantime, there must be no trace left of any of us. Your yacht will be sunk and the corpses of you and your friends fed to the sharks. There must be nobody left for the Djakarta Government to blame—except the crew of the *Bandung*, who will recover, to find the world accusing them of a criminal blunder—or worse. And, when the Americans hear that their leader has been vaporised by a naval vessel of the Republic of Indonesia, they will turn their backs on this country—on Asia, even—for ever.'

'And Kung,' I said, impressed in spite of myself by the mad logic of his plan. 'Is he in your suicide squad as well?'

'That clown?' Max's face darkened. 'I was as surprised to find him here as you were. He nearly wrecked everything but, fortunately, I was able to manipulate 'im also. His infantile attempt to sink this ship was easily prevented, because I 'ad taken the precaution of hiding my pistol on the bridge when we first sighted land. I shot the guard and took my immunisation while your friend Two-tooth was removing the detonators. He was overcome by the gas and will be disposed of shortly. As for Kung, 'e will die in the air attack and his charred bones will be indistinguishable from those of the dead already on Pulau Mati. And, if anyone ever finds a few rusting weapons on the island and the wreck of your yacht, it will mean nothing. This is a plan of genius, Tallon—one man taking over a destroyer without the crew even knowing about it.' His staring eyes remained fixed on me for a moment. Then they narrowed and went cold and empty. 'But now,' he said softly, 'your part in it is over. Soon, the aircraft will be here, and so...' I saw his finger tighten on the trigger. At the same time, Two-tooth came roaring out behind him, desperately trying to cover seven yards in one jump. The gun went off.

But Max's eyes had flicked sideways. The slug fanned my face and, before he could pump the trigger again, I was on to him. He went down under my weight, screamed as his injured left arm hit the deck, and dropped the gun. I squirmed off his writhing, kicking body, grabbed for the P-38 as it scuttered across the deck, missed, and heard it plunk into the sea. Max sprang to his feet, snarling and spitting like a cat, ducked under the ox-felling swing that Two-tooth aimed at him, and ran for'ard. He disappeared through a hatchway and, as Two-tooth started after him, I shouted, 'Leave him! He's gone for a gun.' I hauled myself to my feet. 'We've got to pick up Christina and her brother. At the same time, we'll use the yacht's radio. Over the side, and go deep.'

Max jumped out on deck as we climbed up on the rail. He braced his legs apart, tucked the big Skoda sub-machine gun into his side, and opened up. But, by that time, we were halfway down to the water, Two-tooth going down feet first with his nose firmly gripped in his fingers. He hit the sea like a sack of coal only a second before I went under.

The water was as warm and clear as a swimming-pool, and it gave us no cover at all. In the turquoise underwater world, roofed with sunlit dazzle, I could see the blue fibreglass hull of the yacht quite clearly, nuzzled up to the bulky grey mass of the *Bandung*. A cloud of bubbles marked the spot where a bearded, Neptune-like

280

figure with a retinue of darting, flame-coloured parrot-fish was making for the safety of the yacht's keel. I hugged the destroyer's steel plates, spurred on by the roaring commotion in the water behind me as Max fired a long burst from the rail. I looked back.

And from behind the *Bandung's* rudder slid the long, stream-lined shape of a fifteen-foot tiger-shark, a dark-blue monster marked with darker stripes that gave it is name. It swam slowly, trailing me by scent as it picked up with its hyper-sensitive olfactory nerves the minute traces of blood I must be leaving in the water. But when it saw me...I spurted hard, pumping my tired arms and legs through water that seemed suddenly to have the consistency of treacle.

There was a concussion and a white mass of bubbles at the destroyer's stern. I saw a pair of whitish trousers and a bald head then the area round the rudder came alive with speeding, snapping shapes that churned the sea into turmoil as they fought for Karonides' corpse. Even in death, he was keeping his promise to look after me. He was giving me the few precious minutes I needed—and, if Max had had to cease fire to dump him over the side, it must mean that the Indonesian strike aircraft were very close.

They came in like silent shadows, the banshee wail of their six-hundred-mile-an-hour approach blanketed from us by the destroyer as we trod water on the starboard side of the yacht. For a split second the sky was blotted out as the nine Venom FB1s, in three neat vics of three, flashed overhead, almost at mast height. Then the howl of the Ghost 103 turbojets hit us as the twin-boom fighter-bombers went screeching up into the blue, climbing ten thousand feet per minute. I pulled myself up by the rail and on to the yacht's deck and hauled Two-tooth aboard, my spine crawling with goose-flesh as I waited for the stammering racket of the Skoda from the deck of the destroyer above us. But there was no sign of Max. He wouldn't want to be seen waving his pop-gun, I reminded myself, while the *Bandung* was under observation from the air. Two-tooth, his knife in his fist, ran to cut *Victoria* loose and I made for the bridge, stepping over the body of a Chinese in jungle-green that was lying sprawled in a cloud of flies inside the door.

The bridge was a shambles. Kung's men had smashed anything they couldn't loot, and the radio looked as if it had been struck by lightning. The signal lamp had gone and the door of the empty flag-locker hung askew from one hinge. I hit the starter, breathing a sigh of relief as the diesels fired instantly in a puff of blue exhaust gases. The lives of two people on the island depended on those engines. But, even as they caught, there was an answering pillar of black, oily smoke from the southern end of Pulau Mati. A succession of dull explosions rattled the bridge windows as, shimmering with speed, three Venoms in line astern came whistling low over the water towards us, their first pass at the island completed. Urgently, I slammed the throttles forward, feeling *Victoria* dig her screws in as we surged away from the destroyer.

CHAPTER SIXTEEN

Pulau Mati looked like an active volcano, erupting in gouts of flame-tinged smoke through which the Venoms weaved their wailing pattern of destruction, blasting the island with rockets and napalm until it glowed like a live coal against the black pall that writhed up into the blue, cloudless sky. Trees were burning like torches along the shoreline, crashing in sheets of sparks that settled on our decks as grey, powdery ash. And Christina and her brother were somewhere inside that inferno. A Venom streaked low over the island and there was a white-hot flash followed by a detonation, louder than the rest, that made the aircraft stagger momentarily as it climbed away. A shower of red-hot cinders hissed into the sea alongside and I said uneasily, 'That sounded like Kung's ammo dump. What happened to the explosive he put below?'

'Still there. Fifty pounds of plastic.' Two-tooth peered through the bank of acrid smoke that was rolling sluggishly over us and on to the *Bandung*. 'But I slung the detonators through the porthole. To windward,' he said thoughtfully, 'now I think of it. Which is probably why I only got a whiff of that bloody gas our friend was talking about. I remember the stink of the island blowing in on me face just before I flaked out. Then, when I came round, everything was so flaming quiet. Nobody around except me and him.' He jerked his beard at the sea where he'd dumped the Chinese guard. 'So, when I heard the 'copter, I came to see what was going on.' He grunted. 'Shoulda known. That Max was always a bit of an enema.' Before I could find out whether he meant enigma or the other thing, he asked, 'How did you get Chan out of hock?'

I told him about Chan as we closed the island. I'd hoped the planes might call off their attack when they saw us moving in. But the smoke hid us and, by the time we'd cleared the northern tip of Pulau Mati and come out into the hot sunlight again, the nine aircraft were already dwindling away to the west, their mission completed. It had been a good strike...appallingly good. The jungle at the northern end of the island was burning furiously, and the radiated heat as we approached was like a blast straight from Hell. There was no beach, and the roaring flames licked at the rocks we'd seen the night before—rocks that were now steaming with the heat of the furnace behind them. Two-tooth said, quietly, 'There's nobody there, mate. There couldn't be, not in...' He stopped. Then he grabbed my arm and pointed. 'Look!'

A little further along the coast, there was a point that was slightly to windward of the main fires. There were trees and bushes that had not yet been consumed. And, on the rocks, I could see two figures, one kneeling, one standing. I said, opening the throttles, 'Thank the Lord for that. But we can't go in close—we'd tear our bottom out. They'll have to swim for it.' I nosed the yacht inshore, into the searing heat. Two-tooth pulled off the wet handkerchief he'd tied over his face, waved it, and shouted, 'Jump! We'll pick you up.' The girl, the kneeling figure, waved back.

I shouted, above the roar of the holocaust we were approaching, 'What the hell are they playing at? Those trees'll go off like a bomb any minute.'

'With us perched in the bloody branches

if you don't back your engines.' He gestured frantically. 'Watch it. We got about six inches under the keel.'

Then, above the dull thunder of the fire that was slowly eating back into the trees, I heard Christina scream, 'Clam!'

'God!' I said, alarmed. 'Chan's got his foot caught. Here, quick.' As Two-tooth grabbed the wheel I tumbled down the companion, wrenched the big, red-painted fire-axe from the engine-room bulkhead, tore up on deck and jumped from the rail into the sea. *Victoria*, her engines reversed, backed away from the rocks.

Chan, his flat Chinese face contorted with agony, was standing pinned just above the knee in the jaws of a clam that looked like a steam-shovel, and Christina was beating at it with a rock. She might just as well have been trying to break open a safe. I pulled her back and swung the axe. Chan screamed as the blows jarred his leg, but there was no time for the gentle touch. Already, thick white smoke was gushing out from among the trees, not ten yards away. Any minute now, they would burst into flame and burn like a petrol dump. The heat was so great that the sea-water was steaming off my body and I felt as if I was being barbecued. Coughing in the smoke, my eyes streaming, I struck savagely at the giant shell and at last it broke—only a small break, but enough for me to lift Chan clear. I swung him gently on to my shoulder, averting my eyes from his mangled leg.

And Kung, looking like a demon in a pantomime, came staggering out of the trees, a Kalashnikov automatic rifle in his hands. 'So!' he gasped. 'The yacht. But you must bring it closer. I cannot swim.' His uniform was in rags and all the hair, including his drooping moustache, had been singed off his head. 'Quickly!' he yelled to Two-tooth. 'Bring the yacht in.' He jerked the gun. 'Or I shoot them all.'

There wasn't much I could do about it. I carried Chan, who was now mercifully unconscious, out on to the rocks, choosing a spot where the water seemed deepest. *Victoria* came in and I winced as I heard an ominous scraping from beneath her keel. 'You first,' I said to Christina. 'Take the wheel, try to hold her steady, and tell Two-tooth to give me a hand with...'

There was a dull whoomf and a blast of hot air from behind that made me stagger. Fascinated, I watched the ice-blue paint on the yacht's bows turn to a scorched brown as the jungle ignited with a crackling roar. Kung went up and over the side like a steeplechaser, to shelter on the seaward side of the bridge while the girl climbed aboard. Then, feeling as if my lungs were full of red-hot cinders, I handed Chan up to Two-tooth, who carried the unconscious man below. Christina followed them after I had kicked lumps of burning wood over the side and taken the wheel from her. I backed off from the rocks, grateful for the protection from the direct heat that the windscreen gave me.

When we were a cable's length from the island, Kung appeared in the bridge doorway. 'Now,' he said, breathing hard. He stood at the top of the ladder that led to the saloon, his rifle trained on me. 'You will take me to...'

Where, I never found out. Because a pair of large hands reached up from below, grabbed his ankles and the rifle went clattering across the deck as his head hit the corner of the chart-table with a crack like an auctioneer's gavel. Two-tooth hoisted himself up the ladder, grinning. 'Nasty tumble, that,' he said, surveying Kung's sprawled, unconscious figure. 'Hadn't got his sea-legs, I reckon.' He cocked a steel-grey eye at me. 'What now, mate? Back to the battle-wagon?'

I nodded, looking ahead at the bank of rolling, dirty-grey smoke that hid the *Bandung*. 'We've got a smoke-screen and an automatic rifle. I'm going to board her. Alone,' I added as he opened his mouth. 'You stay to look after the girl.'

'In your bloody gum-boots, mate,' he said energetically. 'Why d'you think Max let us get away before? Because he's got that helicopter, that's why, and I bet you a dollar to a pig's ear-hole he knows how to use it. You go aboard on your Pat Malone and he'll blow your head off, fire off his missile, and then come looking for us. You heard what he said—nobody walks away from this one. So we'll all go aboard. We'll be a hell of a lot safer. And we can lock the girl in a cabin somewhere, so that she'd survive, at least.'

It made sense. It also gave us an element of surprise, since Max would expect us to run for it, not lay the yacht alongside the destroyer like a flea attacking an elephant. And so there was no fluttering burst of machine-gun fire, no snarling face at the rail above us as, shrouded in smoke and with the engines shut off, we coasted in silently to the high, steel-grey cliff that loomed up out of the murk. I went up the ladder fast, the rifle slung over my shoulder.

The smoke was thinner up on the smut-stained, deserted decks. For'ard, I could make out the bridge superstructure with its fire-control tower, anti-aircraft armament and main radar array that soared high above a sharply-raked funnel. Another, smaller, radar tower was situated amidships, with a deck housing aft of the second funnel. And, aft of that again, were the missile-launchers—one of them empty, the other holding a grey, shark-like shape that pointed skywards. I dropped a rope to Two-tooth and unslung the Kalashnikov. He came over the side silently, followed by Christina, and the three of us scuttled for the shelter of a clipped-back hatchway. An Indonesian seaman lay huddled inside—where he'd been dragged off the deck by Max, very likely. I said, 'I'm working on the theory that the missile control centre's in the deckhouse near the launcher. If it is, that's where Max will be. Christina, I want you to go below. When we...'

'No. Please,' she said urgently. She looked at the sailor who, although unconscious, had his eyes wide open. 'I'd go out of my mind down there. Let me stay.'

I looked at her strained, anxious face. 'Then you stay here, with Two-tooth. And, if he tells you to duck below, you'll duck. Things could get rough.' To take her mind off that possibility, I added, 'And you've got a smut on your nose.' I went aft, running silently with the rifle at the ready.

The steel door of the deckhouse was shut. I couldn't hear a sound from inside. What, I thought with the back of my neck prickling, if the missiles were launched from the fire-control tower and Max was up there with my head in his gun-sight at this very moment? I took a deep breath, swung the heavy door open, and stuck the gun-barrel inside.

For a split second, I thought Max's plan had gone wrong. The man bending over the grey-painted console under the viewing port had his back to me, and he was wearing the cap and tunic of an Indonesian Navy four-ringer. Then he turned, and I realised Max had put on the captain's uniform for the benefit of the

Indonesian pilots. He hissed an obscenity at me and made an involuntary move for the Skoda that was propped against a bulkhead. I said, 'Go ahead. Try to pick it up and see how far you can get.' He went rigid, glaring at me like something out of a painting by Hieronymus Bosch, with rage, incredulity and hate chasing each other across his simian face. With what we had at stake, I wouldn't hesitate to kill him, and he knew it. 'Now,' I said. 'Come out on deck. Your hands clasped on top of your head. If you move them, it'll come off.'

Two-tooth came aft at a run, the girl behind him, as I backed away to the rail and Max stepped out on deck. 'Strewth,' said Two-tooth, his gravelly voice cracking with relief. 'I never thought it'd be that easy. What did you do—offer him a photo of Mousey Tung if he came quiet?'

'A moment,' said Max, swallowing. 'Listen to me, you two. How can my failure benefit you? I can give you money—'

'Shove it,' growled Two-tooth. 'And get that off.' He whipped off Max's cap. 'A bastard like you's not fit to wear naval uniform. When the crew of this ship come round, if they ever do, we're going to...'

'You are going to give rifle back to me, butt first,' said a grating voice from behind me. 'Or you all die, the woman first.'

I went very still. He's bluffing, I said to myself. Kung's got to be bluffing, because I've got his gun. I turned my head. He was limping along the deck towards us, his hairless face blackened with smoke and blood running from the cut on his temple. And in his hand he was holding his Tokarev automatic pistol. He jerked it impatiently. 'Hold out the rifle, Tallon. Then all hands behind head, and do not move.'

God, I thought savagely as I passed him the Kalashnikov, how monumentally stupid can I get? Why hadn't I had the sense to remove his gun from its holster when Two-tooth knocked him out?

There was a splash as Kung tossed the rifle over the side without taking his eyes off us. 'What is happening here?' he snapped, a scowl of bafflement on his filthy face. 'Where is crew? And you,' he stared at Max, 'why are you dressed as captain? Why do friends point gun?'

Max grinned at me, a grin of malicious triumph. Then he began to speak to Kung in what sounded like Cantonese. What was left of Kung's eyebrows shot up. He barked a question. Max replied authoritatively, lowering his hands to gesture at the missile, at us, at the sky. All the bounce went out of Kung. He spoke respectfully and, in response to what was obviously an order, went to stand beside Max. And this, I thought detachedly, is the end of the line.

A buzzer sounded stridently from inside the missile-control room. Max looked at his watch. 'Bring them inside. Quickly,' he said to Kung in English, for our benefit. 'The missile radar has an echo. They can be disposed of later.' He stepped over the coaming and we followed, prodded on by the Chinese.

The control-room was lit by an overhead fluorescent strip and, to a lesser degree, by the six-inch-thick glass of the small viewing port that looked out on to the missile launchers. Under the port was the control console, the size of an office desk, against whose matt grey paint the large red firing button stood out like traffic lights among a clutter of dials and switches. Against the opposite bulkhead were a row of radar display consoles and a small computer. Max went straight to the latter and tore off a strip of paper that it had disgorged. Kung stood inside the doorway, his gun fanning in a gentle arc from Two-tooth and Christina to me as we stood with our backs to the radar sets, our hands clasped above our heads.

Max studied his calculations. Then, his eyes on us, he removed the transparent cover from the right-hand firing button. 'Turn round,' he said softly. 'All of you. Tallon, I want you to see this. Look at the radar.'

On the luminous blue screen, the revolving trace had painted a succession of orange blips, match-head size, that marched in a perfectly straight line from the edge of the screen to a point near its centre. With the after-glow on the screen, the blips graduated in intensity, those at the end of the line being brightest. Even as I watched, the trace added another blip to the head of the column, one that glowed brilliantly before it, too, started to fade. 'The Americans,' said Max from behind us. 'Flying at forty-two thousand five hundred feet on a course of two-seven-three degrees, with a ground-speed of six hundred and seventeen miles per hour. You will see from the scale that 'e is thirty...' another small, sausage-shaped blip glowed into life, '...no, twenty-five miles away. Which means that he has less than two and a half minutes left to live. You 'ave about three.' He chuckled.

'Then I might as well light me pipe,' said Two-tooth. 'If,' he added politely, 'it's OK to smoke in here?'

'Smoke?' snapped Max. 'Of course you are not permitted to...' He stopped. 'Turn round. All three of you.' He stared hard at Two-tooth. 'You' he said slowly. 'You were smiling. Why? And do not deny it. I saw your reflection in the screen.'

'Not smiling.' Two-tooth shook his head. 'Touch of the wind,' he explained. 'I always get me guts in an uproar at times like this. Just happen to be highly-strung, see?'

But he didn't look highly-strung. I'd have expected him to look, as I probably did, angry and chagrined and appalled by what was about to happen. Instead, he stared calmly back at Max, as relaxed as a jellyfish. I wondered what the devil he was up to.

And so, obviously, did Max. 'If you are trying to play for time,' he said angrily, 'forget it. The crew will be out for another 'alf-hour. They will not help you.'

'You're probably right,' said Two-tooth agreeable. He looked at the firing-console. 'Coupla minutes to go, eh?'

Automatically, Max's eyes went to the big, fire-engine-red missile-release button, then back to Two-tooth. 'There is something in your mind,' he said slowly. 'Something you are too stupid to conceal. Why...?' He stopped, listening.

We could all hear it in the silence—the faint, far-off whisper of a high-flying jet. The Presidential Boeing, the closest-guarded, most expensively-maintained air-craft in the world, riding to its destruction at ten miles a minute. And nothing—not all the air forces in the world—could save it now.

Suddenly, Max turned to Kung. 'The explosive,' he said rapidly. 'Is it still on the yacht?'

'Who knows?' Kung kept his eyes and the gun on us. 'They stunned me after they had brought the agent Chan aboard and...'

'Chan?' Max's voice rose. 'The girl's brother? You left him alone on the yacht? You stupid animal! Why, he...'

'His leg's paralysed,' said Christina quickly. 'He's lying below, helpless.'

298

'That is so,' Kung grunted. 'I myself saw that leg.'

'And we've no detonators for the plastic, anyway,' said Two-tooth contemptuously.

'*Alors!* The explosive is on the yacht.' Max stared indecisively at Two-tooth then, once again, his eyes flicked to the red button. I knew exactly what he was thinking—that it wouldn't have been difficult to fool Kung into believing that Chan's leg was out of action. Chan could be on board the destroyer at this very moment. He was a rocket engineer, with access to a load of plastic explosive, and there were plenty of fuses and detonators to be had on the *Bandung.*

Just what was going to happen when that button was pressed?

Max glanced at his watch as the whisper of the distant plane swelled in the silence. 'But there is time to check,' he said aloud. He grinned tightly, regaining confidence. 'The missile will still seek out its target, even if the plane has passed overhead.' He turned to Kung. 'Take them out on deck,' he said viciously, 'and shoot them. Get rid of the bodies, cartridge cases, and any mess you make. I have had enough of their tricks.' He picked up the Skoda

299

and went out. A moment later, through the viewing port, I saw him swing up on to the rocket-launcher.

'Out,' said Kung unemotionally. He sidled towards the doorway, the Tokarev rock-steady as he watched us. The minute he backs up to the coaming, I promised myself, I'll go for him. After all, what difference did it make to me? But it might give Two-tooth a chance to get the gun off him.

The whisper of the four-engined jet had become a faint, mosquito-like whine. As if in slow motion I saw Kung, his eyes on me, feel with his left hand for the steel edge of the doorway. His left foot went up and back over the coaming. Did you, I wondered, feel the impact when a nine-millimetre bullet went through your heart? Was there such a thing as instant death, or did you have a micro-second of unbelievable pain that would seem like an eternity while...? I blanked that thought out. This was where I found out for myself.

Abruptly, Kung grunted. The gun-barrel wavered, came up again, and then the Tokarev thumped to the rubber-tiled deck as Kung staggered forward, his back arched. He took two steps towards me, his face twisted in agony, before he pivoted and collapsed face down on to the console so that I was able to see the handle of the knife that protruded from his back. Peter Chan, his face grey with pain, stood in the doorway, hanging on to its steel rim.

Then, even as Two-tooth sprang forward with a shout of alarm, Kung's body slid down from the console. His elbow struck the firing-button. And pressed it.

There was a roar like a furnace igniting from out on deck. With an eerie swish, like the sound of a thousand arrows, the missile flashed away from its rack and hurtled into the blue, riding a column of black, billowing smoke. I watched it helplessly. Its heat-sensors would already be activated and, any second now, it would swerve like a hunting dog scenting a rabbit as it picked up the energy emitted by the American aircraft. And, after that...I saw the trail of smoke swing in a curve to the east and my mouth went dry.

Suddenly, the smoke stopped. For a fraction of a second I saw the missile as a speeding black dot against the sky. And it was falling. Falling into the sea.

Peter Chan said weakly, '...no fuel left. I broke the...' He pitched forward into his sister's arms.

Two-tooth grabbed my shoulder as I went to help her. 'My God!' He pointed through the viewing port. 'Look!'

The area round the launcher was a sea of roaring flame. Horrified, I stared at the ball of blazing rocket fuel that was staggering out of it. Tearing and beating at its body, its hair and clothes burning fiercely, it reeled across the deck screaming—a human torch that, a few seconds ago, had been Max Perrin. He fell against the rail, shedding gobbets of fire, as I seized a foam extinguisher and ran out on deck. And the screams ended with merciful abruptness as Max threw himself into the sea. There was a wisp of steam, then his charred body floated motionless on the water.

Until the sharks came.

The publishers hope that this book has given you enjoyable reading. Large Print Books are especially designed to be as easy to see and hold as possible. If you wish a complete list of our books, please ask at your local library or write directly to: Dales Large Print Books, Long Preston, North Yorkshire, BD23 4ND, England.

This Large Print Book for the Partially sighted, who cannot read normal print, is published under the auspices of

THE ULVERSCROFT FOUNDATION

THE SCAM

BY JANET EVANOVICH

The Fox and O'Hare novels
with Lee Goldberg
The Heist
The Chase
The Job
The Scam

The Stephanie Plum novels

One For The Money	Twelve Sharp
Two For The Dough	Lean Mean Thirteen
Three To Get Deadly	Fearless Fourteen
Four To Score	Finger Lickin' Fifteen
High Five	Sizzling Sixteen
Hot Six	Smokin' Seventeen
Seven Up	Explosive Eighteen
Hard Eight	Notorious Nineteen
To The Nines	Takedown Twenty
Ten Big Ones	Top Secret Twenty-One
Eleven On Top	

The Diesel & Tucker series

Wicked Appetite   Wicked Business
Wicked Charms (with Phoef Sutton)

The Between the Numbers novels

Visions of Sugar Plums	Plum Lucky
Plum Lovin'	Plum Spooky

And writing with Charlotte Hughes

Full House	Full Speed
Full Tilt	Full Blast

JANET
EVANOVICH
AND
LEE
GOLDBERG

THE SCAM

headline
review

Published by arrangement with Bantam Books, an imprint of Random House, a division of Penguin Random House LLC, New York.

First published in Great Britain in 2015
by HEADLINE REVIEW
An imprint of HEADLINE PUBLISHING GROUP

1

Cataloguing in Publication Data is available from the British Library

ISBN 978 1 4722 0184 3 (Hardback)
ISBN 978 1 4722 0185 0 (Trade Paperback)

Offset in Minion Pro by Avon DataSet Ltd, Bidford on Avon, Warwickshire

Printed and bound in Great Britain by Clays Ltd, St Ives plc

Headline's policy is to use papers that are natural, renewable and recyclable products and made from wood grown in well-managed forests and other controlled sources. The logging and manufacturing processes are expected to conform to the environmental regulations of the country of origin.

HEADLINE PUBLISHING GROUP
An Hachette UK Company
Carmelite House
50 Victoria Embankment
London EC4Y 0DZ

www.headline.co.uk
www.hachette.co.uk

ACKNOWLEDGMENTS

We'd like to thank Chuck Knief, Kay Chan, Sam Barer, Kathryn O'Keeffe, D. P. Lyle, Winz Tam, Jim Clemente, Doug Stone, and especially Jim Kochel for sharing their specialized knowledge with us.

1

Kate O'Hare bought her Ford Crown Vic at a police auction for abused cop cars. The dented, Bondo-patched four-door beast wasn't the kind of ride that usually appealed to attractive, professional women in their early thirties. Of course, most of those women didn't accessorize their wardrobe with a Glock, an FBI badge, and a small belly scar from a knife fight with an assassin.

Kate liked used cop cars because they were cheap, low-maintenance, and had options that weren't available on a Prius. Options like Kevlar-lined doors that were great for cover in a gun battle, monster V-8 engines that were perfect for high-speed chases, and steel ramming bars on the front grill that came in handy for pushing cars out of her way.

She'd been heading north on the 405 freeway through the

Sepulveda Pass when her boss, Special Agent in Charge Carl Jessup, called. Nicolas Fox, fugitive number seven on the FBI's Ten Most Wanted list, was trying to make his way up to number six.

"I've been thinking that maybe it wasn't such a bright idea for us to help a world-class con man and thief escape from prison," Jessup said in his amiable Kentucky drawl. "And an even worse idea to give him access to the money we secretly plunder from bad guys and use to pay for our covert ops. Both Nick and a million dollars of our money seem to be unaccounted for."

"I'm sure there's an innocent explanation," Kate said.

"There's nothing innocent about Nicolas Fox."

Kate knew that better than anybody. She was the FBI agent who'd chased Nick for five years before she finally put him in prison. Unfortunately, to Kate's horror, Jessup and Deputy Director Fletcher Bolton had Fox back on the street in record time. They had a plan. Fox would work undercover for the FBI. And Kate would partner up with Fox to keep him honest. Together they were tasked with going after major-league criminals who couldn't be caught through legal means. So Nick remained a major-league criminal himself, secretly working for the FBI, and Kate remained a top FBI field agent, secretly working with an international fugitive.

And that's why Kate was currently taking the curves on Sunset like it was the Talladega Superspeedway. She was hoping to catch Nick in his Sunset Strip penthouse. Technically, the penthouse wasn't Nick's. The IRS had seized it from a rapper who'd neglected to pay his taxes, and then the IRS had left it unoccupied pending sale. Nick had posed as the listing agent and quietly moved in. Thanks to rich tax cheats, Nick could always find a swanky place to stay that didn't require him to show a credit card or his face to a desk clerk.

Kate skidded to a stop in front of the fifteen-story building, jumped out of her car, and ran to the locked lobby door. She rang all of the tenants, held her badge up to the security camera, and looked into the lens with as much authority as she could muster.

"FBI! Open up!"

A tenant with a sense of civic duty, and too much trust, kindly buzzed the door open. Kate charged into the lobby only to come face-to-face with an "Out of Order" sign taped to the elevator.

Just her luck. She dashed into the stairwell and sprinted up the stairs. In a training exercise, it had taken her and a dozen other elite military commandos in full assault gear twenty minutes to rush up to the eighty-sixth floor of the Empire State Building. Kate estimated it would take her three minutes to get up to the penthouse in her sensible shoes.

Her cellphone rang between the fifth and sixth floor. Kate touched the Bluetooth device in her ear and answered the call as she climbed.

"O'Hare," she said.

"Where are you?" It was Megan, her younger sister. "Dad's waiting for you to take him to the airport."

"I'm on my way."

Their father, Jake, lived with Megan, her husband, Roger, and their two grade-school-aged kids in a gated community in Calabasas. That was where Kate had been headed when she received the call from Jessup.

"I told you two weeks ago that the kids have a big soccer game today and it's our turn to pass out the sliced oranges at halftime," Megan said. "You *promised* me that you'd take him."

"Relax, Megan. I'll be there."

"Why are you huffing and puffing?"

The stairwell began to rumble with the unmistakable sound of a helicopter closing in overhead. Kate felt a pang in her stomach, and it wasn't from the exertion of climbing twelve stories in two minutes. It was a powerful case of déjà vu and the dread that came with it. Kate had once chased Nick across a rooftop just as his accomplices were lifting off in a helicopter without him. As the chopper flew away, Nick had leapt off the building and grabbed onto a landing skid to make his triumphant escape. Her fear now was that he was going to try to repeat that death-defying performance.

"I've got to go," Kate shouted to her sister, ending the call and taking the remaining flights two steps at a time, past the penthouse and up to the rooftop.

She burst out of the door to see a green helicopter embossed with a U.S. State Department seal idling on the roof. Nicolas Fox was running toward it, his suit jacket flaring like a cape.

To Kate's relief, the helicopter pilot waited for Nick this time. Nick opened the door to the passenger cabin and turned to Kate as she ran up. There was a boyish grin on his face and a sparkle in his brown eyes. It was pretty much a confession that he was up to no good and enjoying it too much.

He was wearing the kind of off-the-rack, basic blue suit that Jos. A. Bank regularly sold two for the price of one. It was very un-Nick-like. He was a stylish six-foot-tall man with a keen and very expensive fashion sense. This suit made him look like an underpaid bureaucrat. She assumed that was the point.

"Perfect timing," he yelled over the sound of the helicopter blades whirring above them. "I'm glad you could make it."

Kate climbed into the chopper and took a seat. "Where are we going?"

"Malibu." Nick secured the door and sat beside her. They slipped on microphone-equipped headsets so they could hear each other over the noise.

Kate wasn't surprised to see Wilma "Willie" Owens in the pilot's seat. Willie was a fifty-something bleached blonde with enhanced boobs that looked like basketballs with nipples. Her typical outfit was a halter top and Daisy Dukes, but today she wore aviator shades, a white shirt with epaulets, and crisp blue slacks. It was an outfit suitable for a licensed pilot, although she wasn't one. She was a Texan with a natural talent for operating any vehicle on land, sea, or air and an unlawful tendency to steal them for joyrides.

"Have you ever flown a helicopter?" Kate asked her.

"Once or twice," Willie said.

"Which is it?"

"That depends, honey. Does this flight count?"

Kate tightened her seatbelt and turned back to Nick. "We aren't going anywhere until you tell me why you're pretending to be a diplomat and what happened to our million dollars."

Nick pressed a button on his headset that cut Willie off from the conversation.

"Most of the money went into buying and repainting this chopper," Nick said. "The rest went to sending a lucky young man on an all-expenses-paid trip to the Caribbean. It was the grand prize in a contest he didn't even know that he'd entered."

"Or that he was the only contestant."

"You catch on quick. He's staying at a very exclusive, very remote island resort that bills itself as 'the true *Gilligan's Island* experience.'"

"No phone, no lights, no motor car, not a single luxury," Kate said, referencing the show's catchy theme song. "You're keeping him off the grid. Who are you hiding him from?"

"His grandfather, Stuart Kelso, the king of 'the grandparent scam.' Are you familiar with it?"

"Yes. A grandparent gets an urgent email, or phone call, from an official with the terrible news that their grandchild has been arrested, robbed, or badly injured while traveling abroad. The fake official tricks the old and easily confused grandparent into wiring tens of thousands of dollars overseas to get the kid out of trouble."

"That's the one. As fate would have it, Stuart Kelso was recently notified by the State Department that his grandson, Ernie, has been arrested in Cuba on a drug-smuggling charge. The bail is five million dollars. Ordinarily he might have not fallen for his own con, but we had inside information about his grandson. And we landed a State Department helo on his front lawn."

Nick grinned, and Kate tried her best *not* to grin. It was genius and well-deserved poetic justice, and it was totally illegal. It felt oh-so-right but also oh-so-wrong . . . much like her attraction to Nick. And the worst part was that he'd pulled it off under her nose.

"Why didn't you tell me about this con until now?" she asked, eyes narrowed, blood pressure edging up a notch.

"It was just a lark, something to keep myself amused between jobs. Kelso is small-time compared to our usual targets. I didn't think you'd approve."

"So you sneaked around behind my back."

"Yeah."

"We're supposed to be partners. You just made me look like the village idiot."

"Don't take it so personally," Nick said.

"How else am I supposed to take it? I'm responsible for

you. My career hinges on my ability to control you and your larcenous personality. You're only allowed to break the law when you have permission from the FBI. You can't go around breaking the law on a 'lark.'"

"I like when you get all worked up like this," Nick said. "It puts a sparkle in your eyes."

"If you go down, I go down, too. Rest assured I'll do everything I can to make sure it's not a pleasant experience for you. I'll make sure you're locked up and the key is thrown away."

"So you're in on the con?" Nick asked.

Kate blew out a sigh. "Yes."

"Excellent," Nick said. "Can you play an FBI agent?"

"I'll give it a try," Kate said. "But only if we can pick up my dad and drop him off afterward at LAX."

"No problem," Nick said.

2

Jake O'Hare was waiting for Kate and Nick in his gated community's private park. He was wearing a white golf shirt and tan chinos, his hands in his pockets, casually watching as Willie set the helicopter down on the grass. Jake had spent most of his life in the Army, doing covert ops for the government, but those days were long gone. Now he was in his sixties and most of his battles were fought on the putting green.

"Thanks for the lift," Jake said as he climbed in. He took a seat and put on his headset.

"Where are your suitcases?" Kate asked.

"I don't have any. I'll buy what I need when I get there and leave it behind when I go."

"You're going to Hawaii to visit an old Army buddy. It's a vacation, not a covert op."

"Says the woman taking me to the airport in a phony State Department helicopter," Jake said.

"Good point," Kate said. Her father was the only one, outside of Jessup and Deputy Director Bolton, who knew the truth about her and Nick. "Actually, we have an errand to run before we get to the airport."

"That's what I figured." Jake acknowledged Nick with a friendly nod. "What can I do to help?"

"Do you have any experience getting American captives out of foreign countries?" Nick asked.

"Extensive," Jake said.

Nick smiled. "Then just be yourself."

"I can do that," Jake said.

Thirty years ago, Stuart Kelso was an insurance salesman in Dearborn, Michigan, when he got a call in the middle of the night from a cop in Istanbul. Kelso's pot-smoking teenage son Bernie, who was on a backpacking trip through Europe, had been arrested for drug smuggling. If Kelso didn't send the cops $10,000 in twenty-four hours, they'd throw Bernie in a Turkish prison for five years. Kelso did as he was told and his son was put on a plane back to the United States. It was only later, once Bernie was home safe, that Kelso realized how stupid he'd been to act so quickly. *What if it had all been a con?* It was an epiphany for him . . . and the grandparent scam was born.

Kelso chose to target grandparents because the elderly were less likely to think clearly under pressure, and often had access to fat retirement funds. It was a smart move, because now he was ten times richer, fifty pounds heavier, and lived in Malibu with his third wife, Rilee, an aspiring model, in a Southern Colonial mansion on a bluff overlooking the Pacific.

When the U.S. government chopper landed in his backyard two days ago, he was sure the feds were coming to arrest him. Thankfully, he was wrong. It turned out to be a frantic State Department bureaucrat named Nick Burns arriving with bad news. Kelso's twenty-one-year-old grandson Ernie had been arrested smuggling dope into Havana. The Cubans wanted $5 million to set Ernie free or they'd put him on trial to embarrass the United States. Kelso couldn't believe the cosmic unfairness of it all. History was repeating itself. Burns urged Kelso to make the payoff for the sake of his grandson and the good of his country.

Kelso didn't care about Ernie or Uncle Sam, but he was afraid that the media spotlight might reveal his own crimes. That's why every dollar Kelso had was packed into the four suitcases that were currently standing beside him, waiting to be loaded into the State Department helicopter that was landing in his backyard again.

Burns emerged from the chopper, checking his watch as he approached. He was accompanied by a stocky older guy and a fit young woman in a gray pantsuit with her jacket open to show off the gun on her belt.

"Good morning, Mr. Kelso," Burns said. "Is that all of the money?"

The only cash Kelso had outside the suitcases was the twenty-eight dollars in his wallet. All of his other assets were tied up in debt and ex-wives. It was as if the Cubans *wanted* to clean him out. He could no longer run his business, pay his mortgage, or support his third wife and her posse of yoga instructors, hairdressers, stylists, and personal shoppers. But at least he wouldn't be going to jail.

"It was hell getting it all together," Kelso said. "I still don't see why it had to be in cash."

The stocky guy spoke up. "Let's be honest here, Mr. Kelso. You aren't posting bail. It's a bribe being paid to corrupt cops. Bribing is a cash business. Cash doesn't leave a trail."

Kelso looked at Burns and gestured to Kate's dad. "Who is he?"

"Jake Blake. The bag man who is going to spread the bribes around Havana for you," Burns said. "He's done this kind of thing for us before. For obvious reasons, we can't do it ourselves."

"What's to stop Blake from running off with my money?"

"Me," the woman said, flashing an FBI badge.

Kelso felt his bowels seize up with fear. He'd had nightmares about seeing one of those badges in his face.

"I'm Special Agent Kate Houlihan. I'll be with Blake every step of the way."

"You don't trust me, Houlihan?" Blake asked.

"The problem with mercenaries is that they are mercenary," she said. "Loyalty is not in the job description." She shifted her attention back to Kelso. "I'm also the one who will make sure your grandson gets safely out of Cuba."

"I don't know what that stupid kid was thinking," Kelso said.

"The only reason I'm going to bring him to your door and not to prison is because the State Department doesn't want this episode ever coming to light," Houlihan said. "But if I were you, I'd let him know he just used the only get-out-of-jail-free card he's ever going to get."

"I will," Kelso said.

"We've got to get moving." Burns looked at his watch again. "We need to catch a flight to Guantánamo. They're holding a plane for us at Vandenberg."

Houlihan and Blake each picked up two suitcases and carried them back to the chopper. Kelso watched them go. He'd have to crack the whip on his boiler room full of poverty-wage workers in the Philippines and get them to send out twice as many scam emails as usual. He needed to generate as much cash as he could before the workers realized there was no paycheck coming, stripped the place of anything of value, and walked out on him.

Kelso turned to Burns. "When will I hear from you?"

"You won't. If it all goes well, your grandson will show up at your door. If it doesn't, you'll see him on the news being perp-walked in Havana. Either way, this meeting never happened. The U.S. government was never involved. Are we clear?"

Kelso nodded. "Thanks for your help."

"It's what you pay your taxes for."

Actually, Kelso didn't pay his taxes, because he had no

legitimate income to declare. It was one more reason he'd paid the outrageous bribe to the Cubans.

Burns jogged back to the helicopter and climbed in beside the pilot. The chopper lifted up, veered off over the Pacific, and headed north toward Vandenberg.

As the sound of the chopper receded, Kelso heard a car coming up the driveway. He walked around to the front of the house to see who it was. A black Lincoln MKT with livery plates came to a stop, and a lanky guy in a loose-fitting tank top, board shorts, and sandals hopped out of the backseat with a big smile on his sunburned face. It took Kelso a second to realize it was his grandson Ernie.

"Wow, what an amazing trip," Ernie said. "Thanks for sending the limo, Grandpa. How did you know when I was coming back? Did the contest guys call you?"

The enormity of what this meant hit Kelso like a sucker punch in the gut. He staggered, leaning on the house for support. Ernie rushed over, grabbed him, and held him upright.

"Grandpa, what's wrong? Are you okay?"

The helicopter came back and circled low over the house. For a moment, Kelso couldn't breathe. All he could do was gasp for air and look up into the sky. *How could I have been so stupid?*

3

They couldn't fly the fake State Department helicopter into LAX, so Willie flew to Culver City and landed on top of a parking structure for the DoubleTree hotel. From there Jake took the hotel's airport shuttle to his terminal, and Nick and Kate flew back to the apartment on Sunset. They unloaded the suitcases onto the rooftop, and Willie took off again. This time heading north, on her own.

"Where's she going?" Kate asked.

"To a vacant farm up in Ojai that belongs to the IRS. She'll repaint the chopper and keep it under wraps until we need it again."

"We're keeping it?"

"Why not? We bought it."

Pull out my fingernails, Kate thought. It would be less painful than babysitting Nick Fox.

"Okay, we can hold on to it for a while, but only if Willie gets herself a valid pilot's license," Kate said.

"You need to stop thinking so much like an FBI agent," Nick said.

"I *am* an FBI agent."

"Yes, but you're a criminal when you're with me. The law is for people who have nothing to hide. The purpose of a genuine pilot's license is to identify you, prove you have met all of the legal requirements to fly an aircraft, and hold you responsible for your actions. We don't want anyone to know who we are, or what we've done."

"Okay, I get that, but she's had lessons, right? I mean she didn't just get into the helicopter and take off, did she?"

"She's spent hours with a certified instructor. She's absolutely qualified to fly that aircraft."

Nick picked up two of the suitcases full of cash and headed toward the elevator.

"Don't bother," Kate said, carrying her suitcases toward the stairwell. "It's out of order."

"No, it's not." He pushed the call button. "I wanted to discourage realtors and squatters from encroaching on my privacy. And I thought it would be inspiring to see you all sweaty and breathing heavy."

"I wasn't sweaty and breathing heavy."

"I noticed," Nick said. "If you put those suitcases down and let me have my way with you, I could get you there."

"Good grief. Are you flirting with me?"

"Honey, my intentions are way past flirting."

"Your intentions could get you a knee in the groin."

Nick grinned. "At least your mind's on the right body part."

Kate gave a grunt of feigned disgust and stepped into the open elevator. She was an FBI agent, and sleeping with Nick, a wanted felon, was a line she wasn't willing to cross. She'd already crossed so many lines, helping Nick swindle and steal and stay out of prison, that she often wondered what made keeping Nick at arm's length so important to her.

Nick reached past her and slid a key card into the control panel, and the elevator descended. A moment later the elevator doors opened into the penthouse foyer. The penthouse had floor-to-ceiling windows and a terrific view of the Los Angeles basin. Carl Jessup stood at the window, watching the helicopter fly off. There was a thick file folder under his arm. Nick and Kate walked in and set down their suitcases.

"That looks a lot like a U.S. government helicopter leaving here," Jessup said, turning around to face them.

"Looks can be deceiving," Nick said.

"Well, I wouldn't dare argue with you about that," Jessup said. "You're the expert on that subject."

Jessup had the tanned, weathered face and sinewy body of a man who'd spent his fifty-some years outdoors, working a field or raising cattle, but it came from genes, not experience. He'd been in the FBI since he graduated from college.

"What brings you here, sir?" Kate asked.

"I asked myself the same question a few times as I was going up those stairs," Jessup said. "Damn near had a heart attack."

"The elevator is working now," Kate said. "You won't have any issues with it going down."

Jessup cut his eyes to Nick. "So what have you done with the million dollars you took from us?"

"I turned it into five million in less than a week." Nick gestured to the suitcases. "Not a bad return on our investment."

"The goal of our clandestine operation isn't to make money," Jessup said.

"But it doesn't hurt," Nick said.

Jessup frowned and shifted his gaze to Kate. "Who was the target of this swindle?"

"A con man named Stuart Kelso, a major perpetrator of the grandparent scam," Kate said. "He tricks old people into sending him money to get their grandchildren out of desperate situations. Kelso doesn't deserve our sympathy, sir."

"He won't get any from me, but that's not the issue," Jessup said. "How did you get him to give you five million dollars?"

Nick smiled. "I ran the grandparent scam on him."

"Of course you did," Jessup said. "I'm sure you thought it would be great fun."

"It was," Nick said.

"You aren't supposed to be running cons for fun anymore,"

Jessup said. "You're supposed to be doing it to put very bad people in prison. All you did was take Kelso's money and make a fool out of him. He'll just go back to hustling old people out of their Social Security checks."

"Check your email," Nick said. "You've got an important message from your daughter."

Jessup used his phone to browse his email. "She says that she's in Budapest, her wallet and passport have been stolen, and she needs me to wire her two thousand dollars right away. Where did this email really come from?"

"Kelso's boiler room in Manila, where he's got a dozen Filipinos who send out emails to hundreds of grandparents every month using information gleaned from Facebook," Nick said. "One of my associates hacked into Kelso's computers last night. He sent out emails like the one you got to the U.S. attorney general, all nine justices of the U.S. Supreme Court, and the police chiefs of every major American city. Each email is embedded with digital breadcrumbs that lead directly to Kelso's boiler room. I'll bet you five million dollars that Kelso will be in handcuffs within forty-eight hours."

Jessup nodded, not so much with approval than with grudging respect. "I'd wager that it'll be closer to twenty-four hours."

Kate was relieved. Jessup's comment was the closest thing to his retroactive approval that they were going to get. Probably best not to mention the newly acquired helicopter at this time.

"Since you're in a betting mood, you'll like your next

assignment," Jessup said, handing Kate the file folder under his arm. "We want you to take down Evan Trace."

Evan Trace was the forty-year-old owner of Côte d'Argent, the Las Vegas casino where the generation of celebrities who'd never known a world without *The Simpsons* did their gambling, partying, and general debauchery. He was a dead ringer for Brad Pitt, a resemblance he played to the hilt in a series of stylish commercials for Côte d'Argent. He'd made himself the new, hip face of Vegas.

"Trace's boutique casinos in Las Vegas and Macau are laundromats for terrorists, mobsters, drug lords, street gangs, and despots who want to wash their dirty money," Jessup said. "They turn around and use that clean cash to do all sorts of nasty things, like buy weapons, bribe politicians, and finance terrorist attacks."

"It's simple, really," Nick said. "You walk into a casino with some money, buy a bunch of chips, and gamble for a while. Then you hand over the chips that you have left to someone else, say the owner of a vintage Ferrari you want to buy, and he cashes them in. That's it. There is no record that ties you to the transaction. Your money has been washed."

"Sounds to me like you're speaking from experience," Jessup said.

Kate set the file on the massive coffee table. "I know he is. I've seen the Ferrari."

"Playing baccarat is a much more entertaining way to move

cash than working with crooked bankers, crafty accountants, and shell corporations," Nick said. "And you get free drinks while you're doing it, too."

"I get why you do it," Kate said. "But I don't see what's in it for Trace."

"He gets whatever a player loses gambling and a five percent skim at the cashier's cage when the chips are cashed in," Jessup said. "Plus he makes some very powerful friends."

"It seems so easy," Kate said. "I'm surprised that more casinos aren't doing it."

"That's because we closely watch what goes on here, or at least we try to," Jessup said. "But nobody's watching in Macau."

"Why not?" Kate asked.

"There are thirty-five casinos in Macau, and combined they generate forty billion dollars annually in gambling revenue," Jessup said. "The Chinese government takes forty percent of that in taxes."

"That's *their* skim," Nick said. "Not counting the kickbacks and bribes the casinos pay to local cops and government officials."

"That's a lot of incentive to look the other way," she said.

"And they do," Jessup said. "In Macau, ninety percent of the gambling revenue comes from whales: super-rich gamblers who'll bet millions of dollars in one night. We know from our surveillance that most of the whales that gamble at Côte d'Argent are laundering money for al-Qaeda, ISIS, and other terrorist groups who target Americans. That makes Trace a criminal and a traitor. He has to be stopped. But the U.S. has no jurisdiction in Macau, and the Chinese government won't help."

"Seems like a job for the CIA," Nick said.

"The White House won't let them touch it," Jessup said. "They won't take the risk that U.S. spies might get caught sneaking around in Chinese territory."

"But you don't mind risking us," Nick said.

"You're a fugitive, wanted for crimes in a dozen countries, and she's the FBI agent you seduced into bed and into a scheme to rip off Trace's casino," Jessup said. "That will be an easy story to sell if you get caught."

"Nick hasn't seduced me," Kate said.

"Not for lack of trying," Nick said.

"It will be a tawdry scandal," Jessup said. "But not one that will deeply embarrass the United States."

"It will deeply embarrass me," Kate said.

"So don't get caught," Jessup said.

After Jessup left, Kate read through the file on Trace while Nick emptied the suitcases of cash onto the coffee table and counted the money.

She briefed Nick as she went along.

"Trace got his start in the gambling business running a small Indian casino in the desert outside of Palm Springs," Kate said. "Then, six years ago, he bought an unfinished Vegas condo tower, which had stalled midway through construction because the builder went bankrupt. Trace converted it into a 350-room hotel and casino. When he opened up, he hired beautiful young women and hard-bodied young men to hang around his topless pool as eye candy."

"That beats a high-seas pirate battle outside the hotel or a huge fountain of dancing water," Nick said, stacking the money on one side of the vast coffee table as he counted it. "It's also a lot cheaper."

"He also invites celebrities to stay for free," Kate said. "Especially the ones likely to get into trouble and make tabloid headlines."

"Saving him a fortune on publicity. Either he's a tightwad or he was improvising because he was strapped for cash."

"To lure in customers, he offered winning slot machines, bargain buffets, cheap rooms, and very strong drinks. People came in droves. But what really put him over the top were his TV commercials."

"Never saw one," Nick said.

"They were inescapable."

"I was too busy running from you to watch TV."

"Here's the one everybody knows." Kate powered up Nick's laptop, went to YouTube, and played one of Trace's commercials. Nick watched it over her shoulder.

The commercial was set late at night. The colors were so washed out that the picture was almost black and white. Trace walked down the Vegas Strip in a rumpled Armani tuxedo, his bow tie undone and collar open, and dragged on a cigarette, sucking every last molecule of nicotine out of it. He trudged past the erupting volcano, the Eiffel Tower, the New York skyline, all rendered seedy and crass in the harsh shadows, while he spoke to the camera in a voice made raw from a long night of smoking and drinking.

"What a f—king joke," Trace said.

The obscenity was muted, but it didn't really make a difference. It was obvious what he'd said.

"You won't find an authentic experience here. Not on this street. Not in these places."

Trace turned the corner, off the Strip, and there was Côte d'Argent, a slim black tower, untouched by gaudiness or pretense. He opened the door and looked straight into the camera.

"Gambling. Partying. No f—king gondolas."

The obscenity was lost in the bells and coin clatter of a slot machine paying off. He took one last drag on his cigarette, flicked it into the street, and walked into the casino. The commercial ended.

"That's their slogan," Kate said. " 'No freakin' gondolas.' "

"Catchy," Nick said.

"He put it on T-shirts, hats, and coffee mugs," Kate said. "The first two years that Côte d'Argent was in business, Trace made more money off his branded merchandise than he did from his hotel."

Nick went back to counting stacks of hundred-dollar bills. "If we really want to learn about Evan Trace and the inner workings of his casino, we'll need to take a trip to Vegas. Be a couple of whales."

Kate could see where this was going. "We are not going to gamble with the government's money."

"It's not the government's money. It's cash stolen from Stuart Kelso."

"By the FBI."

"Illegally," he said.

"For the greater good," Kate said, thinking that was kind of lame, but it was the best she could do to justify their actions.

"Fine. We're gambling with this money for the greater good," Nick said. "And for the free drinks."

"Will the buffet be free, too?"

"It'll definitely be comped."

"Let's do it," Kate said.

4

Nick and Kate were on a private jet headed to Las Vegas. It had taken two days to organize, but Nick had needed the extra day to set up their fake identities as Nick Sweet, international entrepreneur, and Kate Porter, his executive assistant. It also gave Jessup time to wipe their real identities from various law enforcement databases and temporarily replace them with their new ones.

Nick wore a gray, impeccably tailored Tom Ford suit with a white shirt and blue silk tie.

Kate wore a skin-tight red Herve Leger bandage dress. It had a plunging neckline, cap sleeves, and a skirt that was so short, there was almost no way Kate could get up from a chair without making everyone her gynecologist. Nick had picked it out for her because she had nothing like it. Kate's closet was mostly full of tank tops and jeans and her FBI windbreaker.

Kate picked an almond from a small bowl of heated nuts. "I don't get it. Nick Sweet and Kate Porter. Why are you a dessert, and I'm a beer?"

Nick looked across the aisle at her. "Would you rather be the dessert?"

Kate ate the almond and thought about it. "No."

"What then?"

"I'd rather be a morning glory muffin."

"Hard to fit that on a passport," Nick said.

Kate nodded. "What exactly is the job of an international entrepreneur?"

"To be charming, mysterious, and extravagantly wealthy," Nick said. "Your job is to take care of all the little things that might distract me from being charming, mysterious, and extravagantly wealthy."

"So you get to have all the fun," she said, "while I do all the busy work."

"I swindle while you investigate. We both do what we do best. I've booked the presidential suite for us at Côte d'Argent to announce our arrival. They'll know a whale is coming and send a limo to pick us up."

"How much is this announcement costing us?"

"Thirty-five thousand a night."

Kate choked on a cashew. "Are you insane?"

"It's only one night, two tops, and it accomplishes some very important things. It establishes that we're among the highest of high rollers and it proves that we're not in law enforcement. No cop could possibly justify this expense to his boss."

"*I'll* have to."

He waved off her concern. "Only if the assignment fails. Until then, enjoy yourself."

Easy for him to say. He wasn't wearing a thong and four-inch heels that were pinching his toes.

"You look great in that dress," he said. "It has me feeling romantic."

"Romantic?"

"Okay, maybe that's not exactly the right word."

"And the right word would be what?"

"Hard to boil it down to one word."

"Give it to me in a couple words then."

"I'd like to rip it off you with my teeth."

"Holy cow."

Nick smiled. "Like I said, you look great in that dress."

Kate squeezed her knees together and crossed her arms over her chest.

Twenty minutes later they landed at Henderson Executive Airport, a few miles southeast of central Las Vegas. A black Bentley Flying Spur from Côte d'Argent was waiting for them on the tarmac along with a chauffeur in a black suit and dark sunglasses.

The chauffeur opened the back door of the Bentley for Nick and Kate, and put the four titanium suitcases full of cash and the two Louis Vuitton bags containing their clothes in the trunk. He headed north on Interstate 15 toward the Strip. They hit the Strip and traveled from Mandalay Bay to the Bellagio, exiting at Flamingo Road, turning west over the freeway. Rising above a sea of budget motels, convenience stores, and fast-food restaurants was a forty-five-story black granite tower shaped like a box cutter blade. "Côte d'Argent" was written in lights along the cutting edge.

The driver pulled up to a private entrance behind the building. It was shielded from public view by an eight-foot-high wall of black marble, lined with a thin layer of water cascading down the surface. A doorman who looked more like a Secret Service agent, down to the sunglasses, earpiece, and probably the gun, opened the back of the Bentley for Nick and Kate, and supervised the unloading of the trunk.

Nick and Kate walked into the VIP lobby. The air conditioner was cranked up high against the desert heat, keeping the elaborate ice sculptures of lions taking down gazelles from melting too quickly.

A slim, beautiful hostess approached them. She was dressed in a black frock jacket, a lace peplum blouse, pencil slacks, and ultra-high heels.

"Welcome to Côte d'Argent," the hostess said, guiding them to the registration desk.

The red-haired woman behind the desk wore the same outfit as the other hostesses. She smiled at them as if she'd been eagerly awaiting Nick and Kate's arrival for months.

"I'm so glad to see you, Mr. Sweet," she said.

"Thank you," Nick said. "This is my associate, Ms. Porter. Please extend to her any courtesies that are offered to me by the hotel."

"It will be my pleasure," the clerk said. "My name is Tara. I will be your personal assistant during your stay."

"I've brought a deposit with me." Nick tipped his head to the door, where the bellman was bringing in the luggage. "It's in those four silver cases. I'd appreciate it if you'd exchange the cash for chips and have them on hand for tonight's game."

"Of course. Would you or Ms. Porter like to be present while the cash is counted?"

"Not necessary. It's five million," he said. "I trust you."

"In that case, I'll call for your personal butler, Mr. Covington, to see you to your suite."

"That won't be necessary, either," Nick said. "We like to find our own way around."

"Very well. Mr. Covington will be on call twenty-four hours a day for you, as well as a maid, a bartender, a personal chef, a doctor, a masseuse, a concert pianist, and anyone else that you might need."

"All the comforts of home," Nick said.

"I hope you enjoy your stay. Let me show you to your private express elevator." Tara stepped out from behind the podium and led them to the elevator. She slid a transparent key card into a slot on the wall and then handed it to Nick.

"Please let me know if there is anything I can do to make your stay more pleasurable. I am entirely at your service." She handed another transparent key to Kate and smiled. "Individually or together."

"Good to know," Nick said.

Nick and Kate stepped into the elevator. The door closed and the elevator rose smoothly, but swiftly, up the forty-five floors to the penthouse.

"When she said 'individually or together' . . . did she mean, you know what?" Kate asked.

Nick grinned. "She implied we could have the ultimate group activity."

"Would it show up on our bill?" Kate asked him.

"Would it matter?"

"Jessup would throw a blood clot."

"I'm sure I could have it removed from the bill," Nick said. "Is this a possibility?"

"No!" Kate said. "Good grief." She grimaced at him. "You would do it, wouldn't you?"

"Only one way to find out."

"*Ick.*"

The elevator opened into a circular marble foyer with a massive crystal chandelier. They crossed the foyer into an expansive living room that opened onto a wraparound terrace with an unobstructed view of the Las Vegas Strip. There was an infinity pool along the edge of the terrace, creating the illusion that the water flowed onto the street forty-five floors below.

The living room walls were paneled in walnut and decorated with abstract art, swirls of paint drippings on canvas in the style of Jackson Pollock. Kate squinted at one of the paintings and saw Pollock's signature.

"Is this the real thing or a forgery?" she asked.

"You'll know if it's in my luggage when we leave."

There were plenty of inviting leather-wrapped couches and easy chairs, a wet bar, a sixty-five-inch flat-screen TV, a stacked-stone fireplace, and a Steinway grand piano.

"Well, this explains the on-call concert pianist," Kate said.

"I was wondering about that myself," Nick said. "There are his and hers bedrooms and boardrooms on either end of the penthouse."

"Boardrooms?"

"You never know when you might want to hold a meeting with your personal staff."

Kate checked out a bedroom. It was the size of her entire apartment. There was a couch, two easy chairs, a fireplace, a flat-screen TV, and a massive king-size bed covered with fluffy pillows and a thick comforter. The marble-tiled bathroom had a steam shower built for two, a whirlpool tub, and a massage table.

"Decadent," Kate said.

"Yeah," Nick said. "I especially like the furry pillows. I'm guessing Mongolian lamb. Or maybe a rabbit on steroids."

Kate peeked into the private boardroom. There was a long conference table for eight, another flat-screen TV, and another bar.

"I feel a sudden desire to have a meeting," Kate said.

"Yeah, I've got some sudden desires, too," Nick said. "They have to do with the dress you're wearing and how fast I could get you out of it."

Kate looked down at herself. "It's not that easy. I'm stuffed into this like a bratwurst."

"I like a challenge," Nick said.

"Not this one. It would come with pain. Possibly a broken bone."

"I'm not really into pain," Nick said. "Especially if it's mine."

"You need to focus," Kate said. "This is all about the mission."

"There's all kinds of missions," Nick said.

But first it was all about the buffet. Kate loved buffets. And the one at Côte d'Argent was spectacular. She brought two plates with mountains of food on them back to her booth, where Nick sat with an iced tea and a small Caesar salad.

"I don't know what we're doing here," Nick said. "We have a private chef."

"It's not the same as a buffet," she said, digging meat from a crab leg with a tiny fork. "This is all-you-can-eat. And you can make last-minute choices. And there's all this *stuff*."

"Quantity and quality are not the same things."

"I grew up on Army bases, eating in canteens where food was basic. And now that I'm on my own I mostly eat out of a fast-food container. Getting access to a buffet, even a bad one, is like someone handing me a free pass to heaven."

Nick smiled wide. "You're equating a buffet to heaven?"

"Okay, so maybe not heaven. Maybe to Disneyland."

Nick watched her clean off both plates. "Where do you put it all?"

"I have a very fast metabolism," she said, dabbing her lips with a napkin. "Did I spill anything on myself?"

He looked her over. "Not a drop or a crumb."

"Then we'd better get to the casino before my good luck fades."

They left the buffet and crossed the casino toward the high-limit room. It was separated from the rest of the casino by partially drawn red curtains.

"Tonight we're playing blackjack," Nick said. "We'll take a table for ourselves. There are five seats. I'll play three hands at once and you'll play two."

"I'm not sure that's such a good idea. I could lose twice as much twice as fast."

"Win or lose, it doesn't matter. What we're trying to do is attract attention as whales with money to burn."

The walls of the salon were covered with hand-stitched leather and framed with dark wood. There were eight gaming tables and only seven men gambling. Four of them were at the same table, playing pai gow poker, the other three were playing baccarat. A few women sat drinking at the bar, where backlit multicolored bottles of liquor were arranged by hue on glass shelves.

Nick and Kate were greeted by a round-bodied, round-faced man wearing a three-piece suit. The way he waddled up to them reminded Kate of the Penguin, from *Batman*.

"Good evening to you both. I am Niles Goodwell, manager of player relations." Goodwell took a slight bow and whispered to Nick. "Your credit is good here, sir, up to five million."

"What's your table limit for blackjack?" Nick asked.

"Two hundred and fifty thousand."

"What are your chip denominations over ten thousand?"

"We have twenty-five-thousand, fifty-thousand, and one-hundred-thousand-dollar chips."

"We'd like a table to ourselves. We'll each start with one million to get warmed up," Nick said. "Half in twenty-five-thousand chips and half in fifty-thousand chips."

"Make yourselves comfortable." Goodwell gestured to a blackjack table where a young woman stood, smiling warmly at them. "I'll be right back with your chips."

They went to the table. Kate sat to the dealer's left, what blackjack players called "first base," and Nick took the seat to the right, known as "third base." A waitress came by to offer them drinks. Nick ordered a martini. Kate settled for a Coke. Goodwell brought them their chips on a gold platter.

"Good luck," he said, stepping away, but lingering close enough to keep his eye on the action.

Nick smiled at the dealer. "Let's have some fun."

5

If Nick had chosen craps, Kate would have been lost, but she figured she could handle blackjack. The goal, for both the player and the dealer, was to get as close as possible to twenty-one without going over. Simple, right?

Nick placed fifty thousand dollars on each of the three betting circles on his side of the table. Kate did the same on her two spots and broke into an immediate sweat. There was *a lot* of money on the table. Money for which she was more or less accountable.

The dealer smiled and patted the table. "Good luck."

She dealt the cards from a six-deck shoe. There were two cards dealt face up for each of their five playing positions. The dealer showed a four.

Kate had a sixteen on one of her hands and a seventeen on the other. She decided to stand.

Nick had a nineteen, an eighteen, and a twenty.

The dealer flipped her hole card. It was a six. The dealer dealt herself another card. It was a ten, giving her a total of twenty. The dealer winced politely, and swept up their chips.

Poof. Their two hundred fifty grand was gone.

It wasn't Kate's own money, but she couldn't help thinking of all the things that she could have bought with it. A house in Las Vegas. Or a Lamborghini Gallardo. Or fifty-four thousand In-N-Out double-double cheeseburgers. Instead they had bought two mighty expensive drinks.

"With the way things are going we could be done early and need a couples massage," Nick said to Kate. "Do you remember the conversation we had in the elevator?"

"Vividly."

"And?"

"And I think I'll stick with the game for a while longer."

After a half hour of play, Nick and Kate were up $1.5 million, and Kate was into the game, riding on a steady drip of adrenaline and her competitive nature. She put $250,000 down on each of her spots, and at the bar behind them, Goodwell picked up the receiver on a red telephone and made a call.

One floor below the casino, at the end of a long hallway, behind a door marked "Customer Relations," a wall-mounted telephone rang. Evan Trace stepped out of the shadows and answered it. His face was meticulously unshaven and the sleeves on his handmade monogrammed white shirt were neatly folded up to the elbows.

"This is Trace."

"We've got a couple whales up here," Goodwell said. "Nick Sweet and Kate Porter. They've taken a blackjack table and are betting two hundred and fifty thousand a hand. They're up one and a half million at the moment and they don't show any signs of slowing down."

"What do we know about them?"

"They came into town from L.A. on a private jet, walked in the door with five million dollars in cash, and booked the presidential suite for the night," Goodwell said. "That's it."

"I want to meet them."

"I thought you would," Goodwell said.

"Invite them to my private dining room for a drink when either they've tapped out or we have."

Trace hung up the phone. He wasn't concerned about the couple winning, even if it added up to tens of millions of dollars. He was a firm believer that his profits came from the winners, not the losers. The winners always came back for more, giving up what they'd won and then some. He knew that from personal experience, which brought him back to the task at hand.

He turned to the center of the windowless room. The only furniture was a stainless steel workbench and the chair behind it. They were placed under the room's single light fixture, a naked bulb that hung on a wire from the ceiling. A sandy-haired man in his late twenties sat in the chair. He was good-looking enough to be a model, or at least he had been before the beating. His eyes were swollen nearly shut, his lips were split, and his nose was bleeding.

Trace stepped up to the table and looked down at the terrified man. "You made a mistake, Stan."

"I know that," Stan said, his voice wavering, and glanced fearfully to his right, where another man stood in the shadows. "Mr. Garver can stop hitting me now."

Garver was also in his shirtsleeves and was wiping Stan's blood off his huge, meaty hands with a towel. His face looked like a head of cauliflower, the result of the beatings he'd taken prizefighting in his youth. He also had thick calluses on his walnut-sized knuckles, the result of the beatings he'd inflicted in the forty-odd years he'd spent in customer relations.

"I run an honest casino," Trace said. "Sure, we give the players free booze to make them careless, but we never cheat them. We expect the players to treat us with that same respect. You didn't do that, Stan. You cheated."

"I've had a run of bad luck and I'm deep in debt," Stan said. "I couldn't wait for my luck to turn. So I nudged it along. It won't happen again."

Garver spoke up. His voice sounded like each word was serrated and scratched his throat on the way out. "Show Mr. Trace your hands."

41

Stan placed his shaky hands on the table. He had long, slender fingers and manicured nails. Trace examined them and nodded with appreciation. Garver slipped back into the shadows.

"They're very nice. You take very good care of them, Stan, and that's smart. Your fingers are the tools of your trade."

Garver returned to the table. He'd picked up a wooden mallet somewhere. It was chipped from age and heavy use.

"No, no, no." Stan started to lift his hands from the table but Garver shook his head, warning him against it, so he stopped. He left his hands where they were but looked imploringly at Trace. "Please don't."

"I'm doing you a favor. Twenty years ago, I was the guy in that chair. Garver broke my hands with that mallet. It changed my whole outlook on life," Trace said. "Now I own a casino and he works for me. I owe it all to that night."

Trace held his hand out to Garver, who gave him the mallet, and then pinned Stan's wrists to the table with his massive hands.

"You don't have to do this," Stan said, pleading. "I promise you that I will never cheat again."

"I know you won't," Trace said, raising the mallet over his head. "Think positive. Maybe I'll end up working for you someday."

Nick and Kate played blackjack for three more hours. At one point, they were up by $3 million. But by the time it was over, they'd lost all of their winnings and were out of pocket another $2 million.

Kate's adrenaline drip had slowed to barely a trickle, and she was thinking more about cheese puffs than blackjack.

"Do you think the buffet is still open?" Kate asked.

"You're hungry?" Nick asked.

"Ravenous," she said. "I could eat two million dollars' worth of crab legs and tiny key lime pies."

"I like this side of you."

Goodwell approached the blackjack table. "Pardon me. If you're done for the night, Mr. Trace would like to invite you to his private dining room for drinks."

Nick glanced at Kate, then back at Goodwell. "If he'll throw in a couple of steaks, we'll be there."

"How do you like your steaks prepared?" Goodwell asked.

Trace's private dining room was behind an unmarked door near the high-limit parlor of the casino. Goodwell opened the door for Nick and Kate and waved them through. They stepped into an atrium that was filled with tropical plants and flowers. A sleek Plexiglas-bottomed bridge arched over a koi pond and into the wood-paneled dining room decorated with contemporary artwork. Kate looked down at the pond as they walked over the bridge, taking note of the silver-green fish. They were about five inches long and had red bellies. Piranha, she thought. More appropriate to the setting than koi.

Trace was waiting to greet them on the other side of the

bridge. He wore a midnight blue silk tux jacket, a white dress shirt, skinny jeans, and black crocodile loafers.

"I'm so glad to meet you. I'm Evan Trace."

"We appreciate the invitation," Nick said. "It was an unexpected treat."

"I could say the same about the two of you," Trace said, smiling at Kate, his attention momentarily caught by the red dress. "It's not often that people we don't know walk in off the street, book our best suite, and gamble millions of dollars."

"Surely you don't know everyone with money," Kate said.

"Everyone but you," Trace said.

A table near the atrium was set for three, and a bottle of red wine had been decanted.

Trace pulled out a chair for Kate. "I've taken the liberty of choosing a bottle of wine from my private reserve. I hope that's okay."

"I'm sure it's lovely," Kate said.

Lovely, she thought. She had actually said *lovely.* Good Godfrey, she sounded like a lady.

She was facing the dining room and looking across the table at the artwork on the walls. All large abstract paintings and a familiar painting of seven dogs sitting around a table playing poker. She'd seen the picture a thousand times before. It wasn't something she'd expect to see in Trace's private dining room.

"I like that you've included the painting of the dogs playing poker," Kate said. "It adds some whimsy to your collection."

"A print of that painting was on the wall in the motel room I rented when I first came to Vegas. But what you see there is the original oil painting, created in 1903 for a cigar advertisement. I bought it to always remind me of how I got started."

"How did you end up in the casino business?" Nick asked.

"I like to say it was a sign from God," Trace said. "I'd gone bust as a gambler in Vegas, so I headed for Palm Springs to be a tennis instructor. I was driving across the desert when my Chevette broke down. It was a thousand degrees outside. I had to walk miles to the nearest gas station, which was this wooden shack in the middle of nowhere run by this grizzled old Indian. I staggered in, sunburned and thirsty, and the old coot welcomed me to the sovereign Chuckwalla Indian nation, total tribal population: one. I had a revelation then and there."

"You saw a vision of a casino," Nick said.

"That's right, my sign from God. My burning bush. Once I proved that the old coot's obscure tribe was real, that his barren patch of desert was truly their ancestral land, and that he was the one Indian left, raising the money to build a casino there was no problem."

The butler brought their steaks to the table and, while they ate, Trace talked about running the Indian casino, selling out his shares once it was a huge success, and using his profits to build Côte d'Argent.

"That's quite a story," Nick said.

"What's yours?" Trace asked.

"I'm an international entrepreneur," Nick said.

"I see. And what type of entrepreneurial endeavors do you favor?"

"You could say I'm a professional gambler, only not at cards," Nick said. "I invest in business ventures of various sorts around the world and hope that they work out. Fortunately for me, they usually do."

"What sort of ventures?"

"Moneymaking ones that involve considerable risk," Nick said. "The risk is almost as important to me as the profit potential."

"You're being vague," Trace said.

"Yes," Nick said. "I am."

Trace shifted his attention to Kate. "And you? What do you do, Ms. Porter?"

"While Nick's busy looking for the next big thing, he forgets to take care of the last big thing and everything else that's going on in his life. That's my job. I manage the details."

"I get bored easily," Nick said.

"As do I," Trace said, his eyes drawn to Kate's cleavage.

Trace redirected his focus and cut what was left of his steak into tiny, bloody squares. "I hope, at least, we've managed to keep you entertained so far at Côte d'Argent." Trace tossed the squares of meat into the koi pond, and the water churned like it was boiling. The piranha swarmed on the meat in a feeding frenzy.

"I always thought the idea of a koi pond was to provide peace and tranquillity," Nick said as he watched the seething water.

"Koi just swim around getting old and fat. I don't get any serenity from that," Trace said. "Piranha are the only small fish with any energy, any joie de vivre. I could watch them do this for hours. The hard part is finding someone willing to clean the pond."

"That would be an authentic experience," Nick said.

Trace gave up a tight smile. "I'll be sure to put that in my next commercial."

Kate's cellphone vibrated in her clutch purse. She'd received a text message. Only Nick, Jessup, and her father had the number to her phone. It couldn't be good news.

"Forgive me, gentlemen," Kate said, standing up. "It's been a real pleasure meeting you, Evan, but I think I've had too much excitement for one night. If you don't mind, I'm going to leave you two and head back to my room."

Both men got to their feet.

"I should go as well," Nick said. "You've been a wonderful host, Evan. But we're leaving in the morning and I want a chance to enjoy the view from our terrace pool."

"You're going to love it," Trace said. "I hope we'll see you both at Côte d'Argent again soon."

Nick smiled. "You can bet on it."

6

"You're not going to like what I have to tell you," Goodwell said to Trace when they were alone. "We got some good shots of Sweet and Porter on the security cameras in the high-roller room and ran them through the biometric facial recognition system. We came up with nothing. If they've gambled before, it hasn't been in Las Vegas."

"What about their fingerprints?"

"We lifted perfect prints off their cocktail glasses and I had my contact at the Las Vegas Police Department run them through AFIS. Nothing came up. Sweet has an American passport and lives in New York in a Park Avenue apartment owned by an offshore shell company that exists in name only. They produce no products or offer any services, at least as far as we can tell at the moment."

So Nick Sweet probably made his money illegally. That much Trace knew before Goodwell's report, and it didn't bother him. What did bother him was that it was hard to exploit a man's weaknesses and desires without knowing what they were. Trace believed the key to successfully recruiting high rollers was to get them to see that exploitation as exceptionally attentive customer service.

"What about Kate Porter?"

"She's also a U.S. citizen. Sweet's shell company owns her home in Park Slope. She graduated with an MBA from Stanford and worked for a couple of major accounting firms before he hired her. The details on her are suspiciously thin, too. They clearly don't want anybody to know who they are or what they are doing, and they have the resources to make that happen. That concerns me."

"I don't see why. It means they have plenty of money to spend. Comp his suite and give him your card. I want to be sure he does all of his future gambling with us."

Trace didn't care where Nick's money came from as long as he continued losing it at Côte d'Argent. If that laissez-faire attitude turned out to be a mistake, and Nick ever became a serious problem, it would be Thanksgiving Day for the piranha.

Nick and Kate walked across the casino and stopped just short of their elevator.

"You could have stayed with Trace," Kate said. "I left because I got a text message and thought it might be important."

"Alone time with Trace isn't high on my list of preferred activities," Nick said. "That guy is scary."

"The piranha got to you?"

"The way he thinks got to me. He's a con man and a sociopath. Did you see the hostess take our glasses when we left the blackjack table? She wore gloves and held the glasses by the rim. I don't think she was worried about catching Ebola. She didn't want to smudge our fingerprints."

"Don't worry, Jessup has our back. The prints won't bring up your shameful criminal record or my triumphant accomplishments in law enforcement."

"And the text message?" Nick asked.

"It's from my dad," Kate said. *SOS Bludd's Money.*

"Any idea what it means?"

"None, but I'm a little freaked by it. I've never received an SOS from him before. I just texted him back but it's not getting delivered."

"Try calling."

Kate tapped in Jake's name on her speed dial. No answer.

She tried Jake's friend in Hawaii, Harlan Appleton.

"Appleton residence. Lieutenant Gregg Steadman, Kahuku Police Department, speaking."

Kate felt a twinge of panic. A cop was in Harlan's home, answering the phone. That probably meant the home was a crime scene. More bad news.

"This is FBI Special Agent Kate O'Hare," Kate said. "A couple days ago, my father flew out to visit Harlan. They're old Army buddies. Now I'm having trouble contacting my father."

"Do you know if he arrived before or after the explosion?"

"Explosion?"

"Harlan's food truck blew up while it was parked at the old sugar mill. He's in the Kahuku Medical Center, recovering from the injuries. Nothing serious. He's got some broken bones, and he's a little burned around the edges."

"What are you doing in his house?"

"A few hours ago someone shot the place up with a machine gun. The windows are shattered, and they must have pumped a thousand rounds into the walls. Doesn't look like anyone was in the house when it happened."

Kate thanked the lieutenant, ended the call, and took a beat to compose herself. Her military and FBI training told her to stay calm, to think logically. But this was her father, and she was having difficulty breathing.

Nick watched Kate struggle with emotion. He wrapped his arms around her and held her close against him, waiting patiently while she gained control.

"Are you okay?" he asked.

She nodded. "Yeah, I had a moment, but I'm fine now." She stepped away. "Cash in our chips, and I'll send the bellman up for our bags. We're leaving now."

"Where are we going?"

"I'm going to Hawaii," Kate said. "You're going to have to

stay behind. We can't be seen there together. I've already identified myself to the police as an FBI agent, and I may need the resources of the local field office to help find my dad."

"No way am I staying behind. He's your father and my friend. We're all family. Besides, how many regimes has he helped overthrow in his career? He might be plotting a revolution. Hawaii could declare its independence if we don't do something."

The private jet carrying Nick and Kate landed at Van Nuys Airport at midnight. Nick was met by a chauffeured Rolls-Royce and motored away into the darkness for parts unknown. Kate drove to her apartment in Tarzana, packed a bag, booked a seat on an 8 A.M. flight out of LAX to Honolulu, and stole a few hours of sleep. At 6 A.M. she called Jessup on her way to the airport. "I need to take a couple personal days. I'm having trouble contacting my father in Hawaii. I'm worried something is wrong."

"I'll alert the TSA you're traveling and notify our field office in Honolulu. If there is anything else I can do, just let me know. All I ask is that you please take care of yourself, limit the property damage, and try to avoid killing anyone."

"I'll do my best," Kate said.

Her plane landed in Honolulu a little before noon. Kate rented a Jeep Wrangler and headed for the North Shore, following the directions to the Kahuku police station on her phone's map app.

The freeway snaked up through the mountains, lush with palms and pines, then descended on the other side, passing through vast pineapple fields that led to the sleepy beach town of Haleiwa, the heart of the North Shore.

Haleiwa had a pleasant laid-back, hippie vibe. Oceanfront homes ran along the coastline, buffered from the two-lane highway by groves of banyan trees. There were a few parking lots for public access to the sand and the rocky shoreline. The beaches were stunning, and the waves were huge. On the south side of the highway there were some bungalows, an occasional small restaurant or shop, and beyond that, the thick forest leading back up to the jagged green mountain range.

Kate continued to follow the Kamehameha Highway for a few more miles, and finally came to an old sugar mill. The blackened wreckage of what must have been some sort of vehicle was parked in the lot. She assumed this was Harlan's food truck.

The Kahuku police station was just up the road from the sugar mill—so close that the cops could have arrived at the crime scene faster on foot than in their cars. It was a significant fact to Kate. If the explosion *wasn't* an accident, someone had either big cojones or the cops in his pocket. Neither prospect thrilled her.

Kate parked beside the lone police car, got out, and walked into the station. She flashed her FBI badge to the desk clerk, a bored Hawaiian woman doing paperwork, and asked to see Lieutenant Gregg Steadman. The clerk nodded in the direction of the door behind her. Kate walked through the door into a cramped squad room that looked like a storage unit for surplus office furniture, old files, and obsolete computer equipment. Sitting in the middle of it all, behind a gray metal desk, was a slim, slightly rumpled guy in his thirties.

"Lieutenant Steadman? I'm Special Agent Kate O'Hare." She offered him her hand.

He stood up, shook her hand, and cleared some files off the seat beside his desk. "It's Gregg, and you don't need to play the FBI card. I'm going to help you all I can, and since you're in law enforcement, I'm going to be more candid with you than I would be with a civilian."

"I appreciate that. All I'm interested in is finding my dad and making sure he's safe."

"I don't know where he is, but I doubt he's safe. Harlan Appleton operates a food truck in the old sugar mill parking lot. He makes some tasty barbecue and gets a long line at lunchtime. This doesn't please the locals running the shrimp trucks. I don't have proof, but I suspect Harlan's food truck was blown up because he refused to pay protection money to Lono Alika's gang. Now Harlan's in the hospital, and the next thing I know I'm getting a call that Lono's chromed Ford F-150, the Hawaiian Bentley, has also been blown sky-high. Lono loved that truck. Might be why Lono's gang shot up Harlan's place. If your dad was staying there it's a miracle he got away. They pretty much demolished the house with gunfire."

"So why aren't you sweating Lono and searching for my father?"

"Both Harlan and Lono say their trucks exploded by

accident. Harlan isn't filing charges over the damage to his house, and there's no evidence your father is doing anything but enjoying his vacation."

"You know that's not true," she said.

"Look, Lono Alika owns the North Shore. He's not just running a protection racket. He's the Yakuza's major drug distributor on Oahu and one of the biggest meth producers in Hawaii. I'm sure you're familiar with Yakuza."

"They're members of a Japanese transnational organized crime syndicate. I know of them, but I haven't had any personal contact."

"I've been trying to make a case against Alika for years," Steadman said, "but even the locals are terrified of him. Some of the cops, too. You don't blow up that man's truck unless you have a death wish. Not only will he kill you but he'll do it in the most agonizing, horrible way."

Kate was pretty sure she knew who blew up Alika's truck. It was justice, Jake-style. Jake was fiercely loyal to his friends and had taken on brutal dictators, revolutionary generals, and international terrorists in his career. He wouldn't let some island mobster intimidate him.

"Does the name 'Bludd' mean anything to you? Or 'Bludd's Money'?"

He shook his head. "No. Why?"

"It was a message my dad sent me before he disappeared. I can't figure it out." Kate stood. "Thanks for filling me in. I appreciate you taking the time."

7

Harlan Appleton lived at the end of a dirt road in a one-story eight-hundred-square-foot home that backed up against the dense forest. His home was a typical Hawaiian camp house, built in the early 1900s for the sugar mill workers. It had a tin roof, a long porch, double-hung windows, and thin walls made only of tongue-and-groove redwood planks. The bullets had destroyed all of the windows and punched holes through the wooden walls. Harlan's bullet-riddled Jeep was slumped in the mud like a dead animal, the tires shredded by gunfire.

Kate drove up to find Harlan standing outside in a tank top, baggy shorts, and a single flip-flop. His other foot was encased in a hard cast that ended just above his knee. His broken arm was in a sling and his other arm was resting around a woman's shoulders. She was in her early forties, wore nursing scrubs, and had an arm around Harlan's waist, more to provide comfort than physical support.

Harlan turned as Kate got out of her Jeep. It took him a second to recognize her, but when he did, he broke into a smile.

"My God, Kate, is that you?" With his good arm, he pulled Kate into a hug. "You've grown so much."

"So have you," Kate said, giving his gut a playful pat.

"That's old age, good living, and plenty of BBQ," Harlan said. "This is my friend Cassie Walner, a nurse at the hospital. This is Kate, Jake's kid. I haven't seen her since I taught her how to throw grenades."

"How old were you then?" Cassie asked Kate.

"Twelve," Kate said.

"*Twelve?*" Cassie said.

"Yeah, she was a good four years past the age when every girl should know her way around a live grenade," Harlan said. "But I remedied that. I didn't let Jake forget it, either." Harlan's smile and good cheer faded. "She's an FBI agent now. I'm guessing you've come to find your dad. Am I right?"

Kate nodded grimly and gestured to the house. "I heard about the friends you've made on the island."

"Yeah, I knew Lono Alika was the Hawaiian Godfather, but I didn't think he was stupid enough to mess with me."

"Would you have paid Alika the protection money if you'd known?" Kate asked.

"No, but I wouldn't have let Jake get caught up in my troubles. I'm real sorry about that, Kate."

"Don't be," she said. "He's the one who blew up that truck, isn't he? He probably had a lot of fun."

Harlan nodded. "I know he's out there in the brush somewhere, and I've been trying to figure out how I can help him, but I'm not real mobile, what with the broken foot and fractured leg bone."

"You can help by keeping a low profile right now, and let me work at finding him. Does 'Bludd's Money' mean anything to either one of you?"

They both shook their heads.

"Are you missing anything from the house?" Kate asked.

"No," Harlan said. "But I did notice that the first-aid kit, shovel, and tire iron are missing from the back of my Jeep."

Kate looked at the lush tropical forest and the mountains of the Koolau Range beyond. This might be Alika's island, but her father would have the advantage in the wild. He was trained in jungle warfare and loved a good booby trap.

Even with all that, Kate knew that eventually Jake would get caught if she didn't rescue him first. She was sure that he knew it, too. That was why he'd sent her the SOS text.

"Harlan," Kate said. "I could use a little firepower."

"Good news. My gun safe is still picture-perfect."

Ten minutes later, Kate got back into her Jeep with a Remington 870 twelve-gauge short-barreled shotgun, sixty rounds of 00 buckshot for killing, twenty rounds of number 6 for close-up defense, and twenty rounds of rifled slugs. Jungle fighting was close-quarters combat, and at that range, a shotgun blast beat a rifle or handgun any day. She hoped she wouldn't have to use any of it.

Kate's phone rang, with the caller ID "Nick McGarrett."

"I'm guessing you're here on Oahu," Kate said, answering her phone.

"I am and I've got good news," Nick said. "I know where Jake is hiding out. Meet me in the ruins of the Waialee reform school. It's between Haleiwa and Kahuku on the south side of the Kamehameha Highway."

Vines wrapped around the concrete ruins of the former Waialee Industrial School for Boys, dragging the building into the moist, green darkness of the forest as if the trees wanted to eat it. The roof had caved in long ago, and now the rotted, splintered remains lay across a smashed grand piano, mattress springs, and dozens of empty beer bottles.

Nick stood by the piano and was wearing sunglasses, a floral Hilo Hattie aloha shirt, Faded Glory cargo shorts, white tennis shoes, and a large straw hat. There was an Oahu guidebook sticking out of one of his cargo pockets and an Oahu map in another. He was just another mainland tourist, identical to thousands of others crawling all over the island. No one would ever notice him.

Kate made her way toward him. "You picked a lovely place to meet."

"It was close to you and no one is likely to spot us here," he said. "Besides, I'm a sucker for creepy, abandoned buildings. Any news on your dad?"

"The local mob, run by a guy named Lono Alika, blew up a food truck owned by Dad's friend Harlan to convince him to pay for protection. So Dad blew up Alika's truck for not being very nice to his friend. Then Alika came gunning for Dad, who escaped into the forest."

"Sounds like Jake." Nick pulled the map out of his pocket and spread it open on the piano. It was labeled *Oahu Movie & TV Locations*. "I found out about *Bludd's Money*. It was a cheesy, direct-to-video action movie. The big finale was shot in the forest here, doubling for Vietnam. Turns out hundreds of movies and TV shows have been shot here and have left bits of their sets behind. They're like ancient ruins for film buffs, who've erected signs identifying them. *Bludd* left the fake fuselage of a downed aircraft up there. I think that's where Jake was when he sent you that text."

"How did you figure it out?"

"I Googled *Bludd's Money*, saw that it was a movie, and watched it on Netflix on my flight out here. When I landed, I bought this locations map."

"You should have been a detective instead of a crook."

"It's not as much fun or as lucrative."

Kate folded up the map and stuck it in her own pocket. "I've got to go. I need to reach him before nightfall."

"If you don't come out of that forest within twenty-four hours, I'm coming to get you."

Kate squelched a grimace. It was nice to know he cared enough to risk his own safety, but it was frightening to think of Nick bumbling through the forest. Especially since her dad probably had it booby-trapped.

Virgil Cleet ran a helicopter tour business out of Honolulu, about an hour's drive from Waialee. And Virgil owed Kate a favor from back in the day when they were both Special Forces. So Virgil was happy to give Kate a lift to the *Bludd's Money* location, which was deep in the forest along the slopes of the Koolau Range.

Before hooking up with Virgil, Kate had stopped at an Army surplus store in downtown Honolulu and bought insect repellant, a dozen protein bars, a slim-profile backpack, cowhide-leather rappelling gloves, night vision goggles, a compass, two canteens, a combat knife, a rifle lanyard, four tubes of camouflage face paint, and 120 feet of 44 mm–thick braided polyester fast rope with an aircraft connection ring on one end.

"What are you planning on doing with all of this?" the clerk asked, packing everything in a box for her.

"Survive the zombie apocalypse."

The clerk smiled and nodded as if they shared a secret understanding.

Kate took the box to her Jeep, and stuffed everything but the rope, the knife, and the gloves into the daypack, and then drove around until she found a gas station.

She locked herself inside the gas station restroom with the duffel bag that she'd brought from L.A., sprayed her entire body with the insect repellant, and then put on a long-sleeved brown T-shirt, camouflage cargo pants, and low-quarter hiking shoes. She holstered her Glock on her hip, put the gloves and the knife in her pockets, and got back in her Jeep.

The heliport was on the west bank of the Ke'ehi Lagoon, just south of the Honolulu International Airport. Kate walked in wearing the backpack with the shotgun over her shoulder and carrying seventy-five pounds of coiled fast rope in her hands.

She was met at the door by Virgil, an African American in his forties who was tall enough to play professional basketball and muscular enough to be a linebacker. His hair was cut so short it looked like a shadow on his head.

Virgil gave her a quick once-over. "Looks like you're ready to party. Do you need help?"

"Thanks," she said. "But I can handle this on my own."

"I'll give you a radio. If you change your mind, all you have to do is call and I'll be there, guns blazing." He took the coil of rope from her. "When do you want to go?"

"Now. I'm racing the sun."

Virgil nodded and led her out to the helipad, where a retired MH-6 Little Bird light utility military gunship was waiting, minus the guns. "This isn't what I use for the tourists. It's my personal ride."

Kate loved it. It was the helicopter equivalent of a Crown Vic.

Kate climbed in, and Virgil powered up the chopper. A few minutes later, they were in the air over Honolulu and heading toward the North Shore. Kate applied green, brown, and black camouflage paint to her face and neck in diagonal streaks. This was the only kind of makeup she really knew how to use and was truly comfortable wearing.

The Koolau mountains were steep, craggy, and lush, with dense jungle along the slopes. There was no place to land close to the remains of the *Bludd's Money* set. She'd have to drop in by rope.

Kate couldn't see Alika's men in the jungle, but she did see their off-road vehicles strategically parked in clearings and trailheads to the north, east, and south of the area where the fake *Bludd's Money* airplane fuselage was located. It was clear to her they were trying to corner Jake against the steep ridge to the west.

"We're in position," Virgil said. "If there's anybody down there they're gonna be watching you drop."

"I'll be in the treetops before they have a chance to pick me off."

The chopper was hovering a hundred feet over the canopy of trees. Kate put on her gloves, tightened the straps of her backpack and the lanyard of her shotgun, attached one end of the fast rope to the fixed connection ring, and dropped the other end out the open cabin door of the chopper. The heavy rope ran straight down into the forest of tall bamboo, huge palms, wild guava, banyan trees, and Norfolk pines.

She strung the rope behind her back and around one leg, putting her right hand on the rope above her head and her left hand on the rope below her waist.

"Ready," Kate said.

"Good luck," Virgil said.

Kate jumped out of the helicopter and slid rapidly down the rope, through the thick layer of leaves and branches to the muddy ground below. It took her less than thirty seconds, and gave her an adrenaline rush.

She let go of the rope and immediately crouched down low, listening and waiting. The chopper rose, the rope dangling beneath it, and veered away toward the mountains.

Kate checked her compass and her GPS app to confirm her position. She was roughly fifty yards southwest of the abandoned *Bludd's Money* set. There was a trail, but rather than take it, Kate moved slowly on a parallel course through the brush, keeping her eyes open for trip wires and anything that didn't seem to fit the natural pattern of forest floor. She didn't want to get nailed by one of her father's booby traps.

She moved slowly until she reached a school-bus-sized section of a passenger jet cabin. It was completely wrapped with vines, and a plastic sign was nailed to the fuselage and engraved with the words "*Bludd's Money* 2009."

There was movement in the trees. Kate dropped flat in the mud amid a thick patch of philodendrons. Three Hawaiians emerged from another trail. Two of the men were large enough to be sumo wrestlers and carried machetes casually at their sides. One was wearing flip-flops, the other neon-bright yellow Nikes. The third man had the lean build and stoned demeanor of a surfer. He held an M16 rifle tightly in both of his hands.

The guy in flip-flops squinted at the sign and read it aloud, sounding the words out phonetically, then turned to the two other men. "You ever see this movie, brah?"

"Three times." The surfer pointed his M16 into the fuselage and peered inside for any signs of life. "It could only have been better if Steven Seagal was in it. Steven Seagal is a badass. He's like Alika only he's not fat."

The guy in the Nikes gave a bark of laughter. "I'm telling Alika you said he was fat."

They moved on with Flip-Flops at point, flanked by his two buddies. He'd gone only a couple steps when his right foot plunged into a hole that had been hidden under a blanket of leaves. He pitched over with a shriek of pain, his trapped ankle breaking with a snap.

Small punji-stake pit, Kate thought. One of Dad's favorite booby traps.

Neon Nikes quickly moved away from the trail, breaking a trip wire at his ankles. He instinctively looked down at his feet to see what he'd walked into, heard something move in the jungle, and then straightened up to see whatever was coming at him. It was a coconut tied to a vine like a tetherball. The coconut slammed into his shoulder with bone-breaking force and knocked Neon Nikes to the ground.

The surfer raised his M16, let out a furious banshee roar, and sprayed the dense foliage ahead of him with bullets until he'd emptied his clip. He was reaching into his pocket for a fresh clip when a long branch whipped out of nowhere and swatted him out of his sandals.

Jake sprang out of the mud beside the trail and snatched the fallen M16 and ammo clip, jammed the clip into the rifle, and aimed it at the three men on the ground.

"You have thirty seconds to get out of here," Jake said. "Or I start shooting."

The surfer and Neon Nikes each took Flip-Flops by an arm, and the three Hawaiians staggered away. Once they were out of sight, Jake lowered the M16 and grinned at Kate, who was still lying flat amid the philodendrons.

"What did you think of that?" he asked.

Kate stood up and smiled at her father. "You're having way too much fun, Dad."

"That's what vacations are for."

"Why did you send me such a cryptic message?"

"I didn't mean to. My battery was near death, and there was barely a signal here. I figured I had just enough juice for two or three words. I was right. As soon as I hit send, the phone died. To tell you the truth, I was sure the message didn't go out, so it was a nice surprise when you showed up."

"Why did you go off into the jungle?"

"Alika didn't see the ironic justice of *an eye for an eye,* or in this case *a truck for a truck.* The F-150 was still smoking when he sent his goons out to get me."

"How did he know it was you?"

"We'd had a chitchat prior to the explosion."

"Nice."

"Turns out he has anger issues," Jake said. "Hidden inside all that tattooed fat is an insecure, angry man."

Kate did a grimace. "You could have gone to the police."

"I didn't know if I could trust the police. I knew I could trust the jungle. Problem was I had no exit strategy. Alika has too much of the island covered. So what's *your* exit strategy?"

"We wait until sunrise, hike to a clearing about five miles southeast of here, and then I'll call in a chopper for an extraction."

"It's weak on shock and awe, but it sounds like a fine plan to me." He put his arm around her and sighed with contentment. "I don't know how people can come here and surf when they could be doing this."

Kate grinned. "Neither do I."

8

Nick Fox blew into the office of the Hawaii Film Commission just as Allan Mingus, the only employee still on duty, was about to lock up and call it a day. Nick was in mid-conversation on his cellphone and held up a finger to Mingus, instructing him to wait.

"Tom Cruise is too short and too old. This is a movie about a young, virile action hero." Nick spoke rapidly in a foreign accent of his own creation that he hoped could pass for Swedish, not that many people would know a Swedish accent if they heard one. He'd colored his hair blond and wore sunglasses, a soul patch under his lip, and a pair of phony diamond studs in his ears. "Get me a Hemsworth. Chris, Liam, Luke, Mario, or Zippy. I don't care which one. Nobody can tell them apart anyway."

Nick ended his call and faced Mingus, a stout man in his fifties in the obligatory aloha shirt. They stood in the center of the office, which looked like a small travel agency. The walls were decorated with posters of tropical Hawaiian beaches and movies like *From Here to Eternity* and *Raiders of the Lost Ark* that were shot on the islands.

"Show me what you've got," Nick said.

"I'm sorry, but I was just closing for the day," Mingus said.

"Not anymore. I'm looking for Vietnam, South America, and Florida in one place and I need it quick."

"Who are you?"

"I am Krister Blomkvistbjurman-Malm, of course. Don't you recognize me? Writer, director, and cinematographer of *Sherm de Sherm den Hurf*."

"I am not familiar with that movie."

"It won the Oscar for best foreign picture," Nick said. "How can you call yourself a film office when you know *nothing* about film?"

"Oh, yes, now I remember it," Mingus said, his cheeks flushing with embarrassment. "Great movie. I just forgot the original Russian title."

"It's Swedish."

"Right," Mingus said, his flush deepening. "I'm afraid you'll have to come back tomorrow."

"That's too late. Tomorrow night I go to Australia to see what they have to offer. So tonight you'll show me photos and tomorrow you'll take me on a helicopter and ground tour of the locations I've selected or you're out of the running."

"That's not the way it goes," Mingus said. "We need more advance notice and a lot more details before we go scouting. For one thing, we have to see a script—"

Nick interrupted him. "Nobody sees a script. It's the latest installment in a major billion-dollar movie franchise. Anyone who wants to read the screenplay must come to the studio, surrender their cellphones, and lock themselves in my office."

"Okay, but before we can get started, we need some basic information," Mingus said. "We need to know the production company and studio, where the financing is coming from, whether the project is union or nonunion, whether—"

Nick interrupted him. "Say that again."

"What?"

"What you said before, only this time with coiled rage and greater authority." Nick pointed at him and said, "Go!"

Mingus stared at him for a moment, not sure what to make of the request, so he just soldiered on. "What I'm saying is that I need to make sure that you and your movie are legit. Anybody can just walk in here and claim—"

"Wonderful," Nick said, cutting him off again. "I believed it. Where did you get your training as an actor?"

"I don't have any, but before I got this job, I did some small parts. I was one of the airline passengers in the *Lost* pilot. I didn't have any lines, but I was in the background of every scene."

"Those roles are crucial. They are even harder than speaking parts."

"They are?"

"Of course. They give a film its inherent reality. You have that and natural gravitas, too."

"I do?"

"Inherent reality and natural gravitas are just what I am looking for in the actor who plays Indy's boss."

"Did you say 'Indy'?" Mingus's gaze flicked to the *Raiders of the Lost Ark* poster on the wall. "As in 'Indiana Jones'?"

Nick winced, as if realizing he'd let something slip. "No, I most emphatically did not. Forget I said that. All you need to know is that it's a key speaking part, and I need to cast a local rather than fly someone in. You'd be doing me a big favor if you'd take the role. It's a two-day job, tops. Would you do it for me?"

"I'd be glad to," Mingus said, breaking out in a huge grin.

"Then it's done, assuming we shoot here, of course," Nick said. "What can you show me tomorrow?"

"We have some spectacular locations, among the best on earth," Mingus said. "Let me go grab the binders."

Kate and Jake awoke at dawn and worked their way slowly to the southeast, keeping low and staying off the trails. It took them three hours to slog through the heavy vegetation and reach their destination, which was marked by a pair of iron gates under a massive stone arch with the words "Cretaceous Zoo" carved across the top.

Jake knocked on the arch. It was a molded fiberglass veneer nailed to plywood. "What is this place?"

"The old set for a movie about a zoo filled with genetically re-created dinosaurs and cavemen. The dinosaurs escape and eat all of the guests," Kate said. "The cavemen team up with a retired New York cop, a busty medical student, and a novelist to battle the monsters."

"You saw it?"

"I think it's probably the best work Gunter Jorgenson has ever done. In the finale the survivors fight their way through hordes of raptors to get to the brontosaurus paddock. That's the field where the helicopters landed to get the heroes off the island before the nukes were dropped. If it worked for them, it could work for us."

Kate took the lead, her shotgun at the ready, and sprinted under the arch, then hugged the tree line along the trail that led inside. Jake followed, wielding the M16 he'd acquired the day before. They moved from tree to tree, one person at a time, covering each other as they went.

The *Cretaceous Zoo* Welcome Center loomed at the end of the trail in front of them. It was a two-story Polynesian-style building with a domed glass atrium. The plants in the atrium had grown and broken through the glass. There were several Jeeps that had been crushed by rampaging dinosaurs scattered around the Welcome Center.

Kate and Jake used the Jeeps as cover, going from one to another, as they approached the Welcome Center and then worked their way behind the building, sticking close to the walls. They peeked around the edge of the building to see what lay beyond it.

They faced the zoo itself. To their left was the caveman habitat, a neighborhood of stone-and-log cabins covered in layers of graffiti and arranged in a half circle facing a statue of two raging T. rexes tearing apart a struggling pterodactyl. To their right was a fake hillside, riddled with caves and overgrown with plants. At the far end, directly across from the Welcome Center, was another arch that lead to the next section of the zoo.

"The brontosaurus corral and the clearing are on the other side of that arch," Kate said.

"We'll be out in the open between here and those T. rex statues," Jake said. "Then in the open again to the clearing."

"You go first and I'll cover you." Kate drew her Glock and held it out to Jake. "But I'll need your M16 to do the job right."

They swapped weapons. She gave him her extra clips for the Glock and he stuck them in his pocket. She removed the shotgun from over her shoulder, and moved into position with the M16. She pressed her cheek against the stock, looked down the weld line through the sight, and targeted the statues. She put her finger on the trigger.

"Ready," Kate said.

"That's my girl," he said.

Jake held the Glock at his side and dashed out into the open, zigzagging as he went. He was halfway to the fighting dinosaurs when gunfire rang out and bullets cut divots into the dirt around him. Two shooters with M16s were firing down at him from the hillside caves.

Kate opened fire on the hill, driving the startled shooters back into their caves. She pivoted and sprayed the caveman cabins, too, pinning down two other shooters who were about to let loose a barrage of their own. Her suppression fire gave Jake the crucial seconds he needed to dive for cover amid the legs of the fighting T. rexes. Kate had caught them by surprise, but it wore off quickly.

The instant Jake landed, bullets chipped away at the dinosaurs' legs from both the cabins and the caves, showering him with bits of wood and plaster. Alika's men also let loose on Kate. She ducked back as bullets slammed into the wall beside her.

There were at least two men in the cabins and two in the hillside caves, all armed with M16s. Jake was pinned down. He had a Glock and very little cover. Kate's clip was empty, which left her with the twelve-gauge short-barreled shotgun, a perfect weapon for close-quarters fighting but lousy for situations like this. She'd have to get much closer to her enemy for the shotgun to be effective. The question was whether Jake could hold out long enough for Kate to sneak up on the cabins and start taking the shooters out, one by one.

Her other option was to call Virgil on the radio. Tell him to come in the chopper right away, and bring all the firepower he could muster.

Kate was about to make a decision when she heard the unmistakable sound of a helicopter approaching. She looked up apprehensively, and a white helicopter flew in low over the Welcome Center. As it passed, she could clearly see the Hawaii state seal on the side of the aircraft.

9

"This is where they shot *Cretaceous Zoo*," Alan Mingus told Nick as they flew over the statues of the two battling T. rexes in the center of the park. "Those are caveman houses. You can remodel the buildings or tear them all down. It makes no difference to us."

Nick had a director's viewfinder hanging on a lanyard around his neck. He used it to peer out the window at the set below, and glimpsed what he thought was someone hunkered down among the fighting dinosaurs. He couldn't be sure, and even if it was someone, it didn't mean it was Kate or her father.

"I wish you'd tear the sets down," said Larry Kealoha, the uniformed park ranger who sat across from them. "People love to party up here. Over the years, we've probably had to rescue a dozen drunken fools who've fallen into the raptor pit and broken their legs."

"I would never use another director's sets," Nick said. "The vision of this film must be completely my own. I would be morally and artistically bankrupt to do otherwise. It would be like asking the women in my films to shave their underarm hair."

"Is that a thing in Swedish films?" Kealoha asked.

"It is in mine," Nick said.

The pilot landed the chopper in the center of a field with enormous cages on one end and bleachers on another.

"What was this?" Nick asked.

"The brontosaurus corral," Mingus said. "In the movie, the dinosaurs were in those big cages, and their trainers rode them around this field like horses, doing tricks, while the audience watched from the bleachers."

Nick hopped out, dashed a few yards away from the helicopter, then held the viewfinder up to his eye with one hand and scanned the statues. He could definitely see someone standing with his back against the leg of a T. rex. The man turned to look at Nick. It was Jake, covered in mud and holding a gun. Nick panned the viewfinder up over to the cabins and saw a Hawaiian peek out of a doorway holding an M16. Nick figured Kate was here somewhere, either taking cover herself or moving in for the kill.

Mingus and Kealoha came up beside Nick.

"What do you think of the location?" Mingus asked.

Nick dropped the viewfinder, letting it fall against his chest. "Very nice. Lots of possibilities here. Let's take a closer look."

He tramped purposefully toward the statues, followed by Mingus and Kealoha.

Kate didn't know who the three men were, but they'd arrived in a government helicopter and she doubted Alika's men would dare open fire in front of state officials. The blowback for Alika from the authorities would be too severe. Kate was willing to stake her life on that assumption.

She slung the shotgun over her shoulder by its strap, stepped out from behind the wall into the open, and strode casually toward her father. Jake saw her coming and peeked out from behind one of the T. rex legs to sneak a look at the caves. The gunmen were hiding in the dark recesses of the caves and cabins, wrestling with the decision of whether or not to shoot.

Kate reached her dad just as the three men from the chopper were crossing under the arch from the brontosaurus paddock. That's when she realized that the blond one with the ridiculous soul patch was Nick.

Mingus and Kealoha were surprised to see the couple who'd walked out of the zoo to meet them. The old man was shirtless, covered in mud, and holding a gun at his side. The younger woman's face was painted in streaks like some sort of jungle savage, and she had a shotgun slung over her shoulder.

"My God," Mingus said to Kealoha. "Who are those people?"

"Crazy tourists," Kealoha said. "Maybe a couple of survivalists. We get all kinds out here."

"Sven!" Nick said. "Gita!"

Mingus looked at Nick in astonishment. "You *know* these people?"

"They are two of my actors. They have lived in the jungle for days, immersing themselves in the roles that they will play," Nick said, loud enough for Jake and Kate to hear as they approached. "This is the commitment you must have to be in my movies."

"You didn't mention anything to me about having actors in the jungle," Mingus said.

"We *became* the jungle," Kate corrected him in an accent as unrecognizable as Nick's.

"I'm certain that it will add enormous depth to your roles," Nick said, then turned back to Mingus. "Sven and Gita are huge stars in Sweden, and their total dedication is the reason they are so popular. You could learn something from them. I want you to become the jungle, too."

The color drained from Mingus's face. "Is that really necessary?"

"It is if you want to achieve greatness as an actor. Think about it, because I love this location. This is where I'll make my movie."

"Excellent," Mingus said, his enthusiasm tempered by the terrifying prospect of having to become the jungle himself.

Nick faced Kate and Jake. "You two must come back to Honolulu with me and tell me all about your experiences."

He put one arm around Jake and another around Kate, and led them back toward the chopper. Mingus and Kealoha lagged behind so they could confer in private.

"Out of curiosity," Nick whispered. "How many shooters are there?"

"At least four," Jake said. "With M16s."

"Poor guys," Nick said. "They never stood a chance."

Nick took Kate and Jake back to his two-bedroom suite at the historic Royal Hawaiian Hotel, on Waikiki Beach, so they could shower and change into clean clothes.

Jake was happy to see a white polo shirt, khaki slacks, and a pair of leather loafers, all in his size, laid out on the bed. He was *ecstatic* to find the correct Dr. Scholl's inserts in the shoes, because his feet were killing him.

A luncheon buffet of fresh fruit, kalua pork, and an assortment of desserts that included lilikoi cheesecake and haupia cream pie was laid out on the dining table. The doors to the lanai were open, letting in a gentle breeze and offering a spectacular panoramic view of Diamond Head, Waikiki Beach, and the shimmering Pacific.

"Feeling better?" Nick asked Jake.

"I was feeling great before." Jake took a plate and nodded in approval. "But this isn't bad."

"We'll have lunch, relax on the lanai for a bit, and then you and I will head back to Los Angeles by private jet. Kate will settle up with the local authorities and take a commercial flight home."

"I'm not going anywhere until I take down Lono Alika," Jake said. "He destroyed Harlan's food truck and shot up his house. I can't let him get away with that."

"I met a local cop who I think is a good man," Kate said. "I'll have a talk with him and the agents in the FBI field office. They'll make sure Alika knows that it would be a big mistake to give Harlan any trouble."

Jake shook his head. "That's not good enough."

"I think it's possible that we can take down Alika and Evan Trace at the same time," Nick said. "Since we left Vegas, I've been noodling with an idea for a con to destroy Trace's money laundering operation, but it wasn't coming together. It was missing the key piece, the fulcrum, you might say."

"Fulcrum," Jake said. "Like a seesaw?"

"Like a tipping point," Nick said. "We're going to insinuate ourselves into the money laundering operation at Trace's casino in Macau by becoming junket operators."

"I have no idea what that means," Kate said.

"Most of the major money laundering in Macau is done through junket operators. They are middlemen who bring high rollers to the casinos to gamble in private VIP rooms. The gamblers book their travel, rent their hotel rooms, and buy their chips through the junket operators, who are actually the ones on the hook with the casino for everything."

"So, technically, the players aren't actually gambling in Macau with their own money," Kate said. "They are playing with the junket's money."

"That's how the money gets laundered," Nick said. "The cash the players use to buy their 'vacations' in Macau is dirty. But the money they get when they cash in their chips is clean."

"How do the junkets make money on the deal?" Jake asked.

"By imposing a surcharge on all of their services and by requiring the gamblers to wager a certain amount of money over the course of their VIP play. The junket takes forty percent of whatever the house brings in at the tables. The casino takes the other sixty percent."

"That's crazy," Jake said. "Why doesn't the casino get rid of the middleman and deal directly with the high rollers themselves?"

"Risk avoidance. A lot of these high rollers come from countries like China, where it's virtually impossible for the casinos to collect on gambling debts. But the casinos *can* collect from the junket operator, who assumes all of the financial and legal risks," Nick said. "It's the junket operator, not the casino, who has the relationship with the players. If anybody ever asks, the casino can say they don't have any idea who the gamblers are in those VIP rooms or how much money they're winning or losing."

"So how do we take down Trace by running a junket?" Kate asked.

"We're going to bring a Canadian mobster and a Somali

warlord to Trace's casino in Macau to launder their dirty cash," Nick said. "Only the two bad guys will be our friends playing parts, and the money they'll be washing will be ours. We go in, we gamble, we leave."

"Which will establish our credibility as junket operators if anybody asks Côte d'Argent about us," Kate said.

Jake smiled. "Someone like Lono Alika."

"Now you're catching on," Nick said. "We're going to invite Alika on a gambling junket to launder his money with us. We'll go back to Macau with him and our two fake bad guys, wash his cash and ours, and everybody leaves happy."

"You seem to be missing the part where we put the criminals in jail," Kate said. "So far we're just washing our money and making the bad guys richer."

"We're going to have to bait the trap for Alika first," Nick said. "He isn't going to go all in on the laundering scheme the first time around. He'll gamble only a little of what he has and see how it goes. Once he discovers how well the washing machine works, he'll come rushing back to us to launder all of the cash that he's been hoarding. Only this time, I'm going to run away with his money, leaving him broke and Trace holding the bag."

"That's a dangerous play," Jake said. "I like that you're ruining Alika, but he and his Yakuza backers will be in a bloody rage. They'll go after you and Trace."

"I'm counting on it," Nick said. "That's what makes Alika the key element of this con. We need to scare the crap out of Trace.

We want him to absolutely believe that his life is in serious danger."

"It *will* be," Jake said. "The Yakuza take revenge to extremes."

"It won't come to that," Nick said. "Before there is any real threat, Kate is going to reveal herself to Trace as an undercover FBI agent."

"What will my story be?" Kate asked.

"That you've spent two long years infiltrating Nick Sweet's criminal operation to bring him down, but now that he's in the wind, you're screwed and looking for a way to turn a disaster into a win," Nick said. "So you'll offer Trace protection from the Yakuza, the Canadian mob, and the Somali warlords if he agrees to rat out all of the terrorists, despots, and crooks that he's ever helped. Or you could keep him in business as an FBI front and gather invaluable intelligence. Either way, Trace will jump at the offer."

Kate smiled at her dad. "He's good."

"Not as good as you," Jake said. "Because you caught him."

"Hey," Nick said. "Whose side are you on?"

"Kate's," Jake said. "Always."

Nick nodded. "As it should be."

"I think your scam is great," Jake said, "but in the meantime, I'm not convinced that Harlan will be safe from Alika. So there's something I'd like to do before we go."

"I'm not going to let you blow up anything else," Kate said. "Or kill anybody."

"Don't worry," Jake said. "All I have in mind is some friendly persuasion."

Kate raised an eyebrow. "Because that worked so well last time?"

Jake grinned. "I think we're developing a relationship."

Da Grinds & Da Shave Ice was a dive restaurant with a red-dirt parking lot on the Kamehameha Highway near Kahuku. It was a wooden shack with a corrugated metal roof that extended out over a sagging porch and a few picnic tables. Food was served through a takeout window that had a hand-painted, flaking menu board beside it.

The restaurant was owned by Lono Alika, who was often the only patron besides the occasional ignorant tourists who didn't know any better and never would because they were always politely served and not harassed in any way. But the locals saw it for what it was—Alika's front office, a place you didn't go unless you were summoned, which inevitably meant pain and suffering, or if you sought his help, which also inevitably meant pain and suffering. Everyone on the North Shore knew him but few wanted *him* to know *them*.

Alika sat at his picnic table, eating a plate lunch, when Jake took a seat across from the 350-pound, six-foot-tall, bald-headed Hawaiian. The huge man, who always wore a tank top and board shorts to show off the Polynesian tattoos that covered his arms and legs, looked up from his two scoops of white rice, macaroni salad, teriyaki chicken, and short ribs and regarded Jake with a slow, sleepy gaze.

"Eh, watchu want, buggah?" Alika said, speaking in Hawaiian pidgin English, the local dialect.

"I want you to apologize to my friend Harlan Appleton and buy him a new food truck."

"Last time you say dat I have my men chase you into da woods, you old fut."

"And I put three of your men in the hospital."

Alika showed his teeth like a dog, and started to rise from his seat. "I'm gonna give you da dirty lickin's and put you in da ground."

"I wouldn't if I were you." Jake calmly wagged a finger at him in warning. "Do you really think I'd be here without backup? You're in the crosshairs of a sniper right now." Jake pointed his finger at Alika's chest.

Alika looked down and saw a red laser dot over his heart, then looked up into the dense thicket of trees that was alongside the restaurant and that ran up the slope to the mountains beyond. He sat back down, but his face was tomato red with rage.

"How I know dat's not just some fool wit' a laser pointer in da trees?"

"You don't. So go ahead and make your move, though you're so fat and slow, I could probably save my friend a bullet and kill you myself before you cleared the bench."

Alika snorted. "Oh, yeah? How you do dat, old man?"

Jake tipped his head toward Alika's plate lunch. "I'd shove that fork in your neck and watch you choke to death on your own blood."

Jake was relaxed when he spoke, and his general posture conveyed complete confidence in his safety. It clearly unnerved Alika, who swiped his fork off the table.

"Say what you wanna say," Alika said. "Tink hard cuz dey be your last words."

"First off, Harlan had nothing to do with what happened to your pickup truck. I did that on my own. Secondly, my friend doesn't owe you anything. He's already paid his dues on the battlefield so *mokes* like you can enjoy your freedom. So you're going to show him some respect and back off."

"We have dis talk before. If he fool nuff to go back in business, he pays me or he gets real buss'up. Dat's how it is."

"Harlan has a lot of friends on this island from his days in the military," Jake said. "Whatever happens to him, happens to you. That's how it is. That's how it was with your truck."

Alika looked down at the laser targeting dot on his chest then back at Jake. "I wanna show you something. Come wit' me."

"Only if we stay in the open."

"Chillax," Alika said, rising slowly, the dot moving along with him as he walked off the porch to the red-dirt parking lot. "I want you to meet somebody."

Alika stopped and pointed at the ground. Jake looked down and saw a man buried up to his neck in red dirt, his face sunburned and crawling with ants. The man opened one pleading eye for a moment, then quickly closed it again before an ant could crawl in.

"Dis Kimo," Alika said. "His job was to take care of my truck. Now he got a new job. He fertilizer."

Kimo whimpered.

"It wasn't his fault," Jake said. "Dig him out."

"I will, maybe tonight, maybe tomorrow," Alika said. "Point is, I evah see you again, dat brah be you, only you stay buried till the ants get fat an' I see yo' skull."

Jake drove up the highway for fifty yards, and then pulled over to the shoulder to pick up Kate, who was dressed in camo and carried a rifle case. She climbed in and Jake drove off.

"Thanks for covering me," he said.

"Any time."

"I think Alika will lay off Harlan for the time being. But I'm worried about that guy in the dirt."

"Don't be. Alika won't kill the guy now that he's shown him off to you. It's too risky. You could call the cops. But to be on the safe side, I'll ask Steadman to swing by."

"Were you tempted to shoot Alika while you had him in your sights?"

"Hell, yes," she said.

"What stopped you?"

"The rifle wasn't loaded," she said.

10

Nick and Jake left Honolulu later that afternoon. Kate stayed behind and met with the local FBI agent in charge. She asked him to let Alika know that it would be very bad for his business if any further harm came to Harlan Appleton. The agent said he'd be glad to do it. Next she drove to Kahuku and visited Lieutenant Gregg Steadman at the Kahuku police station to make the same request and to inform him that Jake was safely off the island.

Steadman agreed to have a word with Alika, too, and was confident that Harlan wouldn't be harassed any further, at least not until he opened another food truck in the sugar mill parking lot. Kate was counting on Alika being out of the picture by the time Harlan was ready to open for business again.

The next morning Kate caught the first flight to Las Vegas.

She arrived late in the afternoon and took a taxi straight to the Treasure Island casino to see Billy Dee Snipes, a retired Somali pirate. Billy Dee now lived in a condo complex in Summerlin for "active seniors," and liked to spend his afternoons playing the nickel slots. In the past he had occasionally worked with Kate's father on some black-ops missions in the South China Sea. More recently Billy Dee had worked with Kate and Nick on a con in Portugal.

Kate found Billy Dee sitting at a Blazing Sevens slot machine near the buffet, drinking a cocktail with one hand and tapping the "spin" button with the other. He looked like a scarecrow in a blue tracksuit, propped on a stool to keep birds away from the machines.

Although Billy Dee appeared to be mortally ill or suffering from starvation, Kate had been assured by her father that the pirate had always had zero percent body fat.

Kate sat down at the slot machine next to Billy Dee. "I hope you haven't fed that machine all of the money you made from us."

Billy Dee turned and smiled at her. "I believe my savings are safe at my current rate of play."

"How would you feel about switching your game to baccarat for a while?"

"Well, baccarat is all luck and no skill, like slots, and the house edge is small, but they don't let you play baccarat for a nickel a hand. I'd burn through my retirement money way too fast. So, I think I'll stick to this."

In fact, he hadn't stopped playing for a second while he spoke with her. He constantly tapped the spin button as if it were a necessary part of his breathing.

"How would you feel about playing high-stakes baccarat in Macau with our money? We don't care if you win or lose and we'll pay you a hundred thousand dollars to do it."

"What's the catch?" he asked.

"You'd have to travel to Hong Kong from Mogadishu and pretend to be a ruthless Somali pirate."

"I *am* a ruthless Somali pirate," he said.

She gestured to his feet. "You're wearing sneakers with Velcro straps."

"You need comfortable footwear to be ruthless."

"You'll be playing the part of a Somali pirate who is gambling with the millions of dollars that you've made hijacking oil tankers and cargo ships in the Strait of Malacca," Kate said. "But what you'll really be doing is helping us bring down a casino money laundering operation. If it goes wrong, you don't need to worry about getting arrested. You'll need to worry about getting out of Macau alive."

"That used to be the charm of Macau. You *always* had to worry about getting killed. For five hundred years, it was a Portuguese trading port for smugglers, slavers, and pirates. I sold a lot of stolen ships and cargoes there. But then the Portuguese handed Macau over to the Chinese and they turned it into this." Billy Dee waved his hand around to indicate the casino around them. "Treasure Island. The world is becoming too clean and safe. Soon there won't be any place left where hookers, assassins, and thieves roam the streets and will slit your throat for the coins in your pocket."

"Most people don't have a problem with that change."

"Most people aren't ruthless Somali pirates. We like a little danger in our lives, and since I have absolutely none now, I'd be glad to gamble with your money and my life. When do I leave for Mogadishu?"

"In a couple days," she said. "We still have arrangements to make, identities to create, and documents to forge. Speaking of which, I've got to go back to the airport and catch a flight to Los Angeles tonight."

"How about having a bite with me before you go? My treat." He took his Treasure Island Players Club card out of the slot machine and held it up. "I get a club discount at the buffet and it opens for dinner in five minutes."

Kate checked her watch. "It's only four thirty."

"So you're not going to join me?"

"Of course I will," Kate said. "It's never too early for an all-you-can-eat buffet."

A few blocks from Treasure Island, Evan Trace sat at his million-dollar desk in his office suite atop the Côte d'Argent tower. His desk was essentially an iPad the size of a dining room table, and he was typing furiously on his virtual keyboard and making lots of mistakes. He'd been a lousy typist even before his hands were smashed with a mallet.

Elsewhere on the desktop, hundreds of security camera images from throughout the casino played in thumbnails like a checkerboard tablecloth with animated squares. If he wanted to, he could touch and expand any of the video squares to full screen or shuffle them around like mahjong tiles. But he wasn't interested in that right now. All of his attention was focused on the email he was writing to TMZ, the notorious gossip website and TV show.

He'd logged onto the TMZ site as Emilia Guttierez, a nonexistent Côte d'Argent maid, a character he'd created as a seemingly legitimate front for the anonymous tips that he regularly sent to the media. To make Emilia more credible, just in case anyone decided to snoop, he'd put her on the Côte d'Argent payroll, rented an apartment for her, and had credit cards and various utility company accounts opened in her name.

Trace was tipping off TMZ that a world-famous young singer, a twenty-year-old man who'd once been a Disney star, had just registered in the hotel under the pseudonym *Bolt Stryker* and had two cross-dressers in his room. He attached a photo to Emilia's email of the disguised singer slipping into the hotel through the VIP entrance and another photo of him letting the two "ladies" into his room. Trace added one more line.

He's with them right now!!! You can't ever say where you got this information or hint that it was someone on the cleaning staff. After the last tip I sent you, Trace went ballistic and threatened to fire every single employee.

Trace was sure that the news would go viral on a global scale and would generate a million dollars' worth of free publicity for Côte d'Argent. Of course, he'd booked the room for the singer, he'd arranged for the cross-dressing hookers, and promised him absolute secrecy. But Trace didn't have any qualms about breaking that promise, or lying to the singer about it later when the news broke. The lurid publicity, and with it the constant association of Côte d'Argent with celebrity and scandal, was worth a lot more to Trace than the singer's future business. He clicked the SEND button just as Niles Goodwell, his manager of player relations, waddled in like an enormous penguin.

"I hope I'm not disturbing you," Goodwell said.

"Not at all. I was just catching up on my email."

"I got a call from Nick Sweet, the guy who blew a couple million at one of our blackjack tables last week," Goodwell said. "He's wired fifteen million dollars from a bank account in St. Kitts to our casino in Macau to establish a credit line."

It was amazing to Trace what he could accomplish with his personal touch. High rollers like Sweet were always flattered to get attention from the man in charge, and it took the sting out of their gambling losses. It had obviously sealed the deal this time.

"Make sure he gets the royal treatment," Trace said. "Offer to fly him to Macau on our jet as our guest. Comp his suite and have one of our chauffeur-driven Rolls-Royce Phantoms available for his personal use at all times during his stay. Whatever he desires, he gets, especially if it's kinky and disgraceful. That way we've got leverage to use against him in the future. We want him to continue losing his money with us until we have it all."

"There's just one wrinkle, sir," Goodwell said. "Sweet doesn't want the credit for his own play. He'd like to establish an account with us as a junket operator so he can bring in some high rollers. He's asking for a VIP suite with a baccarat table and all of the amenities."

"We'll still treat him well, but don't offer to fly him in. He'll have to get himself and his guests to Macau and pay top dollar for his rooms," Trace said. "But at least now we know what his short visit here was all about. He wanted to show us his credentials."

"We don't know anything about him," Goodwell said. "All he showed us was his money."

"That's all that matters," Trace said. "Especially now."

Trace was on the brink of a bold expansion in Macau. In addition to his existing property in old Macau, he wanted to build a much larger resort. Monde d'Argent would sit on the Cotai Strip, two square miles of reclaimed land that joined the former islands of Taipa and Coloane into one.

The Cotai Strip was already home to the Venetian Macao, the largest hotel casino complex on earth, and a half dozen other mega-casinos that were either finished or in the midst of being built. If his company was going to survive, Trace believed that he had to be on the Cotai Strip, too. He desperately needed the revenue that came from high-roller play to fund the construction. But there was a problem.

"There's new leadership in China and they're cracking down on high-level corruption on the mainland," Trace told Goodwell. "It's a publicity stunt, and it'll go away in a few months, but until then, the richest people in China are afraid to draw attention to themselves by gambling in Macau. This couldn't have come at a worse time for me. We've broken ground on Monde d'Argent and everybody is fighting over the handful of high rollers that are left."

"I understand that, sir," Goodwell said. "But I don't trust Sweet and Porter. I'm worried that they are working on some kind of a big score."

"I'm certain they are, but I can't let them take their fifteen million dollars and their future business across the street to one of the other casinos," Trace said. "So we'll welcome Sweet and we'll keep our eyes on him. Just make sure that he knows the ground rules. We run the table and the chips need to be rolled three times."

That meant that Nick's whales would have to gamble their chips at least three times, greatly increasing their chances of losing their initial stake and any winnings they got along the way.

"Our dealer in the room will stay on top of it," Goodwell said. "We'll watch every chip and guarantee that the games are honest."

"When is this junket supposed to come in?"

"Next Wednesday."

That was a week away. "What do we know about his guests?"

"Nothing, sir," Goodwell said. "Do you really want to know about them?"

It was a sensible question to ask. It was often better not to know who was in the room, especially if the players were coming to Côte d'Argent Macau to launder their money. The junkets gave Trace plausible deniability if the money was used to finance the bombing of a U.S. embassy somewhere and the Justice Department ever started asking him questions. But Trace's curiosity was stronger than his caution.

"Get whatever information you can," Trace said. "But make sure your inquiries don't leave a trail of any kind back to us."

"Will do," Goodwell said and walked out.

Trace tapped a virtual button that activated the speakerphone on his digital desktop and called Garver, his enforcer and body-guard. Garver answered his phone after one ring.

"Yeah?" Garver replied. He was the only man who worked for Trace who didn't feel the slightest need to grovel to him.

"Pack your mallet," Trace said. "We're going to Macau."

11

Thanks to the success of *The Lego Movie,* there was a mad scramble among Hollywood producers to make films based on children's toys. So perhaps it was inevitable that Mr. Potato Head would inspire a new animated feature. But few people, besides savvy studio accountants, could have foreseen that it would be an all-potato adaptation of Charles Dickens's *Great Expectations.* The novel was in the public domain, meaning that it was free to use, saving the producers the money, time, and creativity required to come up with an original story suitable for talking potatoes. The studio accountants were thrilled.

The movie's cast recorded their parts individually in a studio located in a small office building on Hollywood Way in Burbank. The studio had originally been a dentist's office and still smelled like mint mouthwash. Not because the scent had tenaciously lingered through the remodeling, but because the voice actors were constantly sucking on breath mints and throat lozenges.

One of those actors was Boyd Capwell, a fortyish man with great teeth, a strong chin, and perfect hair who behaved as if he was always playing to an audience or a camera, even when they existed only in his mind. Boyd was in a soundproof booth the size of a closet. He was facing the window into the control room, where the director and the sound editor were watching him.

He'd been cast as the voice of Magwitch, the escaped convict that young Pip encounters one fateful, foggy night in a churchyard cemetery at the beginning of Dickens's tale. Magwitch was described by Dickens as a fearful man in leg irons, wearing wet, filthy clothes and a dirty rag tied around his head, who'd limped and shivered, glared and growled. So Boyd was limping and shivering within the cramped confines of the booth as he recorded his lines into the microphone. He wore tattered clothes and a dirty rag on his head, and addressed a potato in his hand as if it were young Pip. It was a pose intentionally reminiscent of Hamlet.

"You'll bring me a file to cut these chains and food to fill my stomach, you little devil, and you won't say a word to anyone." Boyd spoke with a heavy Irish accent while he glared and growled. "Or else my friend who is hiding in the marshes will cut you into fries and shred you into hash browns for us to eat."

"Cut," the director said into his microphone. His name was Milt Freiberger, and he was a twenty-year veteran of Saturday morning cartoons who was making his first feature film. He took off his tortoiseshell glasses, rubbed his eyes, and ran his hands through his thick, curly hair before speaking quietly and patiently. "Boyd, what are you doing?"

"Acting."

"Yes, I know that. But this isn't the same performance you gave in the audition."

"That's because all I knew then was that I was auditioning for an animated version of *Great Expectations*," Boyd said. "I wasn't aware that the characters would be potatoes."

"What difference does it make?" Milt asked.

"It goes to the essence of the characters. I have to embody that. I've spent the last two weeks eating nothing but potatoes to fill myself with the taste, smell, and texture of the noble tuber."

"I see," Milt said. "Why are you using an Irish accent?"

"Because I did my research. Clearly, Magwitch is an Irish lumper, the prevalent variety of potato at the time. But here's where it gets interesting. Twenty years after this story ends, the Irish lumper crops were decimated by a horrible disease, causing the great potato famine of 1845, so my accent is also dramatic foreshadowing."

"But in the Charles Dickens novel, Magwitch wasn't Irish."

"He wasn't a potato, either."

"Go back to the cockney accent you used in the audition. And please, stick to the lines as written, too. You're supposed to say to Pip that your friend will 'cut out your heart and your liver, roast them and eat them.' You changed it to something about French fries and hash browns."

"Because Pip is a potato," Boyd said, shaking the potato in his hand for emphasis. "He doesn't have a heart or a liver."

"He's got arms and legs and he talks," Milt said. "So he has a heart and liver."

"That makes no biological or botanical sense."

"Mr. Potato Head is a plastic toy potato that you can snap different facial features onto, like noses, eyes, ears, and mouths, to create new characters," Milt said. "It's not an actual potato. None of these characters are. Think of them as people who happen to resemble potatoes."

Perhaps Boyd might have argued the point, or even given in to the director's wishes, but then he saw Nick walk into the studio. Boyd didn't know anything, really, about Nick or his partner, Kate, or Intertect, the mysterious private security company they claimed to work for. All that Boyd knew, and all that really mattered to him, was that whenever they showed up, it meant he'd have a chance to earn $100,000 by playing a character in an elaborate con to capture a criminal. The colorful roles they gave him were played on the stage of life, where a bad performance could get him killed. The danger made the roles even more thrilling.

"I quit," Boyd said.

"You can't quit," Milt said.

"Take it up with my agent," Boyd said, pointing to Nick. "He just walked in."

Milt turned to Nick. "He has a contract. If he walks, I'll ruin him in this business."

"If you had that kind of pull," Nick said, "you wouldn't be directing a cartoon version of *Great Expectations* with talking potatoes."

"*The Lego Movie* made half a billion dollars worldwide, and Legos aren't even characters. They're plastic bricks. Mr. Potato Head is a beloved global personality, an icon. We could top what Lego did."

"If you do, then you won't care that Boyd walked, will you?" Nick said. "You'll be too busy basking in your success."

Boyd emerged from the booth. "If you want success to happen, Milt, you can't pretend the potatoes aren't potatoes. You have to embrace your inner potato."

"I don't have an inner potato," Milt said.

"Then you are the wrong man to be directing this movie," Boyd said and dropped his potato in Milt's lap.

Nick and Boyd walked outside to the parking lot where Nick's Porsche 911 was parked next to Boyd's Cadillac CTS.

"So how much were you making as a potato?" Nick asked.

"It's not about the money, it's about living. I am an actor. I need to act, the same way that I need to breathe, or eat or sleep. I saw playing a potato as a creative challenge. I've played an apple in a Fruit of the Loom commercial, and even a pancake once, but I've never had a chance to be a vegetable, and certainly not with classy material like this," Boyd said. "It's *Great*

Expectations, a Charles Dickens masterpiece. There will never be a better vegetable part. How could I say no?"

"And, yet, you're walking away."

"I can't work with directors who don't have passion for what they're doing. But you certainly do. What role do you have for me?"

"A powerful, vicious, and amoral Canadian mobster who is going to Macau to play high-stakes baccarat," Nick said. "You like the game, but what you're really there to do is launder your money through the casino. You're mixing business with pleasure."

"I'll be Tony Soprano meets Snidely Whiplash."

"The bad guy with the handlebar mustache that Dudley Do-Right, the Canadian Mountie, was always battling in the cartoons?"

"He's a perfect touchstone for my character," Boyd said. "I particularly like the mustache."

"Just don't wear the top hat and black cape," Nick said. "Keep it subtle."

Nick and Kate spent the first part of the week establishing identities for Boyd and Billy Dee.

Kate used her FBI access to create criminal backgrounds for "Shane Blackmore," Boyd's nonexistent Canadian mobster, in all of the key law enforcement databases worldwide. She also sensationalized the criminal files that already existed for Lou

Ould-Abdallah, Billy Dee Snipes's real name, so he'd appear to be an active, brutal power player in high-seas piracy. When the con was over, she'd erase all of her creative writing.

Nick got in touch with his tech wizard in Hong Kong. They planted fake articles and references about Shane Blackmore and Lou Ould-Abdallah on the Internet, and forged the necessary passports, credit cards, and driver's licenses that would be needed.

Once Nick and Kate were done, Boyd flew to Vancouver, British Columbia, on his U.S. passport. In Canada, he switched to Shane Blackmore's Canadian passport and flew to Hong Kong. This established a trail that led back to Canada in case anyone checked into his identity.

Billy Dee flew from Las Vegas to Mogadishu, by way of London, Istanbul, and Djibouti. He spent a night in Mogadishu, and then used his Somali passport to take a flight to Kenya, a two-hour flight to Ethiopia, and finally a ten-hour flight to Hong Kong. It was a belabored way to get from Las Vegas to Hong Kong but, as with Boyd, it was necessary to establish his cover.

Nick and Kate didn't have to worry about leaving a trail. They focused instead on making the right impression. So Nick chartered a private jet for their trip. He met Kate at the Van Nuys Airport early in the morning on their departure day.

"The last time we went to China together, it was in the trunk of a '69 Dodge Charger in the cargo hold of a passenger jet," Nick said. "This time, I thought we should go in style."

Kate climbed the stairs to the G650, said hello to the flight attendant and the pilots, and settled into one of the eight cushy leather club chairs. The crew compartment and galley were in front of her. A credenza with a wine cooler and flat-screen TV were behind her. A couch and the restroom were also behind her.

"This is really extravagant," Kate said. "Couldn't you have chartered something smaller and cheaper?"

"Sure, but we would have had to stop somewhere on the way for refueling," he said. "This baby will take us straight to Hong Kong without stopping and makes a bold statement."

"What does a bold statement cost?"

"Two hundred and fifty thousand dollars."

Kate squelched a grimace. "Jessup is going to pop a hemorrhoid."

They were an hour into the flight, Kate was halfway through her third bowl of heated nuts, and Nick reached for his messenger bag. "I'm going to teach you how to play baccarat," he said. "I packed three decks of cards and a big bag of M&M's for the trip."

"What are the M&M's for?"

"Gambling chips. I wanted them to have some value to you." He handed Kate the bag of candy. "Separate these by color. Yellow M&M's will be a hundred thousand, red will be fifty thousand, blue will be twenty-five thousand, and brown will be five thousand."

"What about the orange and green M&M's?"

"Those are for you to snack on so you won't be tempted to devour your chips."

"My kind of game. I'm liking it already."

"Baccarat is a lot like betting on a sporting event," Nick said, shuffling the cards. "There are two teams, the dealer and the player. You're going to place a bet on who you think will be dealt the cards that come closest to adding up to nine."

"What's the strategy?"

"There is none," Nick said. "It's pure luck. Unlike blackjack or poker, you don't get to make any choices. You're dealt your cards and that's that."

"You mean you just sit there and do nothing?"

"Yep," he said.

"There's no bluffing?"

"Nope," he said.

"So why is baccarat the game that James Bond always plays against the bad guys to prove how clever he is?"

"Because that's not what he's doing. He's showing them that he's willing to take huge risks and that he has unwavering confidence in his own good luck."

"And that he looks great in a tuxedo," Kate added.

"That's the part that takes true finesse. Here's how the game works. To start, you and the dealer are each dealt two cards, facedown." He dealt out the cards to Kate and himself. "An ace counts as one, the ten and face cards count as zero. You subtract ten from any combination of cards that adds up to more than nine. For example, an eight and a three would add up to one. Two tens would equal zero. The player looks at her cards first."

Kate turned over her cards. She had a nine and a three. "So am I stuck with this lousy two?"

"Nope. If the player draws two cards that total zero to five, she automatically gets a third card. You never get more than three cards."

He dealt her a four, giving her a total of six.

"That's better," she said. "How does it work for the dealer?"

"That's more complicated." Nick turned over his cards, revealing a queen and a three. "The dealer isn't allowed another card unless the player has drawn three cards, and it depends on what that third card was. The rules vary from casino to casino, but usually the dealer must stand if he has a seven, eight, or nine and must draw a card if he has a zero, one, or two. If the dealer has a three, like I do, he'll draw if the player's third card is any number but eight."

"Why eight?"

"I have absolutely no idea. But none of it really matters since you're already finished with your part of the game. You just have to go along with it, knowing that the rules are designed to give the house a statistical advantage." Nick drew a card, a five, giving him a total of eight to win the game.

Kate tossed her cards back to Nick. "I'll bet with the house every time."

"If you do that, the house takes a five percent commission on each bet you win."

They played for a couple hours, and Kate eventually started to lose more often than she won. She was down to her last $200,000 in blue and brown M&M's, when she scooped them up and ate them.

"I guess this means we're done," Nick said.

"I'd rather watch grass grow."

"It was kind of sexy the way you ate all those M&M's. I like an aggressive, take-charge woman."

"You should see me in combat gear."

12

In the late 1990s, the few farmers that occupied the small, hilly islands of Chek Lap Kok and Lam Chau, twenty-one miles southwest of Hong Kong, were told to pack up and move. Their tiny villages were razed, the hillsides were shaved off, and everything was dumped into the water between the two islands to create one completely flat piece of land for a new international airport. From the sky, the unnaturally level and squared-off island that was Hong Kong International Airport looked to Kate like a gray rug floating on the sea.

Nick and Kate landed in the late afternoon. They were fast-tracked through customs and walked a short distance to the heliport, where a white Peninsula Hotel helicopter was waiting for them. A young Chinese valet in an all-white mandarin-collared uniform, pillbox hat, and gloves cheerfully

JANET EVANOVICH AND LEE GOLDBERG

relieved them of their suitcases and escorted them to the chopper. They climbed in, the valet stowed their bags and secured their door, and they were off, soaring over the hills, the ports, and the bridges toward the city center.

Within moments, Hong Kong Island loomed up in front of them with its spectacular skyline of densely packed skyscrapers. The island consisted of a narrow strip of land between Victoria Peak and a harbor that was a freeway filled with ferries, jetfoils, yachts, ocean liners, and Chinese junks. The Kowloon Peninsula was just across the harbor. Here the skyscrapers had more shoulder room, but still rose up from a closely packed warren of buildings on overcrowded streets.

The Peninsula Hotel, built in 1928, was on the Kowloon waterfront, facing the harbor. The helicopter landed on top of the hotel's thirty-story tower, a relatively recent addition to the original building, which was an elegant and fiercely beloved relic of Hong Kong's British colonial era. The flight from the airport had taken only seven minutes.

Nick and Kate exited the helicopter and walked into the China Clipper lounge on the thirtieth floor. A crisply dressed female clerk greeted them and presented Nick and Kate with their key cards. She assured them that their bags would be delivered to their rooms while they dined. Nick thanked her, and he and Kate took the elevator two floors down to Felix, the hotel's renowned restaurant and bar.

They emerged from the elevator into a wildly overdesigned restaurant that looked like a SPECTRE villain's secret lair from a 1960s-era Bond movie. It was a big, bold, two-story-tall space, gleaming with bronze, zinc, and undulating aluminum sheathing. There were dramatically lit walls, pillars, and two oval structures that, if this *were* SPECTRE headquarters, would have been stylized silos for nuclear missiles instead of fancy bars. The real grabber in the room was the commanding view of the Hong Kong skyline from the wall-to-wall floor-to-ceiling windows that would have pleased any supervillain bent on world domination. But instead of finding Dr. Evil sitting in the center of it all, stroking his hairless cat, Kate spotted Boyd Capwell at a table, twirling his handlebar mustache.

Boyd's hair was colored jet black to match his well-oiled mustache. He'd mimicked Tony Soprano's fashion sense, wearing a navy blue short-sleeved bowling shirt, with cream panels and two embroidered martini glasses on the left chest, a pair of khaki slacks, and leather loafers with no socks.

"Welcome to Hong Kong," Boyd said, gesturing to three empty chairs with seatbacks decorated with black-and-white drawings of longtime, and mostly deceased, Peninsula employees. "Have a seat."

"You look like you're on Snidely Whiplash's bowling team," Kate said.

"Thank you," Boyd said. "Now Snidely is flesh and blood and embodied in Shane Blackmore, a man to be feared. But because I'm dressed in a relaxed, lighthearted manner, I'll catch people completely off guard with my seething menace." Boyd sat back, smiled, and twirled one end of his mustache.

Kate could feel an eye twitch coming on. "The mustache-twirling bad guy was already a cliché when they were doing silent movies."

"In other words, it's a powerful symbol embedded deep in our collective psyche. By twirling my mustache, I'll provoke primal fear in my adversaries," Boyd said. "That's why this mustache is perfect. Nick gave me the idea."

Kate turned to Nick. "You didn't."

"I did. I may grow one myself. It would hint at *my* inner menace," Nick said.

"I had a goatee once," Billy Dee Snipes said, walking up behind Nick and Kate. "But it was like drawing a circle with a Sharpie around my mouth and saying 'Look at my crooked, yellow teeth.' So I shaved it off."

Billy Dee wore another silk tracksuit similar to the one he'd had on in Las Vegas. The only change he'd made to his wardrobe was the addition of a *koofiyad*, a Somali skullcap embroidered with an elaborate design of interlocking triangles.

"Have you seen the bathrooms in here?" Billy Dee asked Nick. "You pee facing a wall of glass that looks out over Kowloon."

"It's a display of aggression, dominance, profanity, freedom, and exhibitionism all rolled into one," Boyd said. "Urination as performance art and political statement."

"I think it's just a great place to pee. It's the first time I've ever enjoyed having prostate trouble," Billy Dee said. "I've gone twice already and I'm looking forward to going again in ten minutes."

The waiter appeared at the table and passed out iPad menus. Kate scrolled through the selections and examined pictures of dishes such as soy-marinated pigeon and French duck liver with caramelized strawberries. What she really craved was an In-N-Out burger or a bucket of KFC. What she ordered instead was a Kobe steak and fries, and a double-chocolate brownie with espresso ice cream and custard sauce for dessert.

"Your job tomorrow is easy, gentlemen," Nick said over dessert. "Gamble six million dollars each and have a fabulous time."

"I can do that," Billy Dee said.

Boyd added cream to his coffee. "That's easy for you to say. You have the benefit of actually being a Somali pirate, while I must draw on a lifetime of acting experience to deliver a rich and nuanced performance as a Canadian mobster."

"It's okay to win," Nick continued. "But if you're losing, pace yourself. Try to walk away with at least five million if you can. You're here to launder your money, so up to a ten percent loss is acceptable as a washing fee, and I suppose that another five percent loss could be written off to having too much fun."

"I'm going to play baccarat like it's nickel slots," Billy Dee said.

"I've seen you play the slots," Kate said. "You never stop hitting the spin button."

"Come to think of it," Nick said, "if we lose it all, it's only going to make Trace more eager for us to come back, so don't sweat the money."

Kate looked at Nick. "You have a lot to learn about encouraging fiscal restraint."

"Because I don't have any," he said.

"I've noticed," she said.

Nick received a text message just as everyone was finishing dessert.

"Gentlemen, it's been a pleasure, as usual," Nick said. "A small business matter that Kate and I need to attend to has come up. Feel free to continue enjoying yourselves, but remember, we have a big day tomorrow."

Kate left the dining room with Nick and paused at the elevator. "What's up?"

"There's someone in Kowloon that I want you to meet," Nick said. "Sorry about it being so last-minute, but we don't get to Hong Kong very often and we're only here for the night."

They took the elevator to the lobby, and Kate thought the hotel's entryway, filled with neoclassical columns, gilded ceilings, and a string quartet, was reminiscent of an elegant bygone era. That feeling passed the moment she stepped outside and saw the scores of tourists posing along the Victoria Harbor waterfront with their smart phones attached to telescoping selfie sticks, trying to get the perfect shot of themselves against the Hong Kong skyline.

The sidewalks were teeming with people, more than she'd ever seen before on any city street. The roads were clogged with European luxury cars, tour buses, and countless identical red-and-white Toyota taxis.

They stepped into the flow of people and let it carry them up Canton Road, which was lined with flagship stores for such luxury brands as Louis Vuitton, Hermès, Prada, Harry Winston, and Gucci. The stores were packed with customers, desperate for their chance to spend top dollar on the priciest Western goods. Outside the high-end store doors, and at every street corner, there were relentless hucksters whispering offers of "cheap Gucci, cheap Rolex," and handing out cards with directions to back-alley shops that sold bootlegs of everything.

"Who are we meeting?" Kate asked.

"My tech wizard, Lucie," Nick said.

Kate stopped in the middle of the sidewalk and stared at him. "When you made your deal with the FBI, you said you would never do anything that could potentially expose the people you've worked with before."

"You're right, I did. And I won't share her with the FBI. But you're more than the FBI to me. If the day should come where a con goes wrong, you might need Lucie's help to disappear. I would rather see you retire to a beach in Thailand than waste away in some federal prison."

"Wow."

"Yeah, it took me by surprise, too," Nick said.

"Probably we don't want to talk about it."

"For sure. Absolutely. Still, if you're really grateful . . ."

"I don't think so."

A little old man and a young woman bumped into them and said something in rushed Chinese. Nick bowed, gave his apologies to the man, and tugged Kate forward onto a side street, where the sidewalks weren't quite as mobbed. Garish neon signs for restaurants, shops, and massage parlors hung out over the road, cluttering the air above her head and clamoring for her attention in blazing yellow, orange, and red Chinese letters. The signs cast enough light for the tourists to easily read their pocket maps and for some locals to look natural wearing sunglasses at night. Music blared out of electronics stores. Frustrated drivers leaned on their car horns. The humid air was thick, almost chewable, with the smell of cooking oil, fish, perfume, and bus exhaust. The atmosphere was electric, chaotic, and overwhelming.

Nick stopped in front of a glass door set in an elegant, marbled façade that looked out of place amid the garishness of the street. Kate looked up and saw that it was the ground floor entrance to a glass-and-marble-sheathed tower that was about as wide as three parking spaces and rose thirty stories into the night sky. Nick punched a code into the security keypad and the door unlocked.

They rode an elevator up to the twentieth floor. When the door opened, Kate saw two apartment doors that were about a foot apart from each other, and maybe four feet in front of them.

"This is the smallest apartment corridor I've ever seen," she said.

"Real estate is tight in Hong Kong."

"Literally," Kate said.

Nick knocked on the door on the left. It was immediately opened by a young, very thin Chinese woman in her early twenties. She was dressed in a sharp black business suit and white blouse and smiled when she saw Nick. She said something to him affectionately in Chinese, Nick replied back to her in Chinese, and then the young woman turned to Kate.

"It's so nice to finally meet you." She spoke perfect English with a slight British accent. "I'm Lucie Wan. Please come in."

Lucie stepped aside and they walked into a small living area with an amazing view. To their left was a large picture window with a cushioned sill that looked out at the towers along Victoria Harbor. To their right was a single bed, the covers neatly tucked into tight military corners. Directly across from them, not even ten feet away, were two pocket doors, one partially open to reveal a two-burner stove, a mini-refrigerator, and a small sink. Kate assumed that behind the other door was a bathroom, probably about the same size of an airplane lavatory.

"What do you think of my place?" Lucie asked Nick.

"It's terrific," Nick said and kissed her on the cheek. "Congratulations."

"Thank you," Lucie said, beaming with pride. "When this building opened, over two thousand prospective buyers showed up but I was one of only sixty people who scored a place."

"You were lucky," he said.

"Screw luck," she said. "I hacked into the developer's computer and put myself at the top of the list."

Lucie turned to a tiny desk that held her laptop computer and two hard drives.

"The identity for Shane Blackmore is all set if Trace's people start snooping. He's listed in Canadian government databases—birth records, tax rolls, DMV, et cetera," Lucie said. "I've also planted news stories that mention him in the *Toronto Star* and *The Vancouver Sun* archives. Lou Ould-Abdallah's identity was much easier to create, since he really is a Somali pirate."

"Excellent work," Nick said. "As usual."

"Do you create all of Nick's false identities, forged passports, and phony credit cards?" Kate asked.

"I create the identities and accounts in the necessary databases, but I don't do the physical forgeries," Lucie said. "I subcontract that out."

"There's no better place than Hong Kong to get a high-quality knockoff," Nick said, "whether it's a bootleg Hermès bag or a false passport."

"He's right," Lucie said. "This dress is fake Prada. Nick doesn't pay me enough to get the real thing."

"I've paid you enough to get this apartment," he said.

"But now I'm broke," she said. "I may have to go back to picking pockets."

"That's how Lucie and I met," Nick said. "She picked my pocket on the street in Lan Kwai Fong, cloned my identity, and emptied out my bank account within the hour. She was only fifteen."

"It also only took Nick an hour to find me," Lucie said. "I was living in a homemade shelter under an overpass in the Central District and tapping into phone lines with a stolen laptop. Instead of having me thrown in jail, he sent me to boarding school."

"She obviously had a natural gift for larceny and technology," Nick said. "All she was missing to succeed was a real education. Now she works in computer services for an international bank."

"That's my menial day job," Lucie said. "The legitimate front for my real profession, which is keeping Nicolas Fox out of jail. Of course, that's been a lot easier since you stopped chasing him."

Kate felt her throat go dry. "You know who I am?"

"Of course I do, FBI Special Agent Kate O'Hare. It would be hard to create all of those false identities for you if I didn't know your real one."

It was late when Kate and Nick left Lucie and returned to their hotel. Kate staggered into her eighteenth-floor suite, not noticing the amazing view or the lacquered tea blossoms etched on the wall, or the high-tech tablet that controlled everything in the room, or the low-tech nail dryer built into the dresser. She was exhausted and all she saw was the bed. She stripped down to a T-shirt and panties, slipped between the perfectly ironed sheets, and thought about what a different world China was from her own, and how much she missed the comfort of having a loaded Glock under her pillow.

The next morning, before taking the elevator up to the Peninsula helipad, Nick handed out tiny flesh-colored earbud radio transmitters/receivers to Kate, Boyd, and Billy Dee.

"We'll wear these at all times so we can be in constant, simultaneous contact. They're practically invisible."

Nick was wearing a trim-fit gray Armani silk and wool sport coat, white Hermès slim dress shirt, and Dsquared2 jeans. Kate was in a sleeveless Givenchy black satin top with a very deep V-neck that pretty much guaranteed every man she faced would be distracted by her cleavage. That was the intention. Anything that might distract a possible adversary, even for a split second, was an advantage that she might need. Her knee-length skirt with a ruffled tiered overlay was loose enough to allow her plenty of flexibility for a spin kick, which is what she looked for in a dress. Her silver-studded Yves Saint Laurent calfskin ballerina flats were equally practical, being fancy shoes with pointed toes, while still maintaining the capability to haul ass, if the need should arise.

The team slipped the earbuds into their ears and took the elevator up to the China Clipper lounge. They passed quickly through and outside to the helipad, where a white-suited, white-gloved valet stowed their luggage and ushered them into the waiting helicopter for their fifteen-minute ride to Macau.

Billy Dee looked back wistfully at the hotel as the helicopter rose and carried them out over the harbor.

"I'm going to miss that bathroom," he said.

The helicopter soared westward across the Pearl River Delta. Kate's first glimpse of Macau was the Grand Lisboa hotel and casino, a fifty-three-story tower of gold-tinted glass shaped like the feathered headdress of a showgirl.

Macau encompassed a three-mile peninsula as well as the former islands of Taipa and Coloane, which were now joined together by the Cotai Strip. Three two-mile-long bridges linked the city to Taipa, one of which was arched to resemble the back of a sleeping dragon, its tail on the island and its head resting in front of the Grand Lisboa.

They landed on the helipad atop the Macau Ferry Terminal, breezed through the VIP customs checkpoint, and were met outside by a Rolls-Royce Phantom sent by Côte d'Argent. Nick got up front with the chauffeur and Kate sat in the back, sandwiched between Boyd and Billy Dee for the ten-minute drive to the casino along Avenida da Amizade.

"Macau is over five centuries old," Nick said, playing tour guide to his junket guests and their eavesdropping driver. "It was built to resemble Lisbon by homesick Portuguese traders. The Vegas casino moguls came much later, and they also wanted to feel at home."

A twenty-story replica of Evan Trace's Côte d'Argent tower appeared to their right. Directly across the street was Steve

Wynn's small-scale copy of his namesake Las Vegas resort. Both properties faced the harbor and Taipa, where the medieval castle-like spires of the Galaxy Macau on the Cotai Strip peeked out beyond the top of Small Taipa Hill.

"That's real interesting, Nick. Is there a Tim Hortons around?" Boyd asked, referring to the ubiquitous Canadian coffee chain. He spoke with a slight lilt in his voice, his attempt at a Canadian accent now that he was in character as Shane Blackmore.

"I don't think so," Nick said.

"Then it isn't going to feel like home to me," Boyd said. "If Canadians had settled this place, there'd be a Tim Hortons on every corner, a loon on every dollar, and the Grand Lisboa would be shaped like a golden maple leaf instead of Daffy Duck's ass."

"Is that what it's supposed to be?" Billy Dee said, craning his neck to look up at it.

"You know Daffy Duck in Somalia?" Boyd asked as they arrived at Côte d'Argent.

"No," Billy Dee shifted his gaze to Boyd and his eyes turned cold, "but I know an ass when I see one."

Boyd smiled broadly and wagged a finger at Billy Dee. "That was good, Sheik," he said. "I think I'm gonna like you."

The driver pulled up to the Côte d'Argent VIP entrance, and the four of them stepped out of the Rolls-Royce and into the lobby. It was identical to the one in Las Vegas, right down to the ice sculptures and chilly temperature. The slender, long-legged Macanese hostess who approached them wore high heels and a body-hugging black silk *qipao,* a sleeveless one-piece dress with a severe Mandarin collar and a subtle pattern of Chinese symbols.

"I'm Natasha Ling, vice president of guest relations, and I'd like to welcome you to Côte d'Argent," she said, taking a slight bow in front of them. "I will be seeing to your needs throughout your stay."

"That's great news," Boyd said. "What are those drawings on your dress?"

"Chinese lucky charms," she said.

"Do I rub you to get good luck?" Boyd asked.

"You'll find these same charms incorporated into the décor throughout the property," Natasha said. "So good luck surrounds you in Côte d'Argent. Rubbing the staff isn't necessary."

"But it couldn't hurt," Boyd said, twirling his mustache. "Especially the pretty ones."

Kate caught Nick's eye and pretended to gag.

Natasha smiled politely and passed out transparent plastic key cards in paper sleeves with room numbers on them. "These are the keys to your harbor-view suites and the express elevators. They also allow you into your private gaming suite on the eighth floor."

"I thought we'd be higher up," Boyd said. "The penthouse, maybe."

"It's a privilege to be on the eighth floor," Nick said. "Eight is a lucky number that has great power in Chinese culture. It equals prosperity."

"I hope that means for us," Boyd said. "And not the casino."

"We won't find out standing here," Billy Dee said impatiently. "Let's get to the table and play some cards."

"This way, please." Natasha led them through a set of double doors and out into the casino.

The casino floor was filled with hundreds of baccarat tables. Mobs of Chinese men and women crowded around them, cheering and yelling. The gamblers who couldn't find seats were standing, reaching across over the heads of the seated players to place bets. Kate slowed her pace beside one of the tables to peek at a game.

The player who'd been dealt two cards lifted them up very slowly, peeling them up by the edges, as if they were stickers glued to the table. The technique mangled the cards in the process, but the dealer didn't seem to mind, sweeping them into a trash slot at the end of the hand.

"Letting players destroy the cards like that would never fly in Vegas," Billy Dee said.

"The players aren't as superstitious there," Natasha said. "Many players here believe the way they reveal the cards has the power to change the numerical value."

"It didn't work for that guy," Boyd said.

"He may not be a powerful person," Natasha said. "I believe truly powerful men make their own luck."

They continued on across the casino floor toward a bank of elevators, and up to the eighth floor.

13

Dumah was a big and broad-chested descendent of an Indonesian tribe that, as recently as a hundred years ago, had been feared throughout the South China Sea as headhunters and slave traders. Back then, he would have been a warrior, and his traditional dress would have been a necklace of wild boar teeth and tusks, a battle vest of woven rattan and water buffalo bone, and a rigid two-foot-long penis sheath with a sharp pointed end.

Instead, as a security operative for Côte d'Argent, he wore a gray Dolce & Gabbana suit, a Patek Philippe gold watch, a radio transmitter in his ear, and nothing sheathing his penis but bikini briefs. His forefathers would have been deeply ashamed to see him like this.

Nevertheless, Dumah was still a warrior, of sorts. He'd never lopped off a head or traded a slave, but he'd made his living throughout Asia on his muscles, menace, and willingness to commit acts of extreme violence to protect whomever hired him. He'd worked for corporate executives, government officials, Triad mobsters, and, for a short time, a U.S. investment banker who'd embezzled a half billion dollars and fled to a tiny Indonesian island, safe from extradition.

That last job hadn't ended well. It started to go bad the instant a spoiled American heiress and her servants showed up in a bullet-riddled yacht, leading the Bugis pirates who'd attacked them right to the island. The pirates took all the Americans hostage, but they let Dumah go unharmed. He'd bounced around Asia for a few months after that, before ending up as a security guard at Côte d'Argent. It was pure fate that he happened to be standing in the casino when Natasha Ling walked by with her latest group of junket guests.

Dumah recognized two members of the group immediately. It was the heiress and her servant. Only that's not who they were today, and that probably wasn't who they were before. Either way, they deserved agony.

He didn't have a spear to fling at them, or a knife to cut their throats. What he had was a radio. He pressed the button in his pocket, activating the microphone, so that he could speak to his supervisor.

"I need to see Mr. Trace," Dumah said. "It's urgent."

. . .

The only difference between Trace's private dining room in Côte d'Argent Macau and the one in Las Vegas were the paintings on the wall. In Macau, he displayed masterpieces by Qi Baishi, Chen Yifei, and Ai Weiwei to impress his Asian guests. He also had a print of the seven dogs playing poker to amuse himself. The dining room had the same atrium and koi pond, though the only koi that were ever in the pond were ones that he fed to the piranhas.

Trace sat at his table beside the pond, browsing the *South China Morning Post* and eating a breakfast of steamed dim sum, Portuguese egg custard tarts, fresh fruit, and hot milk tea. He sported a carefully groomed three-day beard and was dressed casually in a blue-striped mandarin-collared, knot-buttoned dress shirt that was untucked over faded black jeans. He thought it was a look that straddled East and West but that fit with his devil-may-care image.

Natasha Ling came in, smiling at him as she crossed the Plexiglas bridge that arched over the pond and into the dining room.

"Mr. Sweet and Miss Porter have arrived with their guests," Natasha said, taking a seat at the table. "They are up in the eighth-floor suite and are already gambling."

He set the newspaper aside. "What do we know about their guests?"

"Lou Ould-Abdallah is from Mogadishu. He is a Somali warlord who has hijacked everything from oil tankers to yachts moving through the Strait of Malacca and the Gulf of Aden. Sometimes he sets the crews free and sells the boats and cargo, and other times he holds the crew and vessels for ransom. He's been known to behead his captives when negotiations aren't going to his satisfaction."

"My kind of guy." Trace took a sip of his milk tea. "How much did his last ransom bring him?"

"One hundred million dollars," Natasha said.

Trace whistled appreciatively. "Nice haul. So he's sitting on a pile of cash in the desert and looking to spend it on something besides another camel. What's the other high roller's story?"

"Shane Blackmore is a Canadian mobster. He started in the trucking business, smuggling stolen goods between the U.S. and Canada, then branched out into narcotics distribution and sex trafficking," she said. "He controls the drug and sex trade from Vancouver to Toronto."

"Vancouver and Toronto is about all there is between Vancouver and Toronto."

"That's why he's anxious to expand," she said. "He's got enough money stashed to buy his way into a business, legitimate or otherwise, somewhere else. He just needs to get his cash out of Canada to do it."

"I'm glad to be of service," Trace said. "We could make a lot of money from these two. How did Sweet hook up with them?"

"I don't know yet." Natasha reached for one of the egg tarts on Trace's plate, and he slapped her hand.

She slapped his face, hard enough to draw blood from the corner of his mouth.

Trace licked the blood away and smiled. "That's nice, but it's more fun somehow when you're wearing leather and stiletto heels."

She picked up the egg tart and took a bite out of it before speaking. "I can change my clothes if you'd like."

He was considering the pros and cons of that offer when Garver walked in. Garver moved with a lumbering, slightly hunched gait that looked as if he was fighting the urge to knuckle-walk like a gorilla. He was accompanied by one of Côte d'Argent's security men, a big Indonesian who kept a respectful step or two behind Garver. Trace had seen the Indonesian around the casino but had never actually met him.

"There's something you've got to hear," Garver said. "It's about Sweet and Porter." Garver gave the Indonesian a nod. "Tell him, Dumah."

"I met them two years ago, while I was a bodyguard for Derek Griffin," Dumah said. If a grizzly bear could talk, Trace thought, he would sound like this guy.

"The investment banker who ran off with a half billion dollars of his clients' money? You were working for a celebrity. Why didn't I know that?" Trace looked at Garver. "Do you remember seeing Griffin on Dumah's résumé?"

"I don't read résumés," Garver said. "I read scars."

"I haven't told anyone about that job, Mr. Trace," Dumah

said. "The story I'm about to tell you is the reason why. Griffin was hiding out on an island, safe from extradition, when that woman arrived on a yacht. She said that she'd been attacked by Bugis pirates. The man she was with today was there, too, only he was her servant back then. That night, the pirates invaded the island, took the Americans hostage, and let me go."

"No wonder you don't use Griffin as a reference," Trace said. "I hope you show me more loyalty than you showed him."

"It's true, I didn't protect him. I saved myself instead. But I think by telling you about those two, and revealing my personal shame, that I am demonstrating my loyalty," Dumah said. "I could have just waited for the right moment, slit their throats, and restored my dignity without anyone but me knowing that it had ever been lost."

"Fair point," Trace said. "Go on."

"Two days after I left the island, Griffin was arrested in Palm Springs, California. It made no sense. How did he get there? What happened to the woman and her servant? There was never any news about them. It was as if they never existed."

"I can see why you'd be angry at the pirates," Natasha said. "But why do you want to kill Sweet and Porter?"

"Because they are responsible for my shame," Dumah said. "They either led the pirates to the island through their stupidity, or they brought them there intentionally. I knew something wasn't right about those two the moment they came ashore. I warned Griffin that they were trouble, but he wouldn't listen to me. He just wanted to get the woman into bed."

"Did he succeed?" Trace asked.

Dumah shook his head, no. "Now he's in prison and those two are here, but as entirely different people. They're frauds. Whatever they've told you is a lie. They're here to take something."

Or *someone,* Trace thought. Was it him? Or was it the Canadian mobster and the Somali warlord that they were entertaining upstairs? Or were they after something else entirely?

Trace stood up. "I think it's time we had a candid conversation with Sweet."

"Okay," Garver said. "I'll go get my lie detector."

"You do that," Trace said. "Dumah, come with me."

Another hand was about to be dealt in the eighth-floor VIP gambling suite, a luxury two-bedroom, harbor-view apartment with a baccarat table, a sitting area, and a well-stocked bar. Boyd put $1 million in chips on the betting line. Nick gambled $250,000 on Boyd's hand, and Billy Dee wagered $100,000 with the dealer.

"Thanks for the vote of confidence," Boyd said to Billy Dee.

"I've seen your luck," Billy Dee said. "I'm here to win, not make friends."

They were an hour into play, and Nick and Billy Dee were up about $200,000, but Boyd was already down over a million dollars. This was Boyd's swing for the fences to get it all back in one hand.

Kate sat on a stool at the bar, watching the game and absentmindedly plucking items from the platters of dim sum and Portuguese pastries on the counter. At the rate Boyd was going, she was worried that he'd be tapped out in the next half hour and that she'd eat everything on the bar.

The dealer was a pretty, young Macanese woman named Luisa, who was all smiles and girly enthusiasm on the surface, but in complete command of her table. She dealt the cards with swift efficiency. Luisa was ordered to do that by the casino. The faster the men played, the more they'd bet and the more likely it was that they'd lose.

Standing beside Luisa was a grim-faced Macanese man named Tony who made notations on an iPad and watched the chips.

Boyd flipped over his cards to reveal a pair of twos. He swallowed half of the Bloody Mary that was in front of him.

"Hit me again, honey," Boyd said, though he had no choice but to take another card. "Make it a five."

Luisa gave him a card. Boyd winked at her. She smiled coyly back at him and he flipped the card over. It was a seven. That gave him a measly one.

"Bad luck," Nick said.

"The game isn't over yet," Boyd said and twirled his mustache.

The dim sum was sitting like a rock in Kate's gut. She could face down a two-hundred-pound man attacking with a knife and not break a sweat, but she was terrified at the thought of explaining the loss of a million dollars to her boss. Even without the threat of reprisal, Kate had a hard time justifying this kind of gambling. She was thrifty and law-abiding by nature, and that didn't change just because she zipped herself into a sexpot dress.

Luisa flipped over her cards, dealt herself one more, and came up with a hand that added up to ten, which in baccarat is equivalent to zero. She'd lost the game. Boyd had taken it with a one. It took a beat for it to sink in to Kate. Saved by the luck of the draw, she thought, letting out a *whoosh* of air.

Boyd whooped, pumping his fist in the air. "*That's* how you play the game. Watch and learn, boys."

Evan Trace strolled casually into the suite.

Nick looked over at him. "Well, this is a nice surprise."

"For both of us," Trace said, flashing his warmest smile. "I'm glad our trips here coincided. Now I can personally welcome you and your friends to Côte d'Argent Macau."

Nick stood up and turned to the others. "Gentlemen, I'd like to introduce you to—"

"*No freakin' gondolas!*" Boyd said, shouldering past Nick and thrusting his hand out to Trace. "Gambling straight up, that's how I like it, too. Just deal the cards and screw the show. I'm Shane Blackmore."

Trace shook his hand. "I'll tell you a little secret, Mr. Blackmore. Back when I was a gambler myself, my favorite casinos were the ones off the Strip, the dark rooms so thick with cigarette smoke that you could barely see the cards in your hands, but you could still smell the sweat, beer, and puke in the air."

"You just described my living room," Boyd said. "And my office."

"That does not surprise me," Billy Dee said to Boyd, then offered his hand to Trace. "I'm Lou Ould-Abdallah, but you may call me Lou. I'm glad you settled on a compromise between a casino that reeks of urine and one that's shaken every twenty minutes by the eruption of a fake volcano. This suite is perfect. I couldn't ask for anything more except, perhaps, a change in my luck."

"I can't do anything about your luck, Lou," Trace said, shaking Billy Dee's hand, "but if you do think of something else you'd like, perhaps a masseuse to loosen your muscles after sitting at the table all day, just ask Natasha or one of our other staff members. We will see to your needs immediately."

"I've got some," Boyd said with a mischievous grin. "I'd like a large Tim Hortons Caramel Latte Supreme and a dozen Honey Dip Timbits when you get a chance."

"We'll see what we can do," Trace said and slipped his arm around Nick's shoulder, like they were old chums. "Nick, do you have a few minutes? I'd like to steal you away for a quick chat."

"Of course." Nick turned and winked at Kate as he walked away with Trace. "Keep my seat warm, honey. Win me a quarter million while you're at it."

Billy Dee and Boyd returned to their seats at the table.

"There probably isn't a Tim Hortons within ten thousand miles of here." Boyd grinned at Billy Dee and bet $100,000 on the next hand.

"You like to needle people just to see how far you can push," Billy Dee said, betting $100,000 with Boyd this time. "I've known men like you before, may they rest in peace."

The dealer looked up at Kate.

"Will you be joining us?" Luisa asked.

"Maybe later," Kate said, moving to the bar while she eavesdropped on Nick and Trace through her earbud.

Nick and Trace walked out of the suite, closed the door, and went to the elevator directly across the hall. Trace pressed the elevator call button.

"What would you like to talk about?" Nick asked.

"You, Nick. I'd like to get to know you better now that we're doing business together."

"There isn't much to tell. I'm just an international entrepreneur who takes advantage of new opportunities as they come along."

The elevator doors opened, and there was a Côte d'Argent security man waiting for them inside.

Dumah, Nick thought. *Crap.*

14

"Remember me?" Dumah asked Nick as Nick stepped into the elevator.

"Of course I remember you," Nick said, thinking how to choose his words so Kate would get a grip on this new development. "Congratulations, Dumah. It's good to see you've found a job worthy of your skills."

Dumah caught him with a brutal sucker punch just below the rib cage and Nick folded, unable to breathe. Dumah grabbed him by the arm and propped him up.

"You understand now that we need to have a serious discussion?" Trace asked Nick.

Nick nodded, making an effort to relax, to give his lungs a chance to expand.

"Good," Trace said. "You're going to allow Dumah to assist you across the floor to my office."

Nick nodded again.

Kate heard everything that was happening in the elevator through her earbud. So did Billy Dee and Boyd. They looked over at her with concern, and she smiled at them from behind the bar.

"Go ahead and play without me, gentlemen," she said. "I think I need some air. I'll be right back."

Kate palmed a corkscrew from the bar and walked into the foyer. Natasha Ling was at the door, quietly standing, waiting to be of service.

"I'm just stepping out for some air," Kate said to Natasha.

"I'm so sorry, but you're not permitted to leave the suite at the present time," Natasha said, blocking Kate's path. "I suggest you go back to the bar and enjoy the game. Maybe have an egg tart. They're quite delicious."

"I suppose I could." Kate looked over her shoulder to make sure they were both out of view of the baccarat table before stepping close to Natasha and head-butting her. "But I won't."

The hostess staggered back, stunned by the blow. Kate shifted the corkscrew to her left hand and decked Natasha with a solid right hook, bouncing her head off the door and knocking her out cold. Kate caught Natasha before she reached the floor, dragged the woman into the adjoining bedroom, closed the door, and continued on her way to rescue Nick.

. . .

Nick had recovered by the time the elevator reached the ground floor, but he stayed doubled over, gasping for air, forcing Dumah to support him. He needed a moment to organize his thoughts, to stall for time.

Dumah half-carried, half-dragged Nick out of the elevator and across the noisy casino floor to the VIP salon.

"The VIP salon seems like a nice place to talk," Nick said. "We can have a few drinks, maybe play some cards after I catch my breath."

"I'd like a little more privacy," Trace said. "I'm sure you understand."

He did. He also knew that Kate was listening and he wanted to let her know where he was, and the seriousness of their situation, without being too obvious about it.

They led Nick through the salon, past the bar, to the door leading to Trace's private dining room. There was a security man standing guard at the door. As they approached, the guard took a transparent key card out of his pocket and passed it over a sensor on the wall, and the door unlocked.

"I'm either having déjà vu or the internal bleeding has deprived my brain of oxygen," Nick said. "Isn't your private dining room in the same place in Las Vegas?"

"It's exactly the same building, only with half as many floors," Trace said. "Ironically, it was twice as expensive to build, if you factor in all the bribes I had to pay Chinese officials."

138

Nick wasn't in the mood to appreciate irony. He was trying to think of how he was going to talk his way out of this.

The guard held the door for the three men as they passed, then closed it behind them. They walked into the sunny atrium, over the bridge, and into the open dining room. There was a man waiting for them who looked like he'd used his face to pound in fence posts. He was holding a mallet.

Not a good sign, Nick thought. This guy wasn't wearing a chef coat so you could assume he wasn't going to use the mallet to pound the heck out of a veal cutlet.

Dumah pushed Nick into a chair at the pond's edge and secured Nick's wrists to the arms of the chair with zip ties.

"You already know Dumah, from your experience in Dajmaboutu," Trace said. "This other gentleman is Mr. Garver, our senior customer relations technician. You really don't want to know him."

"At least not until I can put some plastic sheeting on the floor," Garver said, hefting his mallet, enjoying the weight. "This is nice carpet."

"Look, this has gone way too far already," Nick said. "Untie me, pour me a drink, and let's have a civilized conversation about whatever has got you riled up. You don't want to do something you're going to regret."

Trace smiled and leaned close to Nick. "I don't have regrets. Only losers have those. Tell me about the scam you're running. Every detail. Don't leave anything out."

"I'm not scamming anyone," Nick said. "I'm getting into the junket business."

"Wrong answer."

Garver tipped Nick's chair so that the back of the chair was flat to the floor and extended over the pond filled with piranha.

Kate didn't wait for the elevator. She took the stairs down to the casino, listening on the earbud as Nick pointed her to the VIP salon and Trace's private dining room.

She reached the ground floor and opened the door to the casino. A security guard stood in the doorway, his wide body blocking her path. He looked like a Macanese weightlifter stuffed into a Dolce & Gabbana suit that was a size too small.

"Going somewhere?" he asked.

Kate jammed the corkscrew into his crotch, puncturing the fabric of his pants and pressing the sharp point against his shriveling scrotum. His entire body went rigid.

"Unless you want to become a eunuch, you'll step very slowly inside here with me," she said, backing up into the stairwell. He did as he was told, but the instant the door closed behind him, he head-butted her.

Kate fell back, dazed and angry that she'd been surprised by the same move she'd used on Natasha. He swatted the corkscrew away from her and then backhanded her across the face.

Kate retaliated with a brutal kick to the inside of the guard's left knee, buckling him. He toppled to one side, grabbing Kate's other leg while going down and taking her to the floor with him.

Kate pulled his other leg out from under him as they fell, flipped him over on his back, and drove her elbow into his solar plexus with her full body weight. It was an elbow drop. A *WWE SmackDown* move that took the wind out of him. A follow-up punch in the face put him down for the count.

She searched through his jacket pockets and found a five-inch telescoping steel baton. It was a nice trade up from the corkscrew. Kate got to her feet, held the baton down between her arm and her side to shield it from view, and walked out into the casino.

Nick was balanced on the tipped-over chair with the back of his head hanging an inch above the water.

Trace tossed a piece of dim sum into the pond and the water roiled with piranha, fighting over the morsel.

"All it takes is one piranha brushing against your cheek, smelling your flesh, and they'll all swarm on you," Trace said to Nick. "They'll eat your face right off your skull and then start chewing their way into your brain. That could happen any second now."

"I'd like to prevent that from happening," Nick said.

"Then tell me what you and Kate did to Derek Griffin."

"We wanted his half a billion dollars," Nick said in a rush. "We found out where he was hiding and decided the best way to get his money was to kidnap him. Make him pay a ransom to free himself."

Trace tossed another piece of dim sum just under Nick's head, and Nick could actually hear teeth gnashing, as the piranha chewed on one another in their mad lust to get a share of the steamed dumpling. He wondered if Kate, Boyd, and Billy Dee could hear it, too.

Kate could hear it. She didn't know exactly *what* she was hearing, but she knew it couldn't be good. She crossed through the crowded VIP salon toward the guard who was posted at the door to Trace's dining room. As she neared him, she whipped the baton open in her hand. It expanded to two feet of solid tempered steel with a satisfying metallic snap.

The guard reached for his gun. Kate whacked his arm, then his knee, and, as he fell, she brought the baton down across his back, finishing the job.

Kate dropped the baton and took the guard's holstered gun, trading up her weapon once again. If this trend continued, the next guard she disarmed would have a rocket launcher.

She rummaged through the guard's pockets, got his key card, and swept it over the sensor by the door.

"Did Griffin pay?" Trace asked Nick.

"Not the half billion, but we got ten million dollars out of him. We split that with the pirates and set him adrift in international waters," Nick said. "That's it."

Trace sighed in a show of disappointment. "You're still holding back. You haven't explained how Griffin ended up in Palm Springs two days later."

Trace tossed an egg custard tart into the water above Nick's head. The tart broke apart when it hit the water and the piranha went insane. The water boiled with them. The razor-toothed fish were jumping all around Nick's head. One of the monsters was bound to land on his face soon.

"We told some bounty hunters where they could find him," Nick said. "I've got no idea how he ended up in Palm Springs after that."

"Why would you give him to bounty hunters?"

"To protect ourselves," Nick said. "Griffin couldn't come after us if he was broke and in a prison cell."

"So you're just two lowlife swindlers trying to make a buck any way you can."

"Of course we are," Kate said.

Trace, Garver, and Dumah had been so caught up in the piranha frenzy happening around Nick's head that they hadn't heard Kate come in. Now there she was, standing on the bridge, aiming a gun at Trace. She had a strong and natural firing stance. She was firmly in control of herself. Trace saw beads of sweat on her chest, flecks of blood on her knuckles, and stony determination in her gaze. In that moment, she was the sexiest and most dangerous woman Trace had ever seen.

"Who else would have friends like Ould-Abdallah and Blackmore?" Kate said as she walked toward Trace, keeping her gun leveled at him as she did. "Who else would set up a junket to launder money through a casino in Macau? I don't know what kind of people you thought we were supposed to be. Missionaries, perhaps?"

Trace didn't move as she approached. "I see your point."

"Do you? You're making money on this deal and so are we. So what difference does it make what we did in the past? Are you in this business to make money or not?"

She stepped right up to him and pressed the gun barrel against his forehead. Trace looked her in the eye for a long moment. He thought about what she'd said and about the violence that she must have inflicted just to get to this room. He totally understood why Griffin risked everything to get her into bed.

"I guess I lost my head," he finally said.

"Not yet, but you almost did. The only reason your brains aren't all over the wall is because I don't want to jeopardize the money that we're making upstairs." Kate lowered the gun, handed it to Trace, and then looked past him to Dumah. "Don't just stand there, you dumb ape, get Nick out of that chair."

Trace gave Dumah and Garver a nod and the two men lifted the chair upright. Dumah cut the zip ties, freeing Nick's wrists.

"I'm disappointed in you, Evan," Nick said. "I thought you were a smart man. You could have made a lot of money with us. But after tonight, we're taking our business to the Grand Lisboa. Now if you'll excuse us, we've got a game running upstairs."

Nick put his arm around Kate, and they walked over the

bridge just as a bunch of security guards came rushing through the door from the VIP salon. Trace ordered the guards to stand down with a simple wave of his hand. The bewildered guards moved aside and let Nick and Kate pass.

"That was an amazing performance," Nick said once they were clear of the VIP salon and strolling casually through the casino toward the elevator.

"I was going to say the same thing to you," Kate said.

"I had the easy part," Nick said. "I just told them the truth with a lie or two thrown in. You had to intimidate them into folding."

"That's not so hard when you're holding a gun," she said.

"It wasn't the gun that sealed the deal," he said. "It was how you got there and what it revealed about you. I wouldn't want to get on your bad side."

"You have been on my bad side," she said.

Nick broke into a grin. "That's right, and it was a lot of fun. I kind of miss it. And by the way, did you notice you gave Trace a stiffie?"

"That wasn't me," Kate said. "He had it when I came in."

15

Trace sent everyone away except Garver and Dumah.

"I'm surprised that you let Sweet and Porter just walk out of here," Dumah said. "They're playing you."

"I'm a reasonable man and they made a convincing argument," Trace said. "Griffin was fair game, a swindler who got swindled. There's nothing wrong with what Nick and Kate did to him. In fact, I admire how they did it. It shows that they're smart and daring. The fact is, those two have done nothing to me but make me richer."

"It's just a part of their plan," Dumah said.

"I really like that part. But now it could be over because I let my curiosity override my good judgment," Trace said. "I have to find a way to apologize and win back their business."

"You don't want to do that," Dumah said. "They're liars and crooks."

"My best customers are liars and crooks. I can live with that. But do you know what I can't live with?" Trace stepped up to Dumah. "Underlings who question my decisions."

"I'm sorry, Mr. Trace." Dumah lowered his head. "I'm just trying to serve you better than I did Griffin."

"No, you want to avenge your honor," Trace said. "So listen to me very closely. If anything bad happens to Nick and Kate while they are in Macau, I will hold you personally responsible. If Nick stubs his toe and breaks it getting out of bed, it's on you. If Kate gets bitten by a mosquito and has an allergic reaction, it's on you. And the consequences for you will be extreme and disfiguring. Do I make myself clear?"

"Yes, sir," Dumah said.

"You can go now," Trace said.

Dumah nodded and walked out.

Trace watched him go. He would never admit it to Dumah, but he had taken the bodyguard's warning to heart. He wasn't going to act on it the way Dumah, or even Nick and Kate, would expect him to act. He was going to follow Nick and Kate's example instead. He'd swindle the swindlers.

Garver joined Trace at his side and gestured to the chair with a swing of his mallet.

"This wasn't a mistake," Garver said. "Now you know who they really are."

"And they know me," Trace said.

"That's a good thing," Garver said.

It certainly was. Because the next time one of them was in that chair, and Trace believed it was likely that one of them would be, they'd know that they deserved their suffering and that he had every right to thoroughly enjoy it.

Kate went back to her room to change her blood-splattered clothes, making a mental note to do more sucker punches to the throat and hand out fewer broken noses. She discarded the clothes, showered in steaming hot water, and dressed in an indigo cap-sleeved cashmere pullover and white slacks that were like a second skin thanks to a large percentage of spandex. She swiped on some lip gloss and mascara, pulled her hair into a ponytail, and returned to the VIP suite.

The woman who opened the door to the suite introduced herself as Birgita.

"Natasha has fallen ill," Birgita said. "It hit her very suddenly, but she'll be fine tomorrow. May I offer you a cocktail?"

Kate declined and went into the living room, where the game was still in progress. Billy Dee and Boyd were still seated at the baccarat table. They'd each bet $150,000 against the dealer. Nick had joined them.

"You're missing out," Boyd said to Kate. "Birgita makes an amazing lemon-drop martini."

He held up his empty glass to Birgita, who took it with her to the bar. "Another one, Mr. Blackmore?"

"Absolutely," Boyd said. "With lots of sugar on the rim."

"That's a manly drink," Billy Dee said. "Maybe you'd like some whipped cream on it, too? And a little umbrella stuck into it."

Boyd turned to Birgita. "Make sure the martini is shaken, not stirred."

"Now it's manly," Kate said.

The four of them shared a smile. It was an acknowledgment that they were glad to be together again, alive and well.

They could have stayed at Côte d'Argent for dinner, but Billy Dee was eager to explore Macau and see what remained of the dangerous port city he once knew. Kate, Nick, and Boyd were glad to join him after being cooped up in the suite all day. They'd gone from the chopper to the car to the hotel without really stepping outside. They were in Macau, but they could have been anywhere.

They left the casino and followed the tiled sidewalks along Avenida de Almeida Ribeiro toward Senado Square, the heart of the old city. The sidewalk was a uniquely Portuguese mosaic of black and white stones, known as *calçada portuguesa,* that had been painstakingly laid by hand to depict the fish, boats, and sunshine that had been vital to Macau's economy before the casinos came along.

The tiles in Senado Square had a wave pattern that became dizzying, almost animated, when it was revealed in glimpses beneath the feet of the hundreds of Chinese tourists and

Macanese locals in the wide plaza. Kate kept her eyes up, taking in the pastel-colored neoclassical buildings around her, each one filled with history and one with a crowded McDonald's.

Billy Dee shook his head with disgust as they passed the McDonald's. "There used to be a terrific whorehouse in there."

"This is better," Boyd said. "They have a dollar menu."

"They had a dollar menu at the whorehouse," Billy Dee said.

"Do we have a destination?" Kate asked.

"Lorca's Hideaway," Billy Dee said. "Hopefully it hasn't been taken over by a Gap. Back in the day, it was run by a one-eyed fisherman and opium addict. Fabulous Macanese food upstairs and the best opium den in the city in the basement."

"It would be a shame to visit Macau and not sample the opium," Boyd said. "It would be like going to New York and not having a hot dog."

There were several narrow roads spiraling off from the square. Billy Dee started to go up one of them, then abruptly doubled back, choosing to go on a different one. The road that he picked was crammed with people and weaved up through a tangle of side streets and dead-end alleys, toward the ruins of St. Paul's Cathedral. Both sides of the road were lined with *pastelarias,* open store fronts that sold cookies, candies, and sheets of meat jerky that were stacked like reams of paper. The competition between the *pastelarias* was fierce. Shopkeepers cut samples from the jerky with scissors and used tongs to thrust pieces of meat out at the passersby. Other shopkeepers held out baskets and platters of cookie pieces. It created a bottleneck. People bunched up as they stopped to grab samples or avoid colliding into someone.

When Billy Dee doubled back Kate caught three men in her peripheral vision who doubled back with them. She couldn't see their faces, but she had a fix on their clothes and their size. The men were doing their best to stay close but were hugging the walls to avoid being caught behind in the bottleneck or, worse, being shoved up against their quarry.

Kate sampled the thick boar fillet from one *pastelaria,* the top beef filet with black pepper from another, then zigzagged across the street for a taste of spicy pork with abalone sauce. Along the way she managed to steal a pair of greasy scissors from a shopkeeper's apron pocket.

"Where is Lorca's?" Kate asked Billy Dee.

"On Travessa da Fortuna," he said. "It's a side street that's coming up."

"You keep going," Kate said. "I'll catch up with you."

Nick kept his gaze focused in front of him as he navigated through the crowd. "You're worried about the three guys following us."

"When did you spot them?" she asked.

"When Billy Dee changed his mind about which street to take," Nick said.

She wasn't surprised that he'd noticed the tail when she did. He'd been a con man and a fugitive for years, so looking over his shoulder for the police or someone that he'd swindled had become instinctive.

"I picked up a pair of scissors, if you'd like them," Nick said.

That didn't surprise her, either. He was a gifted pickpocket. "Already got my own, thanks."

"I've also got tongs and an entire sheet of pork neck jerky wrapped in paper."

"Now you're just showing off."

They turned right onto Travessa da Fortuna, a tight, dark alley that dead-ended at a retaining wall with a mossy concrete staircase cut into it that went up the hillside. The only light in the alley was cast by the windows of a small restaurant in a lopsided old stone building that seemed to be leaning against the retaining wall for support.

Billy Dee, Boyd, and Nick went on ahead toward the restaurant, but Kate slipped into a dark alcove, pulled out her scissors, and waited. On the stoop beside her, there was a smoking stick of incense in a small bucket of ashes. The bucket was on a decorative platter with a lemon, dried flower petals, and several small cups of tea. It was a shrine, left for good luck by whoever lived or worked behind the closed door. Kate put the scissors in her back pocket and picked up the bucket of ashes. She said a small silent prayer, asking forgiveness from whoever or whatever was in the bucket. And as the three figures passed the alcove, she heaved the ashes on them. She leapt out while they were blinded and coughing, smacked one across the face with the bucket, hit another in the groin, then whirled around, taking out the third with a spin kick. She whipped the scissors out of her pocket and jammed them against the throat of the guy she'd hit with the bucket. His head was covered with ash, but she recognized him. It was Dumah.

"Did Trace send you, or is this personal?" Kate said.

"No, you've got it all wrong," Dumah said, coughing on the ash.

"You boys weren't just out for an evening stroll." Kate looked over at the other two men, who were getting slowly to their feet. One was the man she'd fought in the Côte d'Argent stairwell, the other was the guy who'd been guarding the door to Trace's dining room. They all had good reason to want her dead. "Were you looking for an opportunity to kill me or just give me a good beating?"

"We're here to protect you," Dumah said. "Mr. Trace has put us in charge of your safety. If anything happens to you in Macau, we'll be held accountable."

"So do us a favor and stay out of dark alleys while you're here," the stairwell guy said, slightly pitched forward, his hand cupping his privates.

This was the second time she'd assaulted him today. She almost felt sorry for him.

"And please watch what you eat," the other guard said. "Make sure the egg tarts are fresh and avoid oysters."

"You're in trouble even if we get food poisoning?" Kate asked.

"We don't want to find out," Dumah said.

Kate saw the fear in his eyes and didn't think it was from the scissors at his throat. "Have you ever considered a different line of work?"

"Not until today," he said.

The dining room décor and the menu at Lorca's hadn't changed since Billy Dee's day, but everything else was different. The one-eyed opium addict who'd established Lorca's had died, and the restaurant was now run by his grandson Ernesto, who'd honed his culinary skills in the finest kitchens in Lisbon and Hong Kong. The opium den downstairs had been turned into a coffeehouse and performance space used mostly for poetry readings. The customers appeared to be clean-cut and middle-class. The only pirates, con men, and thieves in the room, as far as Kate could tell, were the four of them.

They ate pork-stuffed squid, grilled sardines, deep-fried salted cod balls, and *minchi,* a bowl of minced meat, onions, cheese, soy sauce, and a fried egg. Kate thought the food was incredible. It was a tasty fusion of Portuguese and Chinese flavors, unlike anything she'd had before. Billy Dee remained sour faced throughout the meal.

"What's wrong with you?" Boyd asked him.

"Macau has lost its charm," Billy Dee said. "All of the danger is gone."

"I almost got killed today," Nick said. "Doesn't that count?"

"It's not the same. The only person attacking anyone in dark alleys with knives these days is Kate, and she lets them live."

Billy Dee tipped his head toward the front window, where they could see Dumah and the two other security men milling around outside, smoking cigarettes.

"Technically it was a pair of scissors," Kate said. "And I let them go because they're protecting us."

"From what?" Billy Dee said. "A painful reading from a desperate poet? Seeing Macau today is like looking at a toothless lion. It's sad and pathetic."

"Your disappointment with Macau aside, this trip has been a smashing success," Nick said. "I toast you all."

He raised a glass of 2011 Douros Muxagat Tinto, a fine Portuguese wine, to them and took a sip.

"But isn't the show over?" Boyd said. "You told Trace that you're finished, that you're taking your business to the Grand Lisboa."

"So that's it," Billy Dee said. "We're done. It would be extremely suspicious if you went back to him after what he did to you."

"You're absolutely right," Nick said. "That's why it's the best possible thing that could have happened for the success of our scam. Now we don't have to entice Trace into our scheme. He'll come running to us. He'll do whatever he can to win back our junket business."

"How can you be so sure?" Kate asked.

"Because his ego won't allow him to let us take our money elsewhere," Nick said. "That would be losing."

"If he's got such a big ego," Billy Dee said, "he's not going to humble himself by apologizing to you and groveling for your money."

"He won't see it that way," Nick said. "He'll see it as using his awesome powers of persuasion on us. And when we say 'Yes, we'll come back,' he'll love us for it. We'll be in solid. Having us around will reinforce his image of himself as absolutely irresistible. Look at it from his angle. Why else would we go into business with him again, and overlook the terrible things that he did to us, unless he was amazing? Best of all, because we walked away, our legitimacy never comes into question again."

"So he's conning himself and doing our work for us," Kate said.

"Wonderful, isn't it?" Nick said.

"It's a thing of beauty." Kate raised her glass to him. "If it works."

And if it doesn't, she thought, by her calculations they'd just given a crook $625,000 to keep up his good work.

16

Kate got out of bed the next morning, opened her drapes, and stared at the Wynn and MGM Grand across the street. To her right, on the tip of the peninsula, was the thousand-foot-high Macau Tower, a Chinese version of the Seattle Space Needle.

She was about to turn away when she saw someone dive off the Macau Tower to certain death. Her breath caught in her throat and she pressed her face against the glass, wincing into the glare, when she saw another person jump. It took her a moment to realize that both people were tethered to bungee cords and that leaping off the tower was some kind of tourist attraction. Even so, it was a startling way to start her day. But at least she could inform Billy Dee that it was still possible to cheat death in Macau.

. . .

She showered and dressed in a sleeveless black knit top, black jeans, and her trusty ballerina flats. Breakfast was being served down the hall, in the VIP gambling suite.

Nick, Boyd, and Billy Dee were already there. They were eating fresh fruit, pumpkin cakes, steamed milk pudding, and eggs that were scrambled with onions, vegetables, and minced *bacalhau,* fried Portuguese salted cod. They were being served their breakfast by Natasha Ling, who greeted Kate with a warm smile, as if she was genuinely pleased to see the woman who'd decked her.

"I hope you had a restful evening," Natasha said.

"Likewise," Kate said.

"What would you like for breakfast?"

Kate took a seat beside Nick. "I'll have whatever they're having."

"Very good. I'll be back in a moment."

Natasha went away to wherever the eighth-floor VIP kitchen was hidden, and Birgita came to the table with a silver tray that held a platter of donut holes and four large red paper cups with the Tim Hortons logo on them.

"Would anyone care for an extra-large Caramel Latte Supreme and fresh Honey Dip Timbits?" Birgita asked.

"I'll be damned," Boyd said. "Where did you get that?"

"There's a Tim Hortons in Dubai. We sent our private jet and one of our chefs there yesterday for you." She handed Boyd a cup. "Careful, it's very hot."

Boyd handled the cup gingerly, cracked open the white lid,

and sniffed the aroma with obvious pleasure. "Nice. Why did you send a chef?"

She used silver tongs to delicately place a few Timbits on his plate as if they were exquisite gourmet pastries instead of glazed donut holes. "It was his responsibility to keep the coffee and Timbits at the optimum temperature to retain their flavor, consistency, and freshness during the seven-hour flight. The jet landed in Macau just a few minutes ago."

"Now *that's* service," Boyd said. "You've all got to try this. Best coffee and donuts on the planet."

Birgita passed out the coffees and Timbits to each of them. Kate tried one of the Timbits and nodded in appreciation.

"It's donut hole perfection," she said.

Billy Dee sipped the coffee. "I must admit that it's a fine cup of joe."

"I agree," Evan Trace said, strolling into the room with a large Tim Hortons coffee cup in his hand. "Maybe I should talk to Horton about opening an outlet here in Côte d'Argent."

Trace probably could have built a Tim Hortons for what it cost him to make that coffee run to Dubai. But in the cosmic scheme of things, Kate knew, the gesture was inexpensive compared to the money he'd already earned from them and the profits he stood to lose if they took their business elsewhere.

"You do and I'll never gamble anywhere else," Boyd said.

"I'll hold you to that," Trace said with a smile. "Nick, Kate, could I please have a word with you in the living room? Bring your coffees with you if you'd like."

Kate and Nick got up and followed Trace into the living room. They were still within view of Boyd and Billy Dee but presumably out of earshot if they kept their voices low. Kate knew Trace did that to make them feel safe. Trace didn't know, of course, that Boyd and Billy Dee could hear every word on their earbuds.

"I understand that you stopped by the Grand Lisboa last night and had drinks with the manager of guest relations," Trace said.

Nick and Kate knew that Dumah had probably dutifully reported that to Trace last night.

"We were in the neighborhood," Nick said. "We didn't want to miss the opportunity to establish a personal relationship with the people we might be doing business with on our next junket."

"I don't blame you," Trace said, a somber expression on his face. "You had a very unpleasant experience here yesterday."

"That's an understatement," Kate said.

"Yes, it is. We've comped your rooms, of course. But that doesn't go nearly far enough. You and your guests lost six hundred and twenty-five thousand dollars at the baccarat table. I have wired that amount, along with the two million that you lost playing blackjack in Las Vegas, to your bank account in St. Kitts," Trace said. "You aren't out a dime to me and you're up six hundred and twenty-five thousand if you choose not to share the refund of yesterday's gambling losses with your guests. Whatever you decide, it will remain our secret. I just hope this small gesture demonstrates my remorse, the sincerity of my apology, and my fervent hope that we can begin a new relationship built on a foundation of mutual trust and respect."

Trace didn't wait for a response to his contrition speech. He bid them farewell with a slight nod and walked out of the suite. It was a classy exit.

Nick and Kate remained stony faced, although they were cheering inside. Natasha and Birgita were watching and would definitely report to the boss.

"He's hooked," Nick whispered.

"Yeah," Kate said. "We should have asked him to reimburse us for the jet."

"Better yet, I think we should let him know there are no hard feelings by bringing him a new whale. Preferably one from Hawaii with Yakuza money."

They went back to the table and finished their breakfast. An hour later the four of them were on a Côte d'Argent chopper headed to Hong Kong International Airport to begin their long journeys back home.

The day after Kate got back from China, she went to her sister Megan's home in Calabasas to relax in Megan's backyard. Megan and her family lived in a Spanish-Mediterranean McMansion on a hillside that overlooked the Calabasas Country Club and the San Fernando Valley. They had lots of comfy outdoor furniture, a pool, a Jacuzzi, and a barbecue island with a smoker, a bread warmer, and a refrigerator. Kate considered the place her own personal resort. So did her father, who lived on the property in a detached garage that had been converted into an apartment.

Kate and Megan were sunbathing on side-by-side chaise longues, drinking homemade sangrias and sharing Nacho Cheese Doritos from a huge bowl on the table between them. Kate was in a black bikini and Megan wore a floral "miracle-slimming" one-piece with a skirt that was supposed to hide her butt, though there was no one around to hide it from. Roger was at work, Jake was on the golf course, and the kids were at school.

"While you've been away, we've been terrorized by coyotes," Megan said. "They're killing pets and crapping all over everybody's yards. Dad wants to shoot them, but that's illegal. So he's come up with another approach."

"He's planting land mines on the hillside?"

"Even better. He and Roger go out at night and pee all around the yard."

"You're making that up."

"It's true. Roger read somewhere that human pee keeps the coyotes away."

"I bet a guy wrote the article just to give other guys an excuse to pee outdoors."

"Men are strange," Megan said, taking a sip of her sangria. "While we're on the subject, anyone new and exciting in your life?"

"Maybe," Kate said.

"I knew it." Megan sat up on the chaise longue. "Have you had sex with him yet?"

"There is no sex."

"But there's heat," Megan said.

"Scalding," Kate said.

It was the first time Kate had admitted to the attraction out loud, and she was surprised that she said *scalding*. *Scalding* was pretty heavy-duty in terms of attraction.

"So what's the problem?" Megan asked.

Kate sipped her sangria. "We're co-workers."

Megan dismissed the comment with a wave of her hand that ended with her scooping a bunch of Doritos from the bowl. "Nobody at the FBI has a life except at the FBI, so don't tell me everybody isn't sleeping with everybody. You'll have to do better than that. What's his name?"

"Bob," Kate said.

"Bob," Megan said, clearly not buying it. She ate a couple of chips and stared at Kate. It was an effective interrogation technique that Kate had used herself.

"I can't tell you his real name because he's an undercover agent. In fact, he's been undercover for so long that he's spent more time as a criminal than an FBI agent," Kate said. "I think he actually prefers being a criminal. He enjoys breaking rules, defying authority, and being unconventional. The thing is, that's what makes him so good at what he does."

"I can see how that would drive you crazy," Megan said.

"I believe the rules exist for a reason."

"I meant crazy horny," she said.

"Oh," Kate said. "There's some of that."

"There's a *lot* of that or we wouldn't be having this discussion," Megan said. "Bottom line, you want to sleep with Bob but you're not. So let's see if we can figure out what's really holding you back. What are his pros and cons? Pros first."

Kate began ticking them off on her fingers. "He's charming, funny, adventurous, romantic, daring, and hot."

"Cons?"

"He's dishonest, manipulative, egotistical, reckless, and hot."

"I noticed *hot* is in both columns. Your problem is that you live for the chase," Megan said. "It's like what happened with Nicolas Fox."

Kate froze for an instant. "What does Fox have to do with this?"

"I saw how happy you were when you were chasing him, and how miserable you were when you finally caught him, and how thrilled you were when he escaped so you could go back to chasing him. It's the Fox Complex all over again."

"You've given it a name?"

"We've talked about this a lot," Megan said.

"We?" Kate said. "Who is *we*?"

"Me, Roger, Dad, and the kids."

"The kids, too?"

"You're afraid if you catch this guy, you'll lose the excitement in your life and the goal-oriented sense of purpose that drives you."

"You've got me all wrong," Kate said, hearing the lack of conviction in her voice.

"So you're telling me that you won't be miserable if you catch Nicolas Fox."

"*When* I catch him, not *if*," Kate said. "It's going to happen."

"Okay, then, if the outcome is inevitable, what you should be thinking about isn't all the ways you can avoid getting what you want, but how to accept it once you have it."

"Are you talking now about me catching Fox or going to bed with Bob?"

Megan looked Kate in the eye. "It's the same thing."

Kate wondered if her sister really knew that it was, or if it was purely intuition or just a coincidence that she brought Nick into the discussion. Not that it mattered. Megan was right.

17

Kate showered, changed into a T-shirt and jeans, and walked into Megan's kitchen to find her sister cutting the crusts off sandwiches, leaving the crusts on the counter, and arranging the sandwiches on a plate.

"Wonder Bread, cold cuts, and Kraft cheese slices," Kate said. "Dad's favorite."

"He's always hungry when he comes back from the golf course," Megan said, sweeping the crusts off the countertop and into the trash masher. "You should have seen Dad when he got back from Hawaii. He was sunburned and covered in bug bites. I've never seen anyone so happy to be uncomfortable."

"That's what happens when you fall asleep on the beach."

"That's what happens when you sleep in the jungle," Megan

said, setting the plate of sandwiches on the center island in front of Kate.

"Why would Dad do that?" Kate asked, playing innocent.

"Nostalgia. Sometimes I worry that he's going a little crazy here."

"He's the same man he always was. He hasn't changed at all."

"I hope you're wrong. Because if that's true, and his pee stops scaring off the coyotes, he *will* start putting land mines on our hill," Megan said. "Where did all of your bruises come from?"

Kate helped herself to a salami and cheese sandwich. "What bruises?"

"The ones all over your body. Your bikini doesn't hide much."

"Kickboxing."

Megan raised an eyebrow, dubious. "Since when do you kickbox?"

"It's a great way to relieve tension."

"So is sex."

"Kickboxing is a lot less complicated."

"But you don't get the Big O."

"I can have all the Oreos I want. Kickboxing burns a lot of calories."

"That's not the 'O' I was talking about."

"You are oversexed."

"And proud of it. Look, Kate, I know a beating when I see one. Dad used to come back from his military missions with the same kind of bruises that I saw all over you. I know it's got to hurt, and I'm not just talking about the injuries that I can see. If you ever want to talk about it, I'm here."

"I know that." Kate gave her sister a hug. "But I can't."

"At least tell me the other guy looks worse."

"Other *guys*," she said. "And yes, they do."

Megan smiled. "That'll teach them to mess with my sister."

They heard the front door open and Jake came in, wearing a bright yellow Greg Norman golf polo shirt and white slacks.

"I thought you were a man who likes to blend in," Kate said. "I need sunglasses to look at you."

"It's a matter of survival. There are a lot of seniors with bad eyesight on the course on weekdays," Jake said. "You have to stand out or you could get hit by a golf ball."

Megan grabbed her car keys off the counter. Her huge key chain had six keys on it, a dozen charms that her kids had made, a tiny flashlight, and countless membership cards from various stores.

"I have to pick up the kids," Megan said.

"They don't get out of school for another hour," Jake said.

"If I don't park in front of Bay Laurel now, I'll get stuck for an hour in the pickup line and the kids will have to wait." Megan gave Kate a kiss. "It was great to see you. Let me know how it goes with Bob."

"You bet," Kate said.

Megan left the house and Jake selected a sandwich from the plate.

"Who is Bob?"

"Nobody you know. How are you?"

"Eager to hear how the con is going." He took a bite out of his sandwich.

"Things didn't quite go according to plan, but we think we've hooked Trace."

Kate told him all about what happened in Macau. By the time she was done with her story, Jake had eaten all of the sandwiches and finished a can of beer.

"Those men are lucky they're still alive," Jake said. "But what amazes me is that you got through all of that without sacrificing the con."

"It might even be stronger now."

"You and Nick are good together," Jake said. "Probably in more ways than you know."

"Let's not go there."

"You keep saying that to yourself, but maybe it's time for a rethink."

"Since when are you interested in my love life?"

"You don't have one. You're all about the job. With Bob, you can have both."

"You don't know anything about Bob."

"I know it's got to be Nick, because there isn't anybody else," Jake said. "Who could possibly compete?"

"Someone who isn't a criminal on the FBI's Most Wanted list for starters."

"How boring would that guy be? He couldn't match the excitement Nick brings to your life. For instance, what's up next in the scam?"

"A few weeks off," Kate said.

"Since when do you take a vacation in the middle of a scam?"

"We can't rush right back into business with Trace. Because if we do, it will seem suspicious after what he did to us. He's got to believe that it was a hard decision for us to go back to Côte d'Argent. Or he needs to come to us in the meantime. So now it's a waiting game."

"You're terrible at that game."

"I'm working on it," Kate said. "They say that patience is a virtue."

"That might be true," Jake said. "But in my experience, the virtuous are usually the first to die."

18

K ate spent the next few days in her cubicle at the Federal Building, catching up on paperwork. Not her favorite thing to do but part of her job. It was especially gruesome now that she was partnered with Nick, because the paperwork involved a secret expense account. She had to itemize and justify Nick's outrageous purchases, and she had to do it in code.

Purchased $1,200 size 5 designer bandage dress to disguise informant in sting operation, she typed as Special Agent Seth Ryerson came up behind her on his way to the coffee machine. He wasn't much older than her and was spending a lot of time cross-training and lifting weights to make up for his rapid hair loss. He was bulking up in direct proportion to how much his hair was thinning out. To cover his bald spots, he'd started using spray-on particles that resembled wet chocolate cake mix dumped on his head.

"I haven't seen you around much," Ryerson said.

"I'm not going to find Nicolas Fox or close my other cases by sitting at a desk," Kate said. "I do my best work in the field."

"The scuttlebutt is that one of those other cases involves high-stakes gambling."

"I can't talk about it," she said. "It's very hush-hush."

"I understand, but if you need help, I'd be glad to jump in. I know my way around a deck of cards."

"You don't strike me as a gambler. You break out in a flop sweat scratching a lottery ticket."

"You haven't seen me play bridge," he said. "Or canasta. I'm a warrior who doesn't take prisoners."

"You know those aren't big casino games, right?"

"Because they're too brutal," Ryerson said. "Anybody can play poker or blackjack. Those are for the timid. Tournament bridge is a blood sport. It's the cage fighting of card games, believe me. I've got the scars to prove it."

He showed her his hands, palms up.

Kate squinted at his hands. "What am I looking at?"

"This." He used his left hand to point at a barely perceptible line on the tip of his right index finger.

"It looks like a paper cut."

"It's a scar," Ryerson said. "It came from bridge. I've felt the sting. The point is, I've got the experience if you need someone to play any card games for you as part of your investigation."

Jessup walked past them toward his office. "Kate, could I see you for a moment?"

"Sure." She got up from her seat and edged past Ryerson. "Thanks for the offer. I'll keep you in mind."

Kate walked into Jessup's corner office and closed the door. He had an unobstructed view of the Sepulveda Pass to the north and could see clear to the Pacific to the west, but she was sure that he rarely ever noticed any of it. His desk was intentionally arranged so his back was to the window and he faced two walls.

"Ryerson just asked me about the gambling investigation I'm doing," Kate said. "You're the only one who could have put that news on the grapevine."

"I'm watching your back in case anyone sees you in Vegas, particularly at a buffet. There's so much illegal activity surrounding the gambling industry that the town is swarming with FBI, DEA, ATF, and IRS agents all investigating something."

"Why the special concern about buffets?"

"Because I've never met a federal agent or an ex-soldier who can resist all-you-can-eat, especially on an expense account."

"Good point," she said.

"How are things going with Evan Trace?"

"We've succeeded in firmly establishing ourselves in his money laundering operation and even got him to reimburse us for almost every dollar we've spent doing it," Kate said, hoping that reminding Jessup that she'd saved money would score her some points. "Now we're in position to set the trap that will take him down."

"That's good, because you're going to have to spring it right away," Jessup said. "The CIA has picked up some intel. A month from now an al-Qaeda representative is going to Côte d'Argent Macau on a junket to pass money to a terrorist cell planning an attack in Europe. We can't let that happen."

"The CIA could kidnap or kill the guy," Kate said.

"Of course the CIA will try, *if* they can ID him, but that would be a delaying tactic at best. Al-Qaeda will just find someone else to be their front man," Jessup said. "The best way to stop the money from changing hands is to destroy Côte d'Argent's money laundering operation."

"If we appear too eager to get back into business with Trace, it could rekindle his suspicions about us."

"That's a chance you'll have to take."

"Would you ever work with someone who'd dangled you over a pool of piranha?"

"Maybe I would if he gave me two million six hundred twenty-five thousand dollars and said he was very, very sorry," Jessup said. "Most criminals I know put money ahead of everything else. Rushing back into business with Trace might just prove to him how crooked you really are and bolster your covers."

"I hope you're right," Kate said.

"Me, too," Jessup said. "I've never had one of my agents devoured by fish before and I'd like to keep it that way."

. . .

Shortly after noon on the following day, Nick and Kate pulled into the red-dirt parking lot of Da Grinds & Da Shave Ice in Kahuku, Hawaii. Nick parked their blazing red Ferrari California convertible beside Lono Alika's brand-new Ford F-150 Raptor, which had a modified grill that resembled shark teeth. A big Hawaiian with his right leg in a cast sat in a folding beach chair in the truck bed, guarding Alika's ride from getting dinged by a tourist or blown up by any retired soldiers.

Nick and Kate got out and walked up to the restaurant's patio, where Alika held court. Kate wore a Versace black-and-violet leopard-print racer-back minidress with a pair of palazzo leather sandals. Nick was Gucci casual from head to toe in white-rimmed aviator sunglasses, a red cotton polo, white skinny jeans, and white canvas sneakers. They'd picked their ride and their designer clothes so that Alika would know they were young, rich, and lived the high life.

The monstrous Hawaiian was eating a multicolored shave ice with a plastic spoon that seemed ridiculously tiny in his massive paw. He was in his usual tank top and board shorts, showing off the Polynesian tattoos that covered his arms and legs. His eyes were hidden behind wraparound shades so dark, they might as well have been blindfolds.

A Hawaiian with a bandaged nose sat at the next table, and Neon Nikes stood nearby, with his right arm strapped to his midsection in a sling, stabilizing his wounded shoulder. Kate couldn't help smiling. Her father had left his mark on Alika's crew.

Neon Nikes glowered at her. "Watchu smilin' at?"

"You look like you were run over by a monster wave," Kate said.

"Why boddah you?" Neon Nikes said.

"Easy, brah, wassamattayou?" Alika said to Neon Nikes, and then he smiled at Kate. "Watchu want, sweet wahini? You likkah da shave ice, yeah?"

"Maybe later, Mr. Alika," Kate said, sitting down across from him. "I'm Kate Porter and this is Nick Sweet. We've come to Hawaii to offer you a deal."

"Wat kine deal you talkin'?"

Nick sat down beside Kate. "A VIP gambling junket to Côte d'Argent Casino in Macau."

"You travel agents, yeah?"

"Of sorts," Kate said.

"This would be more than a vacation," Nick said. "We know you've made a lot of money that you can't spend without attracting the attention of the authorities. Our junket offers you, and your associates in Japan, a way to move large amounts of cash to and from the islands."

"Dat sounds illegal," Alika said.

"For sure," Kate said.

"So, if I were you, I'd assume that we're both undercover feds," Nick said. "Don't say anything now that you wouldn't want to hear played back in a courtroom. All we're asking is that you let us make our pitch. If you like it, then you can check us out and we'll go from there."

Alika scratched one of his sleeveless intricately tattooed shoulders while he thought about Nick's proposition. "'Kay den, you have a shave ice an' talk story wit' me."

Alika told Bandage Nose to bring Nick and Kate each a shaved ice with a scoop of vanilla ice cream and another one for himself. While they ate, Nick explained how money laundering was done through junket gambling at Côte d'Argent Macau and how Alika, and his Yakuza partners, could benefit from it. When Nick was finished, Alika smiled at Kate.

"Wat you tink da shave ice?" Alika asked.

"Onolicious," she said.

Alika grinned and turned his bald, bullet-shaped head to Nick. "If you check out as fo' real, where you be?"

Nick passed a card to him with an address written on it and then stood up. "We'll be there for two days."

"I find out you no fo' real," Alika said. "I da kine come break your face fo' waste my time."

Nick took the threat in stride. He flipped Alika the *shaka*, the sign for "hang loose," his thumb and pinkie extended and his other fingers tucked against his palm, as he walked away with Kate.

Nick and Kate got into the Ferrari and headed south on Kamehameha Highway, the surf on their left, the mountains on their right, and the wind whipping their hair.

"That went well," Nick said.

"We won't know until he comes to us, either to make a deal or to smash our faces," Kate said. "But at least we got to try the best snow cones ever made."

"Where did you learn to understand pidgin?"

"The Navy. It's full of surfers. Where did you pick up what you know?"

"Hawaii Five-O," he said.

19

Evan Trace walked his Cotai Strip property. Right now it was just a ten-acre patch of dry earth and sand, dredged up from the bottom of the Pearl River Delta and moved around by a battalion of bulldozers, but Evan pictured a thirty-nine-story Côte d'Argent tower rising from a lake of fire. Flames would swirl atop the water and reflect off the black glass of the building.

The flaming water would be the signature image of his new resort and a radical departure from his *No freakin' gondolas* philosophy. But that was never based on a deeply held belief anyway. It was based on having *no freakin' money*. Now, in order to remain competitive and lure the international high rollers, he needed to think big, like everyone else around him.

Across the street was the massive Venetian Macao, the seventh largest building ever constructed by man and nearly twice the size of the Pentagon. To either side of the Venetian, Trace could see dozens of construction cranes, hurriedly building mega-casinos, a re-creation of New York's Broadway theater district, and a monorail system that would carry hundreds of thousands of tourists each year to the Cotai Strip. Trace would either become part of that explosive growth or he would be buried by it.

Natasha crossed over to him from one of the half dozen construction trailers on the edge of his property. She wore a white hard hat, which was a ridiculous safety requirement. Grading was the only thing being done now, and there was nothing that could possibly fall on her head. He wore a hard hat, too, but that was because his was gold-plated and identified him to everyone as the boss.

"Are you familiar with the Tiki Palace in Las Vegas?" she asked him.

"It's a cheap downtown casino that caters almost exclusively to Hawaiians, offering them cheap plane tickets, budget rooms, lots of nickel slots, and spam for breakfast," Trace said. "It's strictly small-time."

"Mr. Goodwell called me. He was asked by Sammy Mokuahi, who runs the Tiki, if Nick Sweet and Kate Porter are bona fide junket operators with us here."

There was no reason that Trace could think of for Nick and Kate to be interested in a dump like the Tiki. There wasn't any real money to be made there for junket operators in their league.

"Did Mokuahi say why he wanted to know about them?"

"He was asking as a favor for one of his good customers, a Hawaiian named Lono Alika," Natasha said. "So I checked out Alika. He's a big shot in the Hawaiian mob and runs the Yakuza's heroin, cocaine, and ecstasy sales on Oahu. He also exports Hawaiian-made meth back to Japan for distribution there. What should we tell Mr. Mokuahi?"

Now it all made sense to Trace. He could think of only one reason why Alika would ask somebody he trusts in the casino business about those two. Nick and Kate had invited Alika to Macau on a junket. "Tell him that Nick and Kate do big business with us and that Evan Trace personally and enthusiastically vouches for them."

She cocked an eyebrow. "May I ask why you'd do that?"

"Those two obviously have an amazing range of contacts. Canadian mobsters, Somali warlords, and now the Yakuza as well," Trace said. "Those are some major high rollers they're bringing us. So hell yes, I want their business, and I am going to get it."

Natasha did a slight bow. "Very well, sir."

Once again, Trace was amazed with himself. The $2.6 million that he'd given back to Nick and Kate was a daring gamble, and it was already paying off. It was gratifying to know that his instincts bordered on clairvoyant and that his powers of persuasion were nearly irresistible.

And he had to admit, he was looking forward to welcoming

Kate Porter back into his life and enticing her into his lair. He had romantic plans for her, and he was sure she'd find those plans to be *excruciatingly* pleasurable.

The turquoise water was eighty degrees and clear at Kailua Beach. The stretch of sand was lined with multimillion-dollar homes, widely spaced apart and set back among tall, slender palms, flowering plumerias, and colorful hibiscus hedges.

Nick had rented a plantation-style retreat with an ocean-facing veranda. He and Kate were hanging out on the porch, enjoying the view and sipping pomegranate iced tea. They were side by side on a thick-cushioned wicker chaise longue that was as big as a king-size bed.

"I'm feeling lucky today," Nick said, looking out at the surf. "Let's go swimming."

"How does 'lucky' equate to swimming?"

"You would put on a little bikini, and we'd go into the water together, and then I'd get even luckier."

"That's a fantasy."

"True, but I plan to make it a reality."

"Not gonna happen."

"It's inevitable. I always thought we'd eventually get together," Nick said.

"Well, so did I, but I imagined it would be in an interrogation room, a courtroom, or your jail cell."

"This is better."

"I suppose, but it was fun when I hit you with a bus."

"Yeah, and I enjoyed crashing into you with the armored car." He moved close and kissed her just below her ear. "Thinking about it gets me feeling romantic."

"Listen, mister, there's no romance."

"Okay," he said, "no romance. Just hot, sweaty sex."

"No!"

"Just a little."

"No."

"A kiss."

"Maybe a kiss."

His mouth found hers and some tongue got involved. It might have been Kate's tongue that started it. Or it might have been his. It was definitely Nick who started the groping. Then again, she wasn't far behind. His hand was under her shirt, cupped around a breast when a shadow fell over them.

Kate looked up to see if a cloud was blocking the sun, and gasped when she saw that it was Lono Alika standing over them.

"Mr. Alika," Kate said. "What a nice surprise."

"Dis a bad time fo' you?" Alika asked.

"No, not at all," Kate said, sitting up, rearranging her clothes. "We're glad to see you."

"Da bruddah don't look so happy."

"Maybe you could come back in an hour," Nick said.

"You tink it take dat long?" Alika asked.

"Nick's just kidding," Kate said. "What have you heard about us?"

"Good tings or yo' face be buss'up already, yeah?" Alika sat down on the edge of the chaise. The wicker crackled under his enormous weight, but it held. "I'm in for two mil. When do we go to Macau?"

"In two or three days," Nick said. "I'll make all of the arrangements and get in touch with you."

"One ting," Alika said and held up one of his huge hands. "You see dis?"

"That's a big hand," Nick said.

"Look closah. You see da lines here?" He pointed to faint white scratches that crisscrossed the dark skin on the back of his hands, between the knuckles. "You know wat dat from?"

"Breaking faces," Kate said.

"Dat's right. Back in da day, I used to hammer a lot o' faces, yeah? I'd get all kine o' teeth stuck in my skin. Dat my old life." Alika leaned close to them. "But I will do worse to you if I get screwed."

"We can't guarantee that you won't lose everything," Nick said. "That's up to you and your luck."

"I lose my money, dat's okay," Alika said. "*You* lose it, dat's death. Fo' you, fo' sure."

The threat didn't bother Kate. It reassured her that at least Alika would behave as they'd hoped and that maybe, barring any more bad luck, like Dumah showing up, Nick's ballsy con would go exactly the way they'd planned.

"Fine," Kate said. "We're in business."

·   ·   ·

Nick and Kate spent the rest of the day and the next making all of the necessary financial and travel arrangements to get themselves, Lono Alika, Boyd Capwell, Billy Dee Snipes, and $15 million to Macau.

On the morning of their third day in Hawaii, Nick and Kate met Alika in front of their private jet on the tarmac at Honolulu International Airport. Alika was in his usual tank top, board shorts, and flip-flops, as if he were heading out for another day at the beach instead of to a casino in Macau.

"Ho, brah, dis is choice," Alika said, referring to the plane.

"The only way to fly," Nick said.

"I like yo' style." Alika climbed inside, grabbed two beers from the galley, and dropped himself into one of the big chairs. "I'm gonna chillax, dat okay witchu."

"Go for it," Kate said.

Once they were in the air, Alika washed down a pill with a bottle of beer. Kate assumed it was a sleeping pill, because thirty minutes and three beers later, he was out cold. Loudly snoring and farting his way across the Pacific.

Kate and Nick moved to the rear stateroom, settled onto one of the couches, and watched three of Nick's favorite movies: *The Sting* with Paul Newman and Robert Redford, *The Thomas Crown Affair* with Steve McQueen and Faye Dunaway, and the original *Ocean's 11* with Frank Sinatra and the Rat Pack.

"I'm sensing a theme here," Kate said when the movies were over.

"Just getting myself in the mood."

"For what?"

"For work."

The plane arrived in Macau in the late afternoon of the following day. Two Rolls-Royces, one for Lono Alika and his enormous girth and one for Nick and Kate, were waiting at the airport to transport them the seven miles to Côte d'Argent.

Natasha Ling greeted them in the lobby with the key cards to their eighth-floor rooms. Boyd and Billy Dee wouldn't be arriving until later, so the games in the VIP suite wouldn't be starting until the next day.

"Two questions, yeah?" Alika said. "Where da women an' where da buffet?"

"We're going to leave Mr. Alika in your very capable hands," Nick said to Natasha.

Natasha smiled politely and inclined her head. "Of course."

Kate couldn't blame the hostess for going pale under her makeup. If Kate had been tasked with keeping Alika happy she would have handed in her employee name tag and taken the first plane off the island.

Nick walked Kate to the elevator. "I'm going to the casino floor for some blackjack," he said. "Would you like to join me?"

Kate shook her head. "No. I'm going to my room to take a shower and do some paperwork."

"What paperwork?"

"Our expense account, for one thing. Helicopters, private jumbo jets—"

"It wasn't a jumbo."

"You order expensive wines and caviar. You rent sports cars."

"You should be happy I'm not stealing them."

"And you buy me designer dresses that are too small. How am I going to explain all this to Jessup?"

"They aren't too small. They fit you perfectly, and you look amazing in them."

"Thank you, but that's not the point."

"Of course it's the point. You're a distraction."

"Oh great. Oh joy." Kate flapped her arms. "Now my role is reduced to being a *distraction*. That's all I am in the grand scheme of our partnership."

"You're more than just a distraction," Nick said.

"Oh really? Like what?"

He pulled her flat against him and kissed her. Their tongues touched, and Kate got a rush that rivaled the time she parachuted out of a rust-bucket plane in the middle of the night over Mount Athos.

"This isn't the time or the place for me to go into detail about what you mean to me," Nick said. "So let's keep it simple. You're *everything*."

"Um, okay then," Kate said, inching back, adjusting her shoulder purse. "G-g-good to know."

The elevator doors opened, and Kate stepped inside and pushed the button for the eighth floor.

"Be careful what you put online or on paper," Nick said. "I'm sure the instant we leave our rooms someone combs through them for information."

"Roger that."

The doors closed and Kate slumped against the wall of the elevator. *Everything*. Holy cow. He liked her. Maybe he even loved her. She was pretty sure she'd never been *everything* to anybody before. Maybe her father. Everything was *big*. She wasn't sure if Nick was *everything* to her, but he was definitely *a lot*.

Good thing she was such a badass, dedicated FBI agent or she might still be back there kissing Nick. Or worse, she might have dragged him into the elevator and pressed the hold button between floors. She looked around. Undoubtedly there were cameras, so good thing she didn't have her way with Nick between floors. They would have ended up on YouTube. She'd never hear the end of that from Megan.

She let herself into her suite and found that her bags had already been delivered. Nick had chosen blackjack as a way to unwind from a long flight. Kate opted for a run. She changed into a tank top, shorts, and running shoes and headed out.

Dumah was still on protection assignment and was caught unprepared for her jog. He was forced to keep up with her in his Dolce & Gabbana suit and dress shoes. Kate didn't make it any easier for him by running through the narrow, winding streets of the old town and up the grand staircase to the ruins of St. Paul's Cathedral. A three-story sculpted stone façade was all that remained of the ancient cathedral and was the required selfie backdrop for every Macau tourist.

She paused on the cobblestone plaza to look down at the tangled warren of European-style streets, the Forever 21 and Starbucks at the base of the grand staircase, and Dumah struggling up the steps. She smiled to herself as she jogged west across the plaza and up the much steeper steps to Mount Fortress.

Kate ran alongside the ramparts that bordered the park, all that remained of the fortress that had protected Macau for centuries from invaders. Now the dormant cannons that lined the battlements were aimed south at the Grand Lisboa and the invading forces of greed, democracy, and Forever 21. She noticed that there wasn't a single cannon pointed north anymore toward mainland China.

She headed back down the steps as Dumah was coming up. He was out of breath, his fitted dress shirt drenched with sweat, his wrinkled jacket clinging to his damp back.

He held up a hand to her. "Could we rest up for a minute?"

"Sure." She stood in front of him, bouncing in place to keep her heart rate up.

"Thanks." He leaned his back against one of the stone walls that were on either side of the steps.

"You're out of shape, Dumah."

"I'm a security guard. All I need are muscles and attitude. My work doesn't usually involve chasing."

"I wasn't running from you, I was jogging," Kate said. "If I was running, I would have lost you long before we got to the grand staircase."

"I wish you had," he said. "That was a lot of stairs."

"So what do you do when someone runs away from you?"

"They don't. I hit them or shoot them before they get the chance. Mostly I just need to look menacing."

"I suppose that's enough to handle most people."

"But you're not most people," he said. "I'm still trying to figure out what you are."

"Catch up with me and maybe you'll find out." She started jogging down the stairs.

He took a deep breath.

"At least it's downhill from here," he said to himself and jogged after her.

20

There was a fruit basket and fresh flowers on the coffee table when Kate returned from her run. The handwritten note stuck into the flower arrangement was from Evan Trace, inviting her to his penthouse for dinner in an hour. No mention of an invitation for Nick.

Great. Just fanfreakingtastic. Dinner with the megalomaniacal pervert. She shoved her earbud transmitter into her ear and she could hear the din of the casino floor and people shouting in Chinese.

"Do we still have money left?" she asked Nick.

"I'm on a roll," Nick replied. "I'm up seventy-five thousand."

"That's a relief," she said. "I have flowers and a dinner invitation from Trace. What am I supposed to do?"

"Enjoy the meal," he said. "But don't take the seat next to the piranha pond."

Kate showered and left the bathroom to stare at the clothes in her suitcase. She didn't want to send the wrong message by looking too sexy. A dress was definitely off the table. She didn't want to give Evan Trace an opportunity to slide his hand up her skirt.

She pushed the earbud back into her ear and connected to Nick. "I don't know what to wear," she said to him.

"Wear whatever feels comfortable. Go with your instincts."

"My instincts tell me full body armor, but I didn't bring any."

"Definitely not the red dress," Nick said. "I have erotic dreams about you in the red dress."

"I figured that one out on my own. I'm going with jeans and a T-shirt. I wish you were invited, too."

"I'll be there," Nick said. "You'll just have to be my eyes, ears, and hot body."

"Are you referring to my attributes or yours?"

"Yours, but I can see how that comment might have been confusing if you think I have a hot body, too."

"Now you're blatantly fishing for compliments."

"More like testing the water."

Kate wriggled into the jeans. "Where are you?"

"In my room," he said. "I've got a platter and a bottle of wine coming up."

"Are Billy Dee and Boyd going to be listening in on my dinner when they arrive and power on their earbuds?"

"Nope. I brought my clicker with me," he said, referring to the remote control, disguised as a key fob, that he used to control their transmitters, muting some and keeping others live. "You don't want too many voices in your head when you're trying to think."

"I'm not sure I even want yours."

She pulled out a red blazer that was stuffed into the corner of her bag.

"It would be there anyway, answering you when you ask yourself 'What would Nick do in this situation?'"

"I'd never ask myself that."

"You should when you're conning someone," he said. "I'd ask myself what you'd do if I was ever investigating something."

"Like that'll ever happen."

She checked herself out in the mirror. Her blazer was slightly wrinkled, but that was how she liked it. The only way she could be more comfortable was if she had her Glock holstered on her belt.

"Are you going to iron that jacket?" Nick asked.

Kate narrowed her eyes. "Have you got a camera in here?"

"Of course not. You swept the room for bugs already or we wouldn't be having this conversation."

He was right. She had a nifty device built into her iPhone protective case that detected bugs, audio or video, and it vibrated if it picked up any signal besides the unique one emitted by her earbuds.

"I just know you, that's all," Nick said.

"Then you'd know that I don't own an iron and I've never used one, at least not for ironing."

"What have you used one for?"

"Hitting a guy. He was coming at me with a knife and it was the only weapon handy."

"Irons are also handy for removing wrinkles from clothes that you've rolled up instead of folding."

"That's how we pack for an op in the military."

"Honey, this isn't an op in the military," Nick said.

Kate blew out a sigh. "So sadly true."

She laced up a pair of running shoes and headed to the elevators.

"Going silent," she said. "Showtime."

The elevator doors opened, and she stepped inside, slid her key card into a slot, and pressed the button for the penthouse. When the elevator doors opened again, Evan Trace stood there to greet her.

"Thank you so much for coming, Kate," Trace said. "I was afraid you might not accept."

"Curiosity overwhelmed me."

"You and the cat." Trace led her into the circular foyer that was lined with marble and lit by an enormous dragon-shaped chandelier.

"I'm counting on ending up better than the cat did," she said.

"That's a safe bet," he said.

"Never believe a casino owner who tells you that," Nick said. It was like he was right there, hiding under Harry Potter's invisibility cloak and whispering in her ear. *"There's no such thing as a safe bet."*

The foyer opened onto a wide living room that, like in the penthouse in Las Vegas, opened onto a terrace with an amazing view and an infinity pool that seemed to spill out over the city. On a table in the center of the room was an intricately detailed architectural model.

"I wanted to show you this." Trace stepped up to the table and swept his hand over the model. "It's the Côte d'Argent project that I'm building on the Cotai Strip."

A tiny neon sign atop the hotel tower model glowed with the words "Monde d'Argent." Lights were lit up in many of the windows, and tiny cars moved on the streets to create an illusion of activity. What grabbed Kate's attention were the actual flames that flickered from the water, in front of the casino mock-up.

"What's with the fire?" she asked.

"I was looking for a striking, signature image for the resort so I hired some engineers to create a lake of fire, fed by hidden gas jets. Spectacular, isn't it?"

"Sure," she said. "But isn't it off-brand for you?"

"Brands evolve or they die. The attitude and décor inside the casino will still reflect a straightforward but elegant approach to gambling. But the fire is dramatic and it's going to be a big draw."

"Like the Mirage volcano, which you supposedly hate."

"The volcano is vulgar, crass, and over-the-top," Trace said. "This is a work of contemporary art that's striking, frightening, even sensual. That's a big difference. These flames represent sin in all of its myriad temptations."

"Clever," Kate said, trying not to look horrified. "Very impressive."

"I hope you'll be equally impressed with dinner," Trace said. "We're having a Matsuzaka steak, the best in the world, and also the most expensive. The meat comes from three-year-old virgin cows raised in the Mie prefecture of Japan. The cows are massaged each day, fed tofu and beer, and entertained with classical music. The result is perfectly marbled meat that literally melts in your mouth. I'm willing to pay the price because I appreciate the best of everything. That's why you're here, Kate."

Eek, Kate thought. She was getting massaged like a virgin cow.

"I appreciate the thought," she said, "but you don't know anything about me."

"I know that you're an exceptional con artist and a highly skilled killer."

"He must have read your dating profile on DesperateSingles.com," Nick whispered into Kate's ear.

Kate took a beat to clear Nick's voice from her head.

"What makes you think that I've killed anyone?" she asked Trace.

"I didn't say that you *have,* but it's obvious that you *could.* I believe that my men who fought with you are lucky they're still breathing."

"I had no reason to kill them."

"Did you come to Nick's rescue because you're lovers, or was it simply to protect your business interests?"

"What difference does it make to you?"

"I want to know how committed you are to him," Trace said.

"If you're asking if I'd ever betray Nick, or cheat him out of his share of a deal, the answer is no," she said. "But I'm a free agent."

"In all respects?"

"I don't belong to anyone."

The answer seemed to please Trace. "There's a reason why I wanted you to see the model of Monde d'Argent. It's a huge project, crucial to the future of my business, and it's going to come under attack from my competitors, criminal syndicates, and professional cardsharps. I need someone who can protect my interests from them and any other potential adversaries."

"You're offering me a job?"

"Head of security for Monde d'Argent," he said.

"Even though you think I'm a professional crook and a stone-cold killer."

"That's what makes you exceptionally well qualified for the job. I was a gambler, a swindler, and a cheat before I got into the management and ownership side of the casino business. A criminal background is an asset in this business. It gives you savvy."

"There's nothing like firsthand information," Kate said.

"Exactly. For instance, some of my management style comes from a mistake I made a long time ago. I got caught cheating by a casino, so they had one of their men smash my hands with a mallet."

"Like the man who works for you?"

"It's the same man. He did this to me." Trace held his mangled hand out for her to see.

"Horrible," Kate said. She'd noticed his hands at their first meeting and had tried not to stare, wondering if it was a birth deformity.

"Not at all," Trace said. "It was a learning experience."

Trace moved from the casino model in the middle of the room to a small table by the window. The table was set for two with candles and flowers and linen napkins. He selected a fork from one of the place settings, laid his hand flat to the table, and stabbed the fork hard into the back of his hand.

A wave of nausea rolled through Kate's stomach.

"So what did I learn from this?" Trace asked, clearly undisturbed by the fork stuck in his hand. "I learned that this is an excellent way to deter cheating. I learned that there are more monetarily rewarding ways to make a living than cheating. And I learned that I like extreme sensations." Trace pulled the fork out of his hand as if his hand were just a piece of meat. "My hands work fine, but I hardly feel a thing. Nerve damage."

Kate swallowed back her revulsion and put on her game face. This was a man who fed on fear and suffering. She didn't want to give him the satisfaction of seeing any of her real emotions. And she especially didn't want to show him anything he would interpret as weakness.

"Is stabbing yourself with a fork a regular part of your job interviews, or is that just your favorite parlor trick?" she asked him.

"Both," he said.

He set the fork on the table, and casually pressed one of the linen napkins to the bleeding wound. Natasha swooped in from the back of the room and reset the table with a clean fork and napkin.

"Are you interested in the job?" Trace asked Kate.

"I'll keep the offer in mind," Kate said. "It will be a year or more before Monde d'Argent is built. A lot could happen between now and then."

"I'm prepared to hire you now. You could run security here in the meantime. You've certainly proven that it needs to be beefed up."

"No, thanks," she said.

"We haven't even talked salary or perks."

"Maybe another time. I've had a long flight and I'm afraid the jet lag is catching up with me. I need to get some sleep before we host the junket tomorrow."

"Of course," he said. "You need to be at your best for your guests. Would you like me to send your meal to your room?"

"That would be appreciated."

"My pleasure," he said.

Trace walked Kate to the elevator. "We should do this again soon."

"I can't imagine how you'd top the fork," Kate said.

"Try," he said. "I'd like to hear any ideas you come up with."

She stepped inside the elevator, faced him, and slid her key card into the slot. "They could hurt."

"I hope so," he said, and then the elevator doors closed.

"I'm sorry I missed the hand stabbing," Nick said into Kate's ear. "Next time we'll have to strap a GoPro camera to your head so I get the video with the audio. This guy is freaking nuts."

"He stuck the fork into his hand, and I almost threw up. It was sick."

"Are you okay? Would you like me to come to your suite?"

"You want half of my steak, right?"

"No, sweet cakes, I want all of *you*."

Kate took a beat to steady herself. "I need time."

"The ball's in your court."

21

Natasha was waiting at the door when Trace returned to the suite.

"Mr. Ould-Abdallah and Mr. Blackmore have arrived," Natasha told Trace. "We have eyes on them both. Mr. Ould-Abdallah is visiting an opium den near the harbor and Mr. Blackmore is in the casino playing pai gow."

"What's Alika doing?"

"He's entertaining three prostitutes in his room," Natasha said. "He just had six bottles of champagne sent up."

"Alika has big appetites," Trace said. "I can appreciate that."

"Earlier tonight, he gorged himself on four lobsters and had drinks at the bar with this man." Natasha showed Trace a security camera picture on her iPad of a wiry Japanese man in a tight black turtleneck and black slacks entering the casino. "The man is not staying with us, but our facial recognition system got an ID. He's Richard Nakamura, a sales representative for a Japanese auto parts company that's owned by a senior Yakuza member. He usually gambles at the Galaxy."

"So he came here specifically to meet Alika. That confirms your intel that Alika is a pipeline to Yakuza's money and therefore a man we should make very happy. Make sure he has all the lobsters, champagne, and hookers he desires."

Trace untied the napkin from his deformed hand and examined the puncture wounds. The bleeding had stopped, but the skin was beginning to bruise from the impact of the fork.

"Does it hurt?" Natasha asked, taking his hand in hers.

"I'm feeling no pain."

"Neither am I," she said, squeezing his hand hard, making the wounds bleed again.

"Let's change that," he said and led her toward the bedroom.

Kate walked into the eighth-floor VIP gambling suite in the morning to find an enormous breakfast spread that included an array of Chinese, Portuguese, and Hawaiian dishes. There was also an assortment of Tim Hortons donuts, kettles of his coffee, and stacks of his signature paper cups.

Nick, Boyd, Billy Dee, and Alika were already gambling at the baccarat table, and Luisa was once again dealing cards. Natasha stood behind the dealer and tracked the wagers on an iPad. Birgita stood at the bar, ready to serve the gamblers whatever refreshments they wanted.

Alika was in his usual attire, from the wraparound shades on his head to the sandals on his huge bare feet, and he was the player being dealt the cards. Billy Dee was at the far end of the table, looking groggy.

"Good morning, gentlemen," Kate said. "How is your luck running this morning?"

"I got lucky last night an' it's still wit' me t'day," Alika said, sharing a leer with Boyd that conveyed the kind of luck that he was talking about.

"That's a different kind of luck," Boyd said. "And you paid for that."

"Dey was on da house, but I still got da luck," Alika said, flipping over his cards to prove his point. He had a five and a four. "See? Try beatin' dat rippin' poundah."

It was the dealer's turn. She flipped over her cards. She had a three and a seven.

"Ho!" Alika pounded his fist on the table and rattled everyone's chips. "We pumpin', brahs!"

Boyd nudged Billy Dee. "Wake up, Sheik, you won."

"I'm not sleepy," Billy Dee said. "I'm carefully considering my next wager."

He was also stoned, Kate thought, and set a cup of coffee in front of him.

"There's nothing to consider," Boyd said. "It's all about seeing which way the winds of luck are blowing." Boyd licked his right index finger and stuck it in the air. "It's blowing toward the Big Kahuna."

"Ass right," Alika said. "I plenny lucky."

Kate helped herself to a donut and coffee and joined Birgita at the bar. "What are the chances of getting one of those Matsuzaka steaks with a couple of eggs, over easy?"

"It's no problem," Birgita said.

Nick looked over his shoulder at Kate. "It's one of the best steaks in the world. Why bother with the eggs?"

"That's what makes it breakfast," Kate said. "Plus egg yolk is nature's steak sauce."

"You're going to dip a Matsuzaka steak in egg yolk?" Nick shook his head. "Sacrilege."

"I like da way you eat," Alika said to Kate, then shifted his gaze to Birgita. "Make dat fo' two."

The gambling went smoothly the rest of the day. Billy Dee, Boyd, and Alika established a friendly rapport as they gambled and gorged on the constant supply of food and top-quality liquor. Nick and Kate took turns at the baccarat table, keeping the game moving.

Billy Dee and Boyd each started the day with $5 million, Nick and Kate with $3 million, and Alika with $2 million. By the end of their eight hours of gaming, Billy Dee's slow and thoughtful approach had paid off. He broke even, while Alika was down $175,000, Nick and Kate had lost $500,000, and Boyd was out $1 million. It was a winning day for everyone. The casino was happy to make money. Boyd and Billy Dee were happy to gamble with someone else's money. Alika was happy to launder his illegal profits for a reasonable transaction fee, taken as gambling losses, while indulging all of his desires. And Kate was happy that no one had been killed.

Alika rose from the table and clapped Nick hard on the back. "Dat was to da bomb, bruddah, to da max. Tanks, eh?"

"Glad you had a good time," Nick said.

"How do I cash out?"

"Any way you like," Nick said. "You can trade the chips in with us for cash in any currency or we can wire the money to any account, or to anyone, anywhere in the world."

"What if I want to give some chips to a friend here in Macau?" Alika asked. Kate noticed he'd dropped the pidgin act and wondered if he was even aware of it.

"These chips have no value outside of this room," Natasha replied. "But we'd be glad to exchange them for chips of equal value that can be played, or cashed, in the casino downstairs by your friend."

As if on cue, there was a knock at the door, and Birgita led a lithe Japanese man into the gaming room. He was dressed in all black, including a black onyx ring and a black-faced Rolex Cosmograph Daytona watch.

"My name is Nakamura," he said. "I'm here to see Alika."

Alika lifted the bottom of his tank top to create a pouch,

swept a little more than half of his chips off the table into his shirt, and carried the chips over to Nakamura.

"Dis fo' you," Alika said, stopping in front of Nakamura. Alika shook his shirt, making the chips rattle. "Unreal, yeah?"

The Japanese man stared at Alika as if the Hawaiian had asked him to reach into a latrine.

Natasha quickly brought a silver tray and held it at Alika's waist. "If you'll give me the chips, Mr. Alika, I'll escort your friend to the cashier's window downstairs and exchange these for new chips or for cash, whatever is Mr. Nakamura's preference."

"That would be much appreciated," Nakamura said.

"'K'den, whatevah," Alika said, emptying the chips onto the tray.

Nick offered his hand to Nakamura and flashed his most winning smile. "I'm Nick Sweet. I organized this game. Perhaps you'd be interested in joining us next time."

"Perhaps," Nakamura said.

He declined the handshake and walked away with Natasha to the elevator.

Alika had just successfully laundered $2 million in cash, for himself and the Yakuza, Kate thought. The whole thing took less than two minutes. The FBI had not only let it happen, they'd enabled the unlawful transaction. Jessup wasn't going to like it. She wasn't thrilled about it, either. If the truth ever came out, it would be a huge scandal that would land them both in front of a Senate subcommittee and end with them in a federal prison.

Nick watched Nakamura walk away. "Friendly guy."

"You should see him when he isn't so relaxed," Alika said. "You can cash da rest of my chips an' wire da money to my Cayman Islands account."

"Will do," Nick said.

Alika leaned close to Nick. "Let's talk soon about doing dis ting again, brah."

"Anytime," Nick said. "Would you like to join me, Kate, and our other guests for dinner? I've got us a table at a five-star restaurant in Taipa that usually has a three-month wait."

"No, tanks, I'm going back to my crib an catch da next wave." Alika turned to Birgita, who stood nearby. "I'd like da same kine room service as last night, only one more of everyting."

"It will be our pleasure," Birgita said. "And with our compliments, of course."

Alika shot a grin at Boyd. "My lucky day."

22

Nick and Kate returned to Nick's suite after dinner. Nick switched off the transmission on their earbuds so they could hear Billy Dee and Boyd, but the two men couldn't hear them. Billy Dee was snoring and Boyd was singing in the shower.

"Things couldn't have gone better today if I'd scripted every moment," Nick said.

"The FBI laundered two million dollars in drug money for the Hawaiian mob and the Yakuza," Kate said.

"A key part of the con. We had to do it to draw in a real mobster and create a genuine threat."

"I know, but I still don't like it."

"I've corrupted my principles, too," Nick said.

"You have no principles."

"Not true. I was a criminal, running cons and stealing things for fun and profit. Now I'm doing it to put people like me in jail. I've betrayed the whole notion of honor among thieves," he said.

"Honor among thieves is a bunch of baloney."

"Maybe, but fear of reprisal is real. I'd be a dead man if the people I used to work with knew what I am doing now." He looked out the floor-to-ceiling window. In the distance, beyond the hills of Taipa, he could see the glow cast by the casinos on the Cotai Strip, lighting the sky. "You're still basically doing the same thing that you've always done, arresting people who break the law, only now you're being a bit of a crook to do it."

Kate nodded. She knew this to be true.

"At least we're having some success," Nick said. "Alika is already itching to come back and he hasn't even left yet. As a bonus, we've snagged a Yakuza soldier. After a shaky start, everything is going according to plan. A week from now, I'll run off with all of Alika's money, and the Yakuza will be screaming for blood. All you'll have to do is flash your badge at Trace and he'll run into your arms. Côte d'Argent will be finished, and so will Alika."

They went silent when through their earbuds they heard Boyd abruptly stop singing "Camelot" in mid-chorus. Someone was knocking on his door.

"Hold on, I'm coming," Boyd said. "Be right there."

Nick and Kate heard footsteps, and then a door opening.

"Evan," Boyd said. "What a surprise."

· · ·

Trace had a bandage wrapped around his hand and held a bottle of Evan Williams Single Barrel whiskey by the neck.

"I hope I'm not disturbing you, Mr. Blackmore, but I wanted to have a private chat with you before you leave tomorrow. May I come in?"

"I'm always glad to see a man at my door with a bottle of fine whiskey." Boyd was in his Côte d'Argent terry cloth bathrobe, which was cinched tight, but he cinched it even tighter as he stepped aside and let Trace in.

A new performance had begun, this one pure improvisation, unless Nick and Kate started giving him direction in his ear, which Boyd hoped they wouldn't. He wanted to let his character guide his artistic choices, to live in the moment, to be a trapeze artist walking on a razor's edge.

Trace went to the bar, opened the bottle, and poured out two glasses. "It's a cheap whiskey, only about twenty bucks a bottle, but it's my favorite. Straight out of Louisville, Kentucky. I won't drink any whiskey that doesn't come from the bluegrass state."

He handed Boyd a glass. Boyd took a sip and smacked his lips with pleasure. "Goes down nice and smooth, like caramel with a kick. But you didn't come here to talk whiskey with a bootlegger."

"You're a bootlegger, too?" Trace said. "I didn't know that about you."

Boyd didn't know that about Shane Blackmore, either, until that moment. It was exciting, making it up as he went along.

"I'm sure you know everything about me, right down to the brand of deodorant I use." Boyd sat down on the couch and put one arm up on the backrest, owning the space and showing how relaxed he was. Body language was an important part of his performance.

Trace took the armchair across from him, set his whiskey on the armrest, and ran a fingertip contemplatively around the rim of the glass.

It was bad acting, Boyd thought. Trace wasn't contemplating anything. It was for dramatic effect and it was amateurish, straight out of community theater.

"I have a business proposition for you," Trace said. "I'd like to invite you to come back to Côte d'Argent in a week or two and lose millions of dollars gambling. A colossal loss of ten to fifteen million dollars would be nice."

Boyd laughed. "I can see how that might be good business for you, but how does that benefit me?"

"Because your losses will actually be an off-the-books investment in the Monde d'Argent project that I'm building on the Cotai Strip," Trace said. "Over the next ten years, I guarantee that you'll reap ten times or more whatever amount you invest with me."

"So I get to launder my cash as gambling losses," Boyd said. "And right into a secret moneymaking ownership stake in a Macau casino."

Trace smiled. "Sweet, isn't it?"

. . .

Nick stood ramrod straight and absolutely still, as he listened to the conversation over his earbud. Kate thought he looked like a man in a minefield. And from what she was hearing, he'd already stepped on one and was obliterated.

"We're finished," she said. "Our whole con was built on our gamblers losing all of their money and Alika going after Trace for it. Now he's *asking* them to lose everything as an investment in his new casino."

"It's a brilliant scam," Nick said.

"He's just destroyed our entire operation! This is no time to be impressed."

"Let's not overreact. I want to know more about Trace's scam," Nick said and used his key fob to activate the transmitter in his earbud. "Boyd, get us the details."

"If the profit potential is so great, why share the pie with a Canadian mobster?" Boyd asked. "Why do you need my measly investment?"

Trace shifted in his seat. He was in the difficult position of admitting weakness while trying to demonstrate strength. It was an acting challenge, and Boyd was curious to see how Trace would overcome it.

"I'm a small casino operator and my pockets aren't nearly as deep as my competitors'," Trace said. "Opening Monde d'Argent is my biggest gamble yet but also a necessary risk if I'm going to succeed. The new Chinese president has launched an anticorruption campaign as a publicity stunt. It won't last, but for now, it has made mainland China's high rollers, the titans of industry and leaders of government, reluctant to gamble and draw attention to their wealth. It has hit the bottom line of all the casinos in Macau very hard."

"How much has Macau's gambling revenue dropped?"

"Forty-nine percent from the same month last year," Trace said. Before that bad news had a chance to sink in, he leaned forward and rested his arms on his knees, with an excited smile on his face. "But you have to look at it from a global perspective, Mr. Blackmore. Macau's gambling revenue last month was three billion dollars, and while that's a big drop, that's still half of what all the casinos in Las Vegas combined generate in *an entire year*. We're sitting on a gold mine. I can't let a temporary slowdown in my cash flow stop me from building Monde d'Argent and reaping decades of enormous profits."

Boyd admired the way Trace used his own enthusiasm and body language to mask the dire position he was actually in. Perhaps Trace wasn't as much of an amateur at acting as he thought.

"So because of these temporary, troubled times, you're willing to explore alternative funding options," Boyd said.

Trace grinned, leaned back in his seat, and took a sip of his bourbon. "I like the way you said that."

"It does take the stink off of it," Boyd said, twirling his mustache. "It makes what you're proposing almost sound legitimate."

"I'm going to Billy Dee's room," Kate whispered to Nick. "If Trace is making this offer to one of our players, he's going to make it to all of them. I want to record his conversation with Billy Dee."

"What good is recording the offer going to do us?"

"It's a crime," Kate said. "He's asking them to participate in an illegal conspiracy."

"What *we're* doing is an illegal conspiracy. Whatever you record is worthless as evidence."

Kate was already at the door. "Don't care."

"We need you to buy us some time," Nick said to Boyd. "String him along."

"I'm intrigued," Boyd said to Trace. "It's an ingenious and yet simple scheme."

"Thank you," Trace said.

"But I have some questions."

Trace opened his arms in a welcoming gesture. "Ask whatever you like."

"How would I lose?" Boyd asked. "Are you going to rig the games?"

"I would never do that. I believe in an honest game because the odds are tipped in our favor anyway. Play long enough and you're bound to lose."

"And if I don't?"

Trace shrugged. "You'll come back and lose it tomorrow. When you go home with some of our money, we know you're only taking a high-interest loan because you'll eventually return with what you've won and more. Our biggest profits are from winners, not from losers."

"Where do Nick and Kate fit into all of this?"

"The same way they do now. I don't want to lose their business or their access to potential under-the-table investors like you," Trace said. "Come here next time without them just to gamble . . . and lose big."

"If I make this investment, what's to stop you from reneging on the deal?"

"You'll kill me," Trace said.

"You *do* know me."

Billy Dee answered his door on the second knock.

"Trace is coming over any minute now to make you an offer," Kate said, "and I want to get a video."

The suite consisted of a living room, a small kitchen, a large bedroom, and an opulent bathroom. She stood for a moment, looking around for a place to put her phone that would provide a good angle for filming the discussion, but not draw Trace's attention.

She spotted Billy Dee's phone charging on the kitchen counter. Go with the obvious, she thought, swapping out Billy Dee's phone for her own, tipping her phone in such a way that it faced the living room.

"After you invite Trace in, I want you to sit in one of the easy chairs," Kate said. "Trace will want to sit across from you, not beside you. If you take a chair, that will force him to take the couch. If he does, he'll be facing the kitchen."

Kate didn't have the slightest idea yet how they would be able to use the recordings. The recording would be worthless as evidence in a court, but it might give them an upper hand in other ways.

Nick spoke up in both of their ears. "Trace just left Boyd. You can't leave now, Kate. If he's heading to see Billy Dee or Alika, he'll spot you in the hall."

There was a knock on Billy Dee's door.

"I'll hide in the bedroom closet," Kate whispered.

Billy Dee waited a couple beats before opening his front door to Trace.

"Sorry to bother you at this late hour," Trace said. "But I'd really appreciate a word with you."

"It's your hotel," Billy Dee said. "So make yourself at home."

Trace made the same pitch to Billy Dee that he had made to Boyd, almost word for word. Kate heard it clearly in the closet, thanks to the earbud.

"I like the idea of having a stake in Monde d'Argent," Billy Dee said. "I'm getting too old to hijack ships, and I want to protect what I've earned. But I'm a pirate by nature. I take things. I measure my wealth by what I've got in my hands. What are you going to give me so I know I've got a piece of your casino?"

"For obvious reasons, I can't give you any paper that shows you've invested in Monde d'Argent. No offense, but you're a known criminal and that could cost me my gambling license in the United States," Trace said. "What I can do is sign over deeds to you for condos in the new tower, equal to the value of whatever funds you give me."

"A couple of condos are not going to be as valuable as a percentage of your business."

"No, they're not," Trace said. "But until you see a return, and are assured that you can trust me, having those deeds in your pocket will reassure you that you've actually left Macau with something to show for your money."

"Have you talked to Blackmore? What did that loudmouth Canadian want in return for his money?" Billy Dee asked.

"He took me at my word," Trace said.

"He's a bigger gambler than I thought. Are my hosts in on this, too?"

"No, and I'd appreciate it if you'd keep this between us."

"And Alika, too, I suppose," Billy Dee said.

"I'll be talking to him next. I'm seeking investors with a certain profile, and Nick Sweet doesn't match it. Mr. Alika does."

"So you're using Nick to find guys like me. He thinks he's playing you, but you're playing him."

"Nick is making money out of this, so everybody wins," Trace said. "When does that ever happen in a casino?"

"Never," Billy Dee said.

23

Nick and Kate's flight back to Los Angeles the next morning on their private jet was a somber affair. Alika had taken a commercial flight back to Hawaii, so at least they'd been spared the prospect of spending a dozen hours trapped in the air with a three-hundred-plus-pound reminder of their failure.

"It's so incredibly frustrating," Kate said. "Here Trace is, on video, admitting to a crime. If Billy Dee and Boyd were really big-time crooks, and if this was recorded as part of a legitimate FBI sting operation, then Trace would be finished."

Nick selected a tea sandwich from the buffet that had been set out for them on the plane's credenza. "There was no way to know that Trace would turn this into an opportunity to run a scam of his own."

"We underestimated him."

"True."

"You don't seem very upset by this. We were supposed to take Trace down. Instead, we spent weeks and over a million dollars bringing Trace, Alika, and the Yakuza together so they could all get richer and more powerful while we got *nothing*. This looks to me like a disaster. And the worst part is that the next time al-Qaeda pulls off some horrific terrorist attack on foreign soil that kills scores of people, we'll have to live with the possibility that it was financed with money laundered through Trace's casino and that we blew our chance to stop it."

"We didn't blow our chance. We just hit a speed bump. We need to come up with an even bigger and better con than the original."

"Okay, I like that thinking. At the very least we have incriminating evidence that he's using gambling losses from criminals to secretly finance the construction of his new Macau resort casino. If this video got out, it might not put Trace in jail, but it would certainly cost him his gambling license in Nevada, and that would shut him down in Macau, too."

"The recording is inadmissible in court," Nick said. "Even if it wasn't, you'd have to admit that you were running a con with the international fugitive that you're supposed to be chasing, a retired Somali pirate who did covert ops with your dad, and an actor whose last role was in a talking-potato version of *Great Expectations*. We'd end up in prison, and Trace would still be free."

"As an FBI agent I should be able to do *something* with that video. Organize some sort of sting."

Nick grinned. "I've got it. You're absolutely right. We use the video. The way to save the con is by revealing that it *is* one."

"We're going to reveal to Trace that our junket operation is a scam run by an FBI agent and a con man?"

"Of course not," Nick said. "We're going to reveal it to Lono Alika. We're also going to tell him that Trace is in on it, too. The video is the proof. Why else would there be an incriminating video?"

"But that's a death sentence. Alika will go crying to the Yakuza and they'll come gunning for all of us."

"Exactly, which basically puts us right back where we would have been in our previous scam, if Trace hadn't screwed things up."

"It's insane," Kate said. "But it might work."

They spent the rest of the flight honing the details of the con and by the time they landed at LAX Kate was sold on the scheme. To pull it off, they'd need to work very fast, recruit some old friends, commit grand theft, blow up an $80,000 car, and stage a violent shootout with automatic weapons.

"Those are all the ingredients of a great con," Nick said as they got off the plane.

"Or a disaster that ends with us all in prison or graves."

"At least then you wouldn't have to worry about adding the car to your expense account."

The next morning Kate found her father on the hillside between Megan's backyard and the golf course below. Jake was in the bushes, digging holes in the dirt with a hand shovel. Beside him was an open rucksack full of soda cans that had batteries, electrical wires, and what looked like dabs of clay stuck to them.

She stepped off the patio and noticed a row of freshly dug, and refilled, holes in the slope. "You aren't planting land mines, are you?"

"Of course not," Jake said.

"Then what are you doing?"

"I'm burying small, pressure-activated explosives in the dirt."

"That's a land mine."

"These hardly count. They are no more dangerous than a cap pistol. When weight is put on them, they make a loud pop that will startle the coyotes but won't injure them."

"I still don't think the humane society would approve."

"I've got no choice. Our pee isn't working as a deterrent."

"This is where you and Roger have been peeing?"

"And some of my golfing buddies, too. It's been a great excuse to sit outside and drink a case of beer," Jake said. "There's a severe drought going on but you wouldn't know it by how moist this hillside is."

Kate stepped back up onto the patio and scraped the dirt off her shoe on the rough edge. "I've got something better for you to do. We're ready to make our move on Trace and we could use your help."

"Would the humane society approve?"

"Probably. There are no animals involved in what we're doing."

"I once ran a stampede of cattle through a South American village to free CIA agents being held hostage by rebels," Jake said. "The cattle came out of it fine. Can't say the same for the rebels."

"Our con doesn't involve a stampede. But there are explosives."

"Count me in." Jake put his things back in the rucksack, slung it over his shoulder, and stood up. "The kids can finish up this project."

"You've taught them how to make land mines?"

"I wouldn't be much of a grandfather if I didn't."

"*Suspiria* was a classic," Ainsley Booker said. She was the rail-thin, stringy-haired, flat-chested, braless, twenty-something publicist for the horror flick *The Last Town on Earth*. She was admiring Nick's faded *Suspiria* T-shirt that featured a naked woman hanging over a pool of blood. "Dario Argento is the man."

Nick was posing as a writer for *Fangoria* magazine. To play the part, he wore the *Suspiria* movie poster T-shirt, hadn't washed his hair in the two days since he'd returned to L.A., and drove up to the movie's Closter City location in a 2006 Chevy Cobalt. Closter City was a small central California town that was abandoned in the mid-1980s after it was feared some of the population had developed cancer from pesticide-contaminated groundwater.

"We worship Argento at *Fangoria*," Nick said. "They should carve his face on the Mount Rushmore of horror."

Ainsley gestured to Christian McVeety, the rotund eighty-two-year-old director who was standing in a jacket and tie behind the cameras in Closter City's weed-choked town square. McVeety watched intently as a gang of decomposing zombies with huge fangs chased two buxom screaming girls in halter tops and short-shorts past the cameras.

The movie took place after the human race had been decimated by a virus that turned most of the population into vampires. Now a handful of survivors were battling the last starving vampires, who wanted to breed humans like cattle. The humans were eager to breed, especially with buxom girls in halter tops and short-shorts. They just didn't want to be eaten, hence the conflict.

A production assistant stood directly behind McVeety with his hands palm out in a halting gesture. Nick was about to ask Ainsley what the PA was doing, but it became obvious when McVeety began to tip backward and the PA gently pushed him upright again.

"It's the PA's job to keep McVeety standing," Ainsley said, following Nick's gaze. "It's an honor. Film students line up for the opportunity."

"I'm sure they do. He's a legend."

"McVeety is old school, in the best sense. None of that post-production, green-screen, CGI crap for him. If it's not in front of the camera, it's not in the film. He's all about authenticity. That's why we're shooting in Closter City. You know, for the allegory."

"Allegory and gore," Nick said. "That's Christian McVeety's trademark. I'm going to ask him about that."

"You can interview him after his nap," Ainsley said.

"Cool. I'd like to talk to his special effects guy in the meantime."

"That'd be Chet Kershaw. Follow me." Ainsley led him toward a big tent where several zombie vampires in various stages of decomposition sat in folding chairs, killing time listening to music on their smartphones or reading books. One female zombie vampire nibbled on an Atkins bar, careful not to disturb her makeup.

"Chet's family has been doing monster makeup and on-set special effects since the days of silent films," Ainsley said. "What he does is a dying art."

"So it's ironic that he's using his talents on the walking dead. The same could be said of McVeety."

Ainsley smiled at Nick. "Sounds like you've already written your story."

"I never start anything without an angle," Nick said.

Chet had his back to Ainsley and Nick as they approached. He was a bear of a guy, big enough to be a boxer or a linebacker, but his size was belied by the delicacy he was using to apply latex pustules to the face of the zombie vampire sitting very still in the director's chair in front of him.

"Chet, do you have a minute to talk with *Fangoria*?" Ainsley asked.

"I'm a crew of one who has to make up thirty zombies and rig two exploding heads. I don't have time to pee and I've needed to for an hour." Chet turned around, holding a latex pustule daintily with two fingers. When he saw Nick, he broke into a big smile. "But peeing is overrated."

Ainsley saw the recognition on Chet's face. "You two know each other?"

"I've interviewed Chet before," Nick said. "I'm a big fan of his work."

Kate had drafted Chet for the Derek Griffin con. Chet believed that Nick and Kate worked for a private security firm that pushed the boundaries of legality to get the job done.

Chet stuck the fake pustule on Ainsley's cheek. "Hold on to this for me. We'll be right back."

Chet put his arm around Nick and took him to the far corner of the tent, where they could speak privately.

"It's so good to see you," Chet said. "Seems like just when I'm ready to slit my throat out of boredom and self-loathing, you or Kate show up to save me."

"Is working on this movie really that bad?"

"No, I'm thankful to be here. I've hardly worked since I did that last project for you," Chet said. "I got this gig because McVeety is computer illiterate and my grandfather worked on his first film in the 1950s."

"*Attack of the Flesh-Eating Martians,*" Nick said.

"That's the one," Chet said. "He's been basically making the same movie for sixty years. But God bless him. Once he's gone, I may have to find a new line of work. I've been studying for a realtor's license."

"That would be a tragedy. Maybe I can save you from that, at least temporarily. We'll pay you a hundred thousand dollars to help us take down a bad guy who launders money for mobsters and terrorists."

"What do I have to do?"

"Kill me," Nick said.

Chet smiled. "I'd be glad to."

24

It was early evening when Kate walked into Tom Underhill's workshop in an industrial section of suburban Rancho Cucamonga. It was a cinder block building that had once been a mechanic's garage. The workshop walls were covered with pictures of the imaginative playhouses, tree houses, and dog houses that Underhill built for a living. She saw photos of kid-sized castles, hobbit dens, igloos, gingerbread houses, and even a flying saucer that seemed to have crashed into a tree. What she didn't see were any photos of the structures and vehicles Tom had built for their cons.

In the center of the workshop was a vintage Airstream trailer that had been gutted. Tom was inside the trailer, working on something with a blowtorch, his back to Kate.

"Knock knock," Kate said, raising her voice to be heard over the sound of the torch.

Tom peered out of the trailer and smiled when he saw her.

"Kate!" He dropped the blowtorch, lifted off the goggles, and stepped out of the trailer. "This is a first. It's always been Nick who stops by."

"I wanted to see where the magic happens," she said. "What are you building this time?"

"You know I have three kids, ages four, ten, and twelve," Tom said. "Well, my wife is pregnant again."

"Congratulations," Kate said.

"Thanks," he said. "We're thrilled, but it was a surprise. It means I either have to turn my office into a nursery or buy us a new house. So I'm giving her a nursery and building a man cave on wheels that I can park in my driveway. It's going to be a home theater, game room, and office all rolled into one."

"So you're finally creating a playhouse for yourself."

"I hadn't thought of it that way but, yeah, I guess I am," he said. "It was building that fake oceanographic survey ship and remote-controlled submersible for that con in Portugal that helped pay for this."

"We have another job for you, if you're interested."

"I've got to put four kids through college someday and I'd like to do it without having to sell my man cave on wheels or take a second mortgage on my house," Tom said. "So yes, I'm interested, especially if it pays as well as the last gig."

"A hundred thousand dollars," she said. "But I have to warn you, it comes with the same risks."

"And I hope the same adventure. These jobs make me feel great. My wife notices the change in me, too. She jumped my bones the minute I got back from Portugal. That's how she ended up pregnant again."

"Just a reminder," Kate said. "We're going after a major criminal, but we're using illegal means to get him."

"If he's even half as rotten as the last two guys I helped your detective agency take down, then so be it. There's something wrong with the law if it allows people like Griffin and Menendez to remain free."

"Maybe so, Tom, but if things go wrong, you could end up in prison or worse."

"You keep warning me about that."

"I couldn't live with myself if I didn't," Kate said. "You're a husband and a father. I'm torn every time we come to you. I want your help, but part of me always hopes that you'll turn us down."

"That's why I trust you," Tom said. "What am I building?"

"For starters, you're putting an escape hatch in the floor of an Audi A8."

"That's not much of a challenge," he said. "How about if I also add an ejector seat, machine guns behind the headlights, and a flamethrower in the exhaust pipe?"

"That won't be necessary," she said. "But those would be nice to have in my car."

"I'm sure we could work something out," Tom said. "Where are we going this time?"

"Las Vegas."

"No freakin' gondolas," he said.

"Funny you should say that."

The San Luis Obispo County courthouse looked like a large mausoleum and, perhaps fittingly, Sara Quirk, the twenty-something assistant district attorney, had the pallor of a corpse, the fashion sense of a mortician, and the warmth of a tombstone. She occupied a windowless office that felt as cramped and suffocating to Nick as a coffin buried under six feet of dirt.

"Mr. Petrocelli, your client is charged with grand theft auto, reckless endangerment, and fifty-six counts of kidnapping," she said, sitting across from Nick at a neatly organized gunmetal gray desk. "Your suggestion that we should simply release her with a stern warning is utterly absurd."

"I think it's the only way that your office, and the tour bus operator, can come out of this debacle without embarrassment and ridicule," Nick said, both of his hands flat on the briefcase resting on his lap. It was the day after his visit to Closter City. He wore the off-the-rack suit that he got for free from Jos. A. Bank for purchasing the suit that he wore for the State Department con. "The way I see it, we're doing you an enormous favor."

"You can't be serious, counselor. Yesterday morning, Wilma Owens stole a tour bus carrying fifty-six Japanese tourists from the parking lot of the Camarillo outlet mall and drove it a hundred and twenty-five miles before being apprehended in the parking lot of the Pismo Beach outlet mall by San Luis Obispo County Sheriff's deputies. That's a serious crime."

"Before arriving in Pismo Beach, Ms. Owens stopped the bus in Solvang, and stayed there for over an hour, did she not?"

The question seemed to bewilder Quirk. "Yes, but so what?"

"Well, then how can you say that my client kidnapped the tourists?" Nick said. "She let them all out in Solvang, where they wandered freely through the Danish village buying wooden clogs and eating *aebleskiver,* before happily returning to the bus with powdered sugar all over their faces for the drive up to Pismo Beach. That doesn't seem like the conduct of prisoners or people under duress to me."

Quirk shifted in her chair, making it creak. "Just because they were unaware that they'd been abducted doesn't make it any less of an abduction."

"Did any of the tourists lodge a complaint?"

"They don't speak English, and they were unaware of the jeopardy they were in."

"The only jeopardy they faced was maxing out their credit cards after visiting Solvang and two outlet malls in one day. The fact is, they were so delighted with the trip that they were posing for selfies with my client at the time the deputies arrested her."

"This is ridiculous! Wilma Owens was not the bus driver, nor the owner of the bus, nor does she possess a valid Class B commercial license," Quirk said, tapping the neat stack of papers in front of her with her index finger as she made each point. "She stole a tour bus and took it on a joyride up the California coast."

"'A joyride' is the perfect way to describe this. She brought pure joy to those fifty-six tourists, not to mention the merchants that they patronized in Solvang and Pismo Beach. The one who deserves your scorn is the bus driver who abandoned his vehicle in Camarillo to get high on pot. If anything, my client may have saved their lives. What would have happened if that impaired driver had taken the wheel of that bus? It's his negligence that is the crime here."

Her pale skin had flushed bright red during the course of Nick's argument. He was glad to see it. Because he was beginning to worry that she might be a vampire. She spoke slowly, trying to control her rage.

"There is no evidence that the driver was smoking pot or impaired in any way."

"There's no evidence that he wasn't," Nick said. "Did you give him a drug test?"

Quick bolted up from her seat, unable to contain her anger for another second. "Of course not! He didn't commit any crime."

"Can you prove it?"

"I don't have to prove it."

"You will by the time I'm done raising reasonable doubt with the jury, who will already have seen all of those pictures of smiling, sugary-faced Japanese tourists with their friendly, cheerful bus driver."

"She wasn't their bus driver!"

"She was driving the bus, wasn't she?" Nick said. "Or are you disputing that now, too?"

Quirk leaned forward on the desk, looming over Nick and jabbing her finger at his face. "Stop twisting my words."

Nick smiled and looked her in the eye. "You clearly have no case, Ms. Quirk. So unless you and the bus company crave embarrassment, which is what you'll surely get once I alert the media, share the photos, and present my compelling version of events, then I'd release my client and call it a day."

Forty minutes later, Nick was standing outside the San Luis Obispo County jail as Willie emerged, a spring in her step, as if she were leaving a party instead of a cell.

"Thank you for getting me out," Willie said. "I didn't know you were a lawyer."

"I didn't know you were a bus driver." Nick led her toward his rented Cadillac in the parking lot. "Why did you steal it?"

She fell into step beside him. "It wasn't something I set out to do. I went to the mall to buy some bras and there it was, a new four-hundred-twenty-five-horsepower, forty-six-foot-long motor coach, a big vehicle that I'd never driven before, with the door wide open and nobody at the wheel. It was an incredible opportunity. But before I could drive away, the Japanese started piling in."

"Where was the driver?"

"I don't know. Probably went to get a pretzel or something. Who cares? That fifty-four-thousand-pound monster has a three-hundred-and-fifteen-inch wheel base and a forty-foot turning radius. It's like driving a battleship. It was one of the vehicles on my bucket list."

"If you wanted to drive a bus, you didn't have to steal one. With what we've paid you, you're rich enough to charter a bus for yourself."

She waved off the suggestion. "That's too much trouble."

"Stealing one packed with Japanese tourists from the parking lot of an outlet mall is easier?"

"It was right there," she said. "I couldn't help myself."

"It's your ADD."

"Thirty-four double-D, to be exact. But you're right, it's really their fault." She gave her breasts a gentle heft. "I wouldn't have been at the mall if my bras didn't wear out so fast."

"I wasn't talking about your cup size, but your undiagnosed attention deficit disorder. You have no impulse control."

"You're beginning to sound like Kate."

"Well, occasionally she's got a point. Sometimes there are easier ways to do things than breaking the law."

"You just impersonated a lawyer."

"This wasn't one of those times."

"Because you were in a hurry to get me out to help you with a new scheme," she said. "What do you need me to do for you now?"

"Nothing much." They reached his car and he unlocked it with his remote key fob. "A drive-by shooting."

She laughed. "And you're giving me grief about stealing a bus?"

25

The crew gathered two days later in the sweltering heat of a barn in Ojai, California, to go over the plan. Scattered around them were a half dozen standing floor fans, their heads turning left to right like the audience at a tennis match, but their whirring blades barely moved the heavy, dry air.

Willie Owens, Chet Kershaw, Tom Underhill, Boyd Capwell, and Jake O'Hare sat on picnic table benches facing Nick and Kate, who stood in front of three dry-erase boards covered with blueprints, photographs, and maps. To their left, displayed like the big prize on a game show, was a new black Audi A8 with darkly tinted windows. To their right, like the booby prize, was a mannequin dressed in a blue polo shirt and tan slacks.

"We're here to create a big, violent action sequence worthy of a Hollywood movie," Nick said. "The purpose is to scare the bejeezus out of this man and make him go running to the FBI for protection."

Nick taped a photo of Evan Trace on the board behind him. There was also a photo of the Côte d'Argent tower, which had been cut out and stuck on a blowup of a Las Vegas street map.

"The FBI will throw Trace into prison and shut down his casino, or they'll let him remain free and keep his casino going as a front for a government sting operation," Kate said. "Either way, he's done financing terrorism and organized crime."

"Wasn't that the plan to start with?" Jake asked.

"It was, but how we're getting there has changed," Kate said. "The original endgame was to convince Lono Alika, the Yakuza's man in Hawaii, to join Boyd and Billy Dee and launder his stash of drug profits through another junket at Côte d'Argent. We were going to run off with the cash, crippling Alika's business and leaving Trace to face the Yakuza's wrath."

"And the relentless fury of the Canadian mafia," Boyd said. "We'd hunt Trace down like a moose."

"Is that really a thing in Canada?" Willie asked.

"Moose hunting?" Boyd said.

"The mafia," Willie said.

"Oh yeah, they're fearsome up there," Boyd said. "They say 'Revenge is a dish best served cold' and it's very, very cold in Canada."

"Unfortunately," Kate continued, "Trace ruined our plan by offering Boyd, Billy Dee, and Alika the chance to secretly invest in his casino empire by losing millions of dollars at his baccarat tables. It's a clever scheme that cut us entirely out of the picture."

"But the good news is that Kate has Trace making that offer to Billy Dee on video," Nick said and then pointed to Boyd. "You're going to show that surveillance footage to Lono Alika. You're going to tell him that Trace and I are part of an FBI sting to bring you both down."

"That's a death sentence," Jake said. "Alika will go crying to the Yakuza and they'll come gunning for you both."

"Not if Boyd kills me first," Nick said. "Right in front of Trace's eyes."

Boyd grinned at Willie. "I told you the Canadians were badasses."

"I'm going to meet with Trace in Las Vegas," Nick said. "As I'm leaving in my car, Willie is going to drive by in a van carrying Boyd and his shooters, Chet and Tom."

"They're going to open fire on Nick's car," Kate said, gesturing to the Audi. "He'll lose control, crash the car, and it will explode, blowing him to bits."

"If you're going to do all of that," Jake said, "why do you need to tell Alika about the video? Why take the risk of bringing the Yakuza into this?"

"As a convincer," Nick said. "To prove to Trace that the jeopardy is real."

"Trace will hear from his own trusted sources that the Yakuza wants him dead," Kate said. "After seeing Nick and Boyd brutally killed, that terrifying news will close the deal."

"I get killed, too?" Boyd said. "Who is killing me?"

"I am," Kate said.

"Do I get a death scene?"

Kate pulled a gun from behind her back and fired three times in quick succession at the mannequin, blood spurting out of its chest on impact, splattering the polo shirt.

She lowered the gun and reholstered it. "Whatever performance you can squeeze into those three shots before Chet and Tom pull your body into the van and Willie speeds off."

"Plenty of time to make my death resonate emotionally with the audience," Boyd said.

Willie was still looking at the mannequin. "How did you do that?"

"Kate was firing blanks," Chet said and held up a tiny remote the size of a key fob. "I used this to ignite a vest filled with red-colored corn syrup under the shirt. It's a common Hollywood trick. Or at least it was until CGI came along."

"How are you blowing up the car?" Jake asked.

"I knew you'd have a special interest in that," Nick said.

"Do I get to use my rocket launcher?"

Chet stared at Jake. "You have a rocket launcher?"

"Doesn't everybody?" Jake replied.

"No, you don't get to use your rocket launcher," Kate said. "Or your hand grenades."

Chet looked at Jake again. "You have hand grenades?"

"The bullet hits to the car will be a special effect," Nick said. "The car will be rigged with explosives. But before Chet triggers the blast, I'll escape through a trapdoor constructed in the floor."

"I guess that's what I'm building," Tom said. "Where are you escaping to?"

"The sewer," Nick said. "I'll be crashing the car right above a manhole that will be rigged with a fake cover that you'll design to open when I drop on it. We'll replace it with a real, pre-scorched manhole cover from below immediately after the explosion."

Boyd applauded. "Magnificent. A grand finale."

"I see three problems," Jake said. "The first is that I don't get to use my rocket launcher. The second is Trace's security team. How are you going to stop them from shooting at the van?"

"Nick and I will handle that," Kate said.

"Okay, but that leaves the third, and the biggest problem," Jake said. "The fire department, the police, and the crime scene techs are going to come and they have to find Nick's charred corpse in the car."

"They will," Nick said.

"I'm sure Trace has contacts in the police department," Jake said. "He'll know immediately if it's not a real corpse."

"It will be," Kate said.

"Where are you going to get a body?"

"We have plenty of volunteers already lined up," Nick said.

Boyd arrived in Honolulu the next morning dressed for the part of a Canadian mobster in paradise. He walked off the plane in a wide-brimmed Panama straw hat, yellow bowling shirt, Bermuda shorts, and flip-flops, rented a Cadillac Escalade, and headed for the North Shore.

He'd been to Hawaii once before to host an infomercial for the Smootherizer, a blender that was specially designed to make tropical fruit smoothies. The Smootherizer infomercial aired nationwide, night after night, and Boyd had expected some big residual checks. That was before some Smootherizers that were left plugged in and unattended in kitchens spontaneously combusted and burned several houses to the ground. The infomercial was yanked, a class-action lawsuit was filed, and the manufacturer fled the country. Boyd never saw a dime. Thinking about the betrayal and the injustice of it all put him in the right mindset for the scene he was about to play with Lono Alika.

He parked in front of Da Grinds & Da Shave Ice as if he owned the place and got out of the car. Alika was sitting in his usual spot on the patio.

"Aloha, Lono!" Boyd called out.

Alika set aside the huge slice of lilikoi cream pie that he'd been eating. He wiped the whipped cream off his lips with the back of his tattooed arm, and stood up to greet his friend with a bear hug.

"Brah, dis a big surprise. Si'down, have a lilikoi pie. Make like dis home," Alika said and snapped his fingers at Neon Nikes, who immediately got up from his seat to get another slice of pie from the server at the window. "Watchu doin' here?"

"I came to see you." Boyd sat down across from Alika at the picnic table. "So this is your Bada Bing."

"Bada what?"

"Tony Soprano's strip club. His domain. Mine is a truck stop outside of Vancouver. I got a booth in the back where I do all of my business. Come up sometime and I'll treat you to poutine and some flapper pie."

Neon Nikes set down a paper plate with a slice of lilikoi pie and a plastic fork in front of Boyd and retreated to his seat at the back of the patio.

"You didn't come all dis way fo' talk TV an' eat da grinds," Alika said.

"Don't take this as an insult, but I don't get half of what you say. You're going to have to drop the Hawaiian gibberish and speak plain English, because it's important that we both understand each other." Boyd leaned forward on the table and lowered his voice. "I came to see you face-to-face because I don't trust phones, and we're both in deep trouble."

"What kind of trouble?"

"We've been set up." Boyd pushed aside the plate of pie, took out his cellphone, and held up the screen to Alika. "Take a look at this."

Boyd played a few seconds of the video of Evan Trace making his pitch to Billy Dee.

"*You won't really be losing your money,*" Trace said. "*Whatever you lose gambling will become your off-the-books investment in Monde d'Argent.*"

"I thought laundering my money playing baccarat was a good deal," Billy Dee said. *"But this sounds even better."*

"It is," Trace said. *"Instead of washing your illegal profits, you can make them work for you in the gambling capital of the world."*

Boyd fast-forwarded to another section of the video.

"What did that loudmouth Canadian want in return for his money?" Billy Dee asked.

"He took me at my word," Trace said.

"He's a bigger gambler than I thought. Are my hosts in on this, too?"

"No, and I'd appreciate it if you'd keep this between us."

"And Alika, too, I suppose," Billy Dee said.

"I'll be talking to him next. I'm seeking investors with a certain profile, and Nick Sweet doesn't match it. Mr. Alika does."

Boyd stopped the video and put the phone back in his pocket. "Evan Trace and Nick Sweet are informants for the FBI. They have us on video, too. They're setting us up in return for leniency on whatever charges the feds already have against them."

Alika's face had gone as rigid as stone. He spoke very slowly. "How did you get this?"

"I've been banging Kate," Boyd said.

"Fo' real?" Alika said.

Boyd had startled himself when he said it. He was supposed to say he had an informant in the FBI, but "banging Kate" came out instead. That's what happened when he was totally into character. His instincts took over. He was committed to it now.

"Nobody was more surprised than me. Maybe it started as customer service or maybe I'm irresistible or maybe she's never had a Canadian before. What do I care? Ass is ass."

"Dat's true."

"When Kate got back to L.A., she stumbled on texts between Nick and his FBI handler. It totally freaked her out. So she called me for help. Who else was she gonna call? She's terrified that she'll go down with us."

"We aren't going down. Dey are. Dey gonna die dead."

"Die dead," Boyd repeated. "Is that a Hawaiian thing?"

"Worse kine of dead. Da woman, too."

"Seems like a rotten thing to do to her after she tipped us off."

"If she'd bang you, she'd bang da feds. No disrespect, bruddah. But if dare's no witnesses to testify, dare's no case."

Boyd sighed. "It's such a waste, but you're right. Better safe than sorry. I'll kill Nick and Kate, and I'll go for Trace, too. Problem is, if I miss my shot at Trace, and he hops on a plane to Macau, I can't touch him. My reach doesn't extend that far. How about your business associates in Japan?"

"Nobody can hide from dem," Alika said. "They'd find you if you jumped in a time machine to da future, took a spaceship to a-nudder planet, an hid in a-nudder dimension. An den dey would cut out yo guts, string you up wit' dem, an' set you on fire."

"I'd like to see that," Boyd said.

"Trace will die dead, bruddah," Alika said. "Guaranteed."

26

There's always a surgical conference going on somewhere in Las Vegas and usually it's at one of the major casino resorts. The conferences are sponsored by medical device manufacturers in order to train doctors in the use of their latest high-priced surgical tools and implants. The hope is that those surgeons will then want to use those products, which would force hospitals to buy them. So there's a constant demand on the Strip for cadavers.

One of the companies that served the cadaver need was CorpsSource Services, Inc., which was located in a nondescript building in an office park near McCarran International Airport. Nick drove up to the front door in his 2006 Chevy Cobalt at 11 P.M., two days after Boyd's meeting with Alika. The only other vehicles in the lot were the two refrigerated trucks that CorpsSource used for hauling bodies.

"It looks dead to me. There isn't a living soul in sight," Nick said to Kate and Willie, who were also in the Chevy. The three of them wore white CorpsSource-logo jumpsuits. Willie's jumpsuit was too tight and unzipped to show off her cleavage, purely out of habit, not necessity.

"That's not funny," Willie said. "This whole thing creeps me out."

"All you have to do is hot-wire the truck," Nick said. "If you stay in the cab, you'll never see the body. Kate and I will do the rest."

"At least we're not in a cemetery," Willie said.

"That would be grave robbing, and I wouldn't do that," Nick said. "It would be desecration."

"How's this any different?" Willie asked.

"These people willed their bodies to science," Nick said.

"This isn't science," Kate said.

"It's criminal science," Nick said, and got out of the car.

The women got out, too.

"I'm sure that wasn't the science they had in mind when they made out their wills," Kate said, walking with Nick to the front door while Willie headed for the trucks.

"I'm thinking they no longer care," Nick said.

"Doesn't matter," Kate said. "We're all going straight to hell."

Nick took out a pair of lock picks and opened the door as easily as if he had the key. They stepped into the lobby, and Nick typed a code into the security keypad by the door, deactivating the alarm.

"How did you get the code?" Kate asked.

"I showed up yesterday, posing as a rep for a medical device company, at the same time the office manager arrived here to open up," Nick said. "I saw her punch in the code, and she was even kind enough to give me a complete tour."

Kate went around the receptionist's counter and opened cupboards until she found the DVR unit for the security cameras. She gave it a quick examination. "We're in luck. It doesn't back up to the Web."

"I've seen cookie jars with better security," Nick said.

Kate unplugged the cables going into the DVR, took it out of the cabinet, and lugged it away under one arm. The two of them walked through the front office and down a corridor to the cold storage room. They opened the heavy steel door, pushed aside the clear vinyl strip curtain flaps, and stepped inside what was essentially a very large walk-in freezer. Dozens of cadavers in black body bags were stacked on four long aisles of shelving units that looked like bunk beds. Nick grabbed one of the gurneys that lined the far wall and wheeled it down the first aisle, as if he were shopping at Costco. Kate put the DVR on another gurney and followed him.

Each body bag had a card in a clear plastic sleeve that listed the sex, age, and cause of death of its cadaver. There was also a bar code and some serial numbers. Nick and Kate each took one side of the aisle, checking out the cards on the body bags.

Female, 87, congenital heart disease. Male, 66, amyotrophic lateral sclerosis. Male, 83, lung cancer. Female, 72, kidney failure.

"There are a lot of old people here," Kate said.

"That's the nature of the business, especially in a retirement community like Las Vegas. Here's a possibility. Male, forty-two, massive body trauma." Nick unzipped the bag and immediately reared back. "Holy crap. He's flattened. That won't work."

"Why do they have a body like that here? Don't they prefer them in relatively good shape?"

"Most of the time," Nick said, zipping up the bag. "But they also need bodies for trauma surgery training."

They continued down the aisle and on to the next one, going from body to body. Kate found another contender.

"Male, thirty-eight, heart attack," she said.

Kate unzipped the bag and Nick came over to take a look. The dead man was about five foot five and 250 pounds.

"He won't work," Nick said.

They needed someone Nick's size. Kate zipped it back up and moved to the next bag. And then the one after that. And several more. They were down to the last row of the last aisle before Nick found another possible selection.

"This sounds promising. Male, thirty-eight, cerebral hemorrhage."

He unzipped the bag. The dead man was Hispanic, but roughly Nick's height and weight.

"What do you think?" Nick asked.

She gave the cadaver a quick appraisal. "He'll do."

Nick zipped up the bag and together they picked up the body, set it on the gurney, and strapped it in place. Kate put the DVR on top of the body and they wheeled the gurney out of the storage room, closed the door, and hurried to the loading dock. They lifted the slide-up garage door to find the refrigerated truck already backed up to the loading dock with the engine running.

Kate opened the heavy door to the truck's freezer-like cargo area and pushed aside the plastic strip curtains that kept the cold air inside. Nick wheeled in the gurney. The truck's interior was lined with shelves and belts to secure the body bags to them. Kate set the DVR on the truck's floor, then she and Nick lifted the body bag onto one of the shelves and strapped it in. Nick collapsed the gurney so it was flat on the floor and slid it into place under a shelf.

"This is the first time I've ever stolen a body," Nick said.

"That's not true. You stole a mummy from a museum in London."

"I stole a sarcophagus that had a mummy inside."

"So now you're stealing a body bag that has a cadaver inside," Kate said. "I don't see the difference."

"The difference is the thirty million dollars in jewel-encrusted antiquities that were in the sarcophagus with the mummy."

"Do you still have the antiquities?"

"I didn't keep any of it. The sarcophagus had been looted from an ancient burial site," Nick said. "I returned it to the rightful owner, the Egyptian government, for a handsome retrieval fee. Besides, the antiquities would have clashed with my Rembrandts."

"I hate when that happens," she said.

They got out and closed the door. Kate joined Willie in the truck's cab and Nick dashed across the parking lot to the Chevy Cobalt. Nick drove off first, and then Willie pulled out and followed Nick toward the glow of the Vegas strip.

"I really hope the slogan is true," Willie said.

"*No freakin' gondolas*'?"

"What happens in Vegas stays in Vegas."

It was almost midnight when Willie, Nick, and Kate pulled into a warehouse in an industrial pocket of buildings on the south side of the Côte d'Argent casino. It was close enough to the resort to fall under the black tower's shadow for several hours each day. Willie drove the refrigerator truck into the warehouse, and Nick quickly closed the door behind her. She parked the truck but kept the refrigeration unit running.

Willie and Kate got out of the truck and went to check on the rest of the crew, who were finishing up last-minute details of the con.

Chet Kershaw was applying touch-up paint to the exterior of the black Audi A8 to hide traces of some of his special effects handiwork. Kate leaned in close to the car and examined the finish.

"They're nearly invisible," she said. "It looks like you've just touched up some parking lot dings."

"When these little charges blow, they'll leave M16 impact marks and gunpowder residue behind. Even the crime scene techs will be fooled," Chet said.

"That's above and beyond," Kate said.

"Not the way I look at it," Chet said. "The CSI guys are part of the audience, too. They're just coming late to the show."

Kate moved along to Tom, who was also busy painting, putting the final touches on a Styrofoam replica of a sidewalk manhole cover. He had a genuine manhole cover on the table, next to the fake, that he was using for reference.

"They look identical," Kate said, glancing between the two covers. "I can't tell the difference."

"You'd know right away if you tried to drop through that one," Tom knocked his knuckle against the real cover. "You'd break your feet."

She turned to Boyd, who stood nearby, trying on a vest made up of pouches filled with red-dyed corn syrup. Each pouch had a wire taped to the outside that ran down to a battery pack on his hip.

"This brings back memories," he said, adjusting the Velcro straps on the vest. "I wore one of these in my starring role in *Taken 3*."

"I don't remember seeing you in that movie," Tom said. "Who did you play?"

"Thug number twenty-seven," Boyd said. "I was shot five times by Liam Neeson, but most of my performance was lost due to the director's terrible staging."

"In other words," Kate said, "the camera was on Neeson instead of you."

"The man is a camera hog," Boyd said. "Everybody in the business knows that. He robbed the audience of my indelible performance."

"That won't be an issue tomorrow," Kate said. "I guarantee you'll have everyone's attention."

"But it won't be on camera," Boyd said. "From my professional prospective it's unfortunate that we have to come at the casino from angles that will obscure our faces from security cameras."

"Not unless you'd like to be doing dinner theater in a prison cafeteria for the next five to ten years."

"The long run and captive audience is appealing to me," Boyd said. "But the venue leaves a lot to be desired."

Kate moved on to Jake, who was cleaning an M16, one of a half dozen rifles laid out on a table in front of him.

"That's more weapons than we're going to need," Kate said.

"You can never have too many weapons," Jake said.

"Does that mean you brought your rocket launcher?"

"It's in the trunk of my car in case of a roadside emergency."

"What kind of roadside emergency would require a rocket launcher?" she asked.

"You don't want to find out and not have one handy," Jake

said. "It's also why you should always have a paper clip in your pocket. You can do just about anything with a paper clip."

She gave her dad a kiss on the cheek. "Don't ever change."

"That's a given," Jake said.

Willie popped the hood on a beige panel van parked behind them and examined the engine. Kate joined Willie at the front of the van.

"What are you looking for?" Kate asked.

"I'm checking the belts, fluids, and plugs one more time. I'd hate to have this barge crap out on me when we need to make our fast getaway. I don't see why we couldn't use a Mercedes G500 AMG or a 7 Series BMW 760Li M Sport instead."

"Because we wanted a vehicle that would blend in," Kate said. "Not stand out."

"When Boyd, Chet, and Jake start shooting from the van with M16s, we're going to stand out anyway," Willie said. "We might as well be cradled in soft, Veneto Beige Nappa leather with a raging V-12 twin turbo under the hood when we do the drive-by."

"Look at the upside," Kate said. "You get to drive recklessly at blazing speed through gunfire and flames."

"That *is* my favorite kind of driving," she said. "But it goes much better with a sexy ride."

"You can't have it all," Kate said.

"At least I won't be the one driving with a corpse," Willie said.

Everyone looked at Nick, who stood facing three

whiteboards on easels. The boards were covered with photos of the VIP entrance at the back of the Côte d'Argent casino and street maps of the surrounding area.

Kate walked up beside him. "Going over the choreography in your mind one more time?"

"Trace put the VIP entrance to Côte d'Argent behind the building to provide some privacy for high rollers and celebrities. It's on the southwest side of the building facing this industrial park. There's almost no vehicle or pedestrian traffic on the two side streets that intersect at that corner. He also built an eight-foot-high wall of black marble and cascading water that curves along the corner for additional privacy. All of that gives me confidence that we can control the situation."

As he spoke, he pointed on the map to South Merton Street, which ran along the west end of the Côte d'Argent property and continued down through the industrial area where they were now. South Merton Street intersected with West Norbert, which ended in a cul-de-sac a block east of Côte d'Argent.

Nick tapped the cul-de-sac. "That's where the van will be waiting." He pointed to the southwest corner of the intersection, where he'd taped a photograph to the map. The picture showed the storm drain at the corner, and the low cinder block wall that bordered a parking lot. "And that's where the action ends."

"For you," Kate said. "I've still got to talk Trace into turning himself in to the FBI. I wish you and I could switch roles."

"You make a much more convincing FBI agent than I do."

"That might be true, but smooth talking people is your specialty, not mine."

"You're not smooth talking him," Nick said. "You're tough talking him. That won't be too hard after what he's going to see."

"What if he still doesn't fold?"

"He will as soon as he hears that the Yakuza is coming for him. Worst-case scenario, it takes another day or two for him to run to the FBI for protection."

"If the Yakuza doesn't kill him first," Kate said.

Nick shrugged. "At least he won't be in business anymore."

27

Trace had been back in Las Vegas for almost a week. During that time, he'd often studied the four puncture marks on the back of his hand and thought about Kate Porter. She was smart, beautiful, cunning, devious, and violent. She could take a beating and inflict one with gusto. He'd found women who possessed some of those qualities before, but never one who embodied them all so spectacularly. Thinking about her had him practically bursting out of his Calvins.

So as he sat at his million-dollar desk in his high-rise office that morning, he thought about stabbing his hand with his letter opener. He thought a fresh wound might be just the thing to match the ache in his privates.

That's when he saw Kate's face appear in one of the dozens of live security camera images that flitted across his touch-screen tabletop. It was as if she'd been conjured up by his desire.

Trace immediately expanded her image with his fingertips so it filled half the desk. Kate had just entered the high-limit room, where a few Japanese gamblers were bleeding yen at poker. He zoomed in on her. She wore a long charcoal-colored linen blazer, a loose-fitting white blouse, skinny blue jeans, and leather lace-up combat boots. It was a good look for her that projected sensuality, professionalism, and just a hint of aggression.

Trace watched Niles Goodwell waddle up to Kate to greet her. Trace tapped the "Goodwell" icon on his tabletop and Goodwell immediately reached inside his coat pocket to answer his vibrating cellphone. Before Goodwell could say a word, Trace told him to send her up . . . alone.

"Right away, sir," Goodwell replied.

Goodwell pocketed his phone and led Kate toward the door to Trace's private dining room. Inside was a private elevator that would take her up to his office.

Kate glanced at the security camera as they passed under it and she gave it a sly smile. Trace felt an instant buzz of erotic anticipation. Amazing things were about to happen, he was sure of that. She hadn't traveled to Las Vegas to reject him.

He got up and went to the elevator, timing his arrival so he got to the doors as they slid open.

"Kate," he said. "This is a surprise."

"I hope I'm not disturbing you."

"You've disturbed me ever since you pointed a gun in my face," he said.

"But you like it."

"I do," he said.

Kate walked past him into the vast office, her eyes roaming over the sunken conversation area, the long bar, and the two walls of floor-to-ceiling windows behind his high-tech desk. Trace thought she was like a soldier identifying potential threats and escape routes. Spring-coiled for violence. And for Trace, that was a mating call.

"You're accepting my offer?" he asked.

"I came to discuss it. You didn't mention salary or benefits."

"Name your price."

"I won't negotiate with myself. Hold out your hand."

She drew a lighter from her pocket, flicked it on, and held the flame about an inch below his palm.

"This stays lit until we agree on a price," she said. "And benefits."

"I'd think the benefits would be obvious."

"If you want to play it that way your hand is going to get cooked. If you move your hand away from the flame before we have a deal, I'm gone."

He smiled. The flame was like Viagra. "Half a million dollars a year, an apartment in Macau, and a car allowance."

"That isn't even minimum wage for me. Try harder."

He couldn't get any harder.

"One million dollars, the apartment, the car, free use of the private jet."

Dear Lord, she wished he would negotiate faster. If this went on much longer, she'd throw up.

"I don't want to be just an employee," she said, holding the flame steady and looking right into his eyes. "I want to share in the success of the enterprise."

A blister was forming on his palm, but the only sensations he was feeling were in his pants.

"I'll throw in a hundred-thousand-dollar bonus for each percentage point increase in Monde d'Argent's annual revenue. Plus full medical coverage, with no deductible, and an annual contribution of eight and a half percent of your salary, including bonuses, to your pension plan."

She flicked off the lighter. "You have a deal."

Trace wanted her more in that moment than he'd ever wanted any woman in his life. The only reason he didn't grab her was that he was afraid she'd break his jaw out of reflex.

"Don't you want to hear about the benefits?" he asked.

"I thought you already outlined the benefits."

"I left the big one out," he said.

Before he could demonstrate, a buzzer went off on his desk. It wasn't a sound he could ignore. It was the red alert. Even his desk was blinking red, indicating the severity of the situation. Trace hurried over and touched the tabletop, deactivating the sound and light and simultaneously answering a call on the speaker from the VIP lobby.

It was Tara, the red-haired VIP desk hostess. "Nick Sweet is down here, sir," she said, her voice quavering with fear and from the effort of trying not to show it.

"Damn," Kate said, coming up beside Trace. "He's smarter than I thought."

"He's quite agitated," Tara said. "He's disarmed Guido, the doorman, and he's threatening to shoot the ice sculpture unless you and Ms. Porter come down here."

Trace tapped a button on his table, bringing up the security camera feed from the VIP lobby. Kate leaned over his shoulder as Nick came up onscreen, aiming Guido's Smith & Wesson .38 at the ice sculpture of a hawk grabbing a rabbit in its talons. With his free hand, Nick helped himself to a cheesy canapé from the tray beside the sculpture.

Nick's behavior made no sense to Trace. "Doesn't he know the sculpture is going to melt anyway?"

"It's a stunt, Evan. He wants our attention. Don't send any security men down there, it will just escalate the situation. I'll handle it. Besides, it's my job now."

"I can't tell you how much it pleases me to hear you say that."

Great, Kate thought. And it would please *me* if he didn't have such an obvious boner.

"Good grief," she said, losing the fight not to glare at it.

Trace was glad she'd noticed.

. . .

Kate was relieved that Nick had successfully disarmed the doorman. As far as they knew, Guido was the only person packing a gun in the VIP lobby. If another weapon was stashed somewhere in the lobby, Kate could deal with it.

She and Trace rode the small private elevator down to his dining room. As the two of them hurried out of the dining room, through the high-roller salon, and past the Japanese poker players, Jake gave Kate an update on her earbud. He was outside monitoring the police band from the van.

"No one has reported any trouble at Côte d'Argent to the police. Somebody has stolen a Las Vegas tour chopper, there's a car accident on the Strip, and there's a liquor store robbery in progress downtown, so the police have their hands full anyway," Jake said. "We're in position and ready to go. Good luck, everyone."

Kate and Trace crossed the casino floor and paused for a moment at the door leading to the VIP lobby. It was all riding on her now.

"Keep it casual and friendly," Kate told Trace. "Pretend the gun isn't there."

Trace strolled in first, trying hard to appear completely relaxed. The truth was his sphincters were so tight, he feared it might take the Jaws of Life to open them again.

Tara, Guido, the bellman, and two other hostesses stood to his right with their backs against the wall. Their eyes were on Nick, who stood in the center of the lobby with his right arm outstretched, holding the gun on the sculpture. There was a tray on the floor and several broken crystal flutes in a puddle of spilled champagne.

"Hello, Nick," Trace said as jovially as he could. Kate stepped up beside Trace.

"Oh, for God's sake," she said.

"I'm disappointed in you, Kate," Nick said. "I didn't think you'd jump ship like this. I couldn't believe it when I got your note saying you were coming here to hook up with this jerk."

"It's not a hook-up," Trace said. "I've offered her a position with my company."

"That doesn't make it any better," Nick said.

"C'mon, Nick," Trace said. "We've had much worse misunderstandings than this and moved past them."

"Do you really want to remind me of that while I have a gun in my hand?" Nick asked.

Yes, he did. Trace wanted to show Nick that he could be forgiving, too, though the truth was that he wasn't forgiving *at all*. Very soon, Mr. Garver would be taking a mallet to Nick's hands for this insult. Trace might even invite Kate to watch. Maybe he'd even encourage Garver to take the mallet to a second, even more sensitive body part. That would be strictly for Kate's watching pleasure. And, of course, it would keep Nick permanently out of the bedroom competition.

"Evan is right, it's nothing personal," Kate said. "I saw a career opportunity and I took it."

"You betrayed me," Nick said.

"I'm tired of living like a gypsy," Kate said. "I wanted something steady and lucrative. That wasn't ever going to happen with you."

"I know you're upset," Trace said to Nick. "But nothing has really changed in the grand scheme of things. Your junket business is still welcome here. You'll still work closely with Kate. The only difference is that you won't have to split your take with a partner anymore."

"You haven't just taken my partner," Nick said.

I've taken your lover, Trace thought. Trace tried not to smirk. Yes, he definitely would have Garver take a mallet to Nick's nuts. He might even do it himself.

Nick took a step closer to him, so they were almost nose to nose. "You've also taken the money that Shane Blackmore, Lou Ould-Abdallah, and Lono Alika would have run through my junket and convinced them instead to secretly invest in Monde d'Argent with their gambling losses."

If Trace had a smirk, it was gone now. It was as if Nick had slapped it right off his face.

"How do you know about that?"

"You'll find out soon enough." Nick flipped open the cylinder of the .38, emptied the bullets out on the floor, and set the gun beside the sculpture. "I'd wish you two a happy life together, but I know that it's not in the cards."

Nick smiled, helped himself to another canapé, and walked outside to a black Audi A8 that was parked at the door.

Nick's words were ringing in Trace's ears. Who had talked? Surely, not all three of them. Why would they do that?

Kate followed Nick outside and Trace followed Kate, watching as Nick got into his car and drove around the motor court toward the street. A beige panel van screeched out in front of the driveway. The van's side door slid open and three men with M16s began shooting. One of the men was Shane Blackmore . . . and he was aiming his M16 at Trace.

Kate shoved Trace to the ground just as a spray of bullets raked Nick's car. The Audi was positioned between them and the street. If it hadn't been, Trace knew he would have been killed. Kate had saved his life, instantly earning her pay for the year.

Nick sped out of the driveway and into the intersection, fishtailing in front of the van, bullets riddling his car, shattering his windows, and blowing out one of his tires. He lost control of the Audi, jumped the next curb, and slammed into a low cinder block wall, the trunk of the car popping open on impact.

To Trace's astonishment, Kate reached under her jacket, whipped out a Glock, and began firing at the speeding van. The three shooters continued to pummel the disabled Audi with bullets.

Her steady fire drew Blackmore's attention. The enraged mobster whirled around to spray her with his M16 and Kate shot him three times in the chest. They were great shots, a perfect center mass cluster, and Trace saw the disbelief on

Blackmore's face. The mobster tumbled backward into the fleeing van just as the Audi exploded in a massive fireball.

The force of the blast shattered the lobby windows behind Trace and knocked Kate off her feet. She kept on shooting as she fell, holding her aim steady on the van, which screeched past Nick's car and disappeared behind a veil of smoke and flames.

28

All of the gunshots that were fired during the shootout were blanks. The bullets striking the Audi, the van, and Boyd were illusions, created by tiny charges that Chet ignited by remote control from his seat in the van. It was like another day at work for Chet, only without the cameras, the lights, or the catering.

Nick had opened the trunk on the Audi after the crash to block the rear window so that he could slip out through the escape hatch in the floor, and on through the breakaway manhole cover below, without being seen. He was safely in the sewer when Chet blew up the car with the cadaver inside. The blast was calculated to be strong enough to mangle the car and any evidence of a trapdoor.

After the blast, Nick lifted the real manhole cover into place and scrambled along thirty yards of dry sewer pipe that led to another manhole outside the warehouse they'd used as their base. He climbed out and ran inside the warehouse, where Chet, Ted, and Willie were busy peeling the beige skin off the van to reveal blue paint beneath. Boyd had taken off his shirt, which was soaked with red-dyed corn syrup, and was undoing the Velcro straps on his vest of exploded blood packs.

"Excellent work everyone," Nick said and headed straight for Jake, who sat in the van's passenger seat, monitoring the police band. "Where do we stand?"

"The police are dispatching units," Jake said. "The nearest patrol car is three minutes out. The fire department is on the way."

"Do you copy that, Kate?" Nick asked.

"Gotcha," Kate said as she dashed across the motor court to Trace, who'd risen to his knees and appeared to be shell-shocked. Kate holstered her gun when she reached him.

Car alarms were going off everywhere. Bits of broken glass from the hotel tower were falling on the lobby's broad portico.

"What just happened?" Trace asked. "Why did Blackmore kill Nick? Why did he try to kill me?"

Kate grabbed Trace roughly by the arm, jerked him to his feet, and practically dragged him alongside her into the VIP lobby. Glass shards crunched under their feet. Tara, Guido, and the others were stunned but physically unharmed.

"The police will be here soon," Kate said to Tara and Guido. "Give them your full cooperation."

Tara nodded and Guido stood slack jawed and glassy eyed.

"We need to go somewhere private and talk," Kate said to Trace, pulling him toward the casino's door.

"Why?" he asked. "What?"

Kate opened the door and they stepped into sheer pandemonium. People were screaming and running through the casino toward the main lobby exit. Dealers were hiding under their tables. Pit bosses and security people were watching over the chips.

Kate hustled Trace as fast as she could across the tide of escaping people to the high-roller salon. Goodwell was nowhere to be seen, but the Japanese gamblers were still in their seats at the poker table.

When they reached the door to Trace's private dining room he swiped his key card over the scanner. Kate glanced back at the three Japanese gamblers. Something wasn't right. Why weren't they running for an exit like everyone else? Her gaze locked on one of the men. It was Nakamura, the man from Macau. Out of the corner of her eye, she spotted a pair of shoes. They were on the feet of Niles Goodwell, who lay crumpled on the floor behind the blackjack table.

"Crap," Kate murmured.

She pushed Trace into his private dining room, kicked the door closed behind her, and drew her gun as they crossed the bridge.

"Now what?" Trace asked, noticing her gun.

"Three Yakuza assassins have Goodwell's key card, and they

are coming to kill us," Kate said, more for Nick listening in than for Trace.

Jake also heard the message about the Yakuza and jumped out of the parked van.

"We need to help her," Jake said.

"Not necessary," Nick said. "The police will be there in two minutes."

"And it'll be another five minutes before they can get to Trace's dining room," Jake said.

"You're not going to get there any faster," Nick said. "She can take care of herself, and she has a gun."

"Her gun is loaded with blanks."

"The assassins don't know that," Nick said.

Good point, Kate thought. The bad guys wouldn't know she was firing blanks.

She flipped over the dining table and pulled Trace down behind it. The door to the high-roller room flew open and the Yakuza came in, guns drawn.

She waited until one of them was midway over the bridge, and then she popped up and fired. Two of the Yakuza dropped to the floor. The man on the bridge dropped into the pond. Big mistake. Instantly the water surged with piranha and the man screamed and thrashed around as he was devoured.

One of the Yakuza sat up, staring in horror at the roiling

water. Kate threw her gun at him, fast and hard, catching him between the eyes, knocking him out cold.

Nakamura, the remaining Yakuza, fired two shots at Kate in quick succession. Kate ducked behind the overturned tabletop. Trace crawled as fast as he could toward the elevator. Kate stood and flung a chair at Nakamura. Nakamura dodged the chair and Kate tackled him, knocking the gun from his hand.

Kate and Nakamura went to the floor, and Kate used the momentum of the fall to her advantage. She flipped Nakamura over her and rolled into a crouch, coming face-to-face with him as he rose up.

At that instant, a spinning mallet slammed into the side of Nakamura's head, and split it open like a ripe melon. Kate turned and saw Garver standing in a doorway across the room.

"The police are coming," Garver said.

Trace got to his feet and swiped his key card over the call pad for the elevator. "Stall them, Garver. Kate and I need a few minutes to talk."

Garver picked up his beloved mallet and glanced at the crimson pond, which had begun to calm. Bits of cloth from the consumed man's clothing floated on the surface. Garver gestured with his mallet at the two unconscious men.

"What do I do about these two?"

"What you do best," Trace said. "Make sure they tell no tales."

Nick didn't want his crew hearing Kate reveal her genuine FBI background. Using the key fob remote in his pocket, he cut off the transmission from Kate's earbud to everyone but himself and Jake. "It's a wrap," Nick announced. "Let's get out of here."

Chet, Tom, and Willie piled into the blue van for the drive back to Los Angeles. Jake walked outside with Nick to his Buick. On his way out of town, Jake would drop Nick off in Henderson, where a private jet was waiting for him. Kate would remain in Las Vegas for a few days to tie up the case.

"I can't believe the Yakuza picked today to make their hit on Trace," Jake said. "He's lucky Kate was there to save him."

That was exactly the point Kate intended to make to Trace when they emerged from the elevator into his office.

"Surprise," she said, flashing her badge.

"You're an FBI agent," Trace said. "Could today possibly get any worse?"

"Yeah, you could be dead," Kate said. "But I was here, so you're not."

"You didn't come here to save me."

"I've been working undercover to nail Nick Sweet. But then he came to you, and my mission objectives changed. I can arrest you right now for money laundering."

"No, you can't," Trace said. "The alleged crime happened in Macau, where you have no jurisdiction, and it was done through Nick's junket. My hands are clean. That's the beauty of junkets. The only person you might have a case against was just blown to bits. So we're done."

Trace turned his back to her and went over to the

floor-to-ceiling window behind his desk. He looked forty-five stories down at the police cars and fire trucks converging on the burning Audi and at the hundreds of Côte d'Argent guests streaming out of the main lobby to the parking lot.

Kate stepped up beside him. She noticed a Las Vegas tour chopper heading their way. Côte d'Argent wasn't usually on the sky tour itinerary, but perhaps the explosion changed that.

Trace glanced at her. "You're still here?" he said.

"Aren't you curious why Blackmore and the Yakuza want you dead?"

"Maybe it was you they're after and I just got caught in the crossfire," he said.

"Nick bugged his guests in Macau and recorded your pitch. I got hold of the recordings and passed them on to Quantico to an agent that we suspect is dirty," Kate said. "Now we know that we were right about him. He alerted Shane Blackmore, Lou Ould-Abdallah, and Lono Alika that you and Nick are FBI informants."

"But I'm not one."

"You will be if you want to live. Blackmore is off the field, but the Yakuza will keep coming after you until you're dead." Kate's gaze kept drifting to the chopper. "Wouldn't surprise me if some Somali pirates came after you, too."

"I'll take my chances."

"What happened today is just the beginning. You've been branded as an informant. The killers will keep coming. They will be relentless and unforgiving. You'll need an army to protect you. Fortunately for you, we have one," Kate said. "We can put you on an Army base until you've finished testifying against every mobster and terrorist group you've worked with. Then we'll put you into the witness protection program."

"I'd rather be dead."

His comment made her think about the attempt on his life. The *real* one. The three Yakuza assassins didn't know they'd have the distraction of a drive-by shooting and an explosion to cover their hit. What was their exit strategy after killing Trace?

Once again, her gaze was drawn to the approaching helicopter. In a few seconds, it would be close enough for them to wave at the tourists. Then she remembered the report over the police band about a chopper being stolen from a tour company and she knew the answer to her question. The three assassins had planned to escape off the roof.

"Crap," she said.

She grabbed Trace, turned him around, and ran toward the sunken conversation pit. Behind them, the side door of the chopper slid open and two gunmen with AK-47s started shooting.

Jake and Nick had driven only a block south when they heard Kate say "crap" and knew that she was in trouble. Jake made a sharp U-turn in time to see the tour chopper hovering outside the penthouse and the rapid flashes of gunfire going into the building. Through their earbuds, they heard the hundreds of rounds shattering the windows and obliterating everything in Trace's office.

Kate stood, took the two steps out of the conversation pit, and surveyed the damage. The windows were shattered and wind blew through the office. The storm of bullets had passed over their heads. The million-dollar desk was decimated. The walls and the bar were riddled with hundreds of holes. The control panel for the elevator was destroyed. The only way out was the stairwell, where they were sure to be mowed down by Yakuza assassins.

The sprinkler system burst on. The gunfire must have automatically triggered the sensors in the deluge fire suppression system. The sudden, drenching downpour gave Kate an idea.

She turned to Trace and yelled over the sound of wind and rain. "I'll be back. Stay right there."

Screw her, Trace thought. He wouldn't just sit there while she hid and left him to be executed. There was a gun hidden behind the bar. At least that would give him a slim but fighting chance against the assassins. He scrambled to his feet and immediately tripped on the rain-slicked floor, slamming his knee hard into one of the steps leading out of the pit.

The pain was a shock and a humiliation, and it pissed him off. He tried to stand up again and there they were, the two

Yakuza assassins, charging out of the stairwell into the office, their AK-47s pointed at him. In that instant, Trace regretted telling Kate that he'd rather die, because now that it was about to happen he realized he'd do anything to live.

A thick jet of water came out of nowhere and slammed into the side of the lead assassin like a battering ram, knocking him off his feet and sending him sliding across the glass-strewn floor. Before the second man could fire, the blast of water sent him sprawling, too.

Trace turned to see Kate, wielding the standpipe fire hose.

The first assassin sat upright and fired where Kate had been standing, but she'd moved to one side and pummeled him with 250 gallons per minute at a force of one hundred pounds per square inch. It propelled the assassin across the floor and out the window. He fell forty-five stories without screaming because his nose and mouth were full of water.

The second assassin dove for his fallen assault rifle and grabbed it. When he stood to fire, Kate hit him in the gut with the water, smashing him against a wall like a bug hitting a windshield. He slid to the floor, his head hanging at an unnatural angle. He wouldn't be getting up ever again.

Kate switched off the nozzle and dropped the hose. Trace rose shakily to his feet, one leg unable to sustain his weight, and looked at her. He knew with sickening certainty what he had to do. There was no other option.

"Colt Ramsey," he said.

"Excuse me?" she asked.

"It's the name I'd like to have when you put me into the witness protection program."

It was close to midnight when Kate let herself into her budget room in the budget motel off the Strip. She'd chosen the motel not so much for the price as for the location. She'd wanted something that wasn't in the shadow of Cote D'Argent. And she'd wanted something that was *her* normal and not Nick's. Not that she didn't love the thousand-thread-count sheets and the complimentary champagne and fruit baskets that she enjoyed when she traveled with him. It was more that she needed to re-center herself to a more grounded reality. It had been an exhausting day. Successful but emotionally draining. Everyone on her team had come through unscathed. Thank heaven for that. They'd been paid off and sent on their way, Nick included. She was never sure where he landed after their assignments were done. He could be in Los Angeles or Tibet or Rome or his house in the south of France.

She closed and locked the motel room door, flipped the light switch, and kicked her shoes off. She shed her clothes and headed for the shower, needing to wash the day's grime off her body and soul. She glanced over at the bed and saw it. The Toblerone bar. It was on the pillow.

"Hot damn," Kate said, with a sigh and a smile.

She heard movement in the bathroom, and before she could get to her gun, Nick appeared in the bathroom doorway.

"It's a tradition," he said. "You always get a Toblerone at the end of a mission."

He looked relaxed and fresh from a shower, wearing only a towel wrapped low on his hips.

"This is embarrassing," Kate said. "I didn't expect you to be here. I'm sort of naked."

"Yeah, me, too," Nick said. And he dropped the towel.

29

The parking lot was full, and cars were parked along the shoulder of the Kamehameha Highway for the grand opening of Harlan's Rib Shack, which was now located in the building that only a few weeks before had been Da Grinds & Da Shave Ice.

Many of the customers wore blue surgical scrubs, because they were either coming or going from the Kahuku Medical Center. The crowd also included quite a few other locals, among them Lieutenant Gregg Steadman, who sat with Kate and Jake at the patio table that had once been Alika's iron throne.

"I don't know how you did it," Steadman said.

"I didn't do anything," Kate said. "It was Lono Alika's own decision to walk into the FBI field office in Honolulu and confess to his crimes."

"He did it because he was afraid for his life," Steadman said. "He thought the Yakuza would kill him for getting them involved with Evan Trace."

"He was right," Jake said.

Trace had agreed to fully cooperate with the FBI in exchange for immunity from prosecution and entry into the witness protection program. Based on his testimony, law enforcement agencies in fourteen countries had arrested 230 people, all of them mobsters, terrorists, or corrupt government officials who'd used the casinos to launder money. The arrests and the closure of the Côte d'Argent casinos had a chilling effect on money laundering throughout the global gambling industry.

"What I don't understand," Steadman said, "is how Harlan ended up with Da Grinds & Da Shave Ice."

"The FBI discovered that Alika was using the restaurant as a front to launder his drug profits," Kate said. "So they forced him to forfeit the property to the U.S. government, who made it available for rent pending an eventual auction. Harlan was the only applicant for the space."

"Well, that's no surprise," Steadman said. "There aren't any locals who'd dare move into Alika's place. They'd be too afraid of what he'll do to them when he comes back."

"He's gone for good," Kate said. "After Alika testifies against the Yakuza, the witness protection program will relocate him as far away from here as possible."

"He'll be living in an igloo in the North Pole," Jake said.

"That'd be Alika's version of hell," Steadman said. "He's

spent his life in Hawaii. He's never experienced an outdoor temperature colder than sixty degrees."

Harlan Appleton and Cassie Walner came up to their table. He wore an apron splattered with barbecue sauce and carried a platter piled high with spareribs. She was in her nurse's scrubs and carried their drinks.

"Dig in," Harlan said and set the platter in the center of the table. "For you, it's all-you-can-eat and no charge."

Jake inhaled the smoky smell of the ribs. "I may never leave."

"Great," Cassie said as she passed around the drinks. "Then you can start waiting tables for Harlan instead of me."

"You're working for Harlan now?" Kate asked.

"Part-time," Cassie said. "I want to be sure that he makes enough money to pay his share of my rent."

"You're living together?" Jake asked.

"In separate rooms," Cassie said.

"Most of the time," Harlan said.

"And only until his house is fixed up and habitable again," she said.

Harlan whispered to Jake, "Which may be never."

Cassie went off to see to another order. Jake watched her go and shook his head with disbelief.

"She's got to be twenty years younger than you and two hundred pounds lighter," Jake said. "How'd you win her over?"

"My ribs are an aphrodisiac," Harlan said.

"I'm bringing my wife here," Steadman said.

The talk of romance prompted Kate to check her watch.

She'd expected to hear from Nick by now. His private plane had landed in Honolulu at 4 P.M., and he was supposed to text her after he'd settled in at the beach house. But that was nearly three hours ago and there was still no word.

She hadn't seen Nick since Las Vegas, but they'd stayed in touch by text while she'd led the dismantling of Trace's operation for the FBI. This trip to Hawaii was their first chance to properly celebrate the success of their mission beyond the one unforgettable, sleepless night they'd had together, and they were both looking forward to it. So why had he suddenly gone silent?

Kate sent him a text: *Do you want me to bring you some ribs?*

Over the next twenty minutes, she ate some more ribs, had a Diet Coke, and checked her phone again about a dozen times. But still no reply.

Kate looked up from her phone and saw her father regarding her with concern. She tilted her head toward the parking lot. The two of them got up, said their goodbyes to the others, and met at her rented Jeep.

"What's wrong?" he asked.

"I'm supposed to get together with Nick tonight at a house on Kailua Beach. But I should have heard from him hours ago. I'm going over there now, and I could use some backup."

"I think you can fend off Nick's advances on your own," Jake said.

"That's not the trouble I'm worried about."

"Did you pack an extra gun?"

"Of course," she said. "You can never have too many weapons."

Jake smiled. "I raised you right."

Kate and Jake parked two blocks away from the house and approached it from the beach so they wouldn't be seen in case Nick was being watched by a law enforcement agency or by one of his many enemies.

They stayed close to the ocean-side property lines of the homes, which were spaced widely apart from their neighbors and separated from the beach by patios, pools, and lush landscaping. The shadows cast by the trees and hedges were the only cover that Kate and Jake had on the otherwise open moonlit beach.

It was a perfect tropical night. A warm breeze with a rich, floral scent rustled the tall, slender palms and seemed to move in time with the gentle surf. But it wasn't relaxing Kate. Her heart was racing, jacked up with a shot of pre-combat adrenaline. Her instincts were warning her. She glanced at her father to see if he was feeling it, too, but all she sensed from his posture was reluctance.

"Are you sure you need me?" Jake said. "Maybe Nick just wants to surprise you."

"I've got a bad feeling," Kate said. "Keep your eyes open."

She led the way. Tiki torches illuminated the path from the beach to the backyard, where dozens of candles framed the lap pool, the water covered with flower petals. The house was dark and the shutters were closed on the windows. A gas-fed fire was burning in a lava-stone campfire pit, casting flickering light on a wide-pillowed hammock that was strung between two palms.

"It looks like Nick has a romantic evening planned," Jake said, and started back down the path. "You two have fun."

"Wait," Kate said. She spotted a bottle of champagne sitting in an ice bucket within arm's reach of the hammock. She glanced in the bucket and immediately drew her Glock.

"Your sister's right," Jake said. "You really are afraid of intimacy."

"That's a five-hundred-dollar bottle of champagne sitting in a bucket of tepid water and the candles around the pool are melted," Kate said. "What does that tell you?"

Jake pulled his gun out from under his untucked shirt. "That the evening was supposed to get started hours ago but something got in Nick's way."

Kate moved quick and low to the dark house, her father close behind her, and they flanked the French doors. She reached out with one hand, gripped the door handle, and tested it. The door was unlocked. Jake moved a few steps away from the wall, took a firing stance at a slight angle from Kate, and nodded to her that he was ready.

She opened the door and crept inside in a crouch, ready to shoot at anything that moved in the darkness. Nothing did. But she'd heard shards of glass crunch under her feet and a couch was overturned in front of her. That worried her. So she took the risk of standing up, hitting the light switch on the wall, and making herself a target.

What she saw almost brought her to her knees again. The glass coffee table was shattered and the jagged shards on the bleached-wood floor were splattered with blood. A body had hit the glass. From there, her eyes were drawn to a wide smear of blood that ran from the wrought-iron legs of the coffee table all the way to the front door. There'd been a fight and a body had been dragged outside. Was it Nick? Had he been hurt? Or was he dead?

Jake hurried in behind her and went into the kitchen, methodically moving through the room.

"Clear," he yelled when he got to the other side.

That snapped her out of it. She went across the living room to the entry hall, then into a bedroom, peering under the bed, in the closets, and the adjoining bathroom.

"Clear," she yelled.

Together, Kate and Jake swept the entire house, room by room, until they were sure that there was nobody else there. They ended up in the master bedroom, where Nick's clothes were hanging in the closet above his empty suitcase.

"We know he made it here alive," Kate said.

"There is no reason to think he didn't leave here alive, too."

"You saw the living room," she said. "You saw the blood. A body was dragged out."

"That doesn't mean it was his," Jake said.

She holstered her gun, went back to the entry hall, and cracked open the shutters to look out the front window. Nick's rented Ferrari was parked in the driveway.

"Who did this?" Jake asked. "How did they know he was here?"

"We stayed here before," Kate said. "Maybe he was spotted by one of Alika's gang or by the Yakuza."

"There are no signs of forced entry," Jake said. "His attacker could have been someone he knew."

"Or Nick left the doors unlocked for me so whoever it was just walked right in." Kate surveyed the damage in the living room. "I think Nick was outside, setting things up, and when he came back in, they attacked him . . . and he was either seriously wounded or killed."

"Or he fought back, escaped, and whoever his adversaries were dragged away their casualties."

"Nick's car is still outside."

"All that means is that he didn't have his keys and had to flee on foot."

"If Nick escaped, he would have contacted me already."

"Unless he's still running, or he's unconscious in the bushes or on the beach somewhere, or he's in an ambulance right now, on his way to the hospital," Jake said. "It's too early to tell what happened or where he is."

"Or if he's still alive."

"You can't assume the worst. You've got to assume that he's alive and that he needs you."

"I need him." Kate turned away from her father so he wouldn't see the tears welling in her eyes.

"I know you do."

"I will find Nick, wherever he is, alive or dead and make whoever did this pay. Nothing will stop me."

"Us." Jake put his arm around her.

"Us," she said.

ABOUT THE AUTHORS

JANET EVANOVICH is the #1 *New York Times* bestselling author of the Stephanie Plum series, the Fox and O'Hare series, the Lizzy and Diesel series, the Alexandra Barnaby novels and Troublemaker graphic novel, and *How I Write: Secrets of a Bestselling Author.*

evanovich.com

Facebook.com/JanetEvanovich

@JanetEvanovich

LEE GOLDBERG is a screenwriter, TV producer, and the author of several books, including *King City*, *The Walk*, and the bestselling Monk series of mysteries. He has earned two Edgar Award nominations and was the 2012 recipient of the Poirot Award for Malice Domestic.

leegoldberg.com

Facebook.com/AuthorLeeGoldberg

@LeeGoldberg

ABOUT THE TYPE

This book was set in Minion, a 1990 Adobe Originals typeface by Robert Slimbach (b. 1956). Minion is inspired by classical, old-style typefaces of the late Renaissance, a period of elegant, beautiful, and highly readable type designs. Created primarily for text setting, Minion combines the aesthetic and functional qualities that make text type highly readable with the versatility of digital technology.

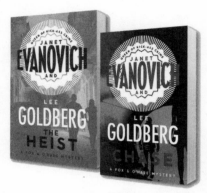

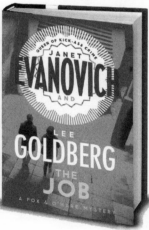

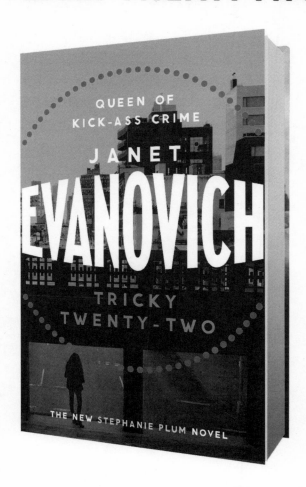

Connect with **JANET EVANOVICH**
on social media!

Facebook.com/JanetEvanovich

@janetevanovich

Pinterest.com/JanetEvanovich

Google+JanetEvanovichOfficial

instagram.com/janetevanovich

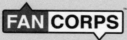

janetevanovich.fancorps.com

Visit **Evanovich.com**
and sign up for Janet's eNewsletter!